Colin Falconer has written over twenty novels, mainly historical fiction and crime. His work is enjoyed by a wide audience and has so far been translated into twenty-three languages. Although he still has his roots in his native London, he now lives in Australia.

LUCIFER FALLS

COLIN FALCONER

CONSTABLE

CONSTABLE

First published in Great Britain in 2018 by Constable

This paperback edition published in Great Britain in 2019 by Constable

A CIP catalogue record for this book
is available from the British Library.

ISBN: 978-1-47212-798-3

Typeset in Times New Roman by Initial Typesetting Services, Edinburgh
Printed and bound in Great Britain by Clays Ltd, Elcograf S.p.A

Papers used by Constable are from well-managed forests and
other responsible sources.

MIX
Paper from
responsible sources
FSC® C104740

Constable
An imprint of
Little, Brown Book Group
Carmelite House
50 Victoria Embankment
London EC4Y 0DZ

An Hachette UK Company
www.hachette.co.uk

www.littlebrown.co.uk

This book is for you, Lise.
You always told me crime does pay.
Thanks, too, to Charlie and George
for the licks and the inspiration.

GLOSSARY

ANPR: Automated Number Plate Recognition
BOLO: Be On the Look Out
CID: Criminal Investigation Department
CPS: Crown Prosecution Service
CS: Crime Scene
CU: Crime Unit
DC: Detective Constable
DCI: Detective Chief Inspector
DS: Detective Sergeant
FLO: Family Liaison Officer
HOLMES: Home Office Large Major Enquiry System
IC3:   code used by British police to describe ethnicity
IM: Intra-Muscular
IR1:   Incident Room 1
LOC: Loss of Consciousness
MAPPA: Multi Agency Public Protection Arrangement
MISPERS: Missing Persons
MIT: Major Incident Team
PACE: Police and Criminal Evidence act
PM: Post Mortem
PNC: Police National Computer
POD: Police Observation Device
SCD9:   Human Exploitation and Organised Crime
            Command
SCO19:   Specialist Firearms Command
SFO: Senior Firearms Officer

SIO: Senior Investigating Officer
TOD: Time of Death
TSG: Territorial Support Group
VGM: Video Game Music
VODS: Vehicle Online Descriptive Search
VPC: Volunteer Police Cadet

CHAPTER ONE

Charlie looked up at the dead man on the cross. His breath formed clouds on the still morning air. He had to squint because of the glare from the pointed Gothic window.

How the hell did he get up there?

The victim's arms were suspended directly above his head, fixed to the rough timber with a nail the size of a railway spike. Blood had leaked down his arms and the top of his chest and dried into a brown crust. His legs had been broken.

He was naked except for a priest's collar and a wooden crucifix around his neck. His expression had been frozen by rigor; he looked as cheerful as a man might, in the circumstances. If he really was a priest, Charlie thought, it was a poignant way to die.

'Jesus Christ,' Greene said.

A moment. Charlie heard the plaintive cry of a crow from the trees.

'Seriously, Jay?'

'It was the elephant in the room. Someone had to say it.'

Charlie shook his head and turned away. One of the CS officers nodded to him and pulled down his face mask. 'Morning, Charlie. I thought we'd had Halloween.'

'What have you got, Jack?'

Jack nodded at the photographer, who was standing on a small, aluminium stepladder, taking close-ups of the stone sill.

'Grooves in the stone, made by a rope or a chain.'

'That's how he got him up there?'

'Looks like it. Take a butcher's at this.' He turned and went outside. Charlie followed.

There was a bit of rubbish strewn around, beer cans and crisp packets and toilet paper; the grass was still crisp with frost. A feathery grey mist hung in the trees.

Under the branches, the gravestones in the cemetery were soured with age and all about the place, in a jumble. Still, the dead had long lost any reason to be tidy. They were actually just fine when they were left alone. He wondered for a moment how many of them had been murdered. One in six hundred and twenty-five, if you believed the statistics.

On the other side of the cemetery railings London was still going about its business, pounding horns, texting, looking at Facebook on the bus.

'See these marks here,' Jack said, pointing at the frozen mud about twenty feet from the Gothic windows. 'What it looks like, he had a van or a truck with a winch. Attached the end of the chain to the top of the cross and hoisted it up, using the wall as a lever.'

'It's a lot of trouble all this. Anything else?'

Jack nodded at two other CS officers in their blue overalls, on hands and knees in the grass. 'Footprints. Good impressions, too; mud must have been a bit softer when he made them and they froze overnight. We've taken casts. There's some smaller tyre prints, could be a mover's trolley.'

'Right. For getting the victim into the church.'

'It would have made life easier.'

'What you mean is, it made death easier. Crucifixion in the twenty-first century. I wonder if he used a nail gun?'

'You'd need a power source.'

'I was joking.'

'Know you were. But that spike wasn't put in here, there'd be blood splatter.'

'You're right. Interesting.'

'Whole bloody thing is interesting, if you aren't the poor sod he did it to.'

'He or she, Jack. Let's not jump to conclusions.'

'It's a he. What would a woman be doing with a winch?'

'Who found the body?'

Jack nodded to the patrol car, parked under the trees, a little way up the gravel drive. A man was sitting in the passenger seat, his head between his knees, holding an emesis bag. Two uniforms were standing over him. One of them was taking notes.

Charlie went over. 'All right?' he said.

'Sir,' they both said, in unison, when he showed them his warrant card.

'Is he OK?'

'Still in shock, sir. We've called an ambulance.'

Charlie squatted down. 'Detective Inspector George, Metropolitan Police. Was it you that found the body?'

The man looked as if he wanted to say something, instead he gagged into the bag. Charlie jumped up and took a step back, didn't want any of that on his Fratelli Rossettis.

'What happened?' he said to the uniform with the notebook, a stocky young woman with an earnest expression.

'He was doing his rounds first thing this morning. He knew something was wrong when he found the chains on the front gates had been broken.'

'Doing his rounds?'

'He checks for vandalism every morning, sir. He's one of the Friends of the Cemetery.'

'The cemetery has friends?'

'Eleven, sir.'

'Christ, it has more mates than I do. So, he comes down here every morning at this time?'

'They have a roster.'

'All right, when he's feeling better get a statement. I want the names and addresses of all the cemetery's Friends. And its enemies as well.'

3

'Sir?'

'It was a joke, Constable.'

He went back inside the chapel. Years since it had been used, by the looks; it was closed to the public these days, most of the windows boarded up with corrugated iron and mildewed plywood, the stained glass all gone. Their perp had used bolt cutters to snap the chain on the padlocked gate in the vestibule.

He stood there for a moment, admiring the way the light angled into the chapel through a hole in the slated roof. Nice. An overhanging tree had worked its inquisitive fingers through one of the high arches. There was the smell of leaf mould. On a transept wall he could make out a piece of ancient graffiti, CASEY LOVES COCK. I wonder if she still does, Charlie thought. She'd be a grandmother by now.

Greene hadn't moved, was still standing there, staring at the body.

'No spear wound,' he said.

'What?'

'Rules out the Romans.'

'What are you doing, Jay? This is not a laugh.'

'I was trying to get inside his mind, guv. The murderer, I mean. It looks like he's arranged everything, like a tableau.'

'A tableau?'

'A tableau's like a representation of a scene from a story.'

'I know what a tableau is, thanks.'

'What I mean, guv, is that if you want to off someone, it's easy enough. You just hit the geezer with a brick. But this, this is like, art.'

'What are you, a profiler now?'

'The thing is, why the bloody performance?'

'That, my old son, is what makes the job interesting. Just when you think you've seen everything, you get a crucifixion in an abandoned church. Brilliant.' His mobile rang. 'DI George.' He listened, said 'right then', and hung up.

'Who was that, guv?'

'Jolly. He's got held up in the traffic. No point in us hanging around then. Let's get back to the nick.'

They walked back to Greene's Sierra, threw their overalls and overshoes in the boot, and climbed in. Charlie let Greene drive, they bumped back down the footpath to the front gates.

Charlie took out his iPhone and did a quick Google search.

'It's a Dissenters' Chapel,' he said.

'What is, guv?'

'The place your artist chose for his tableau. Dissenters were like Quakers and Anabaptists, Christians who didn't believe in the Church of England so they built their own. This one was put up in 1840. Hasn't been used for years. Careful!'

'What?'

'You nearly ran over a squirrel. I like squirrels. You run over a squirrel, I'll get you transferred to traffic duty. Says they recorded an Amy Winehouse video here.'

'Popular little place, then. One of the uniforms said that during the day the locals use it for walking the dog.'

'Is that a euphemism?'

'A what?'

'Look it up. It's in the dictionary next to Tableau.'

There was a jumble of tombs on either side of the path, some collapsed, others overgrown with ivy and brambles. They reached a pair of imposing Victorian gates, blue and white police tape everywhere, three more uniforms from the local nick keeping the curious at bay.

Charlie scrolled down the screen on his mobile. 'God love us.'

'What, guv?'

'It says there's two hundred thousand people buried in here. That's more people than Southend.'

'And they're about as lively.'

They drove through the gates and they were back in North London, a dour streetscape of betting shops and pawn-brokers, a Salvation Army shop squeezed between a Pizza Hut and a Morrisons. There were Hassids in gabardine raincoats and side-curls, Nigerian mothers in bright wraps. Charlie had grown up not far from here; it wasn't like that then.

He quickly checked the Arsenal website before he shut down the phone; Arsène Wenger was still hanging on, he'd been hoping he'd resign. Greene saw his expression.

'What's up, guv?'

'Nothing.' He pointed out of the driver's side window, at the CCTV camera mounted on the other side of the bus stop. 'Let's hope that's working.'

He made a mental note of the row of shops on the other side of the road, flats built over them – someone must have seen or heard something. He didn't want this one getting away from him; people mustn't think they could crucify someone in the middle of London and get away with it. Next thing, everyone would want to do it.

CHAPTER TWO

Dawson, his inside DS, was waiting for him back at the nick, with a mug of coffee. Most of his team were already at their desks, the phones ringing off the hook as usual.

'Who's that?'

'She's our new DC, guv. Lesley Lovejoy.'

'You having a laugh?'

'No, guv.'

'Did I know about this?'

'I sent you an email, last week. She's from CID.'

'Email? You only sit ten feet away, can't you just talk to me?'

He went over. She stood up and held out her hand; cropped blonde hair, a blue trouser suit, sensible shoes, no make-up. 'DC Lovejoy.'

'Sorry, you've got me at a bad moment. No one told me you were coming. You done homicide before?'

'No, guv.'

'You're about to hit the ground running. Where were you before?'

'Kensington.'

'Do they have murders in south west London?'

'The kids knife each other for their Yeezy Mud Rats over there.'

'Well, pay attention, I'm sure we'll find something for you to do.' He went into his office, there was an email from Jack already. He printed off the first shots from the crime scene and went into IR1, started pinning them to the whiteboard.

One by one the rest of the team trickled in. Dawson, Wesley James and Rupinder Singh stood behind him, their arms folded. He heard Wesley swear under his breath.

'OK team, here's one for the ages. Found at around 6.15 this morning in the abandoned chapel in Barrow Fields cemetery. We can't confirm TOD at this stage, but the cemetery is locked overnight so it is safe to assume the crime took place then. The PM will give us a more exact time. Crime Unit believes that the victim was attached to the cross elsewhere and transported afterwards.'

'How did they get in?' Dawson said.

'Bolt cutters.'

'Once he was in,' Rupinder said, 'how the hell did he get him up there?'

'We are speculating that an electric winch was used, and that it was possibly attached to a van or lorry. There were deep grooves in the brickwork above the window.'

'That's mad, that is.'

'What sort of sick batty boy would do something like that? It looks like—'

'You say tableau, Wes, and I'll thump you.'

'I was going to say, like art.'

'That's as bad.'

'He's wearing a dog collar,' Rupinder said.

'That looks like a priest's crucifix around his neck,' Lovejoy said. 'It's too solid for bling.'

'Doesn't mean he's a priest though, does it?' Charlie looked at Greene. 'Could be part of a tableau.' He held out a hand. 'Everyone, if you haven't met her already, this is Detective Constable Lesley Lovejoy, she joins us from Kensington CID, and was lucky enough to arrive this morning for her first day.' He turned and looked at her. 'Our first job is to ID our victim, so as soon as we finish up here, I want you to get on the blower to MisPers, find out if a priest has been reported missing in the last seventy-two hours.'

She got up and leaned in for a closer look.

'Haven't seen a crucifixion before, Detective? You probably don't do a lot in South London, but we get a lot of these, especially in Hackney. This is our third this week.'

She didn't smile; if she didn't have a sense of humour, she wouldn't last long in this unit. He was about to get on with the briefing when she said: 'That's not a proper job though, is it? He meant him to die quick.'

'Meaning?'

'His arms above his head like that. He wanted him to die fast.'

'What do you know about it?'

'I used to be a Catholic, guv.'

'Lot of people used to be Catholics.'

'It's just I was curious about it when I was a kid, so I looked it up. He's done him the quick way.' She walked out, went back to her desk and picked up the phone. Charlie looked at Dawson and nodded. More to that one than meets the eye.

'Rupe, Wes, we need CCTV, everything in a mile radius of that cemetery, business, residential, government.'

They nodded.

'Where's his clothes?' Dawson said.

'There's uniforms from Malden Street combing the cemetery looking for them. Don't fancy our chances. Gale, you and Malik head out to Barrow Fields, there's houses back on to the cemetery and flats that look right over the front gates. Start knocking on doors, someone must have heard something.'

A tall man in a dark blue suit appeared in the doorway, cleared his throat. Charlie looked up. 'Morning, sir.'

'My office. Now.'

He walked off.

'You have been summoned,' Dawson said and grinned.

Detective Chief Inspector Fergus O'Neal-Callaghan reigned over the North London Major Incident Teams from a corner office on the fifth floor of the Essex Road nick. It was all glass and chrome, not a piece of paper in sight, his ceremonial uniform and peaked cap on the coat hanger behind the door.

A small, framed photograph of a smiling family sat on the shelf behind him. It had been there a while; his boys were grown, both off at university by now. Still, having a family at all, it was something to be proud of, in this job.

The walls were filled with citations, and photographs of him with various dignitaries. What was it Greene had said about him?

'If he was a lolly, he would have sucked himself to death.'

From up here the view wasn't spoiled by the train station and the shabby allotment behind Newington Row. The only interruption to the vista were the floodlights of the Emirates stadium.

'Sit down, Charlie. So, what have we got?'

'Bloke with two broken legs nailed to a bit of wood in a derelict church, sir. Know as much as you do at this stage.'

'Who is he?'

'We're still working on that.'

'I don't want to jump the gun, but I feel this could get messy. You think it was some kind of satanic ritual? Some gay BDSM thing? Like that thing with Boy George and that Swedish bloke a few years back?'

'Norwegian. And if it is Boy George, sir, he really did want to hurt him.'

No smile.

Charlie went on. 'As you say, sir, it's too early to make any kind of call. Once we've got an ID and the CS reports from Lambeth, I can set a direction. What are we doing about the media?'

'I'd like to keep the more lurid aspects of this out of the papers.'

'You want me to do the press?'

'Christ, no. I'm not sticking you in front of a camera. I'll

10

brief Catlin to do it. That's what she's paid for. We'll just say we found a body, and we'll keep mum about the cause of death or the journalists will have a field day. What about the fellow who found the body, can we impress on him the need for discretion?'

'We can try. I haven't eliminated him as a suspect just yet.'

'All right, well keep me informed on this one.'

Charlie got up to leave.

'This is a bit close to home for you, isn't it?'

'Sir?'

'Isn't your brother a bit churchy?'

'You mean the one who's a priest?'

'A priest. Oh. I didn't know it went that far. Never picked you for a left-footer.'

'Lapsed.'

'Well, it doesn't matter. Just get a result on this one. This is the sort of nasty business that is not good for our careers.'

He means my career, Charlie thought.

'What are you looking at, Charlie?'

'Your shoes, sir. I've got a pair just like that.' He almost said: I keep them for gardening, but he stopped himself, just in time.

They stared at each other.

'That's all, Charlie.'

'Thank you, sir.'

He went out.

'So, what do you think of the newbie then?' Greene said. They were in the Sierra, driving to the mortuary.

'We don't think anything yet. We don't judge on appearances.'

Greene shrugged, fidgeted. He wasn't done.

'Think she's a gusset muncher?'

'I have no interest in her sexual orientation and, if you've got any sense, Detective, you won't pay it any mind either.'

'Well, yeah, but. You know. The clothes, the haircut. You have to wonder, innit?'

'No, you don't have to wonder. You don't have to do

11

anything. The only thing we are paid to wonder about is the poor sod in the morgue and how he got there, but professionally and privately, I reach the wild borderlands of my wonderment right there. Mind that cyclist. Christ, did you ever have driving lessons? Turn left here. There's a space in the car park over there. Come on, let's get this over with.'

It was refrigerator cold inside the morgue. The buzz and flicker of a fluorescent light put Charlie on edge as they gowned up. They went through a pair of plastic slab doors. He wrinkled his nose at the chemical smell. It turned his stomach.

It wasn't like the new place in Haringey, this was all grim Victorian tile and dull steel sloping towards the drains on the floor. The government pathologist, Henry Jolly, was standing next to a white-coated technician, staring at a display of X-rays in a light box. He was wearing a green apron. Some of his breakfast was still in his beard. He was wearing Crocs with paisley socks and denim jeans, a size too large.

He nodded to Charlie and motioned him over. 'Sorry I missed you this morning. There was a bus versus motorbike on the M25.'

'We didn't mind,' Greene said and nodded to the corpse. 'But this geezer was hanging about for hours.'

Jolly looked at Charlie as if Greene was his fault. No one smiled.

He returned his attention to the light box. 'You are looking at the tibia and fibula bones of the deceased's right leg. As you can see, not a clean break; the bones were shattered at the point of impact. Usually the type of injury seen, for example, from the kick of a horse. This X-ray here is the ulna and radius of the right arm. The joints at the elbow and the wrist have been completely disarticulated. Extraordinary.'

The victim lay supine on a stainless-steel gurney. Paul, the CS photographer, was already at work with a camera, taking video and stills of the injuries. Usually, he would talk to the mortuary technician about the football as he worked – they were both smug Chelsea supporters – but today neither of them was saying very much. Even they seemed a little appalled, and they must have thought they had seen it all. Until this morning, he had thought that too.

'Hell of a job getting him into the mortuary van,' Jolly said. 'His arms were fixed in the position you found him. I had to break the rigor before I could start work.'

Charlie wasn't much interested in his problems transporting the body, or the methods for chemically breaking rigor, but he listened patiently while Jolly explained it all in detail.

'Unusual case,' Jolly said, when he had finished his story.

'Understatement.'

The victim's hands and head had been bagged. Jolly removed the bags and then untied the gag on the victim's mouth. There was another rag inside his mouth, Charlie saw, to prevent the poor sod from screaming. 'Linen,' he said. 'Almost bitten through.'

He took off the dog collar and the cross; they went into the plastic evidence bags that Greene had brought with him. Greene wrote on the labels and attached them.

'Crucifixion,' Jolly said and pursed his lips. 'Interesting history. It was invented by the Persians, apparently, hundreds of years before *the* crucifixion. Alexander the Great once crucified two thousand people at once, outside the walls of Damascus, for having the temerity not to surrender to him. Awful way to die. When the arm muscles give out and are unable to support the body, the shoulders, elbows and wrists all dislocate. The arms can be up to six inches longer when the victim is finally taken down.'

'I've always wondered, what's the cause of death? In crucifixion, I mean.'

'You mean, apart from extreme evangelism,' Jolly said.

'Yeah, apart from that.'

'There are a number of theories. After the shoulders

13

disarticulate, the chest sags and the victim is left in a permanent state of inhalation. Because they can't breathe out, it is only possible to inhale tiny sips of air.'

'So, they suffocate?'

'As a pathologist, I couldn't put it quite that simply. You see, with the onset of anoxia, the carbon dioxide levels in the blood increase and so the body tissues become acidic and start to break down. This causes fluid to leak into the lungs and makes them stiff, so it's even harder for the victim to breathe, which intensifies the suffocation process. But this fluid can also leak into the pericardium, so death might result from cardio-rupture or pulmonary embolus before hypoxia is complete.'

'So how long would it have taken this poor sod to die?'

'This fellow? Oh, not long. No more than an hour.'

'I thought Jesus died after nine hours. That's what they taught me in Bible class.'

'Well, you see, it depends what method is used. With arms outstretched in the classic pose you see in most churches, death may be delayed for twenty-four hours or even more. But whoever did this, knew a little about anatomy.'

'The perpetrator pinioned the arms directly above the head to hasten death,' Charlie said, remembering what Lovejoy had said.

Jolly smiled. 'I see you've been doing your homework. Yes, when the arms are fixed directly above the head, as this fellow's were, it becomes almost impossible to breathe. Also, his legs were broken to ensure that he couldn't support his body weight with his feet.' He nodded towards the pulpy, open fractures on the shins. 'I would say a blunt instrument was used, a tyre iron or a baseball bat.'

'After he nailed him up.'

'That's difficult to say.'

'So, he didn't die from blood loss?' Greene said.

'You mean, from the trauma to his wrists? No, the blood

14

loss from the puncture wounds would not have been significant. The pinion was placed between the junction of the radius and ulna bones, avoiding major blood vessels like the radial artery. As I said, whoever did this knew what they were doing.'

'And breaking his legs was like an act of mercy?'

They both looked at Greene.

'What?' Jolly said.

Charlie looked up at the strip lights, closed his eyes. Jesus, he worried about the lad sometimes. How had he ever made sergeant? 'Yeah, he had a heart of gold, Jay. Proper Saint Teresa.'

'I would venture,' Jolly said, 'that if I shattered the bones in both your lower legs with a heavy, blunt object, you would hardly consider me benevolent.'

'So he did it,' Charlie said, 'to ensure that his victim expired in the manner intended before anyone could find him?'

'It would appear so.'

'Time of death?' Charlie asked him.

'From the extent of rigor, I'd say early hours of the morning. Between midnight and three a.m.'

Jolly took fingerprints and swabs for DNA then began a careful examination of the entire body. 'Look at this,' he said.

He pointed to the soles of the cadaver's feet.

'Brick dust,' Charlie said.

'It's quite different from the limestone in the transept, where he was found. Of course, there's brick in other parts of the church. I'll get samples for comparative testing. You see, there's another patch here on the left elbow.'

'Jack believed he was stripped and nailed to the upright somewhere else, then brought to the chapel.'

'Ah, look at this.' Jolly pointed to a small bruise on the thigh. 'It's a puncture wound, the kind you would expect from a hypodermic needle.'

'He was sedated?'

'Possibly.'

'How long to get a toxicology report?'

15

'Everyone wants everything yesterday, Charlie. This is not the only homicide in London this week.'

'It's the only crucifixion.'

'Doesn't make you special.'

'I'm under a bit of pressure here, know what I mean?'

'Aren't we all?'

Charlie stood in the car park, took a couple of deep breaths, looked up at the sky, enjoying the feel of the icy drizzle of rain on his face. He felt hot and he felt sick. Always the same, no matter how many times he did it. He didn't know how Jolly could do that for a job.

'Act of mercy,' he said to Greene. 'What's wrong with you?'

'Did you see the size of the hole in his wrists? Don't think I'd like anyone doing that to me.'

'I promise you, when the time comes, I'll make it quick.'

Greene lit up. He leaned against the wall and took a long drag at the cigarette. 'Hate this part of the fucking job. Can't get the smell out of my clothes for days afterwards.'

'You're a smoker,' Charlie said.

'It's a different stink.'

'You keep puffing away on those things, you'll be on a tray in there soon. I'll have my prime suspect: Morris, Philip. But you'll be charged as an accomplice, you daft bugger.'

Charlie's phone rang. It was the newbie, Lovejoy; she had a Missing Persons report, a priest who worked with the homeless, a Father Andrew O'Meara, reported missing thirty-six hours ago in Hackney.

'Who reported it?'

'A Father Donnelly. They live in the same presbytery in Holston Road.'

'Get round there now, ask him to come with you to the mortuary in Haringey. You know where that is, right?'

'Yes, guv.'

'We'll need him to make a formal identification.'

16

'Got it. On my way.'

'We'll go and have a coffee and meet you here. Got that?'

'Yes, guv.'

'And Lovejoy. Good work.'

He hung up.

Greene stubbed out his cigarette. 'That was quick.'

'She seems to have her wits about her.'

'So, he is a priest, not a pretend one.'

'Could be. Let's not get ahead of ourselves. First, I need a coffee.'

CHAPTER THREE

Father Donnelly looked pale and a little shaky as he got out of the car. He was stocky, bowed in the shoulder, late fifties perhaps. Without his dog collar, Charlie would have mistaken him for a retired tax clerk with a fondness for puddings.

He went over, nodded to Lovejoy and showed the priest his warrant badge, introduced him to Greene.

'Your detective thinks Andrew is dead,' Father Donnelly said.

'We can't be sure it's him without a formal identification. Can you do this for us?'

The priest nodded, but he looked to Charlie like a man headed to his own execution.

'Wait here,' Charlie said to Lovejoy.

He and Greene buzzed through, and led Donnelly down the corridor to the morgue.

'You sure you're OK with this?'

'I have performed the Last Rites countless times, Detective. I am accustomed to death in all its forms.'

Actually, it's Inspector, Charlie wanted to say, and you have no idea about the different forms of death. 'It's just that it's a bit different in here. None of the people I see day to day have time for the final sacraments.'

'One whiff and down he goes,' Greene whispered in Charlie's ear.

Charlie led him through to the viewing room. A mortuary technician was waiting for them. Jolly had just finished his post mortem and their victim lay under a sheet.

Father Donnelly crossed himself when he saw the body. Charlie nodded to Greene; get ready to catch him.

The assistant carefully drew back the sheet, as far as the chin.

A crucified man, even from the neck up, is not an easy thing to look at. Donnelly groaned and his knees buckled. Greene was ready and caught him before he hit the tiles.

To Donnelly's credit, once he had recovered from the shock he insisted on returning to the room to give his brother priest the final sacrament. He had brought his stole and holy water in Lovejoy's car for just such an eventuality.

For all the grey skies outside, the day no longer seemed quite as bleak as it did an hour ago. Their victim had a name now, was no longer a terrible and mysterious figure nailed to a piece of wood. Charlie told Lovejoy that, after Father Donnelly was done, she was to bring him back to the Essex Road nick to make a statement. He even had a spring to his step as he walked back to the car. Right, now he was going to sort this.

'So, do we have any theories?' Greene asked.

'Too early to start down that road.'

'Bet he was a kiddie fiddler. All those God-botherers are the same. Reckon it's some kid he's had a go at years ago; now he's all grown up and come back to even the score.'

'What makes you think that?'

'It's all so Catholic, innit? You don't off someone that way unless you're a religious nut. I reckon our perp must have gone to a hardcore Mick school. It also accounts for motivation. We do a bit of digging, I bet our Father O'Meara turns out to be a proper bum bandit.'

'Thank you, Sherlock. Want a tenner on that?'

'You don't reckon?'

'Seems a bit too neat.'

'You're overthinking it, guv. Make it twenty.'

Charlie took out his mobile and made a call, told Gale he

was making him FLO for the case. Another good Irish boy, he would be perfect. It was no good sending Malik, even though he had the better temperament for it. O'Meara wasn't family to Donnelly, but if Gale could work a bit of gently gently, they might get a better sense of the deceased from the only person who saw him day in and day out. There was a housekeeper, apparently; he would have Gale interview her as well.

During the interview with Donnelly, he'd said O'Meara's parents were dead, his only family was a sister in Glasgow. He would have to call her and break the news.'

'Weird, innit?' Greene said. 'You don't think of a priest having a family.'

'Don't you?' Charlie said.

'It's like Santa Claus having a brother.'

'Just shut up and drive,' Charlie said.

CHAPTER FOUR

'We appreciate your help, Father,' Charlie said. 'Never easy seeing someone you know in the morgue. This must be a terrible shock.'

'Indeed, it is.'

'Would you like coffee, tea, glass of water?'

'Just a glass of water would be welcome, thank you.' Donnelly had a soft Irish brogue. A Mick priest, Charlie thought, not many of them left. And now there's one less.

'What happened to the poor man?'

'We think he was the victim of foul play.'

'Foul play? You think he was murdered? Are you sure?'

'No room for doubt on that one, I'm sorry.'

'But how?'

'I'll have to spare you the details. We found his body in a disused chapel in Stoke Newington.'

'What? But how did he get there?'

'That's what we need to find out.' He nodded to Lovejoy, who sat beside him with a laptop open. 'We'd like to take a statement from you if you don't mind.'

'Yes, of course. I don't know if I'll be much help, but I'll try.'

They ran through the formalities. Finally Charlie asked him when he had last seen Father O'Meara alive.

'It was the night before last, before he went out on his ministry.'

'His ministry?'

'As I told you earlier, he worked with the homeless, you see. The man was a saint, a living saint.'

'A saint. In what way do you mean?'

'Well, in every way. I don't think I have ever known a man so committed to doing God's holy work on earth. We all do our best, of course, but he was . . . well, he was exceptional. I admit, I was a little in awe of him, of his courage and dedication.'

'What exactly did he do? His "ministry", I mean.'

'You haven't heard of him?'

Charlie shook his head.

'He was a minor celebrity. The BBC made a documentary about him a couple of years back. He started out with a food van, handing out soup and coffee at night to the unfortunates of the parish. These days he has . . . had . . . his own organisation. "Christ is Care", it was called, a play on words, you see?'

'Yeah, I get it.'

'There's a group of around two dozen volunteers who help him. He goes out and talks to people who are sleeping rough, tries to help them with all sorts of problems, and now the weather has turned cold, he often sets up emergency accommodation in the church hall or even in the church itself. I tell you, everyone loved him, *everyone*.'

'Not quite everyone. But let's go back to Tuesday night. What time did he go out?'

'It was about nine o'clock, I suppose. We had dinner in the presbytery together, as usual, then I retired to the living room to read and watch a little television. He got dressed to go out. It was his usual way.'

'He went out alone?'

'Usually he had a volunteer with him, but that night the fellow, Dane, who was on the roster, called in sick. I told him not to go out alone but he said . . .'

Charlie leaned forward, waited.

'He said the Lord was looking over him.'

Yeah, that's my experience of the good Lord, too, Charlie thought. Fickle.

'And that was the last time you saw him?'

'I went to bed around ten o'clock, I believe. He had not returned by then, but I was not alarmed, he often did not come back till after midnight, or so he told me. I got up, as usual, around seven o'clock, went in for breakfast; our housekeeper, Mrs Travis, lets herself in and prepares it for us. When Father O'Meara did not come out of his room, I went in to check on him. I could see that his bed had not been slept in, and that was when I telephoned the police.'

'What happened then?'

'Well, they told me to come to the police station. They took down all the details and said that if I did not hear from Father O'Meara in the next twenty-four hours then I was to call again. They did not seem as concerned about his welfare as I had hoped, to be frank with you, Detective. When your colleague here called me this morning, I hoped it was good news.' He leaned forward and placed a fat forefinger on the desk to make his point. 'I think that someone has not been as diligent as they might be, and it has cost a saintly man his life.'

'We'll look into it, Father. But it is normal for MisPers — missing persons — to reappear, often without our assistance. For that reason, some police officers wait twenty-four hours before activating a report.'

'This is just terrible. There are many in the parish who will take this very hard, very hard indeed. I told him to be careful, I don't know how many times. I didn't like him going out there alone. I believe in the ultimate goodness of the human soul, of course, but this *is* Hackney.'

'We'd better have the full name of the volunteer who called off sick that night. In fact, you'd better give us the names of all his volunteers.'

'You don't think Dane would have anything to do with it? They all loved him, his parishioners.'

23

'Routine. They may be able to help us with our enquiries, that's all. Did they all go out with him a lot?'

'Of course. The roster is on the noticeboard, behind his desk at the presbytery. Mobiles, emails, everything.'

Charlie made a note, he'd have Gale attend to it.

'How did he become involved with this sort of work?'

'From the very first moment he came here, he was much concerned with the plight of the homeless. Well, we all are, but he was a man of astounding energy and dedication. He persuaded the parishioners to contribute to a fund to help him buy a van, and then he organised a roster for making sandwiches and coffee, that sort of thing. He'd collect it all and then park the van outside the church at night. Afterwards he'd go around and talk to the homeless people about their situation, arrange appointments for those of them who would let him; crisis care, drug counselling, doctors' appointments, perhaps contact social services or even their families for them. Next thing I knew he had camp beds set up in the church hall for when the weather turned cold. How he did it all I don't know, but he could charm the birds from the trees, that man. Even the bishop turned a blind eye to some of the things he did, I'm sure they were outside church protocols. But it was all done in the name of charity. He was a man who went about doing good all his life. The rest of us, I'm afraid, just go about.'

'Do you know what he was doing, before he came to the parish?'

'He was a teacher, I believe. At All Saints in Brighton.'

'Did he ever talk much about that?'

Father Donnelly seemed puzzled. 'I don't think so. It was a while ago now.'

'We're just wondering if there might be some connection. A past student, bearing a grudge.'

'What sort of grudge? You don't kill someone for not giving you an A in History.'

'We have to look at all possible leads at the moment. Because of the nature of the crime, we don't think this was a random act of violence.'

'You think someone planned it?'

'We have reason to believe, yes. The body . . . Father O'Meara was transported some distance from where he was last seen.'

'I see what you mean.'

'He never mentioned receiving any threats from anyone?'

'My goodness, no. Like I said to you—'

'Everyone loved him.'

'That man lived and breathed his vocation. His energy, his devotion, well, I have to say he put most of us to shame. He believed that every soul could be saved, that no one was beyond redemption. Of course, as a priest, I believe that, too. But he took that belief into the streets and, one might say, into the heart of darkness itself.'

'One step too far, Father.'

'Perhaps so.'

'Well, thank you for your help.'

'I just can't believe this has happened, seeing him lying there like that, it's . . .'

'Hard to put into words.'

'Yes.' He got to his feet. 'I'm sorry for what happened in there. As I said, I have seen many souls in their last moments, but . . . I expected Father Andrew to look . . . more peaceful.'

Charlie opened the door and called Gale over from his desk.

'This is Detective Constable Tyrone Gale. After we've printed up the statement, we'd like you to sign it for us, then he'll drive you back to the presbytery. While he's there, I think it would be worthwhile for him to interview all of Father O'Meara's volunteers, your housekeeper too, to see if any of them has any useful information for us.'

'You should speak to Sister Agatha.'

'Sister Agatha?'

'They worked closely together, with the homeless. She would know more about what went on out there than I do.'

25

'Where can I contact her?'

'She's at the convent in Holroyd Street. The Little Sisters of the Poor.'

'Thank you, Father. While we're getting the statement ready, why don't you go with DC Gale, he'll make you a cup of coffee.'

'Poor Andy. I will pray for his soul, though I am sure even now he is watching us from heaven. If ever a man deserved to sit at God's right hand, it was him.' He started to follow Gale towards the kitchen and then turned back. 'He didn't suffer, did he, Detective? Please tell me the poor man didn't suffer.'

'I can't say. But at least he's at peace now, and with his God.'

Father Donnelly seemed to understand. He nodded and left. Charlie felt Lovejoy watching him.

'Well, what would you have said?' he said to her.

'I thought it was a brilliant answer actually, guv.'

Charlie nodded, surprised that he still needed reassurance about something like that.

He sat down, watched Lovejoy spell-check the document on the screen.

'So, what do you think?'

'I hate to say this, guv, but a lot of these homeless kids, they've fallen through the cracks. They're addicted to alcohol or drugs and are past helping themselves. They either have mental illness or they've been sexually abused at home. It makes them very vulnerable.'

'You're wondering if he took advantage of that?'

She shrugged. 'Does that make me sound cynical?'

'No, that makes you sound like a good cop. Being cynical does not put you at a disadvantage in a murder investigation, Lovejoy. Playing the saint in public so you can carry on sinning in private, there's nothing new to that game, it was around before Jimmy Savile. But whoever did this was not homeless. They had access to motorised transport and, most likely, private premises. If we found him in an alley with a knife in him, I'd go

26

looking for a psycho in a sleeping bag sniffing petrol. But this is not going to be as simple as that.'

'I'm glad I joined, then.'

'They're not all like this, Lovejoy. And wait until we get a result before you go rubbing your hands together. Because if we don't, watch the organic waste matter hit the fan.'

Wes put his head round the door. 'Guv,' he said. 'I think we've got something.'

Charlie and Dawson and half a dozen of the team all squeezed into a windowless room not much bigger than a store cupboard to stare at a monitor and the ghostly black-and-white images captured from the CCTV camera outside Barrow Fields cemetery.

As the numbers ticked over on a clock in the top right-hand corner, two bright white lights appeared and flickered briefly on the screen. At first the vehicle was anonymous behind the blinding glare of the headlights, but then, as it turned into the driveway, they saw it for the first time in profile. Charlie squinted and angled his head.

'It's a Ford Transit,' he said.

'Fuck,' someone said. 'It would be.'

One of the PCs from the CCTV team kept their finger on the button, fast-forwarding and replaying, trying to get the perfect frame.

'There it is,' someone said.

They could make out the registration plate, but it was too grainy to identify the characters. They'd need enhancement in the laboratory.

As they watched, a man in a balaclava and what looked like a full body jumpsuit got out of the van, holding a pair of bolt cutters. He cut through the chain on the gates and pushed them open. He drove through. Charlie made a note of the time on the clock: 3.10 a.m.

The PC fast-forwarded until the van appeared again; it drove straight out again without stopping. 3.49 a.m.

'So, if anyone ever asks how long it takes to crucify someone,' Greene said, 'there's your answer. Thirty-nine minutes.'

No one laughed. They never did, but that didn't seem to stop him.

'Send the tape to the Transport Research Lab,' Charlie said. 'We want make and model and year. And I want an enhancement of that registration plate, urgent.'

CHAPTER FIVE

At eight o'clock that night Charlie walked into the conference room a floor above IR1. A huge backdrop with the Metropolitan Police logo hung on the back wall. The room was mostly used for media interviews, but tonight he wanted to get everyone together, make sure the whole team was on the same page with him, and this was the only room big enough. They were still inside the magical forty-eight-hour window, the prime time to identify a main suspect.

The room was full. There were nearly sixty cops: his detectives in suits; a surveillance team looking as though they had just been dragged out of bed, as they always did; traffic cops in hi-vis jackets and peak caps; a few uniforms. There was a buzz of conversation. It stopped as he walked in.

Charlie threw his black folder on the desk on the podium and settled himself on the corner of it.

'Welcome everyone. Thanks for coming. This is officially the first briefing of our investigation, which from here on will be Operation Galilee.'

'You're having a laugh, right?' Greene said from the back of the room.

'It's what the computer came up with,' Charlie said. 'We're here today because of Father Andrew O'Meara. I'm sure you have all been shocked by what you've seen on the whiteboard in Incident Room One, but we have to approach this investigation methodically, as we would any murder investigation. Here is what we know so far.'

Charlie ran through the evidence: Father O'Meara had been abducted around 21.30 on Tuesday night, working among the homeless around the Auldminster Estate; his wrists had been nailed to a wooden upright, seven feet long, either in the rear of the van or at an unknown address; he had then been transported to the cemetery at Barrow Fields, where he had been hoisted into position against the church wall, using a winch, which was most probably attached to a large motor vehicle. Two other smaller lengths of wood had then been attached to the timber at forty-five degree angles. His legs had been broken with a heavy blunt object, and he had then been left there to die.

As he talked, some of his more eager detectives took notes; most just shook their heads and stared at the floor.

'We're still waiting for toxicology,' Charlie said. 'Post mortem results show no sign of a struggle, so our initial hypothesis is that he was drugged. There was also debris of unknown origin found on his clothes. Hopefully this will give us further lines of enquiry.'

When he had finished there was a deathly silence in the room.

'A nut job,' someone finally offered.

'A nut job with a very thorough approach to detail,' Charlie said.

'Do we have CCTV?'

Charlie nodded. 'Wes and Rupinder retrieved council CCTV from the High Street that shows a white Transit van pull up in front of the cemetery gates at 3.10 a.m. A man wearing a balaclava and a full body jumpsuit gets out and uses a pair of bolt cutters to break the padlock chain on the gates and drives through. The van reappears at 3.49 a.m. and drives away.'

'Not a Ford Transit?' someone else said.

Charlie saw the looks on the faces around the room. The Ford Transit was the single most stolen vehicle in London. 'The good news is, there is something different about this one. It's too early to be sure but, from viewing the footage, there appears

30

to be something mounted on the front, perhaps a winch of some sort. So, even if it was stolen, it does at least have a distinguishing feature. Some of my team are currently going through all reports of stolen Ford Transit vans in the last three months to see if we can identify it.'

'What about the registration plate?'

'We couldn't read it, we're waiting for the lab to get back to us with an enhancement.'

'No witnesses?'

'We have made extensive enquiries in all the flats and houses in the vicinity, but the people of the borough all sleep like babies, it seems. No one remembers seeing or hearing anything unusual.'

'Well maybe this isn't an unusual crime round there,' Greene said.

'Do we know where he was when he was grabbed, guv?'

'I've had detectives out there all day, crawling into cardboard boxes, talking to every bootsie and gutter nutter we could find. As you'd expect, there's not much help there so far.'

'No one saw him Tuesday night?'

'Wes, they're drinking Skol Super and White Ace. Most of them can't remember their own names.'

'What about his mobile phone? Do priests have them?'

'He did have a phone, we are told, but it was not anywhere at the crime scene.' Charlie looked at Parm from Intel and nodded.

'The last signal placed him in the Auldminster Estate,' she said. 'It was switched off abruptly at . . .' She checked her notes. '. . . 22.16. It has not been reactivated.'

Charlie looked around the room. 'If our perpetrator – or perpetrators – are smart, as they undoubtedly are, then they switched off the phone as soon as they abducted Father O'Meara. It gives us an approximate time for his abduction. We have uniformed teams from the local nick and surrounding areas combing the entire area looking for it, and the search will resume at first light tomorrow. There is also a large pond in a nearby park, Hamersley Flats, and we're going to have a dive team out there first thing.'

The door at the back opened and Gale walked in. He looked exhausted.

'Sorry I'm late, guv.'

'How did you go? Anything?'

He shook his head. 'I interviewed everyone on the volunteer roster.'

'Were they helpful?'

'They wanted to be helpful, but they didn't have anything new to tell us.'

'The housekeeper?'

He shook his head.

'Were they, you know?' Greene made a gesture with the finger and thumb of one hand and the index finger of the other.

Gale looked irritated. 'If they were, Sarge, she's not just going to come out and say so, is she? I talked to everyone over there, there wasn't a hint from anyone that he had anything to hide.'

'You got his computer?'

He nodded. 'It's over in Lambeth right now. Got to tell you, guv, there's a lot of angry people out there. The church is packed, people lighting candles and praying, they've even started putting bunches of flowers outside. It's like Lady Di all over again.'

'Facebook has gone crazy,' Parm said.

'Father O'Meara had a Facebook page?'

'Two thousand followers. Father Donnelly posted a plain white cross on a black background with RIP Father O'Meara. It has almost a hundred comments already.'

'Monitor it. Anything unusual, send it through to the skipper. All right, what we'll do, I'll order a police-marked caravan and trailer over to the church first thing in the morning. It will show everyone we mean business and give all these people a focus; perhaps someone will have something interesting to tell us. We'll reconvene eight a.m. And remember, people, we don't want any of the grisly details getting out. You do not talk about this to your spouses, your family, don't even talk to yourself in the car. The press get hold of this, believe me, it will be a circus. Keeping the methodology quiet means we can eliminate any crazies who come in to confess. Our suspect, when we find him or her or them, they may be mad, but they are not crazy. This may be one of the most brutal and bizarre cases any of us has ever worked on, but it doesn't appear to be random, it has been planned in some detail, probably over months. Questions?'

A shake of the heads. They all looked beat. It had been a long day.

'First thing in the morning, I'm going to talk to Father O'Meara's bishop, see if he can shed any light on his past before he became a priest of the parish. He was a teacher at a boys' college in Brighton for a while.'

There were smiles and raised eyebrows around the room.

'You mean, it could be some ex-pupil taking revenge?' Wes said.

'It's a line of enquiry, that's all. But not all Catholic priests are paedos, like not all of you are divorced alcoholics.' He took a breath. 'Just most of you.'

He even got a laugh out of them for that.

'By this time tomorrow night, I would like to think we will have advanced our inquiry significantly. I don't have to remind you that if you've made any plans for the weekend, you can cancel them right now. OK, that's it.'

They were all about to leave when the DCI strode in.

'FONC,' Wes muttered under his breath, but not loud enough for the DCI to hear.

'Just a word before you all go,' he said, and they all sat down again. No one moaned, but Charlie saw by their faces that no one was best pleased.

He climbed on to the podium behind Charlie and rubbed his

hands together. 'Before you all leave for the night, I just wanted to say a few words. We need everyone to pull together on this. I have complete faith in Detective Inspector George, but I'll be keeping a close eye on everything personally, so you don't have to worry. Follow what he says. Think of him as my mouthpiece, if you like. If anyone has any concerns, you can come and talk to me personally, my door is always open. I cannot stress to you enough how important it is that this case is resolved quickly and quietly. This isn't a random street crime, we have a cold-blooded and grotesque murder here. Anyone who does well on this one can find themselves on a fast track to promotion. That's all. Let's crack on tomorrow and get this case closed. I have every faith in all of you.'

And he walked out.

The officers clattered out of the room, back to their desks or headed to the car park. Lovejoy followed Charlie into his corner office. Witness statements littered the desk, bulging case files tee-tered precariously on the edge of it, there were curling Post-it notes all over his desk monitor. News clippings and inter-office memos crowded for space on the pin board behind his head.

Charlie saw it on her face; most people couldn't see how he got any work done.

'As long as I can see the Arsenal's fixture list, I know I'm still on top of things,' he said.

Lovejoy had the official policy book. She sat down while he dictated his notes to her, brought them up to date. When they had finished, she said:

'Why do they call him FONC?'

'Who?'

'The DCI.'

'Don't know what you mean.'

'Wes just called him that.'

'Oh, that's just his initials. Fergus O'Neal-Callaghan.'

He saw by her face she didn't believe him. Good. She had the makings of someone who would fit right in round here.

'You should go home and get some kip,' he said. 'You've had a right proper first day.'

'I've enjoyed it.'

'You did well with Father Donnelly.'

'Thanks.'

'Are you romantically involved with anyone?' Charlie asked.

She gave him a look. Here it comes, she was thinking, and I've only been here a day.

'Because if you are,' Charlie said, 'working here will fix that. I had a girlfriend, seven years we were together. Nine months after I made Inspector, it was all over.'

'I'll remember that.'

'I didn't have time earlier, to give you your induction talk. So here it is: one week in every eight we're on call. In that time, you don't drink, you don't make social plans. Look at it as a chance to get healthy. If we pull a murder, and we always do, sleep is out of the question until it's sorted. I once did seventy hours straight on a stabbing in Walthamstow. If you don't like it, you don't last. OK?'

'OK.'

'We're a team. Remember that. But also remember, there's thirty detectives in MIT25, and they all want my job, so you'd better learn how to shine.'

'What about you?'

'What about me?'

'Whose job do you want?'

'I want to be chief constable and join the Freemasons and wear a little blue apron every Thursday.' He even said it with a straight face.

She got to her feet. 'You're not off home yourself, guv?'

'You're having a laugh,' Charlie said. 'This is my home.'

After she'd gone, Charlie googled Father O'Meara, and downloaded the BBC documentary about him from YouTube. He put his feet on the desk and watched it, taking occasional notes.

Eerie watching someone you'd only ever seen in the morgue talking on camera, going about their daily life. The documentary was the story of how he had raised money for the food van, and then started Christ is Care. There was footage of him on the streets of Hackney and Haringey and Leyton, squatting in dank doorways talking to homeless people, playing basketball with kids straight out of street gangs. There were interviews with former students at the Catholic college where he'd taught in Brighton, others with youngsters he had helped take off the streets, all saying how they were now off the drink and drugs and living a decent life.

'If you were so fucking good,' Charlie said aloud to the screen, 'why did someone nail you up to a bit of lumber and stack you against a wall.'

Didn't add up. Something had to be missing here.

Father O'Meara must have had secrets.

CHAPTER SIX

A sign faced the road, just above the brick wall around Saint Joseph's church.

Jesus Loves Us.

'Nice to be loved,' Greene said.

'How would you know?' Charlie said.

It was an impressive place, the bishop's residence; Victorian Gothic, like one of those red-brick places that pop stars used to buy in Hampstead. There were bracketed eaves and window headers, and iron cresting above the hooded windows.

'Being a bishop looks like nice work if you can get it,' Greene said.

'Not worth spending all your life on your knees for, is it?'

'I know girls spent their whole lives on their knees never made this much.'

'I'm sure you do.'

They were met at the door by the housekeeper, a middle-aged woman who reminded Charlie of his school nurse. She led the way through the house.

It was like walking into a Brontë novel; walnut Corinthian capitals framed a central staircase, there were carved balustrades, and an ornate chandelier hung from the vaulted ceiling. Under their feet was a tile mosaic of a praying saint.

Halfway up the stairs was a huge gilt-framed oil of Jesus hanging on the cross. Jay looked at Charlie and their eyes met.

'Remind you of anything?' Greene murmured.

The bishop greeted them in a Victorian parlour at the rear

of the house. Several Persian rugs were scattered about the polished parquet floors. I could buy a new flat with just one of those, Charlie thought.

The bishop was standing with his back to a tiled fireplace, he was perfectly decked out in the purple under his tweed jacket.

He extended a hand. 'Robert Holm,' he said.

'Reverend. Detective Inspector Charlie George. This is my colleague, Detective Sergeant Jayden Greene.'

They were invited to sit. They perched on the edge of an Edwardian sofa and the housekeeper was sent to fetch tea.

'Earl Grey or Oolong?' the bishop said.

'Tetley's thanks,' Greene said.

'Oolong would be the business,' Charlie said with an apologetic smile at the housekeeper.

After she had gone, the bishop sat down opposite them and crossed his legs, his fingers steepled under his chin.

'Thank you for making time to talk to us, Reverend,' Charlie said.

'Well, of course. A terrible business. Terrible. We are all still in shock. Times such as these test the faith of each and every one of us, and yet it is only in God do we find comfort.'

'Quite. I'm sorry for your loss.'

'You are the detective in charge of the case?'

'Yes, I am.'

'I shall pray for you and your endeavours, as I shall pray for the culprit also. His soul must be in great turmoil to do such a terrible thing.'

'Souls are your business, Reverend. Mine is catching the person or persons responsible.'

'You think there might be more than one person involved?'

'All lines of enquiry are open.'

'So how may I help you?'

'We are trying to build up a better picture of Father Andrew.'

'What can I tell you? He was a remarkable man.'

'I understand that he was. So, we have to ask ourselves, if he was so remarkable, who would want to kill him?'

'Could it not have been a random act of violence? With his work, he came into contact with all manner of people. Some of them were affected by drugs and alcohol and sometimes severe mental issues.'

'Yes, but this wasn't random.'

'If you don't mind me asking, how exactly did he die?'

'I'm not at liberty to tell you that.'

'I heard he was found inside a disused church, some distance from his own.'

'That's correct.'

'I did find that rather odd.'

'What can you tell us about him? Apart from his goodness, I mean.' Because if someone else tells me what a good man he was, I'm going to throw up on your Persian rug.

'Well, after the seminary, he went to Saint Joseph's Boys' College in Brighton. He taught there for over five years before requesting a transfer to a London parish. When he came here, he obtained a Master's degree in psychology from St Mary's University, as well as a diploma in abuse and trauma counselling. Soon after, he started a charity organisation, using local parishioners as volunteers.'

'Christ is Care.'

'Yes, it received a lot of positive attention. He was mentioned in the Queen's honours three years ago. The BBC made a film about him, it's called—'

'I watched it last night.'

A nervous laugh. 'Then you should know all this.'

The tea arrived on a silver tray. Charlie waited while the bishop's housekeeper poured it for them. A bone-china tea service, Charlie thought; makes a change from instant coffee in a mug.

Greene nudged him and whispered: 'Where's the milk?'

When the door closed again, Greene reached for one of the

digestives, and dunked it in his tea anyway. Charlie saw the Right Reverend Robert Holm raise an eyebrow.

'Inspector, I have to tell you, Father O'Meara was one of those rare souls blessed with the common touch. He could chat with the Queen as easily as he could talk a poor alcoholic into going for counselling.'

'You mean Prince Philip?' Greene said.

Charlie silenced him with a glance.

'As I said, Reverend, the question I have to ask myself is why anyone would want him dead. I cannot divulge the details of this case, but there is not a shadow of a doubt that this was premeditated.'

The bishop shook his large, grizzled head. 'There are many wicked people in the world.'

'That's the conclusion to which my work has also brought me. But, for now, I'd just like to find the one who murdered your priest.'

The bishop put his teacup on the occasional table beside him. 'I don't know what else I can tell you.'

'Let's go back to his days as a teacher. Why did he leave Saint Joseph's?'

'As I said, he himself requested a transfer to a working-class parish in London.'

'So, he jumped, he wasn't pushed?'

'I don't understand.'

'His conduct while he was a teacher. How would you characterise it?'

'Exemplary.'

'You're sure about that? There were never any complaints laid against him?'

'What kind of complaints?'

'Any kind of complaint.'

'What exactly are you asking me?'

'I'm trying to find a reason someone might want to harm him. If he was so good, why was he abducted and murdered?'

'I think I know where you're going with this and, let me tell you, I will not allow you to besmirch that man's reputation in any way.'

'If there's nothing to besmirch, then his reputation has nothing to fear from me. But no one murders a good and holy man.'

'They did it to Jesus.'

'Good point,' Greene said, and reached for another biscuit. Charlie leaned forward and moved the plate out of his reach.

'All due respect, but that was a long time ago. And it wasn't murder, it was a politically motivated government execution. What happened to Father O'Meara doesn't sound kosher to me, if you'll pardon the expression.'

'Are you of the faith, Inspector?'

'Is that relevant?'

'I just wonder why you are pursuing this line of questioning with such zeal.'

'I'm just doing my job.'

'So, you were never one of us?'

'My mother was Catholic.'

'And your father?'

'Every Sunday morning, from the moment he woke up until the pubs opened at lunchtime.'

The bishop gave him a forbearing smile that made Charlie's teeth ache. 'Religion is like following a football club. You can never ever leave it, no matter how badly they play.'

'You have me there, because I'm an Arsenal supporter.'

'Then you understand, Inspector. I realise that you have a job to do, but I believe, as the saying goes, that you are not only barking up the wrong tree, you're in the wrong forest.'

Charlie finished his tea and placed the cup on the table. 'Thank you for your time, Reverend. If you think of anything that may help us, please don't hesitate to call.' He reached into his jacket pocket and laid a business card on the table.

The bishop rang a bell on the occasional table. His

housekeeper reappeared. 'Show these gentlemen out, will you please, Mary?'

Greene went to the door, Charlie followed.

'Inspector. Perhaps you will consider returning to the faith one day. The Church is all that keeps us from the animals.'

'I don't mind animals. I had a spaniel when I was a kid. He never read the Bible but you know what? He never hurt anyone in his whole life, and even when my old man kicked him, he'd still come back and lick his face. That dog taught me how to be a decent geezer more than any Sunday school ever did. No disrespect.'

When they got back to the car, Greene sat there a moment, a hand on the key in the ignition. There was clearly something he wanted to say.

'Come on, Jay, out with it.'

'What does besmirch mean?'

'Stain.'

'Right. That makes sense.'

'What else did you learn from that little exchange?'

Greene straightened his shoulders and considered. 'Did you see the table next to him?'

'What about it?'

'Saw one just like it in an antiques shop in Islington. Rosewood with inlays. Seven hundred nicker. So, what I learned is: crime might not pay but religion does. If I ever get kicked out of the Force, think I'll become a vicar.'

'You'd be very good at it.'

'Thanks, guv,' Greene said, and smiled.

CHAPTER SEVEN

Charlie woke to the first few bars of 'The Ride of the Valkyries', sat up and stared into the darkness, trying to remember where he was. He'd downloaded the ringtone to his personal iPhone, to distinguish it from his work Nokia. It trilled on the carpet beside him, next to the camp bed. He snatched it up.

'Hello.'

'Is that Mr George?'

'Yes.'

'My name's Hannah, I'm the duty nurse at Arlington Mansions.'

'Is my mother all right?'

'Nothing's happened to her, Mister George. But she seems quite distressed. She's asking for you.'

Everything drained out of him. He lay back hard on the pillow, stared at the ceiling, at the shadow of a fluorescent light. Right, he remembered now, he'd spent all day yesterday signing overtime forms, reading and re-reading witness statements and CS reports and poring through intel and, before he knew it, it was too late to go home. He was still in the nick.

'You're not able to settle her?'

'She keeps saying she wants to see you. She's quite agitated and she won't go back to her bed. Would you like us to sedate her?'

'Have you tried ringing my brother?'

'He's not picking up, I'm afraid.'

'Right, OK. No, don't sedate her. I'll be there. Just tell her I'm coming, will you?'

'Thank you, Mister George.'

He hung up, stared out of the window at London emitting a feeble orange sodium glow. He saw his own reflection in the glass. 'Come on, son,' he said to himself. 'You'd have to be up soon anyway.'

It was the start of a cold snap and there was a powdery layer of snow on the ground. As he got out of his car a flurry of it hit him in the face, scratchy and cold. He ran across the car park and punched in the code on the security door. He was met by a rush of hot air, like getting off a plane in the south of Spain in the summer, a shock of heat. He started peeling off layers.

The foyer of Arlington Mansions was like the atrium of a five-star hotel; he almost expected someone to rush up and ask to carry his bags. Well, he supposed Benedict was good for something. He would never have been able to afford something like this on a copper's pay.

God's waiting room, Ben called it; air locked, double glazed, insulated from the world of the living. It was a kind of Netherworld, like his mother told him about when he was little; Fiddler's Green, the place halfway between heaven and hell where all the Cockneys went when they died. The women there drank shandy, or Babycham if they were posh, and played gin rummy.

He went up to the reception, a nurse sitting behind it, just her head visible, a single, angled desk lamp forming a corona around her dark brown hair.

'Hi, I'm Charlie George. I got a call about my mum.'

'Yes, Mr George. We called because we were having trouble settling her. She insisted that we ring you.'

'That's all right. Where is she now?'

'She's in the lounge. You can go through.'

'How have things been?'

She smiled, which wasn't a good sign. 'She had a big row

with Mrs Hetherington about the use of the television. She can be quite difficult.'

'That's not breaking news. I grew up with her.'

'And she lost her purse again.'

'Where was it this time?'

'In her refrigerator in her room.'

'Thanks. Just through here, is she?'

She was sitting in a large pink velvet armchair, stranded in the yellow pool of light from a floor lamp, twisting a Kleenex between her fingers and tearing it into tiny pieces. She was surrounded by a litter of paper tissue, like confetti. Her gaze was fixed on the floor, lost in a reverie he could only guess at.

She had a large handbag on her lap, had both arms wrapped around it, like it had just died. It looked heavy, and he supposed it should be; she took it with her everywhere and inside was her life insurance policy, her birth certificate, her passport – now expired – her purse, three hundred pounds in crisp new five-pound notes, her marriage certificate and three premium bonds from 1978. He'd picked it up once, it weighed as much as a house brick.

'Hello, Ma.'

'Oh hello, son. What are you doing here?'

'They said you were asking for me.'

'Was I?'

'You don't remember?'

'I suppose I must have, if they said so. Where's Nicole?'

'Ma, we split up a couple of years ago, remember?'

'Did you? I don't remember that. Got a head like a sieve, I have. Didn't you like her, I thought she was a nice girl.'

'She was a nice girl. She still is.'

'Who you with now then?'

'I'm not with anyone.'

'What time is it?'

'It's almost five in the morning.'

45

'What are you doing up so early?'

'They rang me and told me you couldn't sleep.'

'Did they?' She leaned forward and lowered her voice to a whisper. 'Someone stole my purse.'

'They said they found it.'

'Well, I've got it *now*. I made them give it back. I don't trust them in here, those nurses would take anything if it wasn't nailed down.'

'The nurses are nice, Ma. They're really good to you.'

He wasn't sure if she had heard him. She went back to tearing up the tissue. 'What are you doing here so early?'

'They called me at the office, they said you couldn't sleep.'

'Do you want a cup of tea?'

'I'll make it.' Charlie got to his feet. 'What would you like?'

'I don't want one. The tea's horrible here.'

He sat down again. He yawned, closed his eyes for a moment. It felt like they were full of sand.

'You all right, son?'

'Didn't get to sleep till two o'clock.'

'Your father was like that, staying up till all hours.'

'Drinking. I've been working.'

'What, till two in the morning?'

'I'm a cop, Ma. That's what we do. Has Ben been in to see you?'

'No, he can't, he's busy at work.'

'We're all busy at work.'

'Yes, but you can come and go as you want with your job.'

'Ma, Ben plays golf twice a week.'

'You could play golf if you wanted.'

'I don't want to play golf.'

'Well, there you are then.'

He looked at his watch. 'I have to get back to the nick. Are you sure you're OK now?'

'When will you come back to see me?'

'Every Sunday and Wednesday, like always.'

A stricken look. He felt as if he was abandoning her in prison or in the terminal ward. He supposed he was in a way, on both counts. He got to his feet. She looked so sad and so small. He wished there was something he could do.

He bent over to say goodbye to her. She clung on to his arm and wouldn't let go.

'Love you, son,' she said.

'I love you too, Ma,' he said.

There was still snow in the air when he got outside, the harsh bite of the living world. The first bus was headed down the High Street, he heard the rattle of a train from somewhere; people would have started posting recipes and pictures of cats on Facebook. They didn't have any of that in there, not in Fiddler's Green.

As he drove out past the Arlington Mansions sign, it occurred to him that it was quite a magical place, in many ways. It was where you could still visit the dead; you just couldn't bring them back with you. Before he'd left, he'd almost been tempted to say to her: if you slip away tonight, and you see Father O'Meara, text me and tell me what happened to him. But that was just fatigue getting to him.

And this was only day two.

CHAPTER EIGHT

Charlie met Sister Agatha in a greasy spoon in Walthamstow. It was piping hot inside and smelled of frying grease; the place was packed with local cabbies and builders in paint-stained overalls, chowing into their fry-ups and butties. Made him nostalgic, it did; all wood-effect Formica, Anaglypta wallpaper and condensation on the windows. Not many good ones left in London any more, it was all Bircher muesli with rhubarb and decaf lattes.

Sister Agatha was sitting in the corner nursing a mug of milky tea and reading the *Independent*. He wasn't sure what he had been expecting; whatever it was, she wasn't it. She had on a long blue pleated skirt, and a crisp white blouse with a silver cross on each collar tip. Her neat haircut looked like a wiry white helmet.

It didn't look like the sort of place where he could get an espresso so he ordered a mug of tea for himself and sat down.

'You'd be the detective inspector,' she said. She leaned back and crossed her arms, as if she was debating whether or not to let him into a nightclub. A big woman, she was, and proper feisty-looking.

'You'd be Sister Agatha.'

'You're not what I was expecting,' she said.

'What were you expecting?'

'Well, you look like one of those fellas that stand behind those Russian billionaires in dark wraparound glasses, cracking their knuckles and pretending to be his accountant.'

'My mother told me never to crack my knuckles, it's bad for me.'

'Good on her.' She shoved her newspaper towards him. 'You can have it. I've been trying to read it, but all I can think about is poor Father O'Meara.'

'You were close?'

'We worked together these last seven and a half years. I would say I knew him as well as anyone alive. I cannot believe he's gone. I still think he's going to walk through the door any moment with that big boyish grin of his. But we cannot question God's intention, or his will.'

Charlie made a face.

'I can see you're not a believer.'

'I believe in forensic science and a well-positioned CCTV camera.'

'We'll agree to disagree then.' She sat back. 'How can I help?'

'I'm trying to put together some sort of timeline up to his disappearance. Can I start by asking you when was the last time you saw him?'

'Two nights ago. I was handing out coffee and sandwiches in the Christ is Care food van. It was parked in the forecourt of Saint Joseph's in Elderberry Lane and I was there until around eight o'clock with Sister Margaret and three volunteers from Father O'Meara's parish.'

'How did he seem?'

'He seemed his normal self. Cheerful, caring and full of the holy spirit.' She leaned forward. 'You are wondering if anything was troubling him. I can tell you now, it wasn't. What I can tell you is this: even though I said I can't believe he's gone, I suppose that's not quite true. This is what I was always afraid would happen. I warned Father O'Meara again and again never to go out alone. He seemed oblivious to danger, that man. He knew the risks but sometimes he flouted the rules of common sense.'

'He put too much faith in God.'

'That is not how I would have put it.'

'"Again and again they put God to the test; they vexed the Holy One of Israel."'

Sister Agatha stared at him for a moment in complete surprise, but then a wariness came to her eyes. 'You know your Bible.'

'I should. I had to listen to it every Sunday for almost eight years.'

'You're one of us, then?'

'If you mean, am I a Catholic, then no, not any more.'

'What drove you away? Was it the girls or the drink?'

'That's for me to know and you to find out, Sister. It's not relevant to our meeting today. I am just trying to find out why someone hated Father O'Meara so badly, they wanted to kill him.'

'As Jesus said, they know not what they do.'

'Oh, whoever did this, they knew what they were doing, believe me. And if it was just some addict or crazy he was trying to help in Hackney Wick, how was it he ended up in a derelict chapel in Barrow Fields cemetery?'

'I wish I could help you, Detective, I really do. As I wish he had called me that night instead of going out on his own.'

'Let me get this straight. He used to wander around at night, talking to the homeless?'

'Sometimes. Some of the people we spoke to were referrals.'

'Referrals?'

'People would call him, say they'd seen someone sleeping out by their bins, or something like that. We took care of them, we'd bandage wounds, take them to the hospital, organise counselling or interviews with welfare, things they weren't able or willing to do for themselves, not at first. At worst Father O'Meara gave them a safe place to sleep and something to eat. He used to say to me, we can't save people from themselves but we can show them that someone cares about them.'

'And who paid for all of this?'

'Well, we had no funding from the government, if that's what you mean. The volunteers who work with us are all from the parish – nurses, teachers, even solicitors.'

'And the food van? That was donated as well?'

'Everything, even the camp beds in the church. He had collected about a dozen of them and they are always full.'

'They say he had the gift of the gab.'

'Perhaps. Most of all, he was a true believer.'

'In God.'

'What he believed, what I believe, is what the Bible teaches us; that we should treat everyone we meet as if they are our brothers and sisters. The story of the Good Samaritan, as Jesus taught it in the gospel, is what true Christianity is all about. Our family, our parish, are the outcasts, the migrants, women fleeing every kind of abuse.'

'Well, he certainly died like a good Christian,' Charlie said.

'Meaning?'

'Meaning, for all his good works, his reward was an untimely death. Anyway, thank you, Sister. If you do think of anything that may help, here's my card. Give me a call.' His Nokia rang. It was Dawson. 'I'll have to take this,' he said, and got up to leave.

'God will help you,' Sister Agatha said.

'Do you think he's got time to call the hotline?'

'You know, you pretend to be different, but you're not.'

Charlie picked up: 'Hang on,' he said, and turned back to Sister Agatha. 'What do you mean?'

'I'm celibate by choice. What about you?'

'I'm not celibate. I was in a relationship for seven years.'

'Why did it end?'

Charlie saw where she was going with this. She was sharp, for a nun.

'You had a choice between work and the girl, I shouldn't wonder. And what did you choose? It's a calling, you see. When it has you in its thrall, there's nothing you can do about it, no matter how you wish otherwise.'

51

'It had nothing to do with religion, though.'

'Whatever you want to call it, you're a believer, same as Father Andrew was, same as I am. Maybe you're not religious, but you're a good man, you're on the side of the angels, just like us.'

Too early in the morning for philosophy. He thanked her for her trouble, and left. He finished the call with Dawson in the street outside. He was wanted back at the nick.

Still not seven-thirty when he got back to IR1, but he was pleased to see most of the team were already at their desks, waiting for Dawson to action them for the day. Sanderson from the CCTV unit and Lovejoy were already waiting to talk to him, so were Greene and Dawson. He took them all down to the canteen for an informal briefing.

The canteen was full, uniforms lining up for cooked breakfasts and the vending machines around the wall doing brisk trade. He got himself a cappuccino from the coffee machine though he had no intention of drinking it. He found a quiet table in the corner and they all sat down.

'I searched VODS for the image we had from the CCTV outside Barrow Hill,' Greene said. He checked his notes. 'Best fit is for a 2100 Ford Transit VM140, produced between January 2011 and October 2011.'

'Plates?'

Dawson frowned and sipped his coffee; it left a froth on his moustache. 'Now then. Lambeth got back to me with an enhancement first thing. I checked on the PNC, they were stolen two months ago. A Fiesta parked in the street in a leafy green in Hampstead.'

Charlie shrugged. He'd been expecting that.

'ANPR?'

'The plates were recorded by a camera on the High Street, 3.58 a.m. Then nothing.'

Sanderson leaned forward. By the bags under his eyes he had

been up all night. 'There is a CCTV on the pub on the corner of the High Street, and we have a white Ford Transit turning into Watts Avenue at 3.59 a.m.'

Greene had a map with him, spread it out on the table. 'This is the area behind Barrow Fields. He drove out of the gates here, to the High Street, turned off here. He must have kept to the back streets to avoid cameras, could have changed the plates and left the estate again by any of these roads. Changes the radius of CCTV capture to more than five miles.'

'What about prior to reaching the cemetery?'

'Nothing on ANPR for those plates.'

'I might have something,' Lovejoy said.

Charlie looked down the table hopefully.

'I checked the PNC, as you said, guv, looked for any modified Ford Transits on the stolen vehicle database. That filtered out the possibles, and then I cross-matched the list with what we got from the VODS.'

'And?'

'Just one, in London. Kennington.'

'Result,' Charlie said.

CHAPTER NINE

The address was a builder's yard, down a back lane not far from the Kennington Oval. It was flanked by a row of terraced houses, and just across the road was a school, built in the twenties from shit-coloured brick. They parked behind a wheel-clamped Mercedes.

'Nice,' Greene said, as he got out, admiring the leaning corrugated-iron fence. It was topped with barbed wire; looked like it was only being held up by a red wheelie bin, full of empty paint tins.

It started to rain.

Charlie followed Greene over the road, watched where he was treading; he had on his new Italian boots. They had been made from one piece of leather, cost him a fortune online. He'd promised himself he wouldn't wear them for work, but the last time he had been home – which was when, exactly, he couldn't remember – and he had been getting dressed for work, he couldn't help himself, had slipped them on. They really looked the business.

It was a decision he was regretting now.

Inside the yard there was an ancient shed with a blue tin sign on the roof. It said: 'GI Moran & Sons.'

It was ciggy time. Two likely lads stood under the awning of a transportable, one of them in tracksuit pants and a t-shirt tucked in, a real belly on him; he gave Charlie the kind of look you get in a pub in Southend late on a Saturday night. The other geezer was a bit sharper, tall and thin –

the owner he supposed, Moran – hoping they might be business.

'All right then, lads?' he called to them. 'How can I help?'

Charlie showed him his warrant card and watched their faces fall. 'Detective Inspector George. This is Detective Sergeant Greene. Got a minute?'

The smile didn't falter but the look in Moran's eyes was suddenly different. He took a drag on his cigarette. 'What's this about then?'

Charlie looked down at his boots. There was mud on them. 'Mind if we step inside?'

The office was a tip, like the yard. There was an ancient desktop PC, a printer, a photocopier, a grey filing cabinet, files piled on the desk with invoices spilling out of them, curled Post-it notes on the threadbare carpet. There wasn't enough room to swing any kind of domestic pet.

But it was the Tottenham Hotspur poster on the wall that really pissed him off.

'Are you the proprietor?' Charlie said.

'Gary Moran,' the tall one said. He nodded at the other one, the fashion diva. 'This is my business partner, James Hodges.'

'Well, Gazza, this is about the Ford Transit van you reported stolen three weeks ago.'

'Has it taken you this long to find it?' Hodges said. 'I told you, Gaz. Useless, the Old Bill.'

'Not my job to find cars,' Charlie said. 'I'm with the Major Incident Team in Islington. That's Murder Squad to you.'

'Murder Squad?'

'We believe the vehicle you reported stolen was recently used in a homicide.'

'Well you should have been quicker finding it, innit?' Hodges said.

Charlie gave him a look. No one spoke for a while. Then

Greene nudged Charlie's arm, nodded at the white Ford Transit parked in the yard, next to a pallet of timber and a stack of cement bags.

'The old one had a winch mounted to the front,' Charlie said.

'What of it?'

'Did it, or didn't it?'

'Jimmy here got the winch cheap. He said it'd be useful.'

'Was it?'

'Yeah, it was, thanks.'

'Mounted it yourself?'

'I saw how to do it on YouTube,' Hodges said.

'Good for you,' Charlie said. 'Pity it got nicked, then.'

Gary sighed and tucked his hands in his pockets. 'What has all this got to do with some bloke getting offed?'

'Where did it get nicked? The van.'

'It was parked in the street outside. Came back one morning and it was gone.'

'So, you've no idea who stole it?'

'Sorry, can't help you.'

'Is that it?' Hodges said. 'You lot never gave a toss about our van until now. Typical Old Bill. We get our means of livelihood blagged and you lot don't get out of the office until some gang-banger gets what's coming.'

Charlie ignored him, reached in his jacket pocket for his card, went through the usual routine, thanks for your help, if anything comes up you think might help us, give us a call.

Just then there was a tap on the glass. A skinny boy in a paint-stained hoodie and trainers put his head round the door. 'Sorry I'm late, boss. I missed me bus.'

'That's all right, Mahesh. Go and get the van warmed up.'

'Yes, boss,' the boy said and slid the glass door shut again. He went over to the Transit van and jumped in.

Charlie looked at Moran. Moran looked at him.

56

'Speaks good English,' Charlie said. 'How long's he been in the country?'

'He was born in Dagenham.'

'That right?'

There was an awkward silence.

'Why did you park your van in the street? It would have been safer here in the yard, locked up.'

'We had a kid working for us. He forgot.'

'That kid, the one from Dagenham?'

'A different kid. Hammersmith.'

'Eleven thousand Fords stolen in the UK last year,' Greene said to Moran. 'Half of them were Transit vans. They make them too easy to nick, in my opinion.'

'But if you've already got the keys,' Charlie said, 'it's no hardship at all.'

'What's that supposed to mean?' Moran said.

'Your employee, the one out there from Dagenham. Have you got his national insurance number?'

'What for?'

'It's a simple request.' Charlie picked up one of the ring binders, let the invoices bundled inside fall out all over the floor. 'I'm sure everything's in order in your business.' He took a step closer. 'Why have you got sweat on your lip?'

'Look, be reasonable. He's applied for his number, it just hasn't come through yet.'

'Perhaps it hasn't come through because he's not legally entitled to one.'

'Don't know what you're talking about.'

'Look Mr Moran, let me be crystal. I don't care if you're employing illegals, that's not my department. I don't care if you lied to your insurance company, they don't pay my wages. However, if you blokes try and obstruct the hand of righteous retribution, i.e., me, when I am after the perpetrator of a homicide, I will bring down on your heads a shit-fight like you just wouldn't believe; Border Force, insurance investigators, the tax office, the fully Monty. And don't expect that van in your yard to pass its MOT either. Know what I mean?'

Moran and Hodges looked at each other.

'This is strictly off the record,' Moran said.

'I'm all ears.'

'The little bastard's name is Sanjay,' Hodges said. 'And if I ever find him, you're going to have another murder inquiry, I swear to fucking God.'

'Tell me about Sanjay,' Charlie said.

'He was working for us two months. He said he'd applied for his number, I swear.'

'Bollocks,' Charlie said. 'He was an illegal and not entitled to a number which is why you paid him sod all. But, like I said, I don't care, just don't yank my chain. I wasn't born yesterday, all right?'

Hodges looked at his boots, nodded that he understood.

'So, what happened?'

'One night he must have pocketed the keys,' Moran said. 'The one to the padlock on the yard as well.'

'How can you be sure it was him?'

'Who else could it be?'

'You went after him?'

'Course we bloody did,' Hodges said. 'He'd done a runner. His mates where he lived reckon he's pissed off back to Pakiland or wherever.'

'Last known address,' Charlie said, and held out his hand.

Moran looked at Hodges, who just shrugged his shoulders: better do it. He checked his phone and scribbled down the address on a piece of paper.

'If we couldn't find him, what makes you think you will?' Hodges said, as they were walking out of the door.

'I'll find him lads. And when I do, I'll get an address for you, you can send him a reference.'

* * *

Charlie walked back to the car humming to himself. Well, that went better than he was expecting. He climbed in the passenger seat of the Sierra, stepping over the puddle at the kerb.

Greene got in behind the wheel. 'How did you know?'

'Know what?'

'That their mucker stole the van?'

'Just a lucky guess. Lesson to you: if you ask people questions, there's no knowing what they'll say in the heat of the moment. If they'd told me to piss off, we would have been no worse off. But it's the guilty conscience, see? Even blokes who think they're proper hard can't help themselves.' He looked at the piece of paper Moran had given him. 'Here, punch this into the GPS. Looks like we're off to Hounslow.'

It was a Victorian squat with bay windows either side of the door, hung with grey net curtains. A green wheelie bin lay on its side in the front yard, which had been paved over to allow for car parking. There was a pathway of concrete slabs, littered with weeds, that led to a door with peeling grey paint and a frosted glass pane.

A strong smell of spice came from inside.

'Fenugreek,' Charlie said, sniffing the air. 'Cumin obviously. Coconut. Wouldn't mind staying for lunch.'

He saw the curtains move. They had been spotted.

'Looks like a bit of fun,' Charlie said.

It was like kicking over an ants' nest. As soon as they started up the path, two Asian teenagers appeared out of a window at the side of the house and took off towards the back fence. One of them clambered over easily, the other got the crotch of his jeans caught on a loose nail and started yelling. Finally, he toppled sideways into the garden on the other side. There was a cry of pain.

Greene was about to go after him, but Charlie caught his arm and made a face. 'Remember your dignity, son. Chasing illegals is for uniforms.'

He nodded at the door, put his hands in his pockets and waited. Greene banged on the door. They could hear them arguing inside, in a language Charlie didn't recognise. He could imagine what they were saying though: don't answer it, we have to, who should go, it can't be me, you go, no you go.

Finally, someone dragged the lock and chain across. An Asian boy, no more than eighteen, wearing a loose t-shirt and jeans, inched open the door and peered out.

Greene showed the boy his warrant badge. 'We're looking for Sanjay Dravid.'

'He's not here.'

'We know that,' Charlie said.

'Did Mister Moran send you?'

'We're the cops, son. No one sends us.'

'Mister Moran said someone would come and break our legs.'

'I'm sure he did. But he's full of bollocks, to borrow a phrase from the Kama Sutra.' Charlie took a step forward. Instinctively, the boy tried to shut the door. Charlie kept it open with his foot. 'Look son, I'm not here to give you grief.'

'I have a British passport.'

'How many of you in there?'

'No one. Just me and my friend.'

'Give over. It's like a football game in there, I can hear it. Now look, we're not the council, we're not Border Force. All we want is a little talk with your friend Sanjay.'

'He's not my friend.'

'What's your name?'

'Dileep.'

'Look, Dileep, we can do this the easy way or the hard way, but you are going to talk to me and so are all your mates. Do you want me to call some heavily armed policemen with bad breath and ungenerous attitudes to foreign nationals, or are you going to let me in?'

'I reckon he's going to let you in,' Greene said.

Dileep let them in.

Charlie made a quick head count: twenty-eight people in a four-bedroom semi, each paying sixty quid a week, if they were to be believed. Nice work if you could get it.

'Almost seventeen hundred notes a week,' Greene said. 'The landlord is quids in.'

They were mostly Indians and Sri Lankans, according to Dileep, though there were two Nepalese nationals and a bloke from Bangladesh who none of them could understand. Charlie gathered them all in the living room, such as it was: a tiny front parlour with a battered brown velour sofa, plaster peeling off the ceiling and a bicycle leaning against the fireplace. There was no heating and the cheap lino on the floor was nuclear orange. There was a Bollywood poster on the wall.

'Is that everyone?' Charlie asked Dileep.

He knew by the way he looked at his feet that it wasn't. So he left Greene to make sure no one else tried to leg it out of the door and followed Dileep down the back path.

There was a damp postage stamp of garden with a neglected sandpit overgrown with weeds, which had been designated as a lavatory by the local cat population. An ironing board and a rusted bike leaned against the fence next to a broken washing machine and a plastic bucket. There was a wooden shed, big enough for a couple of shovels and a lawnmower. Dileep opened the door.

Four more foreign nationals peered out at him from under sleeping bags and between clotheslines, one hunched over a small Primus cooking stove.

'Don't tell me you're sub-letting.'

'We don't even know them. They're Pakistanis. The landlord said we have to let them use the toilet inside.'

'Nice geezer, your landlord,' Charlie said.

'How many people here speak English?' Charlie asked Dileep when they had them all gathered in the living room.

'Not many,' Dileep said.

'Well, you can translate then.'

'Into which language?'

'How many languages are there?'

'Five and two dialects.'

He heard Greene mutter something under his breath.

'Do your best, then,' Charlie said. 'First, tell everyone they're not in any trouble. I just need to find this Sanjay Dravid.'

'Sanjay is a very bad man,' Dileep said. 'He left without paying his share of the rent, and he stole one of my shirts.'

'Well, there are blokes like that,' Charlie said. 'This is why we have policemen.'

'You're not here to report us?'

'Now why would I do that? You told me everyone here has a visa.'

'Oh yes, everyone. Very definitely.'

'Well, I believe you, then. And I will continue to take you at your word as long as someone tells me where I can find Sanjay. Capeesh?'

'I beg your pardon?'

'Do you understand?'

'Yes, yes, I understand.'

'Should we be making those sorts of promises, guv?' Greene said, under his breath.

'Jay, we're not here to solve this country's immigration problems or correct social inequality. Remember that.'

Dileep told everyone what Charlie wanted. There were more than a few blank stares, even after he had said it in several different languages. Finally, a pretty young girl in a hijab and blue jeans put up her hand, as if she was in school.

'Why do you need to find him?' she said.

'He stole a Transit van that was later used in a murder.'

'Murder?' she said, and there was a ripple of alarm through the room.

'He may not be involved. He may have just sold it to someone. I need to find out who to.'

More blank stares.

'Come on, Dileep. Tell them. Sanjay must have had some family here. If someone can't think of something, then I will call the council and you'll all be on the plane back to somewhere hot.'

'It's not hot in Kashmir this time of year, man,' a boy said, at the back. 'It's fucking freezing.'

The girl seemed to hesitate, then her hand crept back into the air. 'Sanjay went home to India. He said his mum was sick.'

'Were you his girlfriend?'

She gave a little wiggle of the head. 'Not his girlfriend. He liked me.'

'He was always trying to impress her,' another girl said.

The Kashmiri boy smirked and crossed his arms. 'He were a proper wanker.'

'Fancy her yourself, do you?' Charlie said, and the girl blushed and her father glared at the Kashmiri boy and there was a ripple of laughter from everyone else and he knew he had won his audience.

It seemed that Sanjay had an uncle who lived in Osterley. No one thought the uncle liked Sanjay very much – perhaps he thought he was a proper wanker, too. The girl even had an address, she said she had been there once.

'In the Ford Transit?' Greene asked her.

'No, on the tube,' the girl said. 'I don't know why he would steal a car. He didn't even have a licence!'

'There are two types of people in the world,' Charlie said when he got back in the car. He punched the address the girl had given them into the GPS. 'There are those that make sandwiches for homeless people and others who make seventeen hundred quid a week out of them.'

'And there's us, guv. Sort of in between.'

63

'Three types then,' Charlie said, and he took out his Nokia and called Lovejoy in the office and asked her to call immigration and try and get an urgent trace on a Sanjay Dravid, Indian national, nineteen years old.

CHAPTER TEN

The High Street was full of halal take-aways and pound stores. There were several shops offering to unblock phones. Why would you need to unblock a phone, Charlie thought, unless you just stole it? There was an empty pub car park, last night's snow still melting in the middle of it, two lonely old geezers sitting at a wooden table outside smoking cancer sticks. The only colour anywhere was the women in rainbow-coloured saris, dripping with twenty-four-carat gold.

They found the address the girl had given them. Sanjay's uncle – Patel, she thought his name was – lived in a three-bedroom pebbledash semi right under the flight path to Heathrow. It had lattice bay windows, a neat and tidy garden, a grey Astra parked in the car port.

The door opened and an elderly woman with a yellow patterned scarf on her head and a green cable-stitch cardigan peered out at them through glasses thick as milk bottle tops.

'We don't have anyone in the shed,' she said.

Greene showed her his ID and she peered at it, but Charlie was fairly sure she couldn't read English.

'Who is it, *nanimaa*?' a woman's voice called from inside the house.

'It's the men from the council,' she called back. 'They want to look in the shed again.'

'Tell them we don't have anyone in the shed.'

'I did, but they won't listen.'

Charlie tapped his foot and waited. Eventually a middle-aged woman in a bright pink sari came to the door and peered over the old woman's shoulder. Greene held up his badge again. 'DC Greene, Major Incident Team. This is Detective Inspector George. Can we have a word with you?'

'Major Incident Team? About the shed?'

'We are not interested in your back shed, ma'am,' Charlie said.

'Then why did you tell our *nanimaa* that you were?'

Greene started to protest but Charlie put a hand on his arm to stay him. 'A word, please. Inside? It will only take a moment.'

She seemed unsure but then she nodded and pulled the old woman after her. Charlie and Greene followed.

'My husband said that Sanjay was always a bad boy, always in trouble. His mother, the heartache he gave her, you have no idea! Always stealing, always in trouble with the police. He was in a gang, you know. In Chennai. The worst sort.'

'Can we speak to your husband?'

Mrs Patel shook her head in confusion. 'He has gone to Sanjay's mother's funeral. In India. He won't be back until next month.'

They were sitting in what Charlie's mother would have called the parlour, a cramped little front room looking out on to the street. The walls were crowded with images of Hindu deities, and there was a shrine on the sideboard with burning incense, fresh flowers and a copper *kalash* with a coconut and mango leaves inside as offerings.

A young man wandered in, wearing jeans, a white t-shirt and dark glasses. He had on more bling than Soulja Boy. A woman, heavily pregnant, followed him in, more traditionally dressed in an emerald green sari, a paste of white ash in the middle of her forehead.

Mrs Patel introduced him as Sunny. She didn't introduce the pregnant woman, who Charlie supposed was Sunny's wife.

'Who's this, *mama-ji*?' Sunny said.

'They're from the council,' the old woman said, looking up from her *Woman's Own*. 'They want to look in the shed.'

'They are not from the council, *nanimaa*,' Mrs Patel said. 'They are policemen, they are looking for Sanjay.'

'Did you tell them?' the young man said.

'Tell us what?' Charlie said brightly.

'He came round here about a month ago, wanting to borrow money from Father.' A wiggle of the head. 'Dirty mofo. Said he wanted to go back for aunty-ji's funeral. Like he cared about his own mother.'

'What did your husband say?' Charlie asked Mrs Patel.

'He told him to go to hell. He said he would only spend the money on drugs.'

'So, you don't think he went back to India?'

'No, of course not.'

The young man leaned in. 'He was here illegal, know what I mean?'

'Yeah, I think I know what you mean. Any idea where I can find him?'

'My husband threw him out. He was no good, that boy. His poor mother he drove to an early grave!'

'I was always the better son,' Sunny said, and strutted out. Mrs Patel heard the door slam. 'Where is he going?'

'To the pub,' the pregnant woman in the sari said, and started filing her nails.

'Something I don't get,' Greene said, when they got back to the car.

'A lot of things you don't get. That's your trouble.'

'Explain this to me. All those little shrines and shiny pictures of people with eight arms the Indians have in their houses. Like a freak show. Everything but the bearded lady. What's that about, then?'

'Google it.'

'I don't need to google it, I've got you.'

'Jesus, Jayden. All right. I think you'll find the bloke with the arms is Vishnu.'

'Why has he got eight arms, then?'

'He's a god. He can have as many arms as he likes.'

'Weird.'

'You want to see something weird, you should have gone in my mother's bedroom, before we moved her out to the old people's home.'

'Your mother was a Hindu?'

'No. What's the matter with you? She had weird pictures, all right?'

'What, like from porn sites?'

Charlie shook his head. Christ's sake. 'Pictures of saints, all getting themselves martyred in horrible ways. Like a Tarantino movie, it was.'

Greene was quiet, which was unusual. Charlie enjoyed it while it lasted. Then Greene said: 'You know a lot about stuff, do you?'

'Just because I'm a policeman doesn't mean I'm ignorant of other cultures and religions.'

'So what's the fat elephant with the shifty expression, then – looks a bit like Boris Johnson?'

'That's Ganesha. Unlike Boris, he's the deva of intellect and wisdom, so you don't have to worry about him, Jay. He won't ever bother you.'

His Nokia trilled in his pocket. It was Lovejoy. Immigration had a Sanjay Dravid leaving Britain on the twelfth of November, on an Air India flight to Chennai. He had overstayed his visa by seven months and was told that he would no longer be allowed entry into the United Kingdom.

Charlie hung up, swore under his breath.

'News, guv?'

'They're right, he's gone back to India.'

'Should be easy enough to find him there. Only a couple of hundred million people, innit?'

'One point three two billion actually,' Charlie said. 'Do you get what's happened?'

'Sure,' Greene said. A long silence. 'Actually, no.'

'He did want the money for the funeral, after all. Here's the scene: he finds out his old mum is about to breathe her last and our bad boy has an attack of conscience. So, he comes to his uncle to ask for the money for the flight home but he won't give it to him, so he nicks the work's van, and sells it to some punter for the airfare. With me?'

'If we could find Sanjay, we could find out who the punter was.'

'If we find the punter, we find the bloke who nailed up the priest.'

'But we can't find Sanjay.'

'Dead end,' Charlie said, and punched the dashboard in frustration.

'Careful,' Greene said. 'You don't want to set off the airbag.'

CHAPTER ELEVEN

Ten days later

Detective Chief Inspector O'Neal-Callaghan was not in a cracking mood, it seemed to Charlie. Face like a half-sucked mango and fidgeting with his Windsor knot like a hangman had put it there. He'd just been chewed out by the bosses up the line, he shouldn't wonder, and now it was time to kick the cat; and me, Charlie thought, I'm the cat.

'How are we doing on the O'Meara homicide?'

'No further progress, as yet, sir.'

The DCI pulled the file towards him, leaned back in his leather chair and went through it, as if the vital clue was in there somewhere, and Charlie just hadn't read it through carefully enough.

'What about this stolen Transit van?'

'We believe it was stolen by a Sanjay Dravid, an illegal. The chief super contacted Chennai in India to request their co-operation in locating him. Still waiting to hear.'

'Perhaps he's back in London by now.'

'I doubt that very much. He overstayed his tourist visa by some seven months, he was told he would not get another.'

'Have the Border Force been told he is to be detained if he arrives here?'

'Yes, sir.' Do I look that stupid, *sir*?

'How did you find this Sanjay David?'

'He stole the van from his former employers. I had a little chat with them. They were quite forthcoming.'

'He already had an arrest warrant current when he left the country?'

'No, sir. His name wasn't mentioned in the original stolen vehicle report.'

'Why not?'

'He didn't have a national insurance number. His employers were worried they would get into trouble if this came to light. They tried to resolve the matter privately.'

'I hope you've followed that up, Charlie? Employing illegal aliens is a criminal offence.'

'But they have been very helpful to our inquiry.'

'They withheld vital information on the insurance claim. That's fraud in anyone's book. They also made a false statement to the police.'

'They gave us the information we wanted, sir. If I start throwing every petty criminal under the bus, no one's ever going to talk to us.'

'It's the thin end of the wedge, Charlie.'

'What wedge, sir?'

'Do I have to do your job for you?'

'My job is catching the sick individual or individuals who tortured and killed Father O'Meara.'

'Your job is to uphold the law. What about his family?' He returned to the file. 'This Mohinder Patel?'

'I interviewed Mister Patel yesterday.'

'Yesterday? Why did you leave it so long?'

'He was out of the country.'

'Out of the country where?'

'In India.'

'Don't tell me. He was in Chennai.'

'He flew back there for a funeral. It was his sister, Sanjay's mother. Funerals are quite elaborate and time-consuming over there, I believe.'

71

'Did he see this Sanjay Dravid?'

'Yes, sir.'

'And?'

'And he thinks he's a toerag, or whatever the equivalent word is in Hindi, and he barely spoke to him. He blames him for his sister's early demise. He said Sanjay came to the funeral, cried a river, and that was the last he saw of him. One of the cousins told him he went to Kolkata the next day.'

The DCI drummed on the edge of the desk with his fingertips. 'What about this van?'

'The night of the murder, an ANPR camera picked up what we think is the same van travelling west on the High Street at 3.57 a.m., and that was the last recording we have. I believe he – or they – planned the escape route very carefully before the crime, and chose the best exit roads to avoid detection.'

'This van has a winch mounted on the front of it.'

'Yes sir, but, due respect, it's still not easy to spot, unless you're standing next to it in the street. It's not like it has a missile launcher mounted on the roof. I've got a BOLO for it, but my guess is that the vehicle is in a garage somewhere and will not appear back on the streets unless . . .'

'Unless what, Charlie?'

'Unless he does it again.'

The DCI swore under his breath.

'Toxicology?'

'Positive for Propofol and ketamine.'

'So he was drugged before he was murdered?'

'Incapacitated, at least.'

'What about this pathology report, the brick dust?'

'London clay, used in the Victorian era, but not the same type used in the construction of the church where his body was found. The most plausible explanation is that the residue came from the premises where he was held captive, prior to being transported to Barrow Fields. It's valuable evidence, but only if we have a suspect whose premises we can search.'

The DCI shook his head, looking profoundly disappointed, as his form teacher used to look when he reviewed his maths results.

'My team has done an extensive door-knock of the area around the cemetery, and spoken to perhaps seven or eight hundred homeless people in the Hackney area. We didn't get a single lead. One gentleman said he saw Father O'Meara being abducted by aliens. Another volunteered to give us a description of his abductor; the finished drawing looked like a purple octopus. The last CCTV images we have of Father Andrew, he was walking along an alley beside the Parkfield estate in Hackney, with his thumbs in his parka, looking like he was off to see the Pope.'

'Somebody must know something.'

'This is not a shut-out, sir. I ordered a POD caravan for the car park of Saint Joseph's and it has been inundated with people who want to help, are desperate to help. None of them can give us anything concrete for the night in question.'

'There must be something we're missing. What has your intel team got on him?'

'I hate to say this, but he was squeaky clean.'

'No one's squeaky clean.'

'This geezer was.'

'What about . . . he may not have been Gary Glitter, but have you looked at that angle? You know what Catholic priests are like.'

'Not a single complaint against him, not even a whisper.'

'You honestly think a crime like this was random?'

'Well it can't be, sir. But there is not enough evidence for us to speculate and it worries me that any theory we come up with at this stage may lead us in the wrong direction.'

'Wrong direction? There is no direction, Charlie. I have to say, I'm disappointed in you.'

So that was it, then; the death sentence.

'I and my team have chased down every possible lead, sir. I

have lived and dreamed this twenty-four seven for the last two weeks. I don't know what to tell you.'

'You realise some journalist has got the story now? Chapter and verse.'

Charlie's heart sank. 'No, I didn't know that.'

'One of the local papers. I had to get the super involved again, he rang the editor. They're holding on to it, for now. But the super wasn't best pleased.'

'How did they find out the details?'

'The bloke who found him, I suppose. He's been talking. I knew this would happen if you didn't get on top of it. It makes us look like idiots.'

'We asked him to keep quiet about this.'

'That's like giving a dog a bone and asking him not to chew it.'

'What if word gets out?'

'You know what Joe Public is like. Unless the papers say it, it's just a rumour. It's not a fact unless it's printed in the *Guardian*.' He tossed the file back on his desk; the only shabby, dirty thing in his immaculate office. He turned away and looked out of the window. 'Thanks Charlie,' he said.

Charlie realised he was dismissed. There goes my career, he thought.

It shamed him to think it was so important. There were worse things than losing your career: losing your life, for instance; hanging on a cross with an iron bolt through both wrists, a gag in your mouth to stop you screaming, while you slowly suffocated to death.

And Father Andrew wouldn't be the last. Of course, he hoped he was wrong about that and the next victim wasn't out there right now, waiting to be grabbed off a night-time street, and nothing Charlie could do any more to help them.

Geraldine Lithgow didn't look like a barrister, with her chill blue eyes and the slightly pained expression of a woman who had been tricked into a date with an overweight bank clerk. She was wearing a leather coat and faded blue jeans; she could have arrived on a Harley. She sat on her own at a table by the window of the Sun in Longacre. Two middle-aged men in Masons' ties were checking her out, but neither of them had the guts to do anything about it.

Her demeanour changed when she saw Charlie.

'Man of my dreams,' she said, and gave his lower lip a play-ful bite as she kissed him.

'How many of those have you had?' he said, tapping her half-empty pint of Lagunitas.

'Just one. Though I had a couple of Café Padron shots while I was waiting. You're late.'

'Just got a Champions League bollocking from my boss. Want another?'

She downed the rest of the pint and handed him the glass. 'Absolutely.' Where did she put it? There was nothing of her.

He bought two more Lagunitas. Why not? He wasn't on call, and half an hour with the DCI made a man want to drink.

'You're attracting attention, Geri,' he said, when he got back to the table with the drinks.

'Why do all Masons look the same? Do you think they're cloned?'

'Do they need to clone white middle-aged men with beer guts? I thought we had enough.' He swallowed half the pint and closed his eyes.

'The priest?'

'Two weeks and no prime suspect. Our best witness is some-where in India.'

'No chance of finding him, I suppose?'

'Even if we could find him, he's not been convicted of any-thing that warrants extradition. My boss even persuaded the chief super to call the director general of police in Chennai who offered his full co-operation. That was ten days ago. Since then, nada. And what good would it do? Even if they went and banged on his poor departed mother's door, assuming she has one, he's not going to be there, is he?'

'You've no other leads?'

Charlie shook his head. 'We can't find the deceased's mobile. We have some grainy CCTV footage of a white van. We got a reg number, but it turns out the plates were stolen from a Ford Fiesta belonging to some old dear in Hampstead. Last footage we have of Father O'Meara, he was walking down an alley in an estate in Hackney. Forensics have some brick traces, and if we had a suspect, that could be very useful, but we don't.'

'How was he murdered, Charlie?'

Charlie made a face. 'Can't even tell you that. Unless you were our brief.'

'That bad?'

'Easy to catch some wet wipe who loses his nut in the street or has some argy-bargy with his missus and goes too far. But this one, he's thought about it, he's planned it. And you know why that gives me nightmares?'

'It may not be a he.'

'It is. I feel it in my water.'

'You're thinking serial killer.'

'You know that Christopher Halliwell, the taxi driver in Swindon? No one had a clue about him. That poor sod Fulcher got him by bending the PACE rules a touch, and they crucified him for it. Now it turns out Halliwell might have killed up to sixty women by the time he got him. No one had a clue. Look, I'm sick of talking about work. How are you?'

She made a face.

'Looking forward to Christmas?'

'Don't.'

'It's the festive season.'

'I have to spend three uninterrupted days with Simon and all of Simon's family. They're all coming down from Scotland with their fucking accents and their fucking cheap whisky.'

'Doesn't Simon have an accent?'

'He gave it up when he joined the bank. Glasgow doesn't go down well in the boardroom, he reckons. I think it says more about Simon than it does about the bank. I need a ciggy.'

They took their drinks out to the alley next to Pho's. Geri lit up. A woman in a camel-hair coat walked up Broad Court holding a vape. 'I'm thinking of getting one of those,' Geri said. 'They do them in all flavours. Strawberry, cinnamon buns.'

'When they do them in pale ale, let me know. Aren't they just as bad for you?'

'I don't know. It's just cigarettes aren't cool any more, are they? They smell and they make a mess. Bit like Simon. Did I tell you, he's told everyone I'm cooking the turkey.'

'Are you?'

'Well, I'll have to now. I've never cooked a turkey.'

'You can always look it up on YouTube.'

'It's his family, why doesn't he cook the turkey?'

'I don't have that problem any more. When it was me and Nic, I used to do all the cooking.'

'Lucky her.'

'Not that lucky or she wouldn't have left.'

Geri finished her beer and stubbed out her cigarette with her heel. Watch her in court, she looked like she went straight home to choir practice. 'Shall we walk?' she said.

Charlie tried to hide his disappointment. 'Sure.'

They cut down to Covent Garden by the tube station. There were half a dozen rickshaw drivers outside hawking for fares, their cabs flickering with coloured lights, all hoping to find a tourist who didn't know any better. 'Look at that one,' Charlie said. 'His cab looks like a Turkish brothel.'

'Well I guess you'd know.'

'What does that mean? Never paid for it in my life.'

'That's because you're thirty-five and reasonably good look-ing, in a rough trade sort of way. Wait until you're middle-aged.'

'I hope to have a wife and an adoring family long before then.'

Geri smiled and deflected the conversation, though he was pretty sure she knew what his point was.

'You shouldn't worry about what your guv'nor says. You're a good cop, Charlie. You tried your best.'

They passed a street performer, a skinny guy with a patchy beard, packing away his pole and his silver Yoda suit. 'There is no try,' Charlie said. 'Only do.'

There was a giant Christmas tree on the cobbles in the middle of the piazza, a full moon behind it, almost as if it had been balanced on top. Theatreland seemed almost subdued, most of the tourists still at shows. When they reached the Strand, Charlie said: 'You could leave him, you know.'

She didn't say anything. He wondered if she had heard him. Finally: 'We've talked about this before, Charlie. You have to give me time.'

'How much time am I giving this, Geri?'

'Don't pressure me, Charlie.'

He'd promised himself he wouldn't do this, and here he was again, worrying at it like a dog with an old bone. They reached Charing Cross Station, stood in the terminus side by side, staring at the departures board. That evening's news highlights played on a loop on the screen beside it, tinsel bright; another terrorist atrocity in Paris, mobile phone footage of bodies being hurried away on stretchers, frightened people sitting on a footpath, covered in blood, open-mouthed in horror.

'What people will do in the name of God,' Geri said.

'I always think: what if God is not there? Every year since Jesus was a boy, all these people getting killed for something that is about as real as Father Christmas.'

'Didn't take you for an atheist, Charlie.'

'Atheists are the kindest, most rational people on earth. Atheists don't put pipe bombs on trains to punish people who aren't atheists.'

'Maybe you're right. I'd miss church on Christmas morning though.'

78

'So would I, I like the hymns. But I'd have enjoyed *Top of the Pops* just as much without Jimmy Savile.'

'Better get my train,' she said, and kissed him on the lips, slipping her tongue into his mouth and parting his coat to slide her hands around his back and run her nails down his shirt. 'I have to go up to Leeds just after Christmas,' she whispered. 'It will mean being away from home for a few days.' The look she gave him; he knew what it meant.

She picked up her bag and ran through gate eleven. He watched her go, cursing himself for not ending it tonight, like he'd told himself he would.

CHAPTER TWELVE

Charlie and Ben in their Arsenal scarves, heading down the Blackstock Road, past the mounted cops in their yellow hi-vis jackets; there was the waft of fresh horseshit, the smell of beer from The Gunners. They went in the Bank of Friendship, before it got too busy. They stood at the bar with their IPAs, getting a bit of a glow on before the game.

'Saw your namesake in here the other week,' Ben said. 'He was with Niall Quinn.'

'We could do with him this afternoon.'

'Could do with him any afternoon; not enough characters like him in the game any more.'

There were jeers and groans from a table of Gooners in the corner. They were watching Tottenham play up at Old Trafford on Sky Sports; the Spurs had equalised just on the stroke of half-time. Two of the blokes got to their feet and flipped the bird at the screen.

'The definition of ambivalence,' Ben said. 'If they draw, we're second by the end of the afternoon. But it's Tottenham, they get a result anywhere it makes me want to throw up. Even in a pre-season friendly.'

'Why do they do that?' Charlie said.

Ben glanced back at the screen, there was a close-up of the new Brazilian forward Spurs had just signed, trotting back to the middle, pausing to cross himself and then look up at the sky and raise his hands in prayer.

'What?' Ben said.

'All these tossers these days, looking up at the sky and blowing kisses whenever they score. What is that about? Like they proper think God supports their football team. Hasn't he got more important things to worry about than Spurs beating Man U?'

'He's religious.'

'Makes no fucking sense. What if the other goalkeeper's a Catholic as well, how does that work then?'

'I don't know, Charlie. It's just a thing.'

'Annoys the shit out of me.'

Ben sipped his beer and frowned. 'What's rattling your cage today?'

'I don't know. Maybe it's the news, did you watch it?'

'Paris, you mean?'

'Everyone thinks God is on their side. It's like a disease. People drone on and on about freedom of religion. What we need is freedom *from* religion.'

'You'll always have nutcases.'

'Right, and religion doesn't help. Like some idiot blows himself up on a crowded train, he really thinks God is up there going, oh well done, proper nice work, I've got just the virgin for you. Everyone thinks there's someone up there watching them, personally. Bollocks.'

'Charlie, finish your beer, you'll give yourself an ulcer.'

'Yeah, sorry.'

'What's the matter, bro?'

'I don't know. Work, I suppose.'

Ben gave him a look.

'You know I can't talk about it.'

'I don't want you to talk about it. Your job sucks. Scraping people's brains off a wall and sticking them under a microscope, looking for fingerprints. I don't know how you stand it.'

'I don't think you quite understand the finer points of forensic science.'

'Don't need to.'

'The victim was a priest. Maybe that's it. You can't have a childhood like we did and not have an opinion about God-bothering.'

'I try not to think about it any more.'

'We all try not to think about it. Doesn't mean it didn't happen. Have you seen Ma lately?'

Ben winced. 'Been busy.'

'Arlington call me up three or four times a week, middle of the night, say she won't settle. Always me she wants, never you.'

'Well, it was always that way,' he said and finished his pint.

Outside, a crowd of Gooners were heading down the street towards the ground. *'Hello, hello, we are the Arsenal boys.'*

'So, how's the love life?'

'About the same. Want another one?'

'She's playing you off the break, Charlie.'

'What does it take to get some service around here?'

'You've got to give it away. She's never going to leave him. Are you listening to me?'

'She's not happy.'

'She's married, of course she's not happy.'

'She says I'm the only one she can talk to.'

Ben held up his index finger and his thumb and rubbed them together. 'See that? It's the smallest violin in the world and it's playing the saddest song, just for her.'

Charlie got two more ales and leaned on the bar, half turned away.

'I know you don't want to hear this, Charlie.'

'She swears she wants out.'

'She says that, but she's still there, isn't she?'

'For how much longer?'

'Seriously? For ever. You really think she's going to leave him and the two kids and a big fucking mock Tudor house in Kent and come and live with you in your grotty little flat in Islington and live happily ever after? Mate, pull a bird like that, hats off to you, you must be the shit in bed, I'll give you that. But women are far more practical than men. They don't marry for sex. Women like that, they know what side of the bread the butter's on. She's having a good time, you do the same, but don't delude yourself she's a long-term proposition.'

'Is that the lecture over?'

'Look, if there's a fight, or someone gets murdered, or the family needs sorting out, I'll step right back, it's over to you. But when it comes to women, trust me, out of the two of us, I'm the expert. And I'm telling you this, bruv, she's fucking with you.'

Charlie drank his pint, pretended to concentrate on the screen at the end of the bar.

'I know you, Charlie. There's a part of you still wants to settle down and play happy families. No problem with that, but this Geri, she's not the girl you're looking for.'

'We've got so much going for us.'

'See, I've only met her the once, and I couldn't see it. She's hot for you, no question, and you both work on the same side of the law. But more than that, you've lost me.'

'Like you just said, you've only met her once.'

'You think you're rescuing her from an unhappy marriage, the white knight riding in to save her from the Indians and carry her off into the sunset.'

'You're mixing your metaphors.'

'Well I don't do metaphors, I'm a numbers man. All I'm saying, she cheats on her old man, she'll cheat on you. Just remember that.'

'I think I love her.'

'Mate, when it comes to women, you are not the brightest bulb on the porch. Listen to your little brother for a change.'

'I can't help how I feel.'

'Of course you fucking can. Charlie, listen to me, you're one of the nicest blokes I know. A proper shirt-off-the-back friend and the best brother anyone could have. When I was a kid I can't remember how many times you got me out of scrapes. And that time you stood up to the old man, stood between him and Ma, I still remember that, we all do. How many fourteen-year-olds would have the bottle to do that? But when it comes to women, no disrespect, you're fucking hopeless.'

Charlie nodded at the screen. 'United are well on top here. Only Lloris keeping Tottenham in it.'

'What about Nic?'

'What about her?'

'If you really wanted to settle down, she was all over that.'

'She left me.'

'Because you were never home.'

'That's my job.'

'That's also my point. Why don't you just stay married to the Force and see this Geri bird when you can, everyone's happy. Stop trying to turn it into *Casablanca*.'

'I won't be a DI for ever. A couple more promotions and I'll land a nice desk job, join the Masons and play golf every Wednesday afternoon.'

'You'd hate being a desk jockey. You'd rather be out there trying to save Goldilocks from the Big Bad Wolf.'

'I think you mean Red Riding Hood.'

'You know what I mean. Look at me, I'm a selfish shit. I want my million-pound flat in Canary Wharf and a new squeeze every six months. I don't care about the world. I see a body in the street, I step over it, try not to get mess on my trouser cuffs. I thank God for people like you even though I think you're off your nut. She is not a victim and her marriage is not a crime to solve.'

'I can't give her up, Ben.'

'You've got to.' He finished his pint and slammed the glass down on the bar. 'Shall we head down Piebury Corner?'

'Not hungry. You can.'

'Drink up, then.' Ben zipped up his Jack Wolfskin coat.

'You should be in the corporate box. How much did that cost?'

'I can afford it.'

'You coming down to Brighton for Christmas?' Charlie said.
A shrug.

'What does that mean?'

'Not sure I can make it.'

'Fuck me, Ben, it's Christmas.'

'Who's going?'

'I'm picking Ma up, taking her down. You can bring your latest, if you want.'

'What about Michael?'

'Priests don't get time off at Christmas, it's their busy time of the year.'

'It's ski season. It's my busy time as well.'

'You are fucking joking me.'

'I'm taking Ashley to Val d'Isère.'

'Who?'

'I met her on Tinder.'

'You can't bail on Christmas.'

Ben gave him an awkward smile. 'Sorry, it's all booked. What's the big deal, Michael's not going either.'

'He's got a reasonable excuse.'

'So have I. We both want to go to heaven, I reckon I'll find it a lot quicker than him. Three times a day if the pills work.' He did a thing with his scarf that made it look like a cravat and headed for the door. Charlie rushed his pint and went after him.

CHAPTER THIRTEEN

The kids in the hall were dancing to Ed Sheeran and Sam Smith; Morton had told the DJ, nothing too edgy, I don't want hard rap, fuck this, fuck that, fuck the cops stuff. It's all police cadets here, no one here's over eighteen except the volunteers I've asked along to keep an eye on things. So don't go stirring things up, the limbo dance is about as edgy as we want it down here tonight.

They had a blue flashing beacon as a strobe, some of the younger kids thought that was cool. It was all pretty harmless stuff, jigging up and down to the music, drinking Coke and other fizzy crap that he personally never touched, only way to keep his weight down.

A mixed bunch they were, some of the girls in hijabs, the boys wearing their cadet issue baseball caps; he made them wear them the right way around. They all had on their blue polo shirts they'd been issued when they joined. Good kids, most of them, but Morton wouldn't want their lives. If they weren't here, they'd be roadmen most of them, hanging around car parks in their hoodies, the lads trying not to get knifed, the girls hoping not to get pregnant.

He looked at his watch, six o'clock, another hour and he could go home, help Debs wrap the kids' presents, put the milk and carrots out for Santa's reindeer. Be just a normal dad again.

One of the volunteers came over and shouted in his ear, over the music. 'Osman's outside with some kids I don't know. I think they're smoking dope.'

'You're joking.'

'I told him to cut it out, but he just gave me the finger.'

'I'll sort it,' Morton said.

It was bitter outside; some early snow had melted and left brown humps at the edge of the car park, the tarmac was black and slick under the orange sodium lights. The shock of the cold made him shudder, he should have put his coat on.

He smelled the sickly-sweet tang of the shit they were smoking first, then saw the glow of the joint, Osman and his scallies huddled in their hoodies squatted on the car-park rail. The little shits. They said they wanted to be police cadets but they thought it was all right to bring drugs to the Christmas show.

He took a deep breath and thought about his options before he went barrelling in, just as he did on the street. The reason he'd brought them under his wing was to try and coax them away from this sort of life. If he threw Osman out, he knew how he'd finish up. But if he didn't, what sort of message would that send to the other kids? Had no choice really.

It pissed him off. Just when he thought he was making progress. One step forward, two steps back, like always.

Osman saw him and stood up. He was a big kid, just sixteen years old, and already he towered over him, skinny as a pole, outgrown most of his clothes, his hoodie barely came down his waist. You never saw a short Somali kid – if there was one, he hadn't seen one on his watch.

'What are you doing?' Steve said.

'Just hanging with my bluds, Steve.'

Morton clocked the other faces in the dark, none of them cadets, that was something. Just Osman then, pulling his usual shit. He just didn't get it, did he?

'What did I tell you? Come on, Osman, I've said it enough times.'

'It's just a little bit of khat.'

'It's drugs.'

'It's bullshit.'

'I say what's bullshit and what isn't. This is police cadets. What's wrong with you, man? You can't be in the cadets and break the law.'

'I'm just telling these guys how they ought to join us.'

'Oh, great. Come along to the cadets and do drugs, that's what we need. I'm disappointed in you, Osman. I'll have to ask you to leave. And don't come back.'

'What do you mean, Steve?'

'Just what I said. We've got rules here. If you're going to disrespect them, then you're out. I've made that very clear to everyone.'

'You can't throw me out,' Osman said, and for a moment Morton thought he was going to square up to him. He saw the other kids watching, faces hidden in their hoodies, hands in their pockets. For a moment he wondered if he should back off a bit. Four against one. They were only kids, but they were big units, and if one of them had a knife, then he could be in a bit of bother.

You couldn't hear the music out here, just the thump of the bass. If he shouted for back-up, every chance they wouldn't hear him inside. Only one thing to do, Morton thought, brass this one out, don't let them see you're worried, last thing you should do.

'You not throwing me out, just for this.'

'What do you mean, "just for this"? You're smoking drugs at a police cadets' meeting. Doesn't matter that it's a Christmas do. In fact, I don't care about your excuses any more, I've heard them all. Now on your bike.'

'But I like coming here.'

'You should have thought of that before you invited your bluds along for a session. I can't have this, Osman. What do you think we're doing here? You having a laugh?'

Osman looked over at his mates, then back at him. Morton heard one of the volunteers come out of the side door, Halpin. Thank Christ.

'You all right, Steve?'

'Osman here wants to say goodbye,' he shouted back. He didn't want Halpin going back inside, not now; needed him to have his back.

He watched Osman's face in the light of the street lamp; at first, he thought he was going to try his luck, then he thought he was going to cry.

'I'm coming back with my mandem and we going to fuck you up, man,' Osman said.

'You show your face back here and I'll bang you up, the lot of you. Now just be a good boy and get off home.'

Osman put his hands back in his pockets and sloped off. The others followed. Morton watched them until they were out of sight.

Bloody shame, he thought. He could be a good kid, he just had the wrong sort of mates.

The DJ got away right on seven o'clock, but it was almost eight before Morton had finished tidying and was ready to lock up. Last out, as always. Debs said he was mad, working Christmas Eve, but it wasn't just a job for him; besides, some of the results of the programme had been brilliant. You just had to give some of these kids a go.

Halpin had offered to stay behind, he was worried about Osman, but Morton said he was all talk – and besides, he had Boris. No one was going to tangle with a bloke with a German shepherd. He walked him out to the car, Boris hopped in the front and Morton climbed in behind the wheel.

It was a raw night, a freezing fog hanging over the football fields, an oily halo around the moon. He started the engine, let it warm up. Freezing in the car. He turned the heat on full and zipped up his parka.

'What are we going to do with that Osman?' he said to Boris. 'You reckon I was too hard on him?'

He turned on the lights and headed down the driveway

towards the road. Christ, what was that? Something lying on the drive, looked like a body. Some kid drugged up and passed out. He got the Maglite from the glove box and jumped out.

He hesitated, was about to go and get Boris. Trouble with him, he'd take the arm off a black kid as soon as look at him, unconscious or not. He didn't like them, never had.

He shone the torch over the body, and on the grass either side; no one else around by the looks. The body was lying face down. He squatted down, pulled back the hood of the parka. 'Jesus,' he said. He thought it would be a kid, but this was an older bloke with a beard, and right out of it by the looks.

Too old for a roadman. He felt a moment's unease.

He took out his mobile to call for an ambulance, felt something go in his thigh, a freaking needle. What the fuck. He jumped to his feet, thinking about AIDS and Hep C. The bloke jumped up, and he tried to grab the scrote's arm, put him down, but somehow he wriggled away.

The bloke took off. It was pure instinct to go after him, he didn't want him getting away and he was pissed off about the needle. He was pretty nimble on his feet but Morton was no stranger to foot pursuit, kept himself fit; he caught up with him just before he reached the road, brought him down.

He twisted the bastard's arms behind his back but somehow he got away again. How the hell did that happen? He took off after him, but his legs wouldn't work, it was like running through sand. The ground rushed up to meet him.

He didn't feel anything as his face hit the gravel. He heard Boris going berserk in the car, then everything went black.

The office was quiet, everyone in his team had gone home except the sad bastards who didn't have anyone at home waiting for them. Charlie locked his office door behind him as he was leaving, saw Lovejoy sitting in front of her computer staring at the ghostly images from a CCTV camera.

'No home to go to?'

'Got an address, guv. Is that the same thing?'

'You'll go cross-eyed staring at that. Haven't we been through everything?'

'Thought we might have missed something.'

'Get home, don't try and impress me, you'll burn out. You're lucky, last year we had to work Christmas Day.'

'I will be anyway.'

'You're keen. How did that happen?'

'DC James asked to swap rosters.'

'Not his sick mother again? Don't get suckered in. He's always pulling that stunt.'

'I don't mind, guv.'

'Don't let them take advantage, just cos you're new.'

'Really. I'm OK with it.'

He was headed for the door, changed his mind and turned back. 'Look, want you to know, you haven't been with us long, but you've done all right. You've got the makings.'

'Thanks.'

'Don't let it go to your head.'

'I'll try not to.'

'The rest of the team treating you all right?'

'Mostly.'

'Anyone gives you a hard time, let me know. Especially DS Greene.'

'DS Greene may be sexist and homophobic, but he's just fine around me, guv.'

'Good.'

'What you doing for Christmas?'

'Down to Brighton, me,' Charlie said. 'Ever been to Brighton?'

'Couple of times. The pier and all that.'

'I bloody hate Brighton. Full of weirdos and self-pitying *Big Issue* poets. I'd rather go to Benidorm.'

'I thought it was supposed to be cool. Julie Burchill. Chris Eubank. Nick Cave.'

Charlie made a face. 'Brighton is an idea people get when

91

they're sitting on the tube, reading in the *Metro* how someone in Brixton just sold their crack baby for bait in a dog fight, and they think: "Oh, I have to get out of London, where can I go? I know – Brighton. It was great when I went there when I was a kid." But it's like group sex; people think, oh that'd be lovely, then when they actually try it, it's just grubby and disappointing.'

'Have you, guv?'

'Have I what?'

'Ever tried Brighton?'

'No, DC Lovejoy, I'm all talk.'

'So why don't you stay in London for Christmas then?'

'Family, innit? My sister lives in Brighton. She's invited my mother down there, so it's my job to pick her up and drive her down. That'll be the fun part.'

'Don't you get on with your sister?'

'We get on fine, she's not the problem, it's the complete drop-kick she married. One of those blokes that goes to the pisser in the pub and takes his pint with him. Looks like Wayne Rooney. Still, family, right? What Christmas is all about.'

'Is that it, then? Just you and your sister?'

'No, got four brothers.'

'Big family.'

'Well, we're London Irish.'

'Charlie isn't a very Irish name.'

'No, it's the name my old man wanted to call me. He was an Arsenal tragic, they had this bloke played for them in the seventies, called Charlie George. I think he only had kids so he could call one of us Charlie. All the rest of the family were accidents.'

'What was he like, Charlie George?'

'You can watch him on YouTube. Proper cool-looking bloke in those days: tall, long hair, bad attitude. People loved him. The old man thought I was going to be like him.'

'In attitude or good at playing football?'

'Both, I suppose. I was a bit of a disappointment to him in

the talent department. Couldn't kick a ball to save me life. Had to settle for watching.'

'You're still an Arsenal fan?'

'Fan is not strong enough a word. Not like my old man, though, he was a proper hooligan, he was. Loved to go the knuckle. Married man with kids, and off he'd go on a Saturday afternoon with a red and white scarf round his neck and a length of bicycle chain tucked in the back of his jeans.'

'So where are all your family, then?'

'My brothers? One lives in a Rubik's cube in Canary Wharf. Works in the City, fiddles around on his computer with a phone stuck to his ear and earns ten thousand a day. Which is why he can't come to Brighton, he's off to a ski resort in France to slalom with a twenty-year-old. Another one lives in Liverpool. He's a priest.'

'A priest.'

'According to my mother, the only one of us to make good.'

'How do you get on with him?'

'Fine. He prays for my soul on a Sunday and I send him a birthday card every year. Proper nice of him really, I don't know if it will do any good, but every little helps, I suppose, as the old woman said as she pissed in the sea.'

He noticed Lovejoy was counting off his family on her fingers. In case he tried to miss one out, he supposed.

'That leaves two more.'

'You work for the Census?'

'I'm just curious, guv. I'm an only child and big families fascinate me.'

'I've got another brother in Australia.'

'What's he doing out there?'

'Not a lot. Last I heard he was growing his own dope and chaining himself to trees to stop Adani knocking down a koala bear habitat.'

'How long since you've seen him?'

'Not since Jesus was a boy.'

There was an awkward silence. He thought she might let it go.

'One more,' she said.

'Liam.'

'What does he do?'

'Not much. He's dead.'

'Oh, I'm sorry.'

'You don't have to be, you didn't do it. He caught the 8.17 to Southend Victoria, if you get my meaning. It was running five minutes late but it seemed he was happy to wait.'

'When did that happen?'

'I was about sixteen.'

'Why did he do it?'

'I don't know, he never left a note. He might have done it on a whim. Maybe he couldn't find anywhere to buy coffee. Some days are like that, aren't they?'

'Are they?'

He stared at her. She was pushing the line here. He hadn't talked about this in a long time, why the hell did she think he would want to talk about it now? 'Well I don't think so, of course, but that's why I'm still here. I can't speak for Liam.'

'That must have been—'

'Case closed, Lovejoy. Goodnight.'

'Goodnight guv.'

As he left, he made another mental note: DC Lovejoy, high proficiency in interrogation technique. Found out a lot about me, gave away nothing about herself.

Be more wary in future.

CHAPTER FOURTEEN

His mother's church looked more like a Victorian pumping station, and the single red-brick bell tower reminded him of Battersea. He sat there, staring at it through the windscreen wipers, waiting for the squall to pass so that he could get her inside. No hush of soft fallen snow this Christmas; it was bleak and miserable with sleet blowing across the car park.

'Why are we sitting here?' she said to him. 'We'll miss the service.'

'I don't want you to get wet, Ma.'

'If we sit here all morning, we won't get a decent seat.'

'It's not a Multiplex.'

'A what?'

'Hold your horses, I'll pull up in front of the foyer. I've got an umbrella somewhere.'

By the time he had her Zimmer frame and the umbrella out of the boot, he was soaked through. He got her inside and parked the car. When he got back to the church, someone had already steered her to a seat at the front. It was standing room only for the Lapsed. He kept a keen eye on her in case she went home with the verger at the end by mistake.

Long time since he'd been in a church, especially one as fancy as this, it belied appearances from the outside. There was a blue and gold awning over the altar, like a poor man's baldacchino, there was abstract stained glass along the nave, even a shrine in one of the transepts to the Virgin Mary, holding what looked like the Champions League trophy.

High above the altar was a statue of the crucified Christ. Charlie couldn't bear to look at it. It made him think about Father O'Meara. Jesus looked merely exhausted; in real life, the rictus of agony on the priest's face had been horrifying.

The service began. It was a different crew from the days when they all sat in a line beside her and the old man, and sniggered when Ben tried to steal coins from the collection plate. No suits and floral print dresses this morning; instead there were kids in pushchairs and women in headscarves and burly men in bomber jackets and jeans and trainers, tearing up as they crossed themselves and shoving twenty quid in the collection plate.

When it was time for the communion he helped Ma up to the altar to get her bit of biscuit and then led her back to the pew. She seemed not to notice he didn't get any wafers for himself.

But it was worth putting up with the cold and the wet and an hour of religion just for the look on her face. Her cheeks were shining like she'd had three glasses of sherry.

When it was all over she stopped on the way out to stare at the two grandmothers minding the little bookstall at the back. They were doing a brisk trade: Polish prayer books, English dictionaries, statuettes of the virgin, a David Beckham biography.

When he got her outside, the sleet had turned to snow and was coming down almost horizontally; he had to guide her to the car with one hand on the Zimmer, the other holding his umbrella over her to keep her dry. Finally he had her and the frame loaded.

'Did you see how full the church was?' she said to him as he inched the car through the snarl-up at the gates and back on to the road.

'Yeah, good turnout,' he said, didn't point out to her that most of the good turnout were Poles. She didn't have much time for Eastern Europeans, the old mum, unless they were the Pope, and even that was a long time ago.

'And they say people are turning away from God!'

He wondered which people she was referring to. The Church of England, of course, was in terminal decline; Britain, he had read, was becoming a Catholic country, because of the influx of Poles and other East Europeans, who took their God-bothering much more seriously than the English. There were parts of London now where churches held up to seven Masses every Sunday, all spoken in Polish.

'Your father would have loved that service,' she said.

Loved it? He wouldn't even have been there, Charlie thought, it would have cut into his drinking time. Sometimes he went to an evening service, after the pubs were shut, but that was only when he'd given her a black eye and he felt badly enough about himself to go to confession.

'I still miss him, God rest his soul.'

It made his blood boil, that. Why would anyone miss that violent, lazy bastard? But there was nothing he could say to her and he didn't want to upset her, not at Christmas, so he kept his mouth shut, and tried to concentrate on the GPS. They would be lucky to get out of London, never mind all the way to Brighton, if this weather didn't ease up.

He turned the heater on full, wiped the condensation off the windscreen. He wondered what Ben was doing in Val d'Isère right now, but he was the good son, the responsible one, so he supposed he would never find out.

CHAPTER FIFTEEN

Brighton

'So how was it?' Julia asked him.

He helped himself to one of Tel's Stellas from the fridge and leaned back against the kitchen bench. He loved the smell of a good roast; Jules might have no dress sense, and her taste in men was questionable at best, but she could proper cook.

'Did you do communion?'

'Did I fuck. You know I can't stand all that stuff.'

'Many people?'

'More Poles in there than Warsaw. Ma didn't seem to notice. What a right load of shite. "Jesus was born to bring light into the world." There are more divorces at Christmas than any other time of the year, more deaths on the road, and wars everywhere.'

Julia put the turkey back in the oven, tucked her hair behind her looped earring. She had dyed her hair purple for the season, was wearing the new FCUK tee that Tel had bought her for Christmas, romantic that he was.

'Listen to you,' she said. 'You sound like that bloke out of the Muppets, Scrooge.'

'Dickens.'

'What?'

'Scrooge was Dickens.'

'No, it was the Muppets, I saw it on the telly last night.'

'Have it your way.'

'Was Ma all right?'

'Got misty-eyed about the old man again. I don't mind Father Christmas, I don't mind microwave neck pillows and Mariah Carey CDs – what gets to me is how she chokes up about him every year. Can't remember one time she ever got through to New Year without a black eye and she talks about him like he was Tom Hanks. Should you be drinking Bacardi breezers when you've got a bun in the oven?'

'It's only one, it's Christmas.'

'Still.'

'You look on edge, Charlie.'

'Of course I'm on edge, I just drove all the way down from London in a blizzard with her going on about how immigrants are taking everyone's jobs and how much she loves Margaret Thatcher.'

'Margaret Thatcher?'

'She was prime minister before you were born.'

'Thought I'd heard of her. Christ, look at the time. Tel will be right pissed off if the dinner isn't ready when he gets home.'

'I'll give you a hand.'

'No, you go and play with Rom, he's been dying to show you his new FIFA game.'

Ma was sunk into the sofa, with a glazed look on her face, as if she was mesmerised by the tree and its trashy lights. Macaulay Culkin was on the telly looking poignantly cute. Must be terrible to peak so early, Charlie thought. Something I'll never have to worry about.

Rom was in his bedroom in the dark, his face reflecting the eerie glow of his PC. 'Hello Uncle Charlie.'

'Hello Rom. What's up?'

'I got the new FIFA game. You want to play?'

'Only if I can be the Arsenal.'

'I'm Watford.'

'I can't believe I have a nephew who supports Watford. It's not a football team, it's a place on the motorway.'

'Dad says they're the best team on the planet.'

'Your dad got concussion twice last year falling off roofs, so I wouldn't take too much notice.' He pulled up a chair next to him. He clocked him from the corner of his eye, didn't want him to know he was checking him out. All skin and bone under that tracksuit.

'What else did you get?'

'Dad got me a football. When I'm better we'll go and kick it about.'

'Yeah, no good for playing football today anyway, snowing like the North Pole out there.'

Charlie picked up the console. They played for a bit and it struck Charlie there was one major benefit to spending half your life trapped in your room; Rom was proper good at playing FIFA football. After ten minutes Arsenal were already two down. These games are getting more and more realistic all the time, he thought.

'Come on, Uncle Charlie, I'm not a little kid, you don't have to let me win.'

'I'm not letting you win!'

'You're hopeless.'

Charlie grabbed him in a headlock, a gentle one, and Rom laughed and still managed to get a corner without even looking at the screen. Just then Charlie heard a commotion in the hall. He let Rom go.

'Dad's home,' the little boy said with a catch in his voice.

The look on his face when he saw him. Tel had clearly forgotten Charlie was coming down for Christmas lunch, or, just as likely, he was just too legless to remember anything. There he was, in his Watford shirt, one freckled hand full of chunky gold sovereigns and tomato sauce stains, holding Julia by the throat against the wall. He had pulled back his other hand.

100

Charlie didn't suppose he was really going to hit her, but you never knew, bloke like that, when he was drunk, he might do anything.

Julia looked more scared of Charlie than she did of her husband. 'Don't do anything,' she said to him. 'Terry don't mean nothing. He's just had a bit too much to drink.'

'I can see that.'

Terry let her go. He stood back, wary. 'Hello Charlie. Sorry mate, just a bit of a domestic.'

'Yeah, when it's my sister, it's not a domestic any more, innit?'

Julia stood between them. 'It's all right, Charlie, he didn't hurt me, he just gets a bit wound up sometimes.'

Charlie put an arm around Terry's shoulder. 'Let's go for a walk.'

'Charlie,' Julia said. He saw Rom watching over her shoulder.

'It's all right, Jules Just going for a bit of a walk along the seafront, bit of sea air, help sober him up. That's all. Right, Tel?'

Terry didn't want to go, but he didn't see how he could say no. Charlie had him hard by the back of that pink bull neck. Charlie kept smiling, his arm muscles bunched and tense under his sleeve. 'Come on, Tel,' Charlie said and manoeuvred him out of the door.

The storm had cleared away, leaving little piles of snow in doorways, the new fall white and crisp on the grass. Overhead the clouds were patterned like mackerel and faintly pink. Terry tried to run first chance he could, but Charlie grabbed him by the shirt and frogmarched him around the corner where no one could see them from the flat.

He held him against the railings. 'How do you feel about a sex change without anaesthetic?'

'Charlie, it wasn't nothing.'

'It didn't look like nothing to me.'

101

He pushed him back over the iron rail spike. A couple went past, wheeling a toddler in a pushchair. Charlie turned and smiled. 'Merry Christmas.'

The man looked terrified. 'Merry Christmas,' he said.

'He got me a Mariah Carey CD for Christmas,' Charlie said.

'You've got a right to be mad then,' the bloke said and they walked on.

Charlie turned back to his brother-in-law. 'Now look, Tel, you're married to my sister, so I can't do to you what I would like to do to you. I can't fucking kill you, not right off. But if you ever, ever, ever, fucking lay a hand on her again, then I will hang you off the pier by your jacobs. Getting minging with your scally mates is no excuse for hitting a fucking woman. Am I being crystal, my son?'

'My back.'

'Sorry, am I impaling you?'

His Nokia rang. Just as well, he thought; might actually do some damage otherwise. He fucking hated men who touched their wives, and when it was his sister, he wasn't answerable.

'DI George,' he said, phone in one hand, Tel in the other.

'Guv, it's DC Lovejoy.'

'Merry Christmas, Detective. How can I help you?'

'Guv, I'm with DI Fenton. There's another body and I reckon it's one of ours.'

'One of ours?'

'I asked the DI if I should call you and he gave me the OK. It's just I thought you should take a look at this.'

'Where are you?'

'Community Centre off Ridgewell Street in Tower Hamlets. Can you get here fairly smartish?'

'I'm in Brighton.'

'Looks like we're going to be here for quite a while.'

Charlie hung up, slipped the phone back into his pocket. 'You're lucky,' he said to Terry. 'Off the hook. Literally.' He let

102

him down and walked back to his car. He clipped the blue light on the roof of his Golf and set off back to London.

Just as well. Christmas lunch would have been a little awkward now, anyway.

CHAPTER SIXTEEN

Charlie signed in, ducked under the police tape, nodded at Fenton and the DCI standing there huddled in their coats, looking as though they'd just come from a funeral. The car park was frosted with ice, and the wind cut right through his Canada Goose. He turned up his collar and went over.

'Merry Christmas, sir. Hello, Bob.'

'Sorry to drag you away from your Christmas dinner.'

'You took your time,' the DCI said.

'I was in Brighton.'

'Well, that'll teach you.'

'What have we got, Bob?'

'Constable from Malden Street station, kidnapped from here last night about ten o'clock.'

'Yeah, it was all over the news coming down this morning.'

'Bad business,' the DCI said.

Charlie looked around. There were still some crime team in overalls poking around behind the hall, uniforms with sniffer dogs under the trees. They had an audience, of course, bystanders watching from the road, nothing better to do on Christmas Day. Charlie supposed if it was a choice between listening to your grandfather snore on the sofa and watching police tape flapping in the wind, he'd probably be down here as well.

'What's this to do with me? MIT23 is up this week.'

The DCI and Fenton looked at each other. 'Tell him, Bob,' the DCI said.

'Down here since midnight last night. Then this morning, your new DC, what's her name?'

'Lovejoy.'

'Right. I had her helping with house-to-house; some geezer reckoned he saw something. He was walking home late last night and a van pulled in to the car park, nearly ran him over. A white Ford Transit.'

'And?'

'And because it nearly knocked him over, he remembered there was something weird about it. Something on the front.'

'A winch?'

'Possibly.'

'He didn't get the plates, I suppose.'

'He was on his way home from the pub, Charlie.'

'Could have imagined the whole thing.'

'Could have. But your DC wanted to call you.'

'And you want to get shot of it.'

'I want to do the right thing, Charlie.'

The DCI shrugged. 'So, what do you reckon? Your team won't thank you for dragging them away from their Christmas dinners.'

'Jack been here?'

'Left a couple of hours ago.'

'Anything?'

'Latents on tyres, probably too many of them, he'll try to cross-match with Barrow Fields. Same with footprints.'

'CCTV here?'

Fenton shook his head.

Charlie tapped his foot; they all knew he was just stalling for time. It didn't make sense, this. 'Every minute counts with a kidnapping,' he said aloud.

'If it's unrelated, then it's another high-profile case,' the DCI said. 'Chance of redemption. If it is related, fresh leads, find a suspect, all is forgiven.'

'My team are all at home with their families.'

'Those that have them. The rest are sitting home on their own, watching re-runs of the "Morecambe and Wise Christmas Special" from 1976 and feeling sorry for themselves. But it's your call.'

'Where are you at with it, sir?'

'This is a brother officer, so we're doing everything we can. I've called in extra uniforms, and a specialised intel team. If another SIO is going to step in, now is the time. Do you want it?'

Charlie looked at Fenton, who looked away. 'Yes, sir, I do.'

'Good. Don't fuck it up this time.'

'Thanks for the vote of confidence, sir.'

'I mean it. No excuses this time, Charlie, only results. Get the bastards who did this.'

'Yes, sir. But.'

'But what?'

'It may be just one bastard.'

'Don't be daft. No one takes a six-two, thirteen-stone copper off the street unless he has help.'

'Well, the toxicology report on Father O'Meara showed ketamine and Propofol. It could be just one person, acting alone.'

'Well, if you're right and it is just one, it shouldn't take you so long to find him. Good luck. I'm going home to my Christmas pudding. Be sure to keep me informed of progress.'

And he walked off.

'Better fill me in, Bob.'

'Missing man's name is Constable Stephen Morton. He works patrol at Malden Street, been there three years, joined straight from cadet school. Used to be a teacher, apparently. Gave up all those holidays every year for the Plod.'

'What was he doing here?'

'He ran the local volunteer police cadets; you know, first aid, band practice, phonetic alphabet, bit of marching. The

Duke of Edinburgh award for those who could hack it. He didn't get paid for it, worked with some local volunteers in his spare time.'

'A cop with spare time. He should have been in a museum.'

'Community policing was his thing.'

'He was teaching them the phonetic alphabet on Christmas Eve?'

'No, it was the end of year wind-up, they had a Christmas party for all the VPCs, hired a DJ, lots of dancing, strictly no alcohol, so you would have hated it. After it was over he stayed behind to clear up. That was the last anyone saw of him.'

'Who called it in?'

'His wife.'

'She came down here?'

'No, she called one of the volunteers. They've got two little kids; they were tucked up in bed, she didn't want to leave them. Anyway, the volunteer geezer came down, saw the car and no Morton, called the local uniforms in.'

'That his motor?' Charlie peered through the side window. 'Jesus, what happened?'

'He had a German shepherd. It was locked in, went mad trying to get out, chewed up the upholstery. Another couple of hours I think it would have gnawed through the engine block. We had to get a vet to sedate it, so we could get inside.'

'Fuck me. Any idea what happened?'

'Come and have a look.'

They got overshoes and white overalls from the crime scene van and went down the driveway. Bob showed him where the gravel had been kicked up. 'See this. Looks like there was a struggle about here. Then there's these drag marks over to the bushes, we think the van was parked behind it on the grass. That's where Jack lifted a tyre impression. There were also a couple of footprints.'

'How long for the results?'

'Who knows, with this last round of budget cuts.'

'Any blood?'

Fenton shook his head.

'What do you have on this Morton?'

'Regular Constable Care. He had a medal for bravery and two kids.'

'What did he get the medal for?'

'Jumped off Southend Pier and saved some kid from drowning. He was off duty at the time. It was in all the papers apparently.'

'He sounds like the proper Superman.'

'Not the first time he's been in the papers.'

'How do you mean?'

'It will all be in the file. About two months ago, the local rag did a feature on the local cadet group, how they were going to the Remembrance Day parade in London to be stewards, and then there was an op-ed piece about how Morton was helping turn kids away from crime.'

'How's his wife?'

'I've got my best FLO with her. She's holding up for now.'

'I'll have to talk to her.' He looked at Morton's motor, then at the car park, trying to piece it together in his mind. 'So Morton gets out of the car, leaves the dog behind – bad mistake – and gets nabbed. Perhaps a fast-working drug, IM.'

'If it was IM, he would have made it back to the car.'

'He would have tried. But our boy didn't need to stop him, just slow him down till the drug took effect. When he's out of it, he drags him to the van and it's goodnight Irene.'

'How did he get that close, that's the question?' Fenton said.

'If it was me, I'd just lie down in front of the car and play dead. Did you find his mobile?'

'It was still in the car. Lucky the shepherd didn't eat the sodding thing.'

'Anything?'

Fenton shook his head.

'CCTV?'

'Not here. I've got teams pulling CCTV in a mile radius.'

'Anything else?'

'He had some kind of bust-up last night with one of the cadets. One of the volunteer PCs, a Nigel Halpin, came outside and saw them squaring up. Halpin had reported the cadet for an indiscretion in the car park during the disco and Morton came to sort it out.'

'What sort of indiscretion?'

'He caught him smoking drugs with his mates from the estate. Naturally, that sort of behaviour is strongly discouraged in the police cadets. Morton told him he was surplus to requirements. The boy threatened to come back with his mates and fuck him up – his words, that's what our witness said.'

'Who was this kid?'

'His name is Osman Balewah, he's sixteen, Somali, been in the country about three years.'

'Form?'

'He has three minors for shoplifting and for possession.'

'And he's a police cadet?'

'At least a quarter of the cadets in every brigade come from a troubled background. They actively look for kids who are vulnerable, try and recruit them before they get into gang culture and start dealing drugs. A Somali minor offender is almost a poster boy for them.'

'Must look great when it works. Have you talked to this little scrote?'

'We grabbed him last night, him and his mother, had them down the nick till five in the morning. His mother insists he was home when Morton was snatched.'

'You believe her?'

'Osman doesn't own a vehicle and he can't drive. You should have seen him. He's no hard case, he was absolutely shitting himself, he thought we were going to attach his gonads to the light socket. Maybe that's how they do things in Somalia.'

'Don't knock it till you've tried it.'

'Well, I've ruled him out of the inquiry.'

'What about the other kids?'

'We got them all in here, to the hall, spoke to each of them, along with their parents. They were all crying, we went through a dozen boxes of tissues. Halpin and the other volunteer, they said the kids all loved him, except for this Osman.'

'This Halpin. Nothing funny there?'

Fenton shook his head. 'He works in a bank. Don't think he's even had a parking fine his whole life. What do you reckon, you really think these two cases are connected, Charlie?'

'Van with a mounted winch. What's the odds?'

'I heard what happened to that Father O'Meara. Nasty.'

'Keep that to yourself.'

'Of course. Brave decision, by the way.'

'You must be relieved you managed to wriggle off the hook. You've got nothing, basically.'

'I'll be jealous as hell if you crack it. Saving a brother officer, there's a promotion and a medal in this.'

'And if I don't?'

'Then I wouldn't like to be in your shoes.'

CHAPTER SEVENTEEN

Charlie rang Greene, told him to call the team in.

'They won't be best pleased,' Greene said, sounding none too chuffed himself.

'Tell them if they wanted an easy life they should have got a job with the government. We have a brother officer relying on us to do our job. Do your best Winston Churchill on it and get everyone in, sharpish. Capeesh?'

'Got it, guv.'

By the time he got back to the Essex Road nick, a few of the team were already there; Lovejoy, of course, looking eager; Greene, Rupinder, DS Dawson, his coat over the back of the chair, his gut over the rim of his belt. He gave Charlie a sharp look.

'It's not my fault, skipper,' Charlie said to him. 'I didn't ask for this.'

'Yes, you fucking did. I got the whole story from Fenton. My wife is going to kill me. I told her I had Christmas off this year.'

'Yeah well, think about this bloke Morton's wife. She'd probably like him home for Christmas too. If we do our job right, maybe he still will be.'

That shut them all up.

Charlie sat down on the edge of Dawson's desk. 'OK, here's the story. You've all heard on the news about the missing cop. A witness thinks he saw a Ford Transit van at the scene, shortly before Morton was grabbed. It had been modified, had a winch on the front of it. Remembers because he nearly wore it across his shins. So, we are looking at the possibility that whoever has PC Morton also murdered Father O'Meara.'

'Makes no fucking sense,' Dawson said.

'Crucifying a priest in an abandoned church made no kind of sense neither, skipper, but that's what happened. Fenton was on duty roster last night, he will be in shortly to brief you all. DS Dawson will action the rest of the team as they arrive. The DCI has put extra resources at our disposal. The clock is ticking, people. We have to find PC Morton, and fast.'

'Does he have any connection to Father O'Meara?' Rupinder asked him.

'That's what we have to find out. Soon as Wes gets here, you two go back to see Father Donnelly, ask him if O'Meara knew Morton, then talk to the nun, what was her name, Sister Agatha.'

'What about his mobile?'

'It was still in the car. Fenton's intel team found nothing, but they've handed over Morton's financials and his hard drive on his work PC to Billy and Parm.'

'What about his laptop?'

'Nothing. But we'll check it again, now that we know what we're looking for, which is, specifically, something that links him with O'Meara. But while we're on that, let's not forget our basics. Could be we don't find that link until we have a prime suspect. The CCTV should be arriving shortly, it will have to be checked, every Transit on Holloway Road from 21.45 to 22.30.'

'Last time it had stolen plates.'

'And most likely it will have stolen plates again. But we'll look pretty stupid in the wash-up if they were the real ones this time and we didn't check. Find the van, get the time, try and get some sort of trace on the exit route. Let's just do our job and perhaps we can join the dots from there.'

'Was he bent?' Jayden said. 'I mean, this could be something weird, or it could just be all about money.'

'There's nothing so far to suggest that he was anything but squeaky clean. We haven't exhausted that possibility, however.'

'What about the media?' someone said.

'The DCI is planning a media conference late this afternoon, just in time for the evening news. We'll put a POD on the street outside the community centre, appeal for help from the public. Any questions?'

'This guy married?' Lesley said.

'Yes, he has two children, three years old and eighteen months.'

'Shit,' Greene said.

'He's not dead yet,' Charlie said. 'The clock is running, so let's find this fella and get him home with his family in time for the Michael McIntyre special. All right?'

'Yes guv,' almost in unison.

'I'm off to talk to his wife, then I'll have a word with his line manager at Malden Street. We wanted a break on the O'Meara homicide, this may be it. I'm scheduling a meeting in IR1 tonight at eight o'clock. Let's get to work.'

The Mortons lived in a quiet residential avenue of semis with bay windows and a privet hedge in the front garden. The street had been cordoned off to keep the media away. Charlie left Greene in the car and signed himself in, nodded to the two patrol officers outside the front gate.

The FLO, a blonde DC called Yardley, met him at the door. She introduced him to the family members crowded in the hall, all talking in whispers, fetching cups of tea for each other, as people seemed to do in these situations.

He clocked the large framed photograph on the wall, Morton with his family. It must have been taken recently, they had both the children with them. They looked so young and fresh-faced, it could have been a commercial for health insurance.

But that was then, he thought; this is now. When Yardley led Charlie through to the front room he found a very different

113

Deborah Morton; pale and aghast, hunched on the sofa with a box of tissues. There was a Christmas tree, presents piled prettily under it; her three-year-old was playing at her feet with a large plastic lorry. A little girl sat on her lap, unnaturally docile.

Deborah Morton looked up as Charlie walked in, and there was a flicker of hope, quickly extinguished.

The circles under her eyes were pronounced. He supposed she had been awake all night.

'Mrs Morton, I'm Detective Inspector George.'

'Did you find him?'

He shook his head. 'We're still looking.'

'Detective Yardley said you were taking over the case.'

'That's right. I want you to know we're doing all we can to find Stephen. I just need to ask you a couple of questions if I may. It might help us.' He sat down. 'I'm sure you've gone through this with the other officers, but I'd like you to think about it just once more. Can you think of anyone, anyone at all, who might want to hurt your husband?'

Her eyes welled up. She couldn't trust her voice so she just shook her head. Yardley took her hand.

'He didn't seem anxious or depressed or worried about anything?'

'He loved . . . being a policeman.'

'No threatening phone calls, nothing happened at work that he mentioned to you?'

Another shake of the head. She stared at the presents piled under the tree. 'Sam doesn't want to open them until his daddy gets home.'

'One last question. Did you ever hear him mention the name, Father Andrew O'Meara?'

'A priest?'

Charlie nodded.

'You think that has something to do with Stephen going missing?'

'We don't know.'

'We saw it on the TV. But we're Church of England.' She choked back tears. 'You will find him, won't you?'

'We're doing our very best.'

Charlie nodded to Yardley. He didn't know how anyone managed that part of the job, he would be completely useless at it. He let himself out. Greene was waiting for him in the Sierra at the top of the street. He heard the click and whirr of press cameras from the other side of the cordon as he got in.

'How did it go, guv?'

'It was the bollocks, Jay, what do you think?'

'Anything?'

'Just drive. Malden Street.'

The Nokia buzzed to life in his pocket. Charlie juggled it, dropped it on the floor, answered it at the second attempt. He saw Greene give him a look. OK, so he was rattled, so what? You sit down with a woman whose husband has gone missing on Christmas Eve.

It was Dawson.

'Now then, guv. Might have something.'

'Go on.'

'Hotline's going off like a frog in a sock. Most of it I've discounted, but got a call just now I thought you should know about.'

'Shoot.'

'Some old geezer lives next to a church. Says the place has been abandoned for years, then he saw a workman there this morning in a white Transit van.'

'When?'

'He wasn't sure, just said it was early.'

'Where's this church?'

'Where are you now, guv?'

'Just leaving Morton's house.'

'Well, it's about five minutes from where you are, on Elmscroft Road. Another one of those Dissenters' Chapels.'

115

Charlie punched the address into the GPS with his free hand. 'Got it. We're on our way.'

'Want to get back-up from the local nick?'

'You call them, we're going right there.' He hung up, tapped the screen. 'Here, quick as you can.'

Greene nodded, he loved the cowboy stuff. He wound down the window and reached under the seat for the blue light, put it on the roof.

Charlie felt his heart-rate lift.

'We've got him,' Greene said and veered into the oncoming lane to go around a Ford Focus that had pulled in front of them.

'Take it easy, Jay. The punter who called it in, he told the skipper he saw it first thing this morning. It won't still be there. Anyway, it may not be the right van.'

The lights ahead of them had turned red; there was a bus in one lane, a taxi in the other.

'Careful,' Charlie said.

Greene turned into the oncoming lane, his fist on the horn. A white Cavalier turned up on to the kerb, just missing a woman pushing a pushchair.

'Christ's sake!'

'Come on, come on,' Greene muttered under his breath, veering around a cyclist. He accelerated down the High Street, glancing at the GPS. Two and a half minutes away. 'We need a break on this one.'

'We're trying to find a murderer, not become one. Slow the fuck down.'

Greene eased off the pedal. His fingers drumming on the wheel, he swore under his breath at anyone who didn't get out of the way fast enough.

Let them still be there, Charlie thought. If we find the van, we find Morton, and perhaps Morton is still alive. Just this one break, that's all we need.

* * *

116

The place looked like the Dissenters' Chapel where they had found Father O'Meara, except it wasn't hidden away in a cemetery. This one was right in the middle of a 1920s housing estate, the number 18 bus stopped right outside. There was a cyclone fence right around it to stop people getting in. Ironic really, the only time anyone round here wanted to go in to a church these days was when it was locked.

As soon as they drove up, Charlie could see from the car that someone had cut through the padlock on the gate. He jumped out.

He could hear sirens down the High Street, the cavalry on their way.

'You want to wait?' Greene said.

'Not really,' Charlie said, and kicked the gate open with his boot and went in.

It hadn't been used for years, must have been built right back in the day. The walls were Kentish ragstone, there was a vestry and a belfry tacked on in ugly orange brick. There was no glass left in any of the arched windows, and the car park was overgrown with weeds. There was a mossy green wall, a drift of rotting leaf mould piled against it.

This looked like just the place.

He ran around the back, hoping to find the van. Nothing.

There was only one way in to the church, but it had been gated off and the padlock was intact. Charlie peered inside.

Hard to see anything in the gloom. Everything had been stripped away: the pews, the altar; just a shell left. It smelled of damp and mould. No one had been in here for a long time. He heard something scampering around inside and he felt a shock of adrenalin. No, it was just a rat.

He looked up. There was a steeple above the west transept, he shielded his eyes. The bell had long since come down or been moved, there were birds nesting in the rusted Victorian guttering. The place would have been grand once, he could imagine it, a hundred years ago, the congregation in their Sunday best, singing hymns, checking their fob watches if the minister droned on too long.

The slates and flushings were loose; some of them had come down in a storm, lay in the frozen grass around the back. Snow was still piled against the footings where the sun never reached. Nowhere to hide Steve Morton here, unless he was inside, but the gates on the foyer were locked, and the chain hadn't been tampered with.

He heard something around the side of the church. He looked back at the car for Greene, couldn't see him, where the hell was he? He realised he should have brought a Maglite with him, it would have been a weapon of sorts. There had been a low iron rail around the car park once, most of it had rusted away. He found a broken length of it and hefted it in his right hand. It would do.

He edged forward.

There it was again.

His mouth was suddenly dry. He could hear the sirens now, at least two patrol cars on their way. Hell with it, he couldn't wait. He jumped around the corner.

A cat.

It snarled at him and scampered away through a hole in the fence.

Nothing, nothing.

But someone had been here. He squatted down, staring at the tyre marks in the gravel. They were that close.

He looked over his shoulder, saw flashing blue lights, a patrol car pulling up on the other side of the gates. 'Keep them out of here,' Charlie shouted to Greene. 'I want a cordon around the whole place, and then call the crime unit. Jack's Christmas pudding will have to wait.'

Charlie looked back at the tyre prints. 'You've been here, haven't you?' he murmured under his breath. 'I can feel you. You came here for something.' Was it to dump Morton's body?

But where? The church was locked, there was just a car park and a few weeds, no sign of a fresh grave.

No, you came here for something else. If only I knew what it was.

CHAPTER EIGHTEEN

Dawson was making coffee when they got back to the nick. He grabbed Charlie's mug with its distinctive logo off the shelf – *You have the right to remain silent, use it* – and poured in hot water and some Nescafé instant and handed it to him. Charlie would rather drink bleach than instant coffee but he dutifully took it from him; he would pour it down the sink later. It was long past the point that he could tell him.

'No luck?'

Charlie shook his head.

Rupinder and Wes walked in, threw a handful of USBs on to the desk.

'What have you got?'

'Footage from the High Street the night Morton was nabbed. The Anchor, the Crown, Lloyds, Barclays, London Court, Domino's Pizza.'

'Now the good news,' Charlie said.

'Someone has to watch them,' Wes said.

'It will take days,' Rupinder said.

'With ordinary people, but you guys are supermen and you're hungry for promotion, so I expect you'll find a way to get a result today.'

'There's specialists supposed to do that.'

'Only half of them here, it's Christmas. Go on, you'd only be at home watching telly anyway. This is probably more exciting.'

Charlie looked at his watch. Already dark outside, people on the sofa at home, falling asleep after a big Christmas lunch.

Except one poor sod, who was trussed up in a basement somewhere or, worse, bleeding out his last in agony somewhere in an abandoned church.

'Here's FONC,' Wes said.

The DCI nodded at Charlie. 'God's here,' he said. 'He wants to talk to you.'

The assistant commissioner? When was the last time he showed his face in the nick on Christmas Day? The balloon had really gone up this time.

Charlie followed the DCI down the hall to the elevators.

They took the lift to the top floor. The furnishings were better up here, Charlie noticed; no carpet squares, for a start, and though the views out of the window were just the same, they were higher up: he could see St Paul's and the Gherkin lit up through the overcast skies. Even the air seemed more rarefied.

They went into the conference room. They were all there waiting for him: the assistant commissioner, Jamieson, at the head of the table with his PA, Chief Super Brownlea next to him, then the media officer, Catlin.

The DCI sat down, left Charlie standing. The naughty chair was at the far end of the table. Charlie took it. He reached for the water, helped himself, wished it was vodka.

'We all know why we're here,' Jamieson said. He drew a file towards him and peered over the top of his glasses at Charlie. 'Greetings of the season, Inspector.'

'Sir.'

'Any progress?'

Charlie ran through the case with him, directing his remarks to Jamieson and Brownlea in turn. He could feel the DCI beside him, itching to interrupt. Finally, he stopped to draw breath and O'Neal-Callaghan jumped in.

'DI Fenton was originally assigned to the case, sir, but I allowed DI George to step in, as he was the SIO on the O'Meara homicide.'

'Is there anything to associate these two cases?'

'We're waiting on the science lab at Lambeth for a CS report on the tyre latent and the footprints. A modified Ford Transit van was used in both crimes.'

Jamieson frowned and returned his attention to the folder in front of him. 'That's not very conclusive, is it?' he said.

Charlie looked up at the clock. They'll be serving tea and biscuits any minute. *What are we doing sitting here? I need to be working.*

Jamieson looked at the DCI. 'I think this is above the level of your DI now,' he said. 'It's time for you to step in.'

Charlie couldn't believe his ears. 'All due respect, sir,' he said, 'but by the time I have fully briefed the guv'nor here on all the lines of enquiry from both investigations, it will be almost midnight and everyone will have gone home. By that time PC Morton may be dead.'

Jamieson stared him down, didn't like being lectured by the rank and file, of course. But fuck it, Charlie thought, I'm not going to give this up without a fight. Jamieson had never led a major investigation in his life, he'd spent his career in intel; a degree in management doesn't make him Sherlock Holmes.

'You don't have any outstanding lines of enquiry though, do you?' Jamieson said.

'Actually, I have several, sir, including a crime lab report on tyre prints found at another abandoned chapel in Hackney just an hour ago. There is an ANPR camera just half a kilometre away and that could give us a registration tag.' He looked at his watch, just to let them all know he thought they were wasting his time.

The DCI found something of great interest on his shirt cuff.

'We can't afford any mistakes.'

'No, sir.'

'The press have set up camp outside. We are now national news.'

Catlin spoke up for the first time. 'We have to tell them

something,' she said. 'We were able to contain the details of Father O'Meara's murder, but the abduction of a police officer in this manner, well, it's now public property. We can't keep saying "no comment".'

'I understand that,' Charlie said.

'Do you, DI George?' The super now, Brownlea, siding with the majority. She gave Jamieson a conspiratorial smile.

Jamieson sighed. 'Well, I suppose you're right, DI George, it's too late in the day for changes now. You have twenty-four hours. DCI Callaghan, you will familiarise yourself with all aspects of the case ready to step in this time tomorrow if we have made no significant progress. Keep the superintendent here fully apprised of all developments, she will report directly to me.' He turned to Catlin. 'You have a press release prepared?'

She took an A4 sheet from her case and handed it to him. 'I do, sir.'

'Good.' He handed it to the chief super like it had dog crap on it. 'Good luck, everyone.'

There were murmurs of 'thank you, sir,' all around the table. Charlie didn't say anything. He loved the way his DCI had defended him against the intimations of incompetence, but he supposed he shouldn't expect any different.

Never mind all that. The only thing that mattered right now was PC Morton, and his wife and two kids huddled by the unlit Christmas tree, staring at the presents, waiting for their husband and father to come home.

His crew had gone down to the canteen for their Christmas dinner; cappuccinos in cardboard cups from the vending machine, and two packets of cheese and onion crisps lying open in the middle of the table. Dawson was still there, with Wes and Rupinder and DS Greene. There was a general scraping of chairs to make room for him.

'All right?' Dawson said.

'This time tomorrow DCI O'Neal-Callaghan is taking over as your SIO. Unless we have a prime suspect.'

'Christ, not FONC,' Wes said.

'Afraid so.'

'What a sorry place to spend Christmas,' Wes said.

He couldn't argue. There was a stunted tinsel Christmas tree on the food counter, next to the empty *bain-marie* trays. Half the striplights had been turned off to save money.

'Did the DJ check out?' he said to Dawson.

'I sent Mayer and Winston to interview him. Nothing on his record. Looks clean.'

Rupinder finished his coffee and rubbed his eyes. 'Better get back to it. I don't know what hurts my eyes more, Michael McIntyre, or four hours of watching the traffic on CCTV.'

'Well, you've got nothing better to do, Rupe,' Greene said.

'What does that mean?'

'Well, you're a Sikh, you don't have Christmas.'

'Of course we have Christmas. We have turkey and Christmas pudding with brandy in it like everyone else.'

'I didn't think it was part of your religion.'

'What's a pudding got to do with religion? You think Jesus had mince pies at Christmas? It's a holiday, man, we do what everyone else does.'

'Anyway, since when have you been religious?' Wes said to Greene.

'I'm Christian, and everything.'

'No, you're not,' Rupinder said. 'You're a Londoner. And if you really want to know, it's tomorrow that's holy for us Sikhs. It's the day the two young sons of Guru Gobind Singh were bricked up alive for refusing to convert to Islam.'

'What ISIS, you mean?'

'It was the seventeenth century, they didn't have ISIS then. You really don't know anything, do you?'

Wes finished his coffee and threw his empty cardboard cup at the bin, missed by half a yard. He looked at Greene. 'Don't say, "I thought you'd be a good basketballer," just because I'm black.'

'I wasn't going to.'

'Good.'

Wes followed Rupinder to the elevators.

'Funny,' Greene said, after they were gone. 'I thought he'd be a good basketballer.'

By the time they got back upstairs, Gale and Malik were back. Dawson had actioned them to interview the witness who had reported seeing a Transit van at the derelict church in Hackney.

'Any good?' Charlie said to them.

'He couldn't help us much,' Mayer said. 'Old bloke, lives alone, spends his whole life watching CSI reruns. He thought it was his lucky day. Didn't want us to go, kept offering us cups of tea and asking us stuff about fingerprints.'

'He knew more about crime scenes than we do,' Malik said.

'Anything?'

'He didn't pay much mind to it this morning,' Gale said. 'Only remembered it when he saw the bit on the telly about the stolen Transit van.'

'I suppose he didn't get a registration?'

Gale shook his head.

'Bugger.'

'Nothing else?' Dawson said. 'Did he see anyone get out of the van?'

'He just remembered it was parked there when he got up to make a cup of tea. When he went back to the kitchen half an hour later it was gone. I checked, his window has a very restricted view of the car park. He couldn't have seen much anyway.'

'Guv!' Parm from intel called him over. She pushed two Xerox sheets towards him, copies of newspaper pages from a local rag; Morton posing with three VPCs in cadet uniforms. He checked the date. Just two months ago. This was the news piece Fenton had been telling him about.

He remembered that Father O'Meara had been a minor celebrity, too. Odd.

His Nokia hummed to life in his jacket pocket.

'George.'

'Charlie, it's Jack.'

'You got a result on the tyre?'

'Still running tests, I'm afraid. Doesn't look too good, though. The transient wasn't as clear as the impression from Barrow Fields.'

'What about the other one, from Elmscroft Road?'

'Charlie, this is Christmas Day. You're dreaming, aren't you?'

Charlie hung up. If only they could have found the little scrote who stole the van. Even if Jack had a stone-cold match on the prints at Barrow Field and the community centre, all it would prove was that the two cases were connected. It wouldn't help them find a suspect. Even ANPR and CCTV were no good to them if their suspect was using several sets of stolen plates.

He looked across at Dawson, the phones had stopped ringing. The press conference was due in half an hour and he still hadn't interviewed Morton's line manager. Too late in the day now, he'd have to do it tomorrow. Their fault: wasting his time in sodding meetings.

Maybe Morton's DI would have something for him. But he suspected that, even if they did everything right out of the manual, they would need to catch a break if they were going to find Morton alive.

CHAPTER NINETEEN

'The time is 20.00, the twenty-fifth of December. This is a briefing for Operation Galilee, which has been re-opened today following the abduction last night of PC Stephen Morton.'

Christ, clock this lot. They all looked like their dog just died. He didn't blame them, dragged in on Christmas Day. This was supposed to be a new lead but really they were no further along than they were before.

It was Lovejoy's fault, she should have kept her mouth shut; his bad as well, of course. He didn't have to take the case off Fenton.

He had been hoping for a quick breakthrough once they matched the tyre prints, but there was still nothing from Jack. The latents from the community centre and the derelict church in Hackney were inconclusive, and all he could tell him so far was that the shoe sizes were a match.

It had been a miracle to get that much out of him that fast, Christmas Day and all.

Charlie started the meeting by running through the results they had so far. He looked hopefully at Billy and Parm.

'I probably know more about him than his wife does,' Parm said. 'He has no secrets, not even any porn or gambling sites on his laptop. Nothing unusual in his phone or banking records either. It's like his line manager told you, he was practically a saint.'

'Funny, that's what they said about Father O'Meara,' Greene said.

'What about imagery?'

Lovejoy leaned forward in her seat. 'A council CCTV camera recorded seven Ford Transit vans on the High Street between 21.45 and 22.45 the night PC Morton was abducted,' Lovejoy said. 'We cross-referenced with an ANPR camera about a mile away. Four of the vehicles are still being checked, two have been eliminated, one had plates that were reported stolen two months ago. They were taken from a Transit van parked on the street in Finchley.'

'That's only about four miles from where the other plates were nicked.'

'That's the one, isn't it?' Dawson said.

Charlie shrugged. 'We can't be sure.'

'One in twelve cars on the road have stolen plates,' Lovejoy said. 'That's what statistics say. When I was in the CID, all our big-time burglaries and robberies used vehicles with blagged tags. Essential bit of kit these days.'

Another lead closing off. ANPR had only had one hit on the stolen plate before it disappeared from the system.

'So what he, or they, are doing,' Wes said, 'is driving somewhere quiet after they've grabbed Morton and then changing the plates again.'

'If you were prepared, it would be easy enough,' Charlie said. 'Don't have to screw them on, just use Velcro or something.'

'Takes planning.'

'Yeah well, if you're going to crucify someone in the middle of London, or kidnap a thirteen-stone copper, you would be pretty handy at planning.'

'Someone must have seen something,' Dawson said. 'Our perp is clever, but no one is infallible.'

'They'll slip up eventually,' Lovejoy said.

And that was the critical thing, wasn't it, Charlie thought: *eventually*. Would PC Morton be dead before they slipped up, or afterwards?

He looked around the room. They had nothing. The AC would take him off the case tomorrow and he would have failed not once, but twice. *Eventually* the case would crack, and the DCI would be the hero; or, if it all went to shit, O'Neal-Callaghan would have Charlie to blame.

Why had he put up his hand for this?

Gale walked in, he was late. Charlie pointed to his watch.

'Sorry, guv. But I think we've got something.'

Charlie held his breath.

'The search team out at the community centre found a Samsung mobile phone in the bushes. Telephony have traced it, it was reported stolen a couple of weeks ago. Different SIM card, but it was readable. There's five calls on it to PC Morton's number. The last one was made at 21.32 the night he went missing.'

'Fingerprints?'

'We're checking them on the database now.'

There was a murmur of excitement in the room. Only Charlie wasn't feeling it. What this is, he thought, is desperation. The kind of person who could plan crimes like these – if they were, after all, connected – is not going to leave an incriminating mobile phone at the scene. But they had to follow every lead.

'All right, let me know the minute you have something. We'll reconvene at 0900 tomorrow. Thank you, everyone, for putting in. I know this wasn't the Christmas you all had planned, but I'm sure Santa has seen what good boys and girls you've been this year and next year you'll get an extra-big pressie. See you all in the morning.'

The room started to clear.

Charlie stayed as upbeat as he could until the last of them left the room. He couldn't let them see how desperate he was. But with every hour that passed, he knew that if he'd missed something, somehow, it might have already cost PC Morton his life.

It was late, everyone else went home; he still had a lot more to do. He and DC Lovejoy went into his office and updated the policy book. After it was done, she still wanted to talk about the case.

He sent her home. He needed some sleep. Nothing more he could do until the morning now.

Archway: the snow was not deep and crisp and certainly not even. What there was left of it was piled in dirty brown crusts against the kerbstones. The gritter had left a murky slush in the street.

He parked his Golf and let himself into his flat; it was all he could afford after the split with Nicki, but it was a step up from the camp bed in his office, and it was somewhere to store his framed Arsenal shirts.

He stopped off on the way to have a guilty fag in the secluded communal garden round the back. He stood there, shivering in the cold, hating himself for giving in. He was supposed to have given them up but, sometimes, in the middle of a murder case, or the night before he was due at the Old Bailey, he cracked. Just when he thought he had it kicked, too.

These things will kill you, he muttered to himself. This is the absolute last one.

Finally, he went upstairs and crawled into bed, put his alarm on for six, and pulled the covers over his head. He had just closed his eyes when the iPhone buzzed to life on the bedside table. 'The Ride of the Valkyries'. Strange motif to choose for your personal life, Charlie, he said aloud, and rolled over and put it to his ear.

'Charlie, it's me.'

He sat up. 'Geri. What's wrong?'

'I just wanted to hear your voice.' She spoke so softly he could barely hear her.

'It's nearly two in the morning.'

'The house is finally quiet. Everyone's gone to bed.'

'Where are you?'

'Out in the conservatory.'

He imagined a room, twice as big as his flat, looking out over a frozen but geometric lawn. In Kent. Must be nice.

'Simon's asleep, snoring his head off. Him and his dreadful brother got drunk and had a blazing row. His sister spent half the night crying and I had to console her. God, I hate Christmas.'

He lay on his back, the phone against his ear, and stared into the dark.

'How was yours?'

'Got called in to work.'

'I thought you were rostered off.'

'So did I. Just as well, my family Christmas wasn't much better.'

He listened to her breathing. He felt himself stir. He told himself again that he couldn't do this any more. He wasn't cut out for affairs.

'I miss you,' she whispered.

'I miss you, too.'

'Call me. Soon. I need you.'

'Merry Christmas.'

She gave a torchy laugh and hung up. He rolled over and tried to get back to sleep, but all he could think about was that old joke: what's the difference between a light on and a hard on?

Answer: you can sleep with a light on.

He thought: Get up and make yourself a cup of coffee, Charlie son, or a whisky. He was just about to, but the next moment he was dreaming about the DCI, who was wearing a tracksuit and telling him he'd been dropped from the school football team; then he was running along a beach. He didn't know if he was trying to get away from something or catch someone. Whatever it was, no matter how hard he pumped his legs, he just couldn't get anywhere.

131

Then the Nokia rang. He fumbled for it in the dark, held it to his ear. 'DI George.'

'Charlie?'

'Sir?'

'You're needed,' the DCI said. 'We've found PC Morton.'

CHAPTER TWENTY

Still dark, a few minutes after six according to the digital clock in his Golf as he made his way over to Hampstead. His iPhone played the first few bars of 'The Ride of the Valkyries' in its slot mount. He answered.

'Jules. What are you doing up?'

'I tried to call you all day yesterday.'

'It was switched off. I was working.'

'I was worried about you.'

'Sorry I missed my Christmas pud. I told Terry to send my apologies.'

'He reckons you nearly killed him.'

'Come on, Jules, you know me. If I'd wanted to kill him, I would have.'

'I told you to leave it.'

'Yeah, well, can't do that, can I? I just had a friendly word with him, no harm done. But if he ever touches you again, he'll be eating Christmas leftovers through a straw. Did you have a nice day?'

'It was awful.'

'Well, Christmas is like that. What are you doing with that tosser?'

'He's my husband, Charlie. Better or worse.'

'Well, you've got the worse covered. I've got to go. Duty calls. There's a lorry in front, it's putting out more carbon monoxide than China. Reckon I should pull him over?'

'Don't leave it too long. Rom likes to see you.'

'Is Ma all right?'

'She fell asleep on the sofa at four.'

'I gotta go,' Charlie said.

He hung up. His sister's situation made him angry. Tel was just like their old man; it was like watching their childhood all over again. How did that work? Better or worse! As if she believed all that bollocks.

He got the blue light out from under the seat, wound down the window and slammed it on the roof. He veered out into the traffic.

Hell with it, he had work to do.

There was a rugby scrum on East Heath Road, he gave up trying to manoeuvre his motor through it, left it on the side of the road and got out. He went to the boot, got his forensic suit and overshoes. Bugger, he'd forgotten his torch.

There were press and rubberneckers everywhere. He pushed his way through, ducked under the police tape, flashed his warrant card at one of the overworked uniforms and signed himself in.

It was a bitter morning, still dark, patches of frost on the hard ground. He headed towards the halogen lamps about a hundred yards from the car park, where the crime unit had set up their yellow tent. It looked like a garden party if you didn't know any better.

He saw a flickering light, heard a familiar voice. 'Guv, that you?'

It was May, the duty officer.

'Have trouble getting in?'

'It's like we're giving away free tickets for Adele. You'll need more uniforms down here to keep the press out.'

'I'll see to it.'

'What's going on?' The mortuary van had parked next to the CU vehicle. He saw them loading a stretcher into the back. 'That was quick.'

'It's a bit unusual, this one.'

'Oh, brilliant.'

'They didn't know it was him until they exhumed him. That's when they called us.'

'Exhumed him?'

'He'd been buried, up to his neck. They only found his uniform and ID after the crime techs had cleared away the dirt.'

Charlie stood with his hands deep in his parka, shivering. He heard one of the mortuary guys say something, and the other one chuckled and tried to cover it with a fake cough. Charlie wished he'd put on another jumper under his parka. He was freezing.

'It's definitely him?'

'They've taken fingerprints.'

'Why?'

'Well, it was his head, guv. It was, well, it was pretty gruesome actually.' Gruesome. That was something, coming from a sergeant with ten years up dealing with road trauma and violent crimes.

They made their way across the grass. It was rock hard, the frost on the grass crunched under their feet like gravel. Now his eyes were accustomed to the dark he could just make out a pond, almost frozen over, a few scattered trees with claw-like branches.

This didn't make sense.

They reached the tent and Charlie thanked May for her help and went inside. There were two figures in white overalls standing next to a trestle table. One of them had to be Jolly; he didn't know anyone else that tall. The other one was Jack. He looked over Jolly's shoulder and raised a hand. 'Hello Charlie. Did you have a good Christmas?'

'Seriously?'

'Sorry to make it worse.'

There were exhibits piled on the table in evidence bags. He

pointed to one of them. Charlie bent down for a better look. It was PC Morton's wallet, his driver's licence and credit card visible through the plastic.

'Who found him?'

'Patrol car on East Heath Road called it in about two this morning. Foxes were already at it, they said.'

'At what?'

'His head.' Jack called over the photographer, had him flick back through the image library on his SLR, show Charlie the images. The pulpy remains of a human skull protruded from the damp earth. A close-up showed frost on an eyelid, an eyeball bulging from a mess of bone and meat. Charlie swallowed back some bile.

'Fuck me.'

'I'd better be going,' Jolly said.

'Time of death?'

'Three to four hours.'

'It seems like an obvious question, I know, but can you confirm for me how he died? I mean, all this mutilation, was this post mortem, or what? And why did they try and bury him?' Charlie stamped his foot. 'The ground's rock hard.'

'I found no other apparent injuries on the rest of his body. Whether he was conscious at the time of death, I won't be able to tell you until we get toxicology results. He had been bound hand and foot and, although it's difficult to tell from these images, he had also been gagged.'

'And then partly buried?'

'What it looks like, Charlie, is he was stoned to death.'

'Right,' Charlie said.

He walked over to the hole. There were a dozen bricks lying around one end of it, splattered with blood and brain matter. They varied in size and shape; he took a closer look. 'London clay, though I'll have to confirm that,' Jack said.

'Like we found on Father O'Meara.'

'Anything else?' Jolly said.

136

Charlie shook his head.

'I'll perform the PM at ten o'clock. Will one of your team be present?'

'I'll send DS Greene.'

'Right then,' Jolly said. He made his way back to the car park.

Charlie looked at Jack. 'What have you got?'

'My lads are still checking the car park. It's gravel, so there's plenty to work with. The ground's too hard for much in the way of prints, but we think we've isolated a couple of impressions in the dirt around the hole over there. And what looks like tyre marks. A bicycle perhaps.'

'Or a mover's trolley.'

'Could be. I'll get you the results soon as I can, of course.'

'But how the hell do you dig a hole this time of year?' Charlie said.

'Didn't have to. The council had just taken out a tree. If you take a look outside, you'll see the digger, it's parked about ten yards away. Whoever dreamed up this little scenario, they knew all they had to do was lie him in the hole and shovel some earth on him.'

'And then chuck house bricks at him?'

'That's what it looks like.'

'So, he – they, she, it – drives in here, puts him on his back on a trolley, drops him in the hole, does the business, then gets off home again in time for a big fry-up and read of the paper. Christ.'

He shivered, partly because it was freezing out here on the heath, but that wasn't the only reason. You couldn't do this job if you were squeamish about what humans were capable of. A knifing down the estate, a husband hitting his wife with a hammer, that was run of the mill; he could understand how that could happen.

But kidnapping a bloke, so you could truss him up and stone him to death in the middle of the heath?

137

Yeah, that was enough to put the screaming abdabs up anybody.

DS May came over. 'Why?' she said, reading his mind.

'Yeah, that's the question, innit?'

She nodded over his shoulder. 'You've got company. Judging by the size of the crowd, it's your guv'nor.'

Charlie waited for him outside the tent. The DCI had brought four uniforms with him, to deal with the public and the press. He strode purposefully across the grass, gave Charlie a look and walked past him, stared into the hole over the shoulder of a CS officer, made another face. 'Was it him?'

'We believe so, sir.'

'You believe so?'

'His face was unrecognisable. But he was wearing his uniform and he had ID in his pocket. We'll need definite confirmation from a fingerprint match.'

'What the hell happened?'

'Initial indications are that he was stoned.'

'What, drugged you mean?'

'No, sir, stoned, as in the biblical sense.'

The DCI stared at him, as if he thought Charlie was having a laugh. When he saw that he wasn't, he grunted and shook his head. 'I'm taking over,' he said.

'Sir?'

'We have a cop killer on our hands. You had your chance, Charlie. The super called me on the way here. She wants me to take over the investigation effective immediately.'

'Yes, sir.'

'You don't look surprised.'

'I'm not.' Funny, but he almost felt relieved. 'Who's going to tell his wife?'

'Oh yes. His wife.'

'Maybe I should do it.'

'No, call the FLO. That would be better.'

'I don't like designating that sort of job.'

138

'Well, you'll have to. I'm scheduling a meeting for Operation Maverick at 0900, in the conference room. Make sure everyone's there.'

'Maverick, sir?'

'I'm not making this murder a part of any other ongoing investigation until I have more conclusive proof.'

'But—'

He held up his hand, gave Charlie his 'no further questions for today' look. 'This has to get sorted,' he said.

Charlie decided he'd already said enough. Besides, all he could think about was two little kids squirming on Deborah Morton's knee, next to an unlit Christmas tree.

A cold yellow sun was inching up over the heath. It would make the search for evidence a bit easier, though it didn't look like the day would be getting warmer anytime soon.

He watched the DCI marching back down the hill in front of him, surrounded by a phalanx of uniforms from Essex Road.

'You're welcome to it,' he said under his breath, even though he didn't quite believe it.

CHAPTER TWENTY-ONE

There would have been less fuss if someone had shot the prime minister. When he got back to the nick, he had to manoeuvre around all the TV vans with satellite dishes mounted on their roofs, almost ran down a talking head standing in the middle of the street practising her live cross for a breakfast show. He heard the whirr and click of cameras, journos peering through the windows, trying to see who was in the car.

Lovejoy was with him. She'd phoned in with car problems and he'd picked her up from the tube on the way through. 'Should I throw a blanket over your head, guv?' she said.

He was in no mood for jokes. He sat there, fuming. Who was he angry at? Himself, he supposed. What a way to die. His fault, he should have been able to do something. This morning, while he was trying to get to sleep, the poor bastard was getting his brains mashed with a rock.

For Christ's sake.

They went up to the fourth floor in the elevator. Every seat in the conference room had a bum on it, and there was a wall of TV cameras set up at the back of the room. A few minutes later the AC and the super walked on to the stage, looking like they were heading out to meet the hangman. They were followed by Catlin and the DCI.

Catlin sat down and read from a typewritten sheet, the usual stuff: condolences to the family, heinous crime, devoted husband and father, respected and hard-working member of the police force.

She described what they knew about the night Morton had disappeared, gave details of the POD they had set up in Hackney High Street, and appealed to the public for any information that might lead them to those responsible.

Almost before she had finished, the BBC's chief crime correspondent fired off his first question and the AC cleared his throat and began a ponderous answer. They barely gave him time to finish before ITV started on him. This was going to be a bloodbath. He couldn't watch.

At least they would have absolute priority at Lambeth now. He reckoned they would have the lab results they had been waiting on by lunchtime, even though it was Boxing Day. But what would really change the game was someone ringing the hotline to say they'd seen some likely lad park their white Transit van outside their house in the middle of the night and start fiddling with the number plates – or, better, they'd seen their next-door neighbour doing it.

But what were the chances? This was a city where men in furniture removal vans parked in someone's driveway, chatted over the fence to the people next door, perhaps even went in for a cup of tea, and then cleared out the house; it was a world where people still sent money to Nigerians who introduced themselves as barristers trying to unload a seven-figure inheritance on the internet.

People famously didn't get involved or else they were as dumb as posts.

What would turn this around was a busybody who spent all day peering through their curtains, not minding their own business.

But it hardly ever happened, not on the tough cases. Sod's law, innit?

Charlie sat down in the conference room with the rest of the team, Dawson on one side, Lovejoy on the other. The team gave him questioning looks; they would all work out for themselves what had happened, he didn't have to tell them.

There was a buzz in the room, as if by murdering a policeman the perpetrator had made a fatal error. Charlie didn't see how; they had nothing startling or fresh to work with. There were still two dozen uniforms on the heath doing a grid search, perhaps they might turn up something.

The DCI bounded in to the room. He had his secretary Jennifer with him, with the decision log. He put a folder on the desk, took out several photographs and posted them on the whiteboard. A murmur went round the room; it was PC Morton, or what was left of him, as he had been found earlier that morning, buried up to his neck in the shallow hole left by a tree stump on Hampstead Heath.

Several of the more junior detectives and a handful of the uniforms turned away or put their heads in their hands.

'Gentlemen,' he said. 'This morning we lost one of our own.'

'He sounds like Theresa fooking May,' Dawson murmured under his breath.

'PC Morton had been missing for around thirty-two hours when he was found around 1.30 a.m. on Hampstead Heath. Two patrol officers from Hampstead Police Station found the body after they received a report of suspicious activity earlier that night.'

'Excuse me, sir,' Charlie said. 'Just to be clear. Is it definitely Morton?'

'Yes, Charlie. I got a call from Crime Unit in Lambeth a few minutes ago. It is definitely PC Morton.' He nodded to Jennifer and she pinned a map of the heath on to the whiteboard. 'The perpetrator gained access via East Heath Road, drove along this footpath here, until they were out of sight of the road. However, this part of the heath is still visible from the windows of these apartments just here. Someone saw vehicle headlights and then heard the sound of digging. They reported it to the local police.'

'What time was it called in, sir?' Charlie asked him.

'Rupinder and Wesley are interviewing the witnesses right now. But from what I understand, it was just after midnight.'

'What time did the patrol get there?'

'It was a busy night. They had received a number of noise complaints for loud parties, and there had been an assault outside the Rose and Crown.'

'So what time?'

'They logged their arrival at 1.24 a.m.'

'We could have had him,' Charlie said.

'Don't blame them, guv,' Dawson said. 'Blame the budget cuts.'

'Those bricks in the photograph,' Greene said. 'Where did they come from?'

'We believe they were transported there by the killer, or killers. They are being analysed at Lambeth right now.'

Dawson rubbed his bald spot. 'These people who called this in, did they actually see anything?'

'As I said, Rupinder and Wesley have gone back to re-interview. But from what I understand, it was just the head-lights and suspicious noises that led to the report. Nothing else.'

'So no CCTV?'

The DCI shook his head.

'Do we know what kind of vehicle they were using?'

'Not at this stage. Again, we are waiting on results from Lambeth. I have asked them to be fast-tracked.'

'Let's talk about those bricks,' Charlie said, but the DCI cut him off.

'We can talk about that in my office. Now, I don't need to tell you how important it is to get a result on this. The whole country is watching us. The next forty-eight hours are crucial for this case. The assistant commissioner has already held a press conference this morning, to appeal for urgent assistance from the public. We have also mobilised enough uniforms to knock on every door in a mile radius in a search for further witnesses.' He looked at Dawson. 'The DS here will task you,

143

depending on what comes in on HOLMES and the crime line. Hopefully by the end of the day we will have a strong lead on this. All right, everyone, let's get to work. Charlie, my office, now.'

Charlie followed the DCI to the elevators and they rode in silence to the fourth floor.

When they got to his office, he took a seat behind his desk, and leaned back, crossing his arms. 'All right, shoot. What's worrying you?'

'We seem to be overlooking evidence here, sir.'

'What evidence?'

'All the evidence, sir. Due respect, sir, but Maverick and Galilee should not be separate operations. There are clear links to the O'Meara murder.'

'Are there?'

'I thought that had been clearly established.'

'Yes, that's the problem.'

The DCI leaned in, fire in his eye. Christ, Charlie thought, he really resents me. I never realised.

'So, one of your team is on night-duty roster, happens to call you in for the kidnapping of PC Morton. You decide to take over, based on a premise that just doesn't hold water.'

'The modified Ford Transit, sir.'

'Charlie, you're chasing shadows.'

'What about tyre prints?'

'First, at the O'Meara murder scene, Crime Unit was able to get a good impression. What they got from the community centre were only latents, and the results are not conclusive. There is a possibility it might be the same brand and size, but inconclusive for identifying features on wear and characteristics. In other words, we could be talking two different Ford Transit vans and, as you know, stolen Ford Transit vans are like red double-decker buses in London.'

'What about Hackney, and this morning's crime scene?'

'I don't give a toss about Hackney, Charlie, that hasn't got

144

anything to do with PC Morton. And we haven't got any results from this morning yet – Jack can't walk on water.'

'We've got footprints.'

'Same size, yes, but not the same footwear. You want me to arrest every bloke in London with a size ten?'

'The bricks, sir. London clay. It's distinctive.'

'Half of London was built in the nineteenth century. Those bricks are everywhere.'

'Microscopy will prove that the dust and those bricks are from an identical source.'

'You know how long it's going to take to get those results back?'

'The truth doesn't have a time limit.'

'This investigation does. It's my call now, and my feeling is that you've misdirected the investigation. You've made the fatal mistake of trying to fit facts to the theory.'

'And the other tracks we found? Jack thinks it was a mover's trolley.'

'Now you sound desperate. Come on, Charlie. Seriously?'

'The weight of probability says these two murders are linked.'

'I'm in charge of the investigation now and I say it's sheer fantasy. We're wasting time. Get down Malden Street and talk to his line manager, let's see if we can identify someone who had it in for him and let's work from there.'

Charlie got slowly to his feet. Shut up, he told himself; every time you open your mouth you just make it worse. But he couldn't help it. 'Time will bear me out on this, sir.'

'We get back to basics, Charlie: motive and means. Once we have that we'll match the evidence with our suspect. Now get out there and start doing your job.'

Malden Street was about as salubrious as any of the east London nicks; there was a reinforced glass door, a bunch of scrotes hanging around on plastic chairs in the waiting room, photos of MisPers staring out from the poster board, scallies screaming at the desk sergeant through the toughened glass.

Charlie was buzzed through. Morton's line manager at Malden Street, Inspector Susan Grace, reminded him of Miss Trunchbull from *Matilda*. He'd taken Rom to see it at the theatre in Seven Dials. Grace was square-shouldered and formidable. She looked Charlie up and down as if she was working out where to hit him first.

Charlie showed her his badge and she made a face, as if she was surprised that Major Crimes would employ someone like him. 'Where did you get the suit?'

'It's an Ermenegildo Zegna.'

'That must have set you back.'

'Fifty quid in a Salvation Army store in Archway.'

She thought he was having a laugh. She turned her back and led him into her office, shut the door behind them. Her office was tidier than his, maps of station wards and a dozen mug shots on the wall, not even any coffee rings on the fake walnut desktop.

'Matthew Vernon,' she said.

'What was that?'

She pulled out a chair for him and went around the desk to her own. 'Soon as I heard the news I came in here, went through Morton's file, and my daily log, tried to find leads for you. Took me all day. I only came up with this one name: Matt Vernon, 26B Caledonian Close, Leyton.'

'What's the connection?'

'PC Morton assaulted him in the pub down on the High Street, the Sow and Whistle.'

'He assaulted him?'

'He'd been coming on to Stephen's wife when he was round their burgh doing some work. He does kitchen renovations. Dragged him out of the pub about two months ago and sorted him out.'

'How bad?'

146

'Vernon couldn't work for a couple of days. He chose not to lay charges, but it came to my attention pretty much straight away.'

'How?'

'PC Morton came and told me what he'd done. He was like that. What you saw was what you got with him.'

'Right.' Charlie stared at the name in his notebook. Really?

'How did he die?' she asked him.

'I'm not at liberty.'

'For God's sake. The whole nick is in uproar. He was a popular bloke. We have a right to know.'

'Not really.'

'What am I supposed to tell his mates?'

'That we're working round the clock to find whoever did for him. The AC is throwing everything at this. We will be talking to this geezer . . .' Charlie checked what he'd just written in his notebook. '. . . Vernon, as soon as I leave here. You really think he's the one?'

'I don't know,' she said, clearly rattled. 'It's all I can think of.'

'Really, no one else?'

Grace leaned forward, her elbows on the desk. 'They don't make them like PC Morton any more. He was tough, as Vernon will tell you, but he had a heart of gold. No end of awards and citations for working with youth groups, and the effort he put in to the cadets was . . . inspirational.' She paused for a moment, swallowed hard. 'He was one of the best community cops I've ever seen. He really cared about those kids, and some of them, if you ask me, were rat-bags.'

'But he must have made a few enemies in the job. I mean, we both know what it's like. You have to bang up some bloke, they don't always take it well.'

A shrug.

'He'd never been investigated, for anything?'

'You mean, was there a chance he was bent?'

147

'Lot of temptations in this job.'

'Have you ever been tempted, Inspector?'

'Not at work, no.'

'There you are, then. He was like that. A good cop. You're wasting your time if you're thinking of trying to dig any dirt on him. Don't tell me you haven't been through his records already. It's all in there.'

The rest of the interview went the same way.

Lovejoy was waiting for Charlie in the car. He got in and took out his Nokia, rang Dawson at Essex Road and told him to send someone to pick up Matthew Vernon.

He had to follow it up, of course. But he knew it wouldn't do any good.

No one crucified priests and stoned off-duty policemen to death over a bit of a set-to in the pub.

Not even the Krays had done that.

CHAPTER TWENTY-TWO

The DCI put his head round Charlie's door. 'My office. Now.'

Not again.

Charlie followed him to the elevators. 'What's up, sir?' he said when they got in the lift.

But he said nothing until they were in his office.

'Shut the door.'

Charlie shut it and sat down.

The DCI opened a folder and pushed an A4 black-and-white photograph across the desk. Charlie looked at the time and date stamp in the top right corner. It was a CCTV still, captured on the night PC Morton was kidnapped, 9.32 p.m.

'Recognise him?'

'It looks like Osman Balewah.'

'It's a capture from the CCTV at the Queen's Head. Didn't his mother say he was home with her after nine p.m.?'

'Yeah, it's in the file, that's what she said.'

'So how is he in the High Street, not a quarter-mile from where PC Morton was abducted?'

'Clearly, she was lying.'

'Clearly.'

He picked up the hardback notebook from the desk by his elbow. 'He was heard making threats to PC Morton an hour and a half before.'

'I believe so.'

'VPC Nigel Halpin.' He read from his notes. '"I'm coming back with my mandem and we going to fuck you up", unquote.'

'Street talk.'

'You think so? Only from what I saw on Hampstead Heath, a bloke doesn't get more fucked up than PC Morton.'

'What's your theory, sir?'

'After the argument with PC Morton, he goes back to the estate, gets a few of his mates together, one of them has a van.'

'A van? From what I saw, they can't afford a bike between them.'

'No, but they can steal one, especially a Ford Transit. So, they go back and wait till he's locking up and he's on his own. They grab him and chuck him in the back, rough him up. Maybe he's unconscious. Then the next night they take him down Hampstead Heath.'

'So, what, he's unconscious for a day and a half?'

'In the back of the van, yes.'

'I don't see it.'

The DCI reached into his folder and produced two A4 sheets, a printout from a web page. It was an old news item about an Ethiopian man who, according to the article, had been stoned to death in Eritrea in front of a thousand bystanders.

'Part of their culture,' he said.

'He does for him because he threw him out of the police cadets?'

'No, because they're all high on khat and they're scrotes. I'm naming Osman Balewah as our chief suspect in the murder of PC Stephen Morton. I want you to go and pick him up.'

'And then what? We have no evidence against this boy.'

'I've got a search and seizure warrant, signed. We interrogate him, we get his phone, his clothes, everything, get them over to Lambeth. He's not smart enough to hide evidence.'

'It's not him.'

'If he's clean, he's got nothing to worry about.'

'Just because his mother lied in interview? She was probably scared.'

'I'm SIO now, Charlie. I'm calling it.'

'We're wasting time, sir.'

'No, you are.' And he looked at his watch, a theatrical gesture that confirmed, in Charlie's mind, that his guv'nor was a prat.

'Yes, sir,' Charlie said.

'Take Greene with you,' he said.

Charlie picked up a tattered copy of the *Independent* from the front seat of the Sierra and turned to the sports pages. He let Greene drive. 'Fuck me,' he said.

'What is it, guv?'

'Wenger reckons there's no value in the January window. He says that every year. Of course good players are overpriced in January, they're overpriced anytime of the year.'

'Shouldn't we be thinking about the job, guv?'

'I have thought about it, my son. But my thoughts are not welcome. FONC's in charge now, I just do what he says.'

'The Ride of the Valkyries'. He sighed and fumbled for the iPhone in his left jacket pocket. He looked at the display before he answered. 'Jules.'

'Charlie, can you come?'

'What, to Brighton?'

'I'm in London.'

'What are you doing up here?'

'It's Rom. He was transferred up here this morning by ambulance.'

'Why didn't you call me?'

'I am calling you.'

'Where's Terry?'

'He said he couldn't get away from work. You know how much time he's had off for Rom.'

'Where are you now?'

'Great Ormond again.'

'How is he?'

151

'They're trying some different drugs on him. I think maybe this time this is it.'

Charlie took a breath. She always thought that, but then, who knew with these things, he supposed one day she would be right.

'I'm working at the moment, Jules.'

'Just when you can. Be good to talk to someone.'

He hung up.

'Detour,' he said to Greene.

Julia was sitting in the corridor outside the ICU. She was chewing her nails, staring at every nurse that hurried past, every doctor in blue scrubs, hoping and dreading one of them was looking for her, he supposed. She looked terrible; no make-up, dark rings under her eyes. She had on a tracksuit and Adidas trainers.

'Jules,' he said.

She got up and hugged him, and held on. He hadn't realised how much weight she had lost recently. He hoped it wasn't the anorexia again.

'Charlie, thanks for coming.'

They sat down on the hard plastic chairs. 'You need a coffee?'

She shook her head.

'How is he?'

'Soon as we arrived they brought him straight up here, they reckon they've seen something on the heart monitor.'

'Have you told Terry?'

She shrugged. 'He's not answering his phone.'

Charlie bit back what he thought about that; it wasn't the time or the place. 'You want a place to stay tonight?'

'Thanks.' She nodded. 'I hadn't even thought about it.'

'Want to go there now?'

'I can't leave until I know Rom's OK.'

'All right. Look, I can't stay, Jules, I'm in the middle of something. You want me to find someone to sit with you?'

'There isn't anyone. Ben's in France.'

'What about Michael?'

'By the time he gets down from Liverpool, it will all be sorted. Besides, you know what he'll say.'

'God is not punishing you, Jules.'

'Sometimes it feels like it.'

She put her face in his shoulder. He had to push away in the end. 'I'll be back as soon as I can. Let me know what's happening, all right?'

'I will. Go on, I'll be fine. Thanks Charlie.'

He went back to the lifts and down to the car park.

'OK boss?' Greene said as he got in the car.

'If I ever think of feeling sorry for myself, just bring me here and show me a bunch of sick, bald kids in wheelchairs. Some people do have it tough, don't they?'

'How's your nephew?'

'I don't know. They haven't finished doing all the tests.'

'What's wrong with him?'

'He's got Bubble Boy disease.'

'What's that then?'

'The proper name is Severe Combined Immune Deficiency. Bubble Boy was some kid in America who had it so bad he had to live his whole life inside a plastic bubble. What it means is, he has no resistance to anything. Catching the flu could kill him. He's sick almost all the time.'

'How do you get that, then?'

'You're born with it, mate. It's genetic. Most common in places where there's a lot of incest. My old man was born just down the road from the Tottenham ground, it's the only family link I can think of.'

'Nothing they can do?'

'When he was a kid, they gave him bone marrow transplants. It's supposed to help.'

'Marrow? Where do they get that?'

'They have to find a close relative who's a match. So, me.'

153

'You gave him some of your marrow?'

'Yeah, so as if Bubble Boy disease wasn't enough, poor little bugger's got some of me in him.'

'Sounds worse than the disease.'

Charlie picked up the newspaper again, thinking to hide in it, dodge more questions, but he couldn't concentrate and, after a minute or two, he threw the paper in the footwell. They were caught up in traffic on High Holborn, more roadworks; they were digging everywhere in London these days. He tapped his foot on the carpet, found himself wanting to talk about it after all. 'He's had the Last Rites more times than I've had hot dinners. But he's a fighter and he always pulls through. Pity his old man is such a complete bell-end.'

'No cure?'

He shook his head. 'He could live till he's a hundred or he could die next week. Makes you realise, life is precious. You have to make the most of it while you can.' He leaned his head back on the headrest, closed his eyes. 'How did FONC ever get to be a DCI? I thought you had to be smart.'

'Maybe he's sleeping with the chief super.'

'That's a picture I don't need in my head. Just drive, Jay. Try and get us there before Easter, all right?'

CHAPTER TWENTY-THREE

The Orchard Estate was a seventies relic, a concrete square slowly falling into decay just a mile from the Hackney Empire. There were a few business units scattered around it, but most of them were shuttered up now and covered in graffiti. Places like this, they were all over London, sprouting satellite dishes and CCTV cameras like mould, grey tower blocks filled with hunched youths shuffling along balconies and brick underpasses in monochrome sweats.

Greene parked across the road outside a low-cost supermarket. There was a run-down caged football pitch outside the flats, the rubber surface coming away in clumps, leaving exposed asphalt.

Charlie was staring at his phone.

'Well, would you Adam and Eve it,' he said.

'What's that, guv?'

'The Arsenal chairman just voted himself a nine hundred thousand bonus for the year.'

'Well, that's nice.'

'It is, isn't it? Because I believe in hard work being rewarded. Nothing worse than blokes who just cream off the top and let others do all the work. It gives you back some faith in the world.'

'It does.'

'I only pay two grand a year to watch a bunch of nancy-boy millionaires making complete cocks of themselves every week. It's nice that the chairman sees some of that. I mean, look at that,' he said, nodding across the road. 'These bloody people. Got their own training facilities right on the premises, inexpensive shopping within yards of their front door, and do they appreciate it?'

'Scandalous,' Greene said as he got out of the car.

Charlie got out as well. A patrol car from the Malden Street nick pulled up behind them. Two uniforms got out, pulling on their caps, zipping up their Met vests, looking like they were well up for it. Maybe they had been mates of Morton. He would have to keep an eye on them, make sure they didn't get too enthusiastic if there was a takedown.

'It's all right, lads,' Charlie said. 'He's only sixteen. We're not expecting much trouble.'

'They've all got knives, these scrotes,' one of the lads said.

'He's right,' Greene said. Charlie looked where he was pointing. There was a community centre further down the street, boarded up, and covered in gang tags. Next to it was a Methodist church, dull red brick, looked more like a bomb shelter. Outside there was a knife bin with a sign: '*Get a life, bin that knife.*'

'Do you think he did it?' Greene said.

'Doesn't matter what I think,' Charlie said.

'You reckon FONC's sent us on a wild-goose chase.'

'Do I?'

'The boys are on your side, any consolation.'

'Thanks,' Charlie said, and sauntered across the road, his hands in his pockets.

'Seen prisons with better views than this,' Greene said as they walked over a patch of frozen mud. An empty crisp packet was curled against a bit of cyclone fence, the collection of fag ends showed it was a popular spot. There was a CCTV camera on the top of a tall grey pole, a football impaled on the spikes underneath it. He caught a whiff of weed.

'It's a fucking slum,' Greene said.

'You're not allowed to call it a slum, if it's vertical.'

156

'I read somewhere that some of the teenagers in Tower Hamlets have never even seen Tower Bridge.'

'Too scared to leave their mandem on the estates, innit? Afraid they'll get offed.'

'Look at that,' Greene said, nodding at two young girls pushing pushchairs. 'They should still be home playing with Barbie dolls; must have got pregnant in primary school.'

Charlie sent the two uniforms towards the concrete steps at the southern end of the estate. 'It's 48C. You go that way, we'll take the stairs over there. If he tries to run, we've got him boxed in.'

They nodded and trotted across the courtyard.

'Shit,' Greene said. 'He's over there.'

Charlie looked across the quadrangle; there were a bunch of kids in hoodies and trainers sitting on some railings. Now they had clocked them as well. One of them was a head taller than the others, had to be Osman, with that stoop and those long skinny legs.

Charlie called out to the uniforms, pointed to the kids, motioning for them to circle around behind them.

'He's going to run,' Greene said.

'Looks like it.'

'What do you want to do?'

Osman took his hands out of his pockets, bird-dogging; he knew why they were there. One of the uniforms already had his cuffs out, the other was reaching for the CS spray and his baton. It wasn't hard to figure out what was going through Osman's head.

'I smell baaa-con,' he heard someone shout. A little kid, couldn't have been more than ten, looked Charlie right in the face and flipped him the bird.

Osman took off. The two uniforms went after him. Charlie didn't see the point. He had the search and seizure warrant in his pocket; if they found nothing in his mother's flat, they didn't have enough to hold him anyway.

157

'Don't waste your time,' he said to Greene, but he couldn't have heard him. He set off after him as well. As Osman headed down one of the alleys next to the tower block, Greene was only twenty yards behind him. Charlie had to admit, for a smoker he wasn't half bad on his feet.

There was a market set up in the street behind the council estate – not much else down there, a couple of betting shops and a Western Union. The permit holders had parked their vans on the kerb; there were a few racks of knock-off dresses and a stall with cheap jewellery and football shirts.

Osman skipped through the crowd, bounced off a purple wheelie bin, vaulted a pile of black bin liners full of rubbish from the greengrocer's, splitting one of them open with his heel. He lost his balance and nearly fell. He kicked over a bike that had been chained to a one-way sign. Greene vaulted over it but one of the uniforms wasn't as nimble, landing on his hands and knees in the gutter.

When Charlie caught up, Osman had reached the High Street, Greene was still after him, the other uniform not far behind. Osman knocked over a woman in a brown chador outside the Balti house. She shouted curses at him in Farsi while her friend screamed for the police. She looked surprised to see two of London's finest get there a few seconds later and rush right past her.

Finally, Greene gave up and stopped, put his hands on his knees, coughing up his last ten packets of Benson and Hedges. Charlie patted him on the shoulder. 'Told you how many times. Those things will fucking kill you.'

Greene wanted to answer but couldn't get his breath.

Charlie wished the other uniform would give it up. Young coppers loved this sort of shit. Too much television when they were kids, he supposed.

A courier came out of a lane on a bike and knocked the copper on his backside. In other circumstances, Charlie might have laughed. 'He's got away,' Charlie said, not that bothered.

Osman reached the local Nails 4U and ran across the street.

Charlie could see what was going to happen next, but there was nothing he could do to stop it. Everyone in the street must have seen the bus except Osman. The driver had no chance of stopping.

There was a squeal of brakes and a loud bang. Instead of bouncing, Osman was dragged under the radiator grille. People were screaming, both sides of the street. The bus driver jumped out of his cabin, stood there holding his head: he didn't want to look.

That onerous duty fell to Charlie. He got down on his knees and peered under the wheels. Then he stood up and called the ambulance. Wouldn't do any good, but someone had to scrape what was left of Osman off the bitumen.

There were red and blue lights flashing up and down the street, television vans arriving surprisingly late on the scene. Charlie had done his best to mop up, got as many uniforms down there as he could to set up a cordon around the scene, had other officers taking down names and addresses of witnesses. They would need them later when the *Guardian* and the BBC said someone had seen a copper push a black kid under a bus.

He clocked Greene sitting in the passenger seat of a patrol car, his head between his knees, a silver blanket around his shoulders. Right after it happened he had told Charlie he blamed himself; it's just shock, Charlie told him, don't you fucking say another word to anyone without a union lawyer next to you – there'll be enough people agreeing with you even before the body hits the morgue.

The ambulance pulled away, crawling through the banked-up traffic. Not an easy job for them either, peeling him out from under the wheels. The second ambulance was still there, the bus driver sitting on the back steps, face grey as cement, staring at nothing. No winners here today.

Everyone in Hackney had come out for a look, trying to get some pictures for Facebook, something to talk about on Twitter. He heard a few people in the crowd shouting shit at the uniforms in the cordon. He supposed it was fair enough: the Met had form with the black community around here.

A black Mercedes with a blue light on its roof eased through the cordon, a cop with braid on his uniform got out. He was from Malden Street, he had the DCI with him. O'Neal-Callaghan came over, he looked grim but also pleased.

'Result,' he muttered to Charlie, though he didn't actually see his lips move.

'Sir?'

'You know what I mean.'

'Don't think I do.'

'Did he say anything before he died?'

'Didn't have the chance, died instantly.'

The DCI nodded, satisfied. He held out his hand. 'Have you got the search and seizure warrant?'

'Are you going to do it now?'

'We'll get his family off down the nick first. All very tragic, I know, but there's an ongoing murder inquiry here.'

'I don't know that his mother even knows yet. Someone should get round there and inform her before she hears it on the street. We're only three streets from the estate.'

'I've got a team on the way.'

'There could be a lot of trouble here later, sir, especially after lights-out. It was only last year that young West Indian kid died during an arrest.'

'Thank God the bus driver's black then. Don't blame yourself.'

'I don't sir.'

'How did it happen?'

'Detective Sergeant Greene and the two boys from Malden Street saw him leave the estate and pursued him on foot. He tried to evade them and ran into the street without due care and attention.'

'Right under the number 38 bus.'

'Yes, sir.'

'Did you tell Greene to pursue him?'

'No, I didn't give him a direct order.'

'Did you tell him not to chase him, then?'

'I told them all to desist, but I don't think they heard me. I had already pointed him out to them as the subject of our arrest warrant, so they were acting with due diligence.'

'Nicely put. Remember to use that phrase with the IPCC.'

'It's the truth, sir, I won't need to remember it.'

'He wouldn't have run if he didn't have something to hide.'

'He ran because he's scared of the cops.'

A tight smile. 'We'll see, Charlie.'

He held his hand out for the warrant. Charlie gave it to him. 'I could let you handle this,' he said to Charlie.

'I don't want to steal your moment of glory.'

He stepped closer and hissed in Charlie's ear. 'We're only doing our job, remember that. I'd be a lot sorrier about what happened here if we didn't have a damned fine policeman in the morgue right now.'

'Yes, sir.'

'You'd better get home. I'm putting you on stress leave. You look like shit.'

'I'm all right, I've seen worse.'

'Yes, but it's not about you, is it? Besides, I want you out of the way until you've been cleared by the internal affairs people. They'll be giving you a call tomorrow, I don't doubt. I'd take a union lawyer to the interview with you.'

'I will.'

Charlie turned to go. The DCI called him back. 'Charlie, I don't understand why you didn't bring more officers along with

161

you. I told you he was a prime suspect in a murder case. You might have anticipated this.'

Right. He could see the way this was going to go. Someone would have to take at least a reprimand for this and it wasn't going to be FONC. You didn't get to his rank without knowing how to play the game.

'Where's your car, Charlie?'

'It's over on the estate.'

'I'll get one of the Malden Street uniforms to drive you over there.'

'What about Jay?'

The DCI looked over at him. 'He's in no condition to drive. He'll come back to the station with me when I'm done. Now get out of here.'

CHAPTER TWENTY-FOUR

Charlie sat in the Sierra, staring at his hands on the wheel, feeling numb. Despite what he'd told the DCI, he actually hadn't seen much worse than that. Somehow looking at dead bodies for a living wasn't quite the same as watching someone die right in front of you.

He heard yelling from inside the estate, saw a squad of armed police up on the third floor, tussling with a woman. Mrs Balewah was screaming, her kids were out there now, the neighbours pouring out too, a couple of them started tussling with the coppers. Christ, they'd need the TSG up here soon; by tonight there would be bonfires in the street and cars getting trashed.

He shook himself from his torpor. Get home, son, he said to himself, kick off your shoes, get out your bottle of single malt and forget about all of this for a few hours. You're not indestructible, even though you make out you are.

Then he remembered he couldn't do that. He picked up the phone and dialled Julia's number.

She answered on the second ring.

'Jules.'

'Charlie. Thanks for calling.'

'How is he?'

'He's out of ICU. They say he's responding to the drugs.'

'Thank God. How are you?'

'I feel worn out.'

'I'll come and find you.'

'Thought you were working.'

'I've finished for the day. Sit tight, I shouldn't be more than half an hour.'

'Thanks Charlie. You're all right.'

As he drove he wondered what the DCI would do if they didn't find any evidence at Mrs Balewah's flat. He wouldn't fit him up, would he? He didn't like thinking like that, but there was a lot riding on this.

What a fucking travesty.

The Nokia rang in his pocket, he'd forgotten to put it in its cradle. He found a park on Queensbridge Road and pulled over. 'DI George.'

'Hello Charlie, it's Jack.'

'Jack, before you start, I'm off duty. Stress leave, the boss called it.'

'You, stressed?'

'Things have all gone to shit here.'

'It's about the Morton homicide.'

'I'm not SIO on that any more.'

'But you've still got Operation Galilee running, yeah?'

'OK, what have you got, then?'

'We had several good impressions from the crime scene at Barrow Fields; Calvin Klein Berkes, high-top trainers, size eleven. Also a distinctive over-sole pattern.'

'And?'

'We have been working up a latent we found at the car park where PC Morton was abducted. Quite a difficult job. What we had to do was—'

'That's OK, Jack. You can tell me, but I won't understand. The latent is a match?'

'No, but there's a high degree of probability.'

Charlie shook his head. The DCI was just going to love this. 'Have you told FONC?'

'Not yet. Thought I'd let you know first, off the record,

164

of course. But as it may affect your investigation into Father O'Meara's murder, you'll be copied in on the email.'

'See, the thing I don't understand, Jack, he told me you'd been working on the tyre prints and you couldn't confirm any similarities.'

'No, I can't. At the time I told him we were still testing; it was too early to give him an answer.'

'That's not what he said.'

'What did he tell you?'

'That the likelihood of an evidential match was remote. That's a bit different, isn't it?'

'He's under a lot of pressure, I suppose. He heard what he wanted to hear.'

'Thanks for the call, Jack, you're a proper legend.'

'You all right?'

'Yeah, I'm all right.'

'You don't sound all right.'

'Enjoy the rest of your Christmas.'

'What fucking Christmas?' Jack said and hung up. Charlie thought: well, nothing I can do about any of this right now. The boss has ordered me home.

He checked his watch, he'd told Julie he'd be at Great Ormond Street by now. He put the Sierra into gear and headed south down Queensbridge.

CHAPTER TWENTY-FIVE

Great Ormond Street Hospital

Time appeared to have stood still. The man scrolled endlessly through his phone, while the woman's eyes darted around the room, returning every few seconds to the clock, willing the hands to move faster. They seemed to have stuck in place.

The woman had startling red hair, tied in a simple ponytail at the back of her head. There were dark rings under her eyes where her mascara had run and she had forgotten to wipe it off. Her hands squirmed in her lap, like a nest of puppies searching for a nipple to latch on to; her foot tapped ceaselessly on the carpet, without cadence, until eventually her husband could bear it no longer and put a hand on her knee to still her.

How long had it been?

She closed her eyes, remembered saying goodbye to her little girl before they wheeled her in to the operating theatre, telling her to be brave, telling her how much she loved her. But did she know how much? What if that was the last time she would ever be able to tell her?

A post-op nurse pushed open the door, and nervous energy propelled the woman to her feet. But the nurse ignored her, made her way to another family, spoke to them in whispers. The woman put her hand to her mouth and uttered a small cry, her husband put his hand on her shoulder. Bad news.

So this was what it looked like.

They followed the nurse out of the door, their two small boys following behind, eyes big as soup plates.

The door closed and everyone in the waiting room fell to silence again. The man beside her scrolled even faster through his Facebook feed while she closed her eyes and made a silent bargain with God: *please get my baby through this, and I will do anything, anything.*

She got up to fetch a coffee, then sat with the plastic cup in her hands staring at the clock until the coffee went cold. After a while she looked around at her husband, who had the phone still clutched in both hands but was now staring at the wall. She went to pee again, though she had drunk nothing all morning.

She came back, sat down, studied the Styrofoam tiles on the ceiling, imagined God up there watching, deciding her fate. *I'll do anything,* she said silently, over and over. *Anything. Please don't take her, please, please don't take her away from us.*

She opened her eyes and looked at the clock. Was it really just five minutes since she last looked?

Someone's mobile rang, though all phones were supposed to be turned off in the waiting room. A man conducted a whispered conversation, staring at the floor, while she glared at him for daring to intrude on the sacred silence.

The walls crowded in. Out there, somewhere, just a few streets away from where she was sitting, shoppers and tourists were walking along Southampton Row and High Holborn, hunting for souvenirs, as if nothing had happened, as if the whole world hadn't perhaps changed for ever.

The door opened, and a post-op nurse came towards them. No, she thought, not yet, I'm not ready.

'James, Kerry. Little Hannah has just come out of surgery. Everything went well. Her vital signs are recovering and we've taken her to post-op. Doctor Cruz would like to speak with you.'

She might as well have spoken to her in a foreign language. Does that mean Hannah is all right? Her husband had to help her to her feet. She could barely move her legs. She followed the nurse into the corridor, James holding her firmly by the arm.

Doctor Cruz came out of Operating Room number seven, in his blue scrubs. She thought he would smile, but he just nodded to them, as if he had performed a routine service on their car.

'Your daughter is in recovery,' Cruz said. 'The operation was successful. She is no longer reliant on the Berlin heart and her new heart is in place and fully functioning. She will go to the cardiac intensive unit next and her chest will remain open with a plastic cover for two days, while we assess it.'

'She's going to be all right?' James said.

'It's a very hazardous procedure and there are sometimes complications, post-operatively. But I am very pleased.'

It took a moment for the news to sink in. The woman felt her knees give way. She clung on to James. 'Oh my God. Thank you, thank you.'

'It is a team effort,' he said. 'The surgical team here in the cardiac unit is one of the best in the world.'

'How can we ever thank you?' she said.

'I'm just doing my job.'

'Do you have children, Doctor Cruz?'

His spectacles flashed for a moment, catching the glare of the strip lights. 'I have a boy and a girl.'

'Then you understand what this means to us. It's a miracle.'

'Your daughter is very fortunate,' Cruz said. 'Around thirty per cent of children with dilated cardiac myopathy do not survive long enough for surgical intervention.'

'God answered our prayers,' she said to her husband. 'He was looking over her.'

Cruz nodded and turned away. He pushed open the swing doors into the scrub room and disappeared.

The nurse took the woman's arm. 'Why don't you and your husband go down to the cafeteria and get yourselves something to eat? Hannah won't be fully awake for a couple of hours yet.'

And she directed them towards the lifts.

'Are you all right?' Julia said to Charlie as he walked in.

He sat down, threw his car keys on the plastic table. 'Yeah, I'm all right.' It was what he always said, even if he'd just come from a double homicide. The funny thing was, mostly it was true, he *was* all right. Most of the time the job didn't really touch him, and it didn't help anyone if it did.

But today had bothered him; not just because it had all been so unnecessary, but because he'd been forced to watch it.

And Julia had enough problems of her own right now, so he wasn't going to burden her with any more.

'Tough day?' she said.

'Not as tough as yours.'

'They say he'll be home again in a couple of days.'

'You must have spent half your life sitting around in hospitals.'

'Rom's worth it. Still, he'd be just as worth it if he was well, innit?' They saw a woman with red hair walk in, her husband gripping her hand. Their faces were grey. 'I wonder what their story is?'

'Don't think I want to know,' Charlie said, and he thought about Osman's mother. Osman was a scally, but he felt sorry for her and for him all the same.

'Poor little Rom,' Jules said. 'When I saw him this morning, all those tubes going in and out of him, he looked so tiny. He said to me, Mum, don't worry, it'll be all right. Ten years old and he's trying to take care of me. He never complains, never says, why me? Just gets on with it.'

'He's resilient. Part of the DNA if you're in the George family.'

'You ever think about God, Charlie?'

'I try not to.'

'I do. I think about God a lot, about what he does, what he thinks.'

'And what have you come up with?'

169

'Nothing, really. I mean, nothing new. It just makes me wonder. I mean, if there is a God, why does he let little kids suffer, know what I mean?'

'Well, you find an answer to that one, let me know.'

'I mean, when we were kids, Father Brian said God was kind and compassionate and all of that, but he's not, is he? Only some of the time. Even Tel is all right some of the time.'

'Is he? You want a coffee, Jules?'

'No, do you?'

'Not really. Want to talk about something else?'

'All right. Tell me about you. We haven't caught up for ages. How's that woman you're seeing?'

He shrugged.

'Ben says she's a bitch. Has she got another fella?'

'She's married.'

'Fuck me, Charlie.'

'I know, I know. Ben has already given me the lecture. I'm a big boy, I know what I'm doing.'

'Do you?'

'What else do you want to chat about?'

'I know you don't like to talk about your job and everything, but you know, people say to me, what do your brothers do? And I say, oh one's a priest, one's a professional dickhead and one's a murder detective. Guess which one they're interested in?'

'It's not that I don't like to talk about my work, it's that I can't. Murder investigations are confidential, Jules. I can't go gossiping about potential suspects, can I?'

She just shrugged her skinny little-sister shoulders, unimpressed.

'If you must know, I've been given stress leave for a couple of days. Last couple of weeks have been probably the toughest time I've had since I joined the Force.'

'And you haven't told anyone, I bet.'

'It wouldn't change anything if I did.'

'It might.'

170

He leaned in across the table. 'All right, how's this? There's a monster loose in the parish. I mean a proper sadistic, possibly deranged, killer. I have no fucking clue at this stage where he is or who he is. So, my question to myself is this: can I, can anyone in our department, find him and stop him grabbing someone else off the street and torturing them to death? Because he is going to hurt someone again, and he won't stop until we do find him. That's why I'm on stress leave.'

Julia put a hand on his. 'Charlie, why don't you take up broking like your brother?'

'Trading futures? It would be easier for me to be a priest, like Michael.'

'I don't know what to say.'

'You don't have to say anything. You wanted me to talk, I talked. You see, there's nothing you can say, nothing anyone can say. Shall we go and see Rom? Then I'll take you back to my place, you can have a shower and I'll make you something to eat.'

'You reckon it's weird if I go to the chapel first?'

'They got a chapel here?'

'Yeah, it's proper amazing.'

'What do you want to go to the chapel for? I thought you were an atheist like me.'

'There aren't any atheists in a kids' hospital, Charlie. Ever.'

Julia was right about the chapel, it *was* proper amazing. She led him past the reception and the pharmacy, then headed down a plain hospital corridor towards the lifts and suddenly there it was. It was as if someone had torn out a little chunk of Venice and put it down in the middle of a modern hospital.

There was a hefty chunk of marble above the door, Jesus blessing all the little children with an inscription: *I was glad when they said unto me, let us go into the house of the Lord.*

He followed Julia inside; it was like stepping inside a Fabergé

171

egg. Even after a crude, bloody day in Hackney, it took his breath away, the fucking grandeur of it. It was all gold and glitter, red Devonshire marble columns with gilded capitals, an alabaster altar screen, a terrazzo floor, like walking on veined glass. There was a central dome with angels playing musical instruments; in the apse, a stained-glass window with a picture of Jesus as a little child.

'All right, innit?' Julia said.

He nodded, dumbstruck.

'They paid for it with the profits from that movie with Dustin Hoffman, *Hook*.'

'It says on this plaque here that James Barrie donated all the royalties from *Peter Pan*.'

'Yeah, I knew it was something like that.' There was a prayer tree on the right of the door. Julia took one of the cards, a blue one, and wrote something on it, and hung it on one of the branches. There were a dozen others hanging there. Charlie wondered how many of them would fall.

'OK, let's go,' Julia said.

'You're not going to pray?'

'Not while you're standing there.'

'I don't mind.'

'No, it's all right,' she said. 'I'm done.'

As they were leaving, they passed a tall and distinguished olive-skinned man with glasses and a goatee beard, headed inside. Charlie noticed the suit he was wearing first: it was navy blue, hand-stitched, virgin wool, probably bespoke, it fitted him like a second skin. He was wearing a maroon Sulka tie.

Charlie watched him for a moment. He went to the front aisle and got down on to his knees. Mind that suit, Charlie thought, and then Julia called him and he hurried along after her.

Doctor Salvador Cruz stared at the teddy bear choir above the altar: a Paddington bear, a tattered pink elephant, an ancient and dusty ted with one eye, left behind by parents long ago, either in thanks or as memorial.

Cruz closed his eyes in prayer, and when he opened them again his eyes fell on Jesus in the alabaster frieze below the choir, suffering all the little children to come unto him, even little Alice Liddell, there with him in Wonderland.

It was the Jesus who was going to save them all, the Jesus who promised all those little ones so much if they only believed, and chose to serve.

Cruz looked him in the eye and whispered something so softly, his lips barely moved.

'Fuck you,' he said.

CHAPTER TWENTY-SIX

He met Geri at a patisserie on Baker Street. She was power-dressed, a navy-blue suit and white silk scarf, D&G shoulder bag, no bling except for a single gold bracelet that could have paid his mortgage that month. Nice.

She had her barrister face on, scary and to die for, all at once. The façade fell away when she saw him; he got a wide-eyed look and a chaste kiss on the cheek. He'd call it a one-all draw, away from home.

'Charlie.'

'All right, then? Want another coffee?'

'No thanks, I'll want to pee on the train. You look tired.'

'You look good enough to eat.'

'You look good enough to eat me,' she said, loudly enough for the man in the suit at the next table to look up from his *Guardian*.

Charlie sat down, helped himself to water.

'No coffee?'

'I've been drinking coffee all day, heart rate's already three thousand a minute.'

'Tough week?'

Their knees touched under the table. The first time it was accidental, the second time she did it deliberately. She gave him her special come-to-bed smile, which would have been all very well, if there had been a bed handy. He moved his knee out of the way.

'I've been ordered off site, suppose you'd call it. Apart from a quizzing from Internal Affairs, I've had sod-all to do.'

'What happened?'

'I don't want to talk about it much. How are you?'

'I had to take a deposition from a Russian billionaire at the Dorchester.'

'Tasty.'

'He wanted me to stay. Offered me an oil well in Georgia for a head job, but you know how it is, how many oil wells does a girl need?'

'Tell me his room number, I could do with an oil well.'

'He's not your type, Charlie. He's sixteen stone and he's not blonde.'

'But he's got a spare oil well. That counts for a lot.'

'The deponent should be on trial himself, scumbag. He's helping us because he's helping himself. Getting rid of business competition. You can imagine what business it is.'

'All part of the game. How was your Christmas?'

'Fucking awful. How was yours?'

'Brilliant. Took my mother to church, had a fight with my brother-in-law, then worked till two in the morning.'

'I missed you.'

'Yeah, don't say that. If you'd really missed me, you would have been here.'

'Well, even if I was, sounds like I would have spent it on my own anyway. It's why we get on so well, we're both married to our work.'

'No, you're married to your husband.'

'Let's not start that.'

Well, he never meant to, in fact, he'd promised himself he wouldn't. But there was a tipping point in any relationship, he supposed, when you thought about the next step. Only with Geri, Ben was right, there wasn't one. Not that he was an expert about affairs, he'd never had one before. He wasn't so sure about her; he'd never asked, in case she told him the truth.

She looked at her watch, a gold Piaget. 'I'd better be getting back to the office.'

'Sure,' he said.

They walked up Baker Street, neither of them saying much. 'You're in a mood,' she said.

'I don't think I can do this any more.'

'You've been talking to your brother again.'

'Ben.'

'Yeah, the one who's telling you to leave me.'

'I can't leave you, you're not with me, not even technically. Anyway, he's in France, skiing with a girl he met on Tinder.'

'You sound jealous.'

'Of course I'm jealous. Everything is so simple for him. He's a complete hedonist. He just does things to please himself.'

'You could do that.'

'No, I couldn't.'

'Why not?'

'Because.'

'That's not an answer. If you keep on like this, the judge will hold you in contempt.'

Charlie laughed.

'What's funny?'

'That was a courtroom joke, right? Only it's sort of true. I can't be like Ben because I feel like I've got someone judging me all the time.'

'Who?'

'I don't know, it's just a conscience thing.'

'Do I trouble your conscience?'

'Maybe. You're the thing I do and hope no one is watching.'

She liked that. She linked her arm in his as they turned the corner on to Marylebone Road. The old Trinity Church was on the other side of the road, on a traffic island, its four Ionic columns and lantern steeple out of step among the bustle of red buses and London taxicabs. Geri pointed to a poster, advertising an art exhibition. 'That looks interesting.'

'Actually, it looks too sinister for words. Anyway, I thought you had to get back to the office.'

'You're in a better mood, so I've got more time.'

The church hadn't been used for years, but it wasn't derelict like the Dissenters' Chapel in the Hackney cemetery; instead it had been upscaled for events and wedding receptions. Even though the interior had been gutted, the soaring dome, bright-coloured mosaics inlaid around the marble wall and the stained glass above the altar were beautiful.

It was like the cool room at the morgue inside, and he turned up the collar of his coat. The sculptures on display were chilling enough on their own; the Virgin Mary laid out naked on a table like a body in the morgue; a crucified ape hanging on a cross that had been fixed in a pile of rocks and dead branches; Jesus sitting bloodied and tortured on a wooden chair.

The centrepiece itself was so chilling, he had to stop and draw breath; an oily black demon with immense tattered wings, thrashed in a net of high-tension power lines above the altar steps. Its corpse-like skin gleamed in the half-light and the tortured wax face seemed to beg for release while at the same time uttering a silent curse on anyone who came near.

Charlie stared at the plaque below it and read aloud: '*Lucifer, Morningstar*. This work signifies the fallibility of the human condition, the chaos and terror of one's own making. Made from anodised aluminium, silicon rubber cord, feathers and aluminium.'

'Amazing.'

'What do you think the artist was trying to say?' Charlie said.

'I have no idea. Lucifer is the devil, isn't he?'

'"How you have fallen from heaven, morning star, son of the dawn! You said in your heart, 'I will ascend to the heavens; I will raise my throne above the stars of God; But you are brought down to the depths of the pit.'"'

She stared at him in surprise, and Charlie wished he'd kept his mouth shut. 'That sounds like the Bible.'

'Book of Ezekiel. I don't know the chapter and verse.'

'I would hope not. How did you know that anyway?'

'I had a very religious upbringing. When we did something wrong, the old man gave us a choice – he'd beat us with his belt or we could learn verses from the Bible. It's very effective. They should try it in Sunday school.'

'Tell me you're joking.'

'I'm joking,' he said.

'So, you know the story of Lucifer?'

'I know *a* story. Lucifer, see, was the most beautiful of all the angels. God's anointed. But it wasn't enough, he wanted more. Thought he could do things better than God.'

'And that led to the fall.'

'Well, he didn't really fall, he was pushed.'

'So the story of Lucifer is about the danger of pride.'

Charlie shook his head. They stepped outside into the cold and the light. He squinted against a cold yellow sun.

'What is it, then?' Geri said.

'It's about grief, innit?'

'Grief?'

'Yeah. We all grieve – losing someone we love, losing our looks, losing things that others destroy. But my old man taught us that the only creature in all creation who really understands grief, I mean really gets it, is the devil, Lucifer. He's the only one who is perfect in his agony. That was how he put it. Very eloquent when he was sober, the old man. Should have been eloquent more often.'

'I don't understand.'

'Lucifer grieves because he lost heaven, see? Because of his pride, he lost more than anyone on earth could ever dream of. He lost paradise.'

'So, he was sent to hell.'

'No, he wasn't sent to Hell, he was sent here, down to earth. Bethnal Green or Bengal or Bali, it don't matter. Hell was what he carried inside him. He can't ever get away from it, can't ever escape it. He knows he's lost everything and can never, ever, get

178

it back. And so he's down here, and he is suffering so fucking bad, all he can do is try and drag everyone else down with him. Misery needs company; no one can bear to suffer alone.'

He turned and looked back into the gloom of the church. He could feel Lucifer watching him, forever trapped in his web of exquisite pain.

'Charlie, you never fail to surprise.'

'Ah well, I'm a surprising man. I'll walk you to the station.'

He left her at Baker Street and went for a walk in Regent's Park. A long time since he had had nothing to do on a Tuesday afternoon. He was so bored he almost went to the Sherlock Holmes museum, but instead he just went to the Royal Oak and drank three pints of IPA.

He had meant to break up with Geri that afternoon, but if he remembered right, he had arranged to meet her in Holborn the next day after work.

He didn't want to lose her, see, not yet, even though it was hurting him. Simple, really.

Lucifer would have understood.

CHAPTER TWENTY-SEVEN

Charlie wandered the backstreets of Chinatown for almost half an hour before he found the place where he was supposed to meet Ben, then realised he had already walked past it three times. The place was faux-speakeasy, with exposed brickwork, baroque mirrors on the walls and dark velvety banquettes.

Ben was already there, fiddling with his phone, a drink in front of him that looked like a salad.

'Sorry I'm late,' Charlie said, 'I couldn't find the place.'

'You're a detective.'

'There's no numbers on any of the fucking doors. I thought this place was a brothel until I saw a bunch of people smoking cigarettes outside.'

'How many brothels do you know have a doorman with a clipboard? What are you drinking?'

Ben called over one of the waiting staff. Charlie wondered if she was really French or she put on the accent to try and get tips. He couldn't make sense of the drinks menu.

'What's that you've got?' he said.

'It's called a Renaissance,' Ben said. 'It's rhubarb and Aperol.'

'That's not a drink, that's a dessert. Do they have beer?'

Ben looked up at the waitress. 'Another Renaissance and an Old Cuban, thanks.'

'What's in an Old Cuban?'

'Old Cubans,' Ben said. 'Delicious.'

Someone had left a copy of the *Independent* lying on the banquette. Charlie read the headline: *SOMEONE KNOWS*

WHO KILLED MY HUSBAND. He saw Deborah Morton's photograph in a sidebar, making another tearful appeal for witnesses. The funeral was tomorrow, the report said.

'Did you see the Liverpool game last night?' Ben said.

'I didn't watch it.'

'Were you working?'

'No, I'm on stress leave.'

'You're pulling my chain.'

'Ask me what I did today.'

'What did you do today?'

'I sat home on my Jack Malone and drank a bottle of very presumptuous red and two cans of Guinness and watched *Love Actually* on Netflix.'

'Fuck off.'

'It's true.'

'You missed a brilliant game. Did you hear about Liverpool's goal? Clear hand ball from Stevie Dodd. The papers are calling it—'

'Yeah, I know, I read it. The hand of Dodd. These journos are clever as all get-out. Should be a Pulitzer Prize for that one. How was Val d'Isère?'

'I sprained my knee.'

'Skiing?'

'Of course, skiing. What do you think of this one?'

He held up his mobile to show Charlie a Tinder profile.

'What about this girl you took to Switzerland?'

'France. What about her?'

'Have you broken up with her already?'

'Not yet. What about this one? No, you're right, too horsey. How was your Christmas?'

'Bloody awful.'

'That's the shot. So how come you're on stress leave? I thought nothing bothered you.'

'It doesn't. It's regulations. Did you know Rom ended up in hospital?'

'I heard about that.'

'Did you ring Jules?'

'Course I did, I'm not a complete bastard. She also told me you beat up Terry even before she'd had a chance to give out the presents. I would have loved to have seen that.'

'You could have.'

'I didn't want to see it that badly. You sure you're OK? You look like you've lost weight. Most people put it on at Christmas.'

'Most people don't have the Christmas I just had, know what I mean?'

'Charlie, sometimes I think you'd be better off in a different line of work. You can't save everyone, you know. Who's going to save you?'

'I don't need saving.'

'Don't you? I think you're getting yourself mixed up with me.'

'What does that mean?'

'Face it, mate, in every family people have a role to play. Will is the sacrificial goat, the exile. Jules is Mother, she even looks like her a bit. Michael is Father's chosen one, the sanctimonious prat. I'm the rebel.'

'You're a broker.'

'I rejected family and poverty, that makes me a renegade in anyone's language. You, you're the martyr. You even sacrifice yourself for people you don't know.'

'Where did you get all that, then? You sound like Doctor Phil.'

'You know your trouble, Charlie?'

'No, but somehow I feel you're about to tell me.'

'You don't know what you want.'

'Am I paying for this? Because you know, Ben, they've got professionals in the Met who do this full time if I wanted to get my head shrunk.'

'Bro, I know you better than anyone. You don't need some stranger telling you what's wrong with you. That's what your family is for.'

'Yeah, cheers.'

'See, you're conflicted.'

'Who are you, Eckhart Tolle or something? Are you going to start quoting bits from *The Power of Now* and the *Tai Ch'ing*? Give it a rest.'

'Just saying, you got to sort yourself out. And this Jodi.'

'Geri.'

'She's not for you.'

'You want her number, is that it?'

'She'd do better with me. I'd take what was on offer and I wouldn't give her grief like you do. Only, thing is see, I wouldn't go out with her.'

'You're yanking my chain now.'

'No, I mean it. Too much grief. Plus, it's immoral.'

'Immoral? That's rich, coming from you.'

'It's true though, innit? I only go out with single girls. I don't go paddling in someone else's pool.'

Charlie finished his salad. Bad as it was, he wanted another one.

'You tell yourself you're proper hard, don't need anyone. *Look at me, I'm Charlie George.* You flash your warrant card, people get out of your way. But what you want is a missus, two point four kids and a white picket fence.'

'Can you imagine a white picket fence in Archway? They'd pull it out of the ground and hit you with one of the fence posts for your iPhone.'

'Joke all you like, Charlie, but you know I've got you pegged.'

'You done?'

'Just trying to be the voice of reason. Look at you. You're not a bad-looking bloke, even though you've let yourself go a bit lately.'

'Let myself go?'

'I mean, you're no oil painting, but some women like a bit of rough trade.'

'I have not let myself go.'

'Don't justify it to me – if women worried about the way a man looks, cage fighters wouldn't get any dates on a Saturday night. I'm just saying you're wasting your time on this woman. Meanwhile the years are passing you by. What does she do, this . . . what was her name again?'

'Geri.'

'See, that's a boy's name, for a start. She's a QC or something.'

'A junior barrister. She works for the CPS.'

'Mate, that's practically incest. Look Charlie, I'm not trying to do your head in. I worry about you. You're my big brother, I don't want anything to happen to you.'

'Like what happened to Liam? That's not me though, is it?'

'I hope not.' Ben's turn to reach for his drink. 'Do you have to keep bringing that up? I just wish we could all put down the past.'

'It's not as easy as that, though, is it? Seems to me, the past is like getting chewing gum on your shoe, never get the bloody thing off, not all of it anyway.'

'Another Cuban?'

Charlie thought about it: not so bad once you hacked your way through the jungle on top. Good to have a bit of a glow on for a change. 'All right,' he said. 'Your buy.'

He wanted to be anywhere but where he was.

A bitter morning, grey overcast, perfect for a funeral. The officers lined up along the route shuffled their feet to try and keep warm. The weather had got it right, for once, just the right amount of dreariness and cold. A hangover, too, the perfect thing.

Charlie clocked the police van with the surveillance camera. The theory was that psychopaths couldn't stay away and would show up among the mourners at the funeral. He didn't know about that, he hadn't dealt with many real head cases; violence bred of ignorance and stupidity, that wasn't the same thing. It scared him a bit, this case. He was right out of his depth; he was almost glad it was out of his hands now.

Two motorcycle riders in fluorescent jackets and white helmets appeared around the corner, their headlights on. The police guard on the road stiffened to attention. The motorcade came into view. He could hear the whirr and click of press cameras in the eerie silence, a hundred television cameras following the black Daimler hearse as it made its way along the street and in through the gates. There were French, German, even US TV crews out there.

No jokes from Greene today. He looked grey. Internal Affairs had given him a good grilling, he'd heard; he had even put his hand up for counselling, somehow blamed himself for Osman's death.

A half-dozen of Morton's fellow officers from Malden Street had been chosen as pallbearers. They were in their dress uniforms with white gloves. They carried the coffin up the steps and through the guard of honour at the church entrance. The coffin was draped in the Metropolitan Police flag, dark blue with a silver star. A wreath of red and white carnations spelled out his shoulder number. His constable's helmet had been placed on top.

Deborah Morton followed the coffin inside, her parents either side, her daughter in her arms, holding the little boy with her free hand. Charlie couldn't watch it. This was the sort of thing that kept you awake at night.

Charlie followed the brass into the church. He and Greene sat behind the two rows of gold braid and listened to the vicar as he read the service.

'. . . neither death nor life, nor angels nor demons, neither the present nor the future, nor any powers, neither height nor depth, nor anything else in all creation, will be able to separate us from the love of God that is in Jesus Christ our Lord.'

Sounds good, Charlie thought. But I wonder what it means, especially if you're that poor woman over there with two little

185

kids to raise. Not feeling the love of God too much right now, I bet.

One by one the family came up. Someone put a framed picture of Morton on the coffin, another draped a West Ham scarf across it. His wife placed a single red rose on top. Fuck me, Charlie thought. Can we get this over with? He put his dark glasses on.

Morton's brother tried to read the eulogy but didn't make it past the first page. Someone helped him down from the lectern and Deborah Morton took over, read it right through without a break in her voice. Charlie spared one glance at the kids, too young to really understand what was going on, he supposed. This wasn't right, just not right at all.

As they were leaving the church, the DCI took him aside. 'Back at work tomorrow,' he said.

'Thank you, sir. What will I be working on?'

'You'll be working with me in Gold group.'

Gold group, the task force the AC had set up to investigate Morton's murder. They had to report to him and the chief super twice a day. The DCI must be working up a sweat, he thought; a week now, and all he had to show was a minor riot in Hackney the day after Osman Balewah died. The family had taken their case to the newspapers, which had given the breakfast shows something new to fuck around with. They were having a proper day out on it.

'I'm looking forward to getting back into it,' Charlie said.

'See if you still think that way if we don't find the bastard who did this.' He walked away.

Greene came over. 'Everything all right?'

'Back to work for me, looks like. How are you, Jay?'

'Proper knocked me around, this has. Haven't been sleeping.'

'It happens.'

'Shrink reckons I have PMT or some fucking thing.'

'PTSD.'

186

'Says it's cumulative. Bollocks. Like I've seen lots of this shit, never had any problems before.'

'Take it easy. We miss you down at the nick.'

'Really?'

'No, I was just saying that. You're a pain in the ass.'

The hearse and the cortege had left, for a private graveside ceremony, but a lectern had been set up on the steps and the assistant commissioner was reading a prepared statement to the press. His voice was indistinct, because of the buffeting of the wind in the microphone. Charlie didn't stay to listen to it.

Had to get home, iron a few shirts. Big week coming up.

CHAPTER TWENTY-EIGHT

He got in the next morning right on early change, squeezed his Golf into one of the last spaces. His doors were bound to get scratched, but he'd given up worrying about it. A couple of the secretaries were out by the back door having a quick smoke, the early turn were waiting with their bags ready to load up. Night duty were still pulling bags from the boots of their patrol cars and signing them back in.

The DCI was already in his office, looking a little less slide-rule than usual. There were bags under his eyes and he had the look of a man on a speeding train who couldn't get off. Not that Charlie felt sorry for him. He threw me under the bus, he thought, now the bastard knows what it feels like. I reckon he got a right bollocking upstairs over Osman Balewah, and bloody right, too. Still, FONC will move on; Osman won't have the opportunity.

'Sit down, Charlie,' he said.

Charlie sat.

'Ready for work?'

'Am I still on the naughty step?'

'You were not being disciplined, Charlie. It was stress leave.'

'Right.'

'Do you still feel stressed?'

'No, sir.'

'Good.'

The DCI drew a thick file towards him, as if it was a detailed log of his life's sins. He drew a small breath before he opened it. 'Operation Galilee,' he said.

'Sir?'

'You were right, Charlie. Forensic results have confirmed that the same vehicle was used in the O'Meara and Morton homicides. They also found high probability on the footprints. It hasn't advanced the case in any significant way. But it's nice to be proved right, isn't it?'

'Not really, sir. Not if we don't have any suspects. What about that bloke his DI told us about?'

'Vernon?'

'That's the one.'

'We tracked him to an address in Leeds, where he was having a family Christmas with his in-laws. Two detectives from the West Yorkshire Police interviewed him. He has a rock-solid alibi.'

'Another dead end, then.'

'We do have this, however.'

He passed Charlie several printed sheets across the desk.

'We checked on the MAPPA system, everyone recently released from prison into the London area, cross-matched them with arrests made at the Malden Street nick. These four are of interest to us.'

Charlie flicked through them; mug shots, form. Joe Shiels, serious assault, three and a half years; Mohammed Costi, burglary, three years; Nicolai Popescu, trafficking, procurement; Michelle Canavan, drug possession and distribution, two and a half years.

'They've all been released from custody in the last couple of months. PC Morton was involved in all of those arrests. Costi was caught while engaged in a crime; Shiels was arrested following a pursuit by Morton on foot, after he was found hiding in a garden shed.'

'Popescu?'

'Morton was the one that tipped off DI Grace about Popescu's activities.'

'How?'

'Anonymous source.'

'And Michelle Canavan?'

'Same thing.'

'Any of these have any connection to Father O'Meara?'

'There's nothing in the files to indicate it. DI Grace says she never heard of O'Meara before she read about his murder in the papers.'

'If we can find a connection with one of these, then we have a prime suspect.'

'You've interviewed all these scrotes?'

'I've got the transcripts of the interviews right here: Costi, Shiels and Canavan.'

'What about Popescu?'

'He was an illegal, deported upon release.'

'Deported where?'

'Romania.'

'And still nothing?'

'Canavan has a cast-iron alibi for the night PC Morton was abducted.'

'Sir?'

'She was in a holding cell at Charing Cross police station. Drunk and disorderly.'

'Costi and Shiels?'

'Costi couldn't punch the skin off a rice pudding; Shiels is an out-and-out thug. Still, we cannot implicate or eliminate either of these two. They remain persons of interest.'

'But neither of them have any connection whatever to Father O'Meara?'

The DCI shook his head. 'Not that we've found.'

'Right.'

'Over to you, then.'

Charlie thought about it on the way down in the lift. Seemed to him there was only one person who knew Father O'Meara well enough to join the dots for them. He

190

wondered where she was and what she was doing right now.

Sister Agatha wasn't easy to find. In the old days, Charlie thought, nuns didn't go anywhere; you wanted to talk to a bride of Christ you just went to a convent, simple. But no, these days he had to go traipsing down by the reservoir and the North Circular, getting mud all over his new Santoni black leather oxfords.

There were two blokes sitting on bits of cardboard by an overpass, drinking cans of Żywiec. Some teenagers in hoodies came barrelling down the steps, jumped over them, like they weren't even there.

He fumbled in his pockets for the packet of ciggies he kept for such situations and offered them one. They looked wary but they both took two, stuck one behind their ears for later.

He lit their cigarettes, worried that the rocket fuel on their breath might blow them all up. 'Do you know Sister Agatha?' he said.

One of them gabbled at him in some language he didn't understand. The other one said: 'You mean, nun. Holy lady. Grey hair.'

'Built like a brick shithouse. That's the one.'

The bloke gave a jerk of his head to a hole in the fence and a long muddy embankment. 'Down at river. Always there every morning, this o'clock.'

Not so much a river, Charlie thought, as he scrambled down the slope; it was part marsh, part spillage pond. The mud was frozen hard underfoot, once the melt came this would turn into a proper bog. He heard voices and followed the path through a tangle of brambles, rusting Tesco trolleys, crushed beer cans and nettles.

'Well, look what the cat dragged in.'

Sister Agatha was squatted next to a homeless man who

191

looked like he had just lost a cage fight. One eye was swollen shut and he'd dribbled blood and spit all over the hood of his sleeping bag. He stank like a goat.

'All right, then?'

'I'm in pretty good shape for the shape I'm in,' Sister Agatha said. 'And yourself?'

'Freezing.'

'Well then, thank the good Lord it's not yourself having to doss down out here.'

'What happened to him then?'

'Lord only knows. Been in a fight, I suppose. I'm trying to persuade him to come to the drop-in centre to have his bruises looked at, but I don't think he understands me.'

'That's because he's unconscious.'

'No, I think it's because he's Polish.' She stood up, peeled off the blue medical gloves and put them in a plastic bag. She put the bag in her pocket.

'So this is what you do all day?' Charlie said.

'Well, it keeps me off the street. That was a joke.'

'Yeah, I get it.'

'This is my faith, Inspector, what you see around you. This is not just what I do all day, what you are looking at is what I believe.'

'Human misery and degradation?'

'No, kindness in the face of it. I believe you know your Bible, young man.'

'A bit of it.'

'For me, the heart of Christianity is enshrined in the story of the Good Samaritan. I'm sure you know that one.'

'Gospel of Luke.'

'Very good. When the man was lying by the side of the road, naked and bleeding, a priest and a fellow Jew both went right past, ignored him. It was a foreigner who stopped to help him, the Samaritan. And you know, the Jews and the Samaritans hated each other, that's the significance of it. Even Martin

Luther King made reference to the story in his great speeches. Did you know that?'

Charlie nodded.

'Some people will tell you that the whole thing is an allegory. I believe it is a lesson in ethics. It is what I have based my whole life upon.'

'You're the good Samaritan.'

'As Father Andrew was.'

'A saint.'

'Other people called him that, he never thought of himself that way. He just saw that he was doing God's work, not by trying to make them believe what he believed, but by acting like Jesus Christ would have done.'

'Well thank God for people like you, Sister. There's not enough of you. Most people would do what I do, walk past every day and pretend not to notice. Compassion fatigue, I suppose.'

'You don't pretend to be something you're not, I'll give you that. The worst ones are the Christians. They're the ones that scare me.'

'The Christians?'

'All they care about is heaven, not kindness. They go to church so they can be first through the door when God opens the gates of Paradise, that's all.'

'How did you get into this? I mean, didn't you ever want to have your own family?'

'Well, of course I did. I didn't always have grey hair and thick hips. I was quite attractive when I was a young girl. I had my offers. There was this young fella when I was seventeen, we went out for a while, his sister told me he wanted to marry me. Don't look at me like that, it's true.'

'I wasn't looking at you like anything.'

'Most people think a woman becomes a nun because she can't get a man or because she's a lesbian without hope.'

'I wasn't thinking that.'

'It wasn't that I didn't want a family, I did. My sisters got themselves husbands, with varying success. A couple of them did well enough at it, they have grandchildren now, and I must admit there's times I wonder what it would have been like. I think I would have been a good wife and mother.'

'If you'd been my mum, you would have terrified me.'

'I reckon you would have been the kind of little boy who needed terrifying. I'd have brought you into line and no mistake.'

'But you didn't do it.'

'I wanted to help other people more than I wanted to help myself.'

'A martyr to the cause.'

'There is nothing wrong with martyrdom, young man. Our Saviour and our greatest saints have all been martyrs.'

'No regrets?'

'Whatever path you choose, there are always regrets. But you'd know all about that.'

'Me?'

'I told you before, we're not unalike, you and I. You cuss more than is good for a man, and drink as well, I don't doubt. But you're a martyr for your cause, same as I'm a martyr for mine.'

'I don't follow.'

'People think chastity is the hardest thing about my job, but when was the last time you were with a woman?'

'You made your point the last time.'

'I'll make it again. Why aren't you swinging off the chandeliers every night, or whatever it is people do when they're not in orders? Because of your work, am I right?'

'I haven't sworn off it.'

'If you don't mind me saying, face like that, I wouldn't blame you.' She laughed. 'But I suppose there's women that go for that sort of thing. Only they can't get near you, can they? You're always at work, same as I am. And what about money? Raking it in, I bet.'

Charlie made a face.

'You should have taken a vow of poverty like me, at least I get board and lodging. You see what I mean?'

This bloody woman, Charlie thought, she proper knows how to get under my skin. 'I'm no saint.'

'Far from it, but like I said, you are a true believer.'

She stood there, smiling at him, like she knew him better than he knew himself. 'Penny for your thoughts,' she said.

'There was this time, when I was a kid, the old man came home, swearing and staggering all over. I told my younger brother to call the cops, before he did some damage.'

'Did they come?'

'No, they got there too late. They never got there on time – well, not soon enough to make any difference. Sometimes they never showed up at all.'

'Sounds like a confession.'

'If you like. Never talked about this with anyone much before.'

'If it is or it isn't, I can't give you absolution.'

'Not looking for any. I absolved myself a long time ago.'

He heard a couple of the old Poles singing, sounded quite lovely and plaintive really, like a gypsy ballad, the wind rustling in the nettles and everything. 'What they all doing down here? Can't be much fun if it rains.'

'I don't think it will rain,' Agatha said, sniffing the air. 'If it does, they'll head for the underpass over there. They like it here because it's safe, no one to bother them.'

'Not much small change to be had over there.'

'They're homeless, Inspector, they're not beggars like you see up your end of town. See that fellow over there, in the red gloves?'

Charlie clocked a young bloke with a ginger beard, lying in a red sleeping bag, reading a paperback novel. He took a closer look. *Remembrance of Things Past.*

'What's a Pole doing reading Proust?' he said.

195

'He's from Nottingham. Very smart fella, that one, he has an honours degree in Literature from Cambridge and schizophrenia. Neither of them have served him very well. He was sleeping in a doorway in Stoke Newington last month and someone thought it would be funny to set fire to his hands. That's why he's wearing the gloves.'

'Did you get them for him?'

'After I took him to the hospital.'

'Why did they set his hands on fire?'

'For a laugh, I suppose. People do like their bit of fun. He told me someone went into a Pret once, bought him a sandwich, but they spat in it before they gave it to him. Bit of a dilemma, isn't it, when you're starving hungry. What to do?'

'What did he do?'

'What do you think he did? He wiped the spit off the chicken best he could and ate the damned thing.'

Charlie looked around. There must have been half a dozen of them that he could see, lying around in sodden and stained sleeping bags, on tattered pieces of cardboard and rank duvets, surrounded by take-away boxes and plastic bottles. One old man, drinking Tetley Rhino, was in a violent confrontation with someone who wasn't there.

'Where did he get the money for the booze?' Charlie said.

'I bought it for him.'

'Should you be encouraging him?'

'Well if I don't, what he does is sneak into St Leonard's Hospital over there, don't ask me how he does it, and he squirts hand-wash from the dispensers into a two-litre Coke bottle and drinks it. Have you any idea what that stuff is like? They tell me it's like getting hit in the back of the head with a brick. At least the Rhino won't kill him, not straight away.'

'He can't be long for this world anyway.'

'He's only forty-five. Used to service Bentleys until depression got the better of him.'

'I thought he was eighty if he was a day.'

'There's a lesson for you then, Inspector. If you want to stay young, don't drink hand-wash.'

He shook his head. 'Reminds me of *Les Mis* all this.'

'Do you see that fella over there?'

'Nice jacket. Army surplus, is it?'

'Polish Army, the real thing. It was his brother's. Last Christmas Kostek had a job and a family and his own Christmas tree to sit round. Then he lost his job down the mine, and he was afraid he was going to lose his house. So he came here. The other side of the German border, people still think they can take the night bus to a better life. There's illegal labour exchanges all over London, he went to one, got a job washing cars for some Albanians, he thought his troubles were over, he was going to send his wages back to his family and everything would be fine. They weren't paying him much but he could live like a king on it back home, is what he says.'

'He didn't get his wages, did he?'

'Of course not. When he asked for his money, they beat him black and blue and told him not to come back. He can't go to you fellas and complain, because he's got no national insurance number, and to get an insurance number you need an address and to have an address, you need a job. Besides, he only has twenty words of English. So Kostek does what every man does when he feels hopeless and washed up, he drinks himself into oblivion.'

'Why doesn't he go home?'

'He's too ashamed. And what is he going to do at home? There's no work. He's given up, you see. They've all given up. Their hopes and dreams have turned into a soiled mattress under a flyover.'

'Poor bastards.'

'Not quite how I would have said it, but I appreciate the sentiment. But this isn't what brought you down here getting mud on those fancy shoes of yours. I take it that you are no closer to finding whoever killed Father Andrew?'

'Not yet. We're still working on a few things.'

'I pray for him every night.'

'Father Andrew?'

'Yes, but I also pray for the man who took his life. His soul must be in terrible torment.'

'To be honest, I don't give two tosses about his rotten soul. I just want to get him banged up before he hurts someone else.'

'And how can I help? Does it have something to do with that envelope you're holding? It looks important.'

'It might be. These are photographs of people who are presently helping us with our enquiries.'

'You think one of them is your man?'

'Or woman,' he said. She raised an eyebrow at that.

Charlie hesitated. He wasn't supposed to divulge information about the case, but if he wanted her help, then he would have to tell her something. 'I need to tell you something in strictest confidence.'

'Of course.'

'You would have seen on the news, about the copper who was found murdered in Hampstead.'

'Yes, the poor man. Terrible.'

'We think there may have been a connection between that murder and what happened to Father O'Meara.'

'Do you now? And that's why you'd like me to look at these photographs for you?'

Charlie took out three eight-by-ten black-and-white head shots, enlargements of the arrest photographs of the three individuals MAPPA had thrown up. He handed Sister Agatha the first one.

'Oh my word, what's this? He looks like a right hard nut. Is it human?'

'His name is Joe Shiels. Ring any bells?'

'Not a single one.' She held out her hand for the next one. 'And who's this?'

'His name is Mohammed Costi. He's just been released from Pentridge, three years for a number of burglary offences.'

'Don't know him. Sorry.'

'This is the last one.'

'A woman? I don't like the tattoo. Why do women do that to themselves?'

'Michelle Canavan. She's a drug dealer from Stoke Newington.'

'Sure and I don't know her either. Any more?'

'No, that's it.'

'You've got one more in there.'

'Don't think he's relevant.'

'Let me have a look anyway.'

'You're very pushy for a nun, don't mind me saying.'

'Is it Bernadette of Lourdes you're mistaking me for?' She held out her hand and made a wiggling motion with her fingers, let me see. He took out the last photograph and handed it to her. She spent longer staring at it than the others.

'Another handsome one. Where did you find these people?'

'All the attractive, charming blokes are in the police.'

'You're kidding me, aren't ya? You look a bigger thug than the lot of them.' She peered more closely at the photograph. 'Who is he?'

'His name's Nicolai Popescu.'

'Popescu. They're all called that, aren't they?'

'Familiar?'

'No.'

'Well, it doesn't matter, it's not him, he was deported back to Romania a couple of months ago after they let him out of stir.'

He went to take the photograph from her but she shook her head.

'Sister?'

'You know I never saw the fella, so I don't know. I can't be sure if he's the same one.'

'The same one?'

'What was this chap in prison for?'

'Sex trafficking. He was kidnapping teenage girls in Romania and bringing them to London, forcing them into prostitution.'

'It's a wicked world. It could be him, I suppose.'

'Sorry, could be him, what? You think you know him?'

She handed him the photograph. 'I do remember, a few years ago, Father Andrew telling me he came across these two girls who were sleeping rough, scared out of their wits, they were. They told him about this fella they met in Bucharest, a real charmer they said, said he could find them work in London as models. When they got here, he beat them up and took away their passports and made them work in one of those, what do you call them these days, pop-up brothels, is that the word?'

Charlie felt a tingling down his back. It could be the link they had been looking for. 'Go on.'

'Well, that's it, really. He found them a place in a women's shelter, then he went to the police.'

'He went to his local nick?'

'No, he didn't want it getting lost in mountains of paper-work, he said. Father Andrew never trusted the police.'

'Thanks.'

'Not because he thought you were bent, he just thought you were inefficient.'

'Well, that's much better then.'

'He talked to this copper he knew, he said he was all right, that he'd sort it out. I suppose he must have, I never heard anything more about it.'

Charlie took the photograph from her, put it back in the envelope with the others. The wind had picked up, coming at them right across the water, courtesy of the North Pole by the feel of it. Cut right through. He stamped his feet and tried to think.

The DCI had wanted him to find a connection between

Father O'Meara and PC Morton and he had found it. But would someone go this far to even the score? If he was a nutter, he might, and the way the two men had been murdered, that was certainly a nutter's MO.

But Popescu was supposed to be back in Romania.

Yeah, right. Unable to get through the UK's cast-iron immigration barriers.

'Have I been any help to you, Inspector?'

'Maybe,' Charlie said.

'Because I hope you haven't got mud on those fine shoes of yours for nothing.'

'They're only shoes,' Charlie said, and walked back through the marsh to the road.

CHAPTER TWENTY-NINE

Geri was staying at one of those hotels that had a DJ and a bar in the foyer; all the people coming in with luggage were a bit of a nuisance really, Charlie thought. The foyer was overrun with young blokes with beards and ink, yo-pros in suits and sneakers, busy with their MacBook Airs, drinking cold pressed fig juice. Of course it would be the sort of place Geri would stay when she was supposed to be in Leeds. Or perhaps she really was going there after; he should be flattered.

He was conscious of the mud on his Fratelli Rossettis. Pity they didn't have shoeshines in Holborn, that would be a real public service, instead of those cycle rickshaws, pissing everyone off. London needed those like Custer needed more Indians.

Surreal coming in here after the day that he'd had. Smell the money and self-satisfaction in here. It was like Sister Agatha said, he supposed, life could turn on a dime. One minute you could be sitting there with your mates, discussing which club to go to on Friday night, and then something happened out of your control, a global financial crisis or your company downsized, or the pills you took for the black dog stopped working. All it took. A few months later you're squatting on a bit of cardboard outside a Barclay's ATM asking people for change.

Geri was sitting by the window, playing with her iPhone, she looked up and saw him and waved. She was wearing a simple black dress, not much make-up and perfume. Read what you will into that, Charlie boy.

'Want a drink?' she said.

'What's that you've got?'

'It's gin.'

'Doesn't look like gin. What's the horticulture?'

'It has basil and elderflowers. Try it.'

He shook his head. 'I had salad the other night with my brother. Too much lettuce gives me a hangover. Do they have beer?'

'They have mead. It's made with honey from local bees.'

'I wouldn't want anything made from the bees round here. Get their nectar straight off the beanie of some wino in the doorway next to the Holborn Tesco.'

'Aren't we the grouch today?'

Yes, he thought, why was he behaving like a prat when he had been looking forward to seeing her all week? Was it because of Sister Agatha and her Polish down-and-outs, or was there another reason?

'Bad day,' he said, giving himself an out.

'What happened? Can you talk about it?'

'I spent the morning tramping around some marshes next to a sewage treatment facility.'

'Too much information. Is that what's on your shoes?'

He thought she might not notice, but of course she did. He shuffled his feet further under the table. 'I think we have a breakthrough, though.'

'On Operation Galilee? Congratulations.'

'Well, mustn't be too hasty. We'll have to wait and see.'

'So, you've got the night off?' she said, her voice suddenly husky.

'Looks like it. How long are you up in town?'

'I have to go up to Leeds in the morning.'

'That's bad luck.'

'Depends how you look at it,' she said, and took a long sip of her gin through the straw, her eyes making all sorts of promises. 'How do you think your luck might hold up?'

'Not sure.'

'If something needs holding up, you've come to the right girl.' She finished her gin and set the glass on the table. 'I shouldn't drink gin, really. It makes me horny.'

'How many have you had?'

'Two. It feels like four or five. Oh, look at your poor shoes. The hotel has a shoe-cleaning service, if you're a guest. I'll put it on my tab. And if you've been tramping round the country, you probably need a shower.'

'While I wait for them to bring back my shoes.'

'They're kind of busy. They may not be ready until the morning.'

'It takes as long as it takes, I suppose.'

'Well, of course. If you're going to give something a good polish, you don't want to rush it. Do you, Charlie?'

She stood in the middle of the room and held out her arms, as if she was an estate agent and he was a prospective buyer. 'What do you think?'

'Very nice. Did you do it all yourself?'

'The wallpaper is decorated with scenes from Charles Dickens novels.'

Charlie looked closer. Looked more like Monty Python to him, but he said, 'I think I've got *Great Expectations* here.'

'So have I,' she said.

If the foyer was quirky, the room was quirkier. There was a huge circular mirror and a floating arm lamp, a copper tone desk with dozens of old Penguin paperbacks stacked in the writing hutch.

'I'll have first shower,' she said, and unzipped her dress at the back.

His eyes went to the massive leather headboard. 'That'll stop you hitting your head on the wall.'

'Who said I'll be the one on my back?' She slipped out of her dress, stood there in a pair of Chantilly lace panties and a demi cup bra, a towel poised on the end of her finger. 'I'm going to go industrial on you, Charlie.'

He tried to grab her but she squirmed out of reach and went into the bathroom.

He heard the shower running. Christ, he needed a drink. Where the hell was the fridge? He tried opening things, found hanging space, a safe, some drawers with stuff, including shoe polish. He sat down, took off his shoes. Look at them, he'd do them himself while he was waiting, he'd be too embarrassed to give them to housekeeping.

He heard the shower turn off and then the bathroom door opened, and she was standing there, wearing a silver wrist bangle, dripping wet. There was a butterfly tattoo just above her pubic bone, always a surprise. Her nipples were pink and hard, but that could just be the air conditioning.

'You're polishing your shoes,' she said and smiled.

'Couldn't find the fridge.'

'We're both at a loose end then,' she said. 'I couldn't find the power point to dry my hair.'

'I'll have to have you wet, then.'

She put a finger between her legs, and then touched it to the tip of her tongue. 'Dripping. Do you want to see for yourself?'

He nodded.

She ran a hand down his shirt and down to the crotch of his trousers. 'How are you holding up, Charlie?'

'I'm holding up all right.'

'It feels like you are. It feels like you're holding up rather well.' She grabbed his shirt and wrapped her naked thighs around him and pulled him towards her. She opened her mouth to let him kiss her, then her hand snaked out and she turned on the shower, adjusting the hot and cold taps and biting his bottom lip at the same time. Impressive how women can multi-task, he thought.

She wrestled his clothes off, his Battistoni shirt ending up on the floor next to a sopping wet towel. Fuck, never mind. His suit trousers were around his ankles, she slipped a finger under the waistband of his Calvin Kleins. 'Charlie, that's nice.'

'Will that do?'

'I'm keeping you from your shower,' she said, and stood on tiptoe to unhook his tie from round his neck. Christ, how was his tie still on? Then she knelt down and he felt her brush against him with her lips, just a tease, no more.

'Let's get you soaped up,' she said.

'I don't want to put you to any trouble.'

'Oh look, how did all this shower gel get in my hand. Where shall I put it?'

He swallowed hard.

'That seems about right. A little here, as well. Am I rubbing the soap in too fast, Charlie? I'll do it a little more. Slowly. Or even, even, slower. Slower still.'

'Oh for fuck's sake.'

'I need some of that gel here on my breasts. Will you rub it in for me?' She stood up and bit him on the shoulder, hard, and he winced. She turned around, the water ran over her face, she watched him over the shoulder. 'You can fuck me now, if you want.'

It was what he'd wanted, wasn't it, what he'd waited for? But all he could think of was: I have to do this better than he does. He slipped his hand between her legs, the other on her nipple, her hands with their scarlet nails slapped against the tiles, then screwed into tight fists. I cannot lose control now, not when there's so much at stake. She's the business, everything I ever wanted. I'll make her want me so bad, she'll never leave.

He threw back his head, let the water run into his face. She came, and a few minutes later she came again. Ben's wrong, he thought. I can do this.

'What are you thinking, Charlie?'

'Thought you were asleep.' They were in the bed; the velvet drapes were drawn, he could still hear the thud of bass from the

DJ downstairs. He looked at the luminous dial of his watch; not even ten o'clock yet.

She rolled over, put her head on his chest. 'I can hear you thinking.'

'Not thinking anything.'

'Yes, you are.'

'I was thinking about my shirt. It's ruined.'

'It's just a shirt.'

'It's a Battistoni. Probably worth two hundred quid.'

'How do you afford to dress like that on your salary?'

'I got it in an Oxfam shop in Stoke Newington for a fiver.'

'A fiver? What are you worried about, then?'

'Do you know how long it took to find a Battistoni for five pounds? It's like winning the pools.'

'You've just had the best sex you've had in your life and all you can think about is your sodding shirt.'

'Fourth best,' he said, and laughed.

She grabbed his balls and squeezed. 'Want to say that again, big boy?'

'Best, absolutely, best by miles. No question.'

'That's better.'

'Doesn't mean you have to let go completely,' he said.

She sat up, straddled him, started to run herself along the length of him. 'Is this the fourth best time any woman's done this to you?'

'Oh my God.'

She leaned over him, he felt her hair tickle his face. She breathed in his ear: 'Ready?'

'I'm ready,' he said.

'You just think you are,' she said and laughed. 'We'll have to find out.'

The cold was breathtaking on King's Cross station at a quarter to eight on a winter morning. Geri looked up at the board, waiting for the platform announcement. 'Come on,' she murmured into her Costa take-away coffee cup. 'Sodding train is leaving in five minutes. Are they having a laugh?'

'Guy's probably up there in the control room watching the platform, likes to see everyone running, probably has bets with his mates on who's going to miss it.'

'I'm sore,' she said.

'So am I.'

'Men aren't supposed to be sore, Charlie. You'll never be a cage fighter, sweetheart.'

'I'm a lover not a fighter.'

'Well, you're not bad at it, I suppose. About fifth best I've ever had.'

He smiled at that one. 'Have you really got an appointment in Leeds?'

'Of course I have. Why else do you think I'm going up there?'

A shrug. 'I don't know.'

'You don't think people make appointments north of the Watford gap?'

'Maybe they do.'

'I'm taking a deposition from a witness.'

'Can't they come to London?'

'Not really, he's in Armley jail.'

'I thought, you know, when you said you had to go to Leeds, it was like, an excuse.'

'To spend last night with you?'

'Yeah.'

'It was. I could have sent someone else.'

'Your husband, does he ever get suspicious?'

There was a garbled announcement over the PA that no one could hear, but then a number flashed up on the board. 'Platform three,' Geri said. 'Five minutes to get on the sodding train and find my seat. Goodbye, sweetheart, I'd better go.'

She kissed him quickly on the lips and hurried off, the wheels of her black executive Aerolite clipping on the concrete behind her. A quick wave from the other side of the barrier and she was gone. So that was twice she'd called him sweetheart this morning, but he didn't want to read too much into it.

He walked back down the platform to the Gents. He checked his look in the mirror, oh Christ, he'd seen better-dressed blokes drinking Tetley Rhino in Waterloo. The Oxfam could have the Battistoni proper this time, same for the Loro Piana. He would have to go home and get changed before he went in to the nick. The DCI would already be looking at his watch. He'd be right for it when he finally got to work.

The tourists' queue was already fifty deep by Platform 9¾. He thought about what Sister Agatha had called him that first time: a good man. Not if she saw him today. He felt a bit like his shirt: something bought cheap for charity and dragged across a wet floor. He had the appearance of quality, but not the threads or the stitch for it.

He caught the Northern line to Archway, picked up a *Metro* from the seat, stared at the headline. MONSTER, it said. The papers had made the connection between Father O'Meara's murder and PC Morton's death; well they'd known for a long time, but they'd finally given up censoring themselves; after a community paper had broken the story they had no choice, he supposed.

He got out at Archway and hurried down the street. He thought about Geri, she'd be in first class right now, tapping away on her MacBook Air, saying no to the complimentary coffee, replete and without a care in the world. Ben was right, she should have picked his brother to have the affair with, he would have been far less complicated, wouldn't have lain awake all night, thinking about a future they were never going to have.

Reads better than it lives all this sex-on-the-side business. Never felt so fucking lonely in my whole life.

CHAPTER THIRTY

'You wanted to see me, sir?'

'Come in, Charlie, sit down,' the DCI said. He was a different man from yesterday, Charlie thought, almost likeable. 'Want a cup of Earl Grey?'

I fucking hate Earl Grey, Charlie thought. Tastes like maiden's water, any way you look at it. 'Yes, please.'

The DCI pressed a button on his intercom and got some civilian staffer to get a fresh pot of tea. That was the life. All he got downstairs was a chipped mug with coffee stains and sorry sir, all out of instant.

The DCI pushed a file across the desk. There were a number of photocopied sheets, grainy head shots, documents written in a language that he didn't recognise.

'The assistant commissioner has been in touch with the police principal quaestor at the Directorate of Organised Crime in Bucharest. It's the file on this man of yours, Nicolai Popescu. There's another attachment there with a translation. There's also his file from the PNC. But you're already familiar with most of that.'

Charlie leafed through the pages. 'Impressive,' he said.

'Yes, he's quite the lad.'

The civvy knocked and came back in with a tray. Charlie didn't know the Metropolitan Police owned trays. There were two cups of tea, in bone china. After she left, the DCI reached into a drawer and produced a packet of bourbons. He couldn't believe it, this was like being back at the bishop's.

'As you can see, Popescu has a history of kidnapping and heavy-duty violence. He once broke a rival's legs with a baseball bat. Sound familiar?'

'Father O'Meara?'

'Exactly. And listen to this: three years ago, there was an explosion at a block of apartments in Bucharest, it was believed one of the flats was being used to manufacture illicit drugs.'

'Sir?'

'Didn't Father O'Meara have narcotics in his system?'

'Ketamine.'

'The source of the explosion was traced to an apartment owned by Nicolai Popescu. Unfortunately, the charges were later dropped.'

'Why?'

'Not all coppers are as squeaky clean as us here in London, Charlie. The point of the story, this boy has serious form.'

'Do the Romanians know where he is?'

'No, he could be anywhere.'

'I see.'

'His family are still in the UK. He has a mother living some-where in Harrow and a brother, Bogdan. Our last address for him is in Stratford.'

'You want me to go and talk to his mother?'

'You could have stumbled across the breakthrough we're looking for.'

'What about Bogdan?'

'I'll task Wesley and Rupinder with finding him. Well, hurry up. Finish your tea and get moving. There could be a promotion in this for us both. What's the matter?'

Charlie hesitated. It had all seemed so promising yesterday. 'I don't know, sir. Something doesn't feel right.'

'What does that mean?'

'What he did to O'Meara and Morton. It's so personal, know what I mean? Crucifying someone for grassing you up. Bit over the top.'

'Not for a nut job.'

'I don't like it.'

'You don't have to like it. Just do what it says on the tin, all right?' He looked at his watch. 'Now tick-tock. Finish your tea, and get moving.' He grabbed the packet of bourbons before Charlie could take any more, put them in his drawer and shut it.

The last address they had for Popescu's mother was over a charity shop in the High Street. The door had blue paint peeling off it, a buzzer fixed to the wall. Charlie couldn't tell if it was working or not, so he hammered on the door with his fist. Five minutes of that and they still didn't get an answer, so they went into the charity shop and he told Lovejoy to ask the woman behind the counter if Mrs Popescu was home.

'Mrs who?'

'The woman who lives in the flat upstairs.'

'I don't know what she's called. I just work here.'

'But there is someone up there?'

'Why, what's she done? Is she a pikey? She looks like a pikey.'

'We would just like to have a word with her. She may be able to help us with our enquiries.'

'You should ring the bell, then, see if she's home.'

'We've tried that. We didn't get an answer.'

'She's probably out, then.'

Charlie could hear Lovejoy sigh from the other side of the shop. He came back to the till holding a leather belt. 'How much is this, then?'

'You want to buy it?'

'This is a shop, isn't it?'

'I thought you were the police.'

'We still have to buy things, same as everyone else. How much?'

She took the belt, tried to read the price label, but she couldn't see what was written on it. 'Give me five quid.'

'Done,' Charlie said.

They walked out, crossed the road to Lovejoy's car. 'Look at that,' Charlie said. 'Bottega Veneta, that is.'

'Is that rhyming slang?'

'No, it's the brand. Bottega Veneta. This would be worth a thousand US dollars online.'

'You'd pay a thousand dollars for a belt, guv?'

'No, I wouldn't, that's the point.'

'You really think a belt is worth a thousand bucks?'

'You're missing the point.'

They got into the car. Lovejoy started the engine. Charlie put his hand on the wheel, told her to turn it off. 'We'll wait,' he said.

'We don't know when she'll be back. We don't even know if it's her.'

'If we don't wait, we'll never know, will we?'

'Don't they have surveillance teams for this?'

'Not to chase around after middle-aged Romanian women, no.'

The tube station was over the road. He watched the punters going in and going out, some of them Africans on their way to jobs in the City, industrial cleaning was their long suit, the Poles and Albanians just headed home after a long day digging basement ballrooms in Kensington and Chelsea. There was a gang of Ukrainian girls in leggings and baseball caps hanging around outside a fried chicken shop.

They sat there and studied all the faces, one eye on that door.

A young woman with a ponytail and a bubble jacket was giving out pamphlets about a fracking referendum in Lithuania. When he was in school, even the teachers didn't know where Lithuania was.

There was a Polish supermarket next to a Kurdish internet café, a Job Centre, a McDonald's. Women in thick padded plastic coats plodded towards the bus stop, loaded down with Morrison's bags, pushing trolleys piled with huge bottles of pickles.

213

'Like Little Poland,' Charlie said. 'They don't like them much, down my way. My mother talks about them like they're in league with Satan.'

'Burglars love the Poles.'

'How do you know that?'

'Working CID. The Poles are hard workers, see, and most of them work in construction, so they get a lot of black money. But they don't like paying tax and they don't trust the banks so a lot of them hide their dosh in shoeboxes under their beds. So, if you're a professional, what you do is sit outside and wait till they've gone off to renovate another five million quid townhouse and then break in and take it. It never gets reported because they don't want the government to know how much they're making.'

'Haven't they ever heard of dead bolts?'

'They cost money.'

A Mercedes pulled up outside the off-licence and a man the size of a refrigerator wearing industrial-strength gold chains and holed fashion jeans got out and went inside. Charlie checked the glossy six-by-four in the file he had on the back seat. 'It's not him,' he said to Lovejoy.

The thud of the bass made the car shake. There was a woman in the passenger seat in a fake fur collar and fake blonde hair. The man came out again, counting a handful of banknotes. 'A shake down,' Charlie said.

'Shall we go over?'

Charlie made a face. 'We can report it if you like. But you're not in the CID now, Lovejoy. That hasn't got anything to do with us. We've got better things to do with our time.'

'I need something to eat,' Lovejoy said. 'I'm starving.' She opened the driver's door. 'You want anything?'

Charlie shook his head.

Lovejoy crossed the road to the supermarket. It was gloomy inside, saving money on power bills, she supposed. There was a magazine rack at the front, *Viva!* and *Playboy* alongside *Cztery*

Kąty and *Cienie I Blaski*. She wandered along the aisles of juice cartons and tins of ham and packet noodles. Doner kebab flavour, she'd never seen those before.

A young girl stood behind the deli counter. Lovejoy smiled at her. 'I'll have a "cappuccinno",' she said, pointing to the Kawa Coffee blackboard and resisting the urge to lick her finger and cross out the extra 'n'. 'And they look delicious. I'll have one of the *pączek*. That must be Polish for "doughnut". Did I say it right?'

The girl just stared blankly at her which probably meant she hadn't.

While she waited for her coffee she looked at Charlie in the car on the other side of the road, his head back on the head rest, his eyes closed, pretending to relax.

She thought she was over men, but there was something about her guv'nor that could perhaps change her mind. Still, that could never happen. Hadn't she learned by now, you should never mix work with pleasure?

The girl looked up and yelled something. There was a woman at the back of the shop, she had on a shapeless coat, a scarf on her head. She was holding a blue plastic bag of Lech beers.

'I saw you!' the girl said. 'You just put that tin of ham in your coat.'

'Like I'm going to eat any of this dog shit in here,' the woman said.

'I saw you!' the girl repeated, standing her ground. 'Show me your pockets.' She tried to reach into the woman's coat but she shrugged her off and made to swing the beers at her. The girl jumped back. 'You took the ham!'

'I didn't take. You think I take, why not you call the police.' She turned to Lovejoy. 'Fucking Poles. Why you people give benefit sixty pound a week and free flat for these people. All lazy bitches.'

Lovejoy felt sorry for the girl standing there, red-faced and outraged. Lovejoy didn't doubt the stolen ham was going to come out of her wages. The woman with the Lechs turned and walked out of the shop.

'You could call the police,' Lovejoy said, feeling a little guilty that she wasn't in a position to get involved.

'Can't trust police,' the girl said. She finished making the coffee and put a doughnut in a brown paper bag. Lovejoy gave her the money and the girl slammed the till. She was tearing up. Poor kid.

Lovejoy went back to the car. Charlie opened one eye. 'You took your time.'

'Sorry guv.'

'Don't be sorry.' He took the doughnut out of the bag and took a bite. 'Delicious.' He took the coffee out of her hand. 'You haven't got time to drink that. Mrs Popescu just got home.'

'When?'

'Just now. You were standing next to her in the Polish deli, Sherlock. Come on, we've got work to do.' And he walked across the road, his hands in his suit jacket pockets, whistling.

CHAPTER THIRTY-ONE

Charlie knocked on the door, waited. It opened, a middle-aged woman in a loose-fitting cardigan peered out at them. She had more lines on her face than a Goodyear re-tread. Too much scowling at people will do that to you, Charlie thought. He showed her his warrant card.

'Mrs Popescu. Detective Inspector George, Major Incident Team. This is DC Lovejoy. May we speak with you a moment?'

'*Nu înţeleg engleză*,' the woman said and tried to shut the door.

But Charlie was ready for her and already had his foot in the jamb. Lovejoy stepped forward. '*Căutăm fiul tău. Şi nu spune că nu înţelegi, te-am auzit vorbind perfect în supermarket.* Now please let us in or we will have to break down the door and arrest you, like we did with your Nicolai.'

'I haven't done anything,' she said.

'We still need to talk to you.'

She doesn't look frightened, Charlie thought, just pissed off. Interesting. We're not going to do any good here. She stepped back and let them in.

The flat was tiny, cluttered and smelled of cats. Mrs Popescu waddled down to the living room, nodded towards the sofa; you want to sit, then sit, her expression said. But there wasn't anywhere, really, not with the empty can of Timişoreana, the newspapers and magazines in what he supposed was Romanian, and the two cats.

'We can do this standing up, Mrs Popescu.'

217

'Nicolai is not here. He is gone back to Bucareşti.'

'That your shopping?' Charlie went through to the kitchen, good Christ it stank in here. He looked into the plastic bags. 'You drink a lot of beer, Mrs Popescu. It's not good for you, you know.'

She just looked at him.

'Expecting visitors?'

Nothing.

Charlie looked around the flat. There were cheap religious pictures on all the walls, little icons on top of the television and on the mantle. 'Religious, are you?'

Mrs Popescu glared at him.

'Good to have a moral code to live by.'

Mrs Popescu looked at Lovejoy. 'What he says? He is a crazy man.'

Charlie pushed aside an icon of the Archangel Michael and picked up a framed photograph of two burly men with shaved heads, standing either side of Mrs Popescu with their arms around her. 'Oh, this is nice. Are they your sons? No wait, don't tell me. This one here is Nicolai. I recognise him from his photograph. Funny thing, he looks much younger in the one we have, so this must have been taken since he got out of prison. You see what I'm thinking here, Lovejoy?'

He smiled at Mrs Popescu.

'Where was this taken?'

'Bucareşti.'

'Doesn't look like Bucharest. That looks like Southend Pier in the background. Does that look like Southend Pier to you, Lovejoy?'

'Yes, sir.'

'Have they got piers in Bucharest?'

'I don't understand. My English not so good.'

'Neither is mine, Mrs Popescu. I was born in Hackney.'

'Mrs Popescu,' Lovejoy said, 'we are looking for your son.'

'Bogdan?'

218

'No, not Bogdan. Nicolai.'

'Nicolai is in Bucareşti now. You make trouble for him, you people.'

'I didn't make trouble for him. Did I make trouble for him, DC Lovejoy?'

'No, guv.'

'He's a good boy, my Nicolai.'

'Good boys don't do hard time for sex trafficking, Mrs Popescu.'

She waved a finger right in his face. 'Not my boy. *Au fost acele cunti polonese.*'

'What did she say, Lesley?'

'Word for word, guv, she said that it wasn't Nicolai, it was those Polish cunts.'

Charlie shook his head. 'Can't stand racism, me. Where does it all come from, all this, Lovejoy?' He turned back to the woman. 'Is it possible that your son is not in Bucharest, but has instead returned to England illegally?'

A shrug and a shake of the head.

'Where's Bogdan?'

'He is at work.'

'Where does he work then?'

'I don't know.'

'Does he live here?'

A shake of the head.

'Where can we find him?'

'I don't know.'

'Not a very close family unit, is it, Lovejoy?'

'Perhaps they just like to give each other a lot of space, guv.'

Charlie rocked back on his heels, hands in his pockets. There was a fresh packet of Pall Mall on the pantry shelf, between a tin of pickles and a jar of cherry preserve.

'You smoke, Mrs Popescu?'

She nodded and forced herself to cough.

219

'Very good, you should be on the stage. All right, thanks for your help, Mrs Popescu. We'll be off now.'

'Nicolai is in Bucareşti. I don't see my son because of you. He's a good boy.'

'We'll show ourselves out,' Charlie said.

Charlie crossed the road and headed back to the car. 'One minute, guv,' Lovejoy said, and she pulled a tin of ham out of her jacket. The label said Krakus.

'Where did you get that from then? Did you just blag that?'

'It's all right, Mrs Popescu said she doesn't eat this shit.'

She went into the Polish deli. Charlie saw her give the young girl behind the counter the tin of ham and then come out again.

'What was that all about?'

'Nothing.'

'Must have been something. She's tearing up in there.'

'You know these East Europeans. A very emotional people. Now what, guv?'

'Our job here is done, Lovejoy. Surveillance can take over from here.'

Charlie called the DCI on the phone. They waited outside the flat until the surveillance team were in position, then drove back to Essex Road. Nothing to do now but wait, drink terrible coffee, eat fast food at their desks, watch reality shows on the TV in the Incident Room.

'Like being in a war,' Charlie said to her on the way back to the nick. 'Sixty seconds of adrenalin, twenty-three hours of boredom.'

'What about the other fifty-nine minutes, guv?'

'Sleep,' Charlie said. 'You don't want to get unhealthy, innit?'

CHAPTER THIRTY-TWO

At eight o'clock that night, they all sat around the IR, feet on desks, clicking pens, a few of them making comments about what was happening on the television. The skipper had a rogan josh curry in the microwave, Rupe was eating a chicken burger and spilling salad on the keyboard. His desk was littered with take-away containers.

The DCI walked in and they all sat upright, a few of the younger lads even jumped to their feet, like they were in the army. FONC had a mobile in his hand. 'It's Martin, from Surveillance,' he said. 'You were right, they think they've seen him, Nicolai. He's at his mother's just now. They saw him go in.'

He looked at Charlie, almost like he was asking him what to do.

'So, he isn't in Bucharest, then?'

The DCI just shrugged.

'They're sure it's him?'

'Ninety per cent.'

'Let's get him then,' Dawson said.

'Wait a minute,' Charlie said. 'How did he get there?'

'On foot. Why?'

'Well, grabbing him now, what good will that do? We need the van, we need the shoes, we need evidence to tie him to the bodies. We can grab him, but we've got nothing on him, unless he talks. Why would he do that?'

'Need those London clay bricks,' Lovejoy said, bless her heart.

221

'But we've got him in sight,' the DCI said, like he was thinking aloud.

'We don't have to rush this, sir,' Charlie said. 'Let's follow him, see where else he goes.'

'What if he doesn't go anywhere, guv?' Wes said. 'What if he's staying with his muma?'

'We still haven't lost anything. If that's where he is, we can pick him up any old time. But what if he's just visiting? Let's keep our meat pies on him, see where he goes.'

'It's risky,' the DCI said.

'It's sensible,' Charlie said.

The DCI hesitated, then seemed to make up his mind. He brought the phone back to his ear, took the call off hold. 'Keep him under surveillance,' he said. 'Once he's on the move, let me know immediately.'

Charlie and Lovejoy went down to the canteen to drink rubbish coffee they didn't need and wait it out. Dawson came down with them, bought a packet of cheese and onion crisps from one of the machines. 'Just what you need, skipper,' Charlie said.

'What?'

'Shouldn't be eating those, you need to get your weight down. Look at you.'

'Can't all be lean and mean like you. Don't know how you do it.'

'I worry all the time and I don't sleep. Keeps me looking young.'

'What about you, Lovejoy?' Dawson said.

'What about me?'

'You want a crisp?'

She shook her head.

'You don't have to worry about your weight.'

'Thanks.'

'Am I being politically incorrect?'

'Didn't know they had that word in Yorkshire,' Charlie said.

222

'Two words,' Dawson said. 'Just because I'm from up north don't mean I can't count.'

'How's DS Greene?' Lovejoy asked Charlie.

'Still on stress leave,' Charlie said.

'Because of that Somali lad?'

'Think so.'

'Just shows you,' Dawson said. 'Always the hard nuts that crack first.'

'Maybe that's why all the jokes,' Charlie said.

'What were this Mrs Popescu like, then?'

'A piece of work,' Charlie said.

'Did you see the walls in her flat?' Lovejoy said. 'All those icons everywhere. It was like being in a church.'

'My old mum's place in Stratford was like that before she went into the home. Well, Catholic pictures, saints and all that, not that weird Eastern European stuff.'

'Christ Pantocrator.'

'What was that?'

'Christ Pantocrator. It means Almighty or Omnipotent. You always see him with a massive halo behind his head and pointing with two fingers in the air, like Donald Trump. The other one was the Archangel Michael. He's like the assistant commissioner in Heaven.'

'How do you know all this stuff?' Dawson said.

'My former partner was Romanian.'

Partner, Charlie thought. That was suitably non-specific. There was a beat and he knew she was waiting for him to ask her to elaborate. But it was her private life and he wasn't Jay; it had nothing to do with him. He decided not to pursue it, just to be perverse.

'So, your familiarity with the Romanian tongue has nothing to do with your time in the CID.'

'Theft crimes aren't a big thing among the Romanians. They like the flashy strong-arm stuff: sex trafficking, drugs, that sort of thing.'

'Must be a proper bugger to learn,' Dawson said.

'Romanian isn't actually a Slavic language, it's a Romance language. It comes from Vulgar Latin, so not as hard as you think.'

Just then Charlie's phone rang. 'It's Wes,' he said. 'We're wanted upstairs. Popescu is on the move.'

When they got upstairs, FONC was standing by the desk in IR1, holding the phone to his chin, a slightly panicked look on his face. Gale was watching him, arms crossed, Wes was leaning on a filing cabinet, Rupe was making tea. Could be another false alarm.

He hung up.

'Where is he?' Charlie said.

'Headed for the tube. They have a three-man team on it.'

'Better not lose him,' Gale muttered.

'They won't.'

Ten minutes later, his mobile rang again, his hand snaked out and grabbed it. The fastest DCI in the west, Charlie thought.

FONC listened, straight-faced, and said just one word: 'Wait.'

Then he hung up.

'They've followed him to a house in Willesden.'

'Is he alone?'

'There's two cars in the driveway. They're going to keep the place under surveillance, report in every thirty minutes.'

'What are you going to do?' Dawson said.

'I'm not going to wait.' He started punching numbers into his phone. 'I'm getting SCO19 and we're going in.'

'Do we have to be in such a hurry?' Charlie said.

'I don't want to lose him.'

'It's too soon,' he muttered under his breath, but it wasn't his call to make any more.

CHAPTER THIRTY-THREE

The DCI ordered two firearms teams to Essex Road for an urgent briefing. No one wanted this op to go pear-shaped, not after what happened to Osman Balewah. The SCO19 team would use Google Earth to get an accurate picture of the house and the surrounds, and the DCI would show them Popescu's booking photograph from four years before. Finally, the SCO19 Inspector would remind them yet again of the requirement under the Human Rights Act to use only appropriate force. The briefing would be tape-recorded, just in case.

No mistakes on this one.

Charlie was sent ahead with Lovejoy, with Wes and Rupe as his back-up in another car. His instructions were to wait until the firearms teams were in place, then follow them in and make the arrests.

And stay out of trouble.

It was a smart suburban semi in Willesden, lattice bay windows, two doors down from the Welsh Congregational Church. The front garden had been bricked over for extra parking and there were two imported cars parked there, a red Italian job and a black Porsche Macan. There were three wheelie bins lined up outside like soldiers on a parade ground. 'If only all pop-up brothels were as house proud,' Charlie said. Sodium streetlights threw an orange glow over the wet pavements. He pushed his fists further into the pockets of his Stone Island jacket.

The ghostly blue shadows of TV screens flickered in the

windows of the houses up and down the street. They'd soon be getting some real entertainment, he thought.

'What's a Welsh Congregational Church?' Lovejoy said.

'Do what?'

'The church over there.'

'They're non-conformists.'

'They wear odd socks and stuff?'

'I don't know, Lovejoy. They believe in God but they don't believe in the Archbishop of Canterbury.'

'Fair enough, too. I don't think he exists. If he did, I would have seen him. I've been to Canterbury lots of times.'

It started to rain.

'So what do they say about me, Lovejoy?'

'Guv?'

'The talk, you know, in the canteen. They must have told you stuff. You're the newbie, they would have warned you about not making northerner jokes to the skipper, right, and not to take Jay too seriously, what an absolute prat he is. Am I right?'

'Maybe.'

'So, what did they say about me?'

'Honest?'

'No, lie to me. Of course, honest. I've got broad shoulders.'

'They're all terrified of you.'

'Of me? Why?'

'Look in the mirror, sir. You look like a debt collector for the Albanian mafia.'

'I'm a teddy bear.'

A shrug.

Charlie listened to the sound of the rain on the car roof. Across the road, the semi had its curtains closed but the lights were all on. A bloke came out, still tucking his shirt into his trousers. Charlie listened to the traffic on his earpiece. It wasn't Popescu.

He turned on the wipers to clear away the mist of rain and they squeaked as they arced across the windscreen.

'Detective Chief Inspector Fergus O'Neal-Callaghan,' Lovejoy said.

'What about him?'

'You told me that's how he got his nickname, because of his initials.'

'Yes?'

'Only I don't think so.'

'You think your commanding officer is telling you a porky, Lovejoy?'

'I do, guv.'

'Well, I'll tell you what. You're a detective. If you find a plausible alternative explanation, you come and tell me, and if I believe it has a ring of truth to it, I shall make you my deputy SIO on the next case. How does that sound?'

'It sounds like you're hiding something.'

'Everyone's hiding something,' Charlie said. 'If they weren't, we'd be out of a job.' Charlie put a hand to his earpiece to listen.

'We going in?' Lovejoy said.

He shook his head, made a waving motion, not yet. 'Two minutes,' he said.

Lovejoy tapped her foot on the floor. 'So, how did you become a cop, guv?'

'I saw an ad in the local off-licence.'

'Seriously.'

'Why do you want to know?'

'I'm interested.'

Charlie sighed and looked out of the window. 'Rain's getting heavier.'

'Is that my answer?'

'Looks like it.'

'I heard you once played football with Prince Harry on the back lawn of Buckingham Palace.'

'How did you know about that?'

'Apparently you got legless one night and told the skipper. It was when you were still in uniform and you were doing guard duty. Is it true?'

'Hearsay. Not admissible as evidence. What else have you got on me?'

'You joined the CID in 2005 and Homicide in 2009. You've been a DI for three years. You should be a chief inspector but you keep pissing people off. Also, you don't have the right look.'

'The skipper told you all this?'

'Some of it. The rest is in your file. Well, it is if you can read between the lines.'

'And you reckon you can read between the lines?'

'Maybe.'

'What does it mean anyway, the "right look"?'

'You've got a broken nose and you dress like a drug dealer.'

He stared at her.

'Sorry. Just an observation, guv.'

There was a long silence. Charlie rubbed the condensation off the windscreen. 'You know all my deep, dark secrets, now it's your turn. Why did you join up?'

'You're going to laugh.'

'No, I won't.'

'You promise?'

'I promise.'

'I wanted to make a difference.'

Charlie laughed.

He stared out of the window. An urban fox trotted along a wall, not a care in the world. Clever animals, foxes; people took away their old habitats, so they adapted to the new ones.

'A metaphor for the modern world,' he muttered.

'What was that, guv?' Lovejoy said.

'Nothing.'

Within a quarter-mile radius of where they were sitting, he thought, there were seven police cars, two police vans and a London ambulance, all parked, waiting, with their lights off. Four of the cars were ARVs, black Beemers with nine firearms officers waiting in the dark, their Heckler & Kochs on their knees and Glocks strapped to their thighs.

'The people round here would shit themselves if they knew,' Lovejoy said, reading his mind. 'We've got enough firepower in this street to start a small war.'

'Don't remind me,' he said. 'It makes me nervous.'

There they were. The first stick of four men made their way up the path. They were all in black, visors down on their helmets, and armed with Heckler & Koch assault rifles, the absolute business. They had on goggles and body armour, were walking in a close-linked single file. The two rear officers trained a rifle and a pistol at the upstairs window. Desperate suspects had been known to hurl themselves out to avoid getting caught.

The stick, led by an SFO holding a bulletproof shield, pressed themselves against the wall. So far, they had maintained complete silence. Suddenly all hell broke loose as two of the SCO19 team rushed forward with an enforcer and beat in the front door.

'That's us, then,' Charlie said and he got out of the car.

It didn't look much like a brothel, but he supposed that was the point. There was a living room with a bay window, a cheap IKEA sofa with about four mobile phones lying on the cushions, an entertainment system and a *Sound of Music* DVD lying on the carpet next to some cheap pink nylon underwear.

'Armed police. Everyone on the floor! Let's see your hands!'

He could hear arrests being made all over the house, one of the search teams thumping up the stairs. Two SFOs were in the hallway, one had his knee in the back of a man with a shaved head and a Fred Perry shirt. His partner had the bloke's arms behind his back and was slapping on a pair of speed cuffs.

Charlie bent over him. He wasn't the one they were looking for. 'Where's Popescu?'

The man shouted at him in what could have been Romanian.

Charlie looked around and saw Lovejoy standing by the door. 'What did he say?'

'He said your mother has unnatural relations with goats.'

'Tell him not to give away family secrets,' Charlie said, and left him to the two SFOs and headed down the hall.

The girls were being herded into the kitchen. Some of them were just in their underwear. It must have been a shock; one of the poor girls just stood there shaking, with pee running down her legs. She didn't look as if she was more than ten. There was a heavily tattooed blonde with them. He didn't like the look of her.

'Where's Popescu?'

She shrugged and blew a smoke ring at him. He grabbed the cigarette out of her hand and dropped it on the carpet and ground it in with his heel. That was petulant, he thought. Calm the fuck down, Charlie boy.

A punter with a gut like a fat hairy saddlebag staggered out of a downstairs bedroom in a pair of very brief lilac underpants. 'OK, OK,' he was yelling. 'No problem.' In moments, he was flat on his face with his arms cuffed behind him.

The armed containment and call-out was under way, a careful search of the place in case anyone was hiding in a cupboard. A handler came bundling in with a police dog, searching under beds, throwing open cupboard doors. Finally, they ripped open a kitchen cupboard, there was a bloke lying in the foetal position, wearing a Superman t-shirt. He was dragged out and cuffed.

'Is this the one?' an SFO said to Charlie.

He bent down and peered at his face. Similar, but he couldn't be sure. 'Are you Nicolai Popescu?' Charlie said.

'Fuck you,' the man said. He had a heavy Eastern European accent. Never sounded nice when people swore at you with an accent, Charlie thought.

'You know what, guv?'

He looked up, it was Lovejoy. 'What?'

'I don't think that's Nicolai. I think that's Bogdan.'

'Close enough is good enough,' he said, but privately he was fuming. This wet wipe wasn't their target. Charlie waited twenty minutes for the SCO19 team to finish the search, still hoping they would find Nicolai hiding upstairs, but they came up empty.

Charlie got back in the Sierra, and slammed the door. He reached into his pocket and turned on his Nokia. As an afterthought he reached into the other pocket and turned on his iPhone as well. He stared at the screen and swore under his breath. Five messages, all from Arlington Mansions.

'How did he get away, guv?'

'I don't think he was there.'

'Surveillance seemed pretty sure.'

'I'll bet they're sure now. They want it to look like SCO19 screwed up and not them.'

His phone went off, 'The Ride of the Valkyries'. Charlie sighed. 'Charlie George.' He listened for a few moments. 'Did you try Ben? Right. Can I call you back?' A pause, then he said: 'I'll call you back. Thanks.' He hung up.

'Everything all right, guv?'

'Telemarketing,' he said.

'You call telemarketing back?'

He looked out of the window, tapping his foot very fast on the floor. There were beacons flashing up and down the street, the most action Willesden had seen for a while, Charlie thought.

He clocked the DCI, he was talking to a bloke in a hoodie and trainers who was leaning against one of the patrol cars, smoking a cigarette. At first, he wondered how the public had found a way through the cordon, then he realised it was Martin Amery, the head of the surveillance team. When the DCI had finished, he turned away and came over to Charlie.

'No Popescu,' he said.

'The surveillance team said he was here.'

231

'We should have nabbed him when he was at his mother's.'

'Perhaps that wasn't him. It might have been that other geezer, Bogdan. They're brothers, they look alike.'

'No, he must have slipped out the back just before SCO19 went in. We missed our chance. Why do I listen to you, Charlie?'

'Are you blaming me, sir?'

'Don't worry, I'll go easy on you in my report.'

He walked off.

After he'd left, Martin wandered over. 'Hello, Charlie. You look pissed off. What's the matter, old son?'

'Our suspect wasn't on the premises.'

'No. Bad luck, that.'

'Are you sure it was him you clocked at the flat in Harrow?'

'It was dark, Charlie. We saw a man matching the description we were given. We tracked him to this house. But I couldn't give you a gold-plated promise it was the bloke in the photograph.'

'Fuck.'

'Sorry, mate. This is not an exact science. Wish it was. There were men coming and going all night. I told your DCI that. We couldn't follow them all, I don't have enough soldiers. None of them looked like Popescu, all I can say.'

'Thanks, Martin.'

Charlie wanted a drag of Martin's cigarette but talked himself out of it. He'd been off them for nine months – well, except for that one night outside his flat. Tonight's little fiasco was bad enough without getting addicted to nicotine again.

The only thing they could do now was sweat Popescu's brother, get him to tell them where he was. But something nagged at him. There were such things as coincidences, and perhaps the tenuous connection between Father O'Meara and PC Morton was one of them.

He just hoped they weren't going to waste all their resources chasing this scrote, and then wake up in the morning and find another body hung up on a cross somewhere. You shouldn't rely too much on intuition in this game, how many times had he told the young guns that? But his own gut was working overtime on this one.

You've got it wrong, Charlie boy, it was saying. You've got this seriously wrong.

CHAPTER THIRTY-FOUR

The interview room was airless and windowless. It always made Charlie feel claustrophobic. There were four hard plastic moulded chairs and a black box recording machine that had been doing service since the 1980s.

The duty solicitor was the only new addition; she looked as if she had come fresh from the day spa, fresh pink gloss on her lips, her hair shining. Her leather briefcase was propped against the leg of the chair. It looked new, probably a Christmas present.

She had a yellow legal pad on her lap and was tapping her Parker on the edge of the desk either to signal impatience or to annoy him. She obviously didn't know him very well.

She sighed and looked around the room, to signal her boredom. Her foot tapped the air.

'Manolo Blahnik's?' Charlie said.

'Perhaps.'

'Well they are, or they aren't.'

'I didn't look. I have so many shoes.'

'Don't like that colour red,' Charlie said. He screwed up his nose. 'Makes you look . . .'

She stopped tapping her foot. 'Makes me look what?'

'Like you've got red shoes.'

'What are mine?' Bogdan said, beside her, joining in the game.

'Adidas, son. They look brilliant with those track pants and the Superman t-shirt. You're a classy guy.'

Bogdan nodded, like he agreed.

Charlie smiled at the solicitor.

A duty officer came in with four coffees. Charlie picked up the plastic cup, with its scum of instant nodules floating on top. He sniffed. 'Real Colombian coffee,' he said.

'Can we get on,' the solicitor snapped.

There was a pile of fresh tapes on the table, and a box of tissues, as well as some torn tape wrapper and a screwed-up piece of paper from the last interview. Charlie had the duty sergeant tidy them away. He saw Bogdan staring at the box of tissues.

'What they for?'

'They're for when you start crying, my old son. You look to me like you could tear up any minute.'

'You're a real fucking joker, yes?'

'Oh, bundle of laughs, me. Isn't that right?' he said to the duty solicitor.

He unsealed the tapes and slotted them into the machine. He pressed record. He waited for the buzzing to stop. 'We are in Interview Room Two, Essex Road Police Station. My name is DI Charles George. Also present is . . .'

He looked at Lovejoy. 'DC Lesley Lovejoy.'

'Gabriella Crosse-Leavesley, solicitor.'

Charlie took a moment. That was some handle. He looked at Bogdan.

Silence.

'Say your name aloud, please sir.'

Sounding bored: 'Bogdan Popescu.'

'Thank you. Bogdan Popescu, you have been arrested on suspicion of conspiracy to traffic and two counts of conspiracy to control prostitution under the Modern Slavery Act of 2015. You do not have to say anything but it may harm your defence if you do not mention when questioned something which you later rely on in court. Anything you do say may be given in evidence. Do you understand the caution?'

A whispered conversation with his solicitor.

'My client would like a translator,' she said.

Charlie stared at the relay screen. Bogdan was still slouched in his chair in the interview room, dead-eyed, his feet pushed out in front of him and crossed at the ankles. The DCI walked in. 'What's the hold-up?' he said.

'He's asked for a translator. Which is bollocks, sir, he speaks English better than what I do.'

'Everyone speaks English better than you, Charlie. But it's his legal right.'

'He's stalling.'

'Of course he is.' He stared at the monitor; Bogdan was yawning, tapping out a rhythm on the interview table with his fingers. 'Can't imagine it, can you?' he said. 'Being beaten and forced to have sex half a dozen times a day.'

'Doesn't sound unlike my mother's life to be honest, sir.'

What was that look the DCI gave him? Was he repelled, or did he think he was making it up, just for the sake of it? A lot of people did.

Charlie heard a commotion in the corridor, four blokes in suits out there, carrying briefcases and looking important.

'Who are those other blokes?'

'They're from the Modern Slavery and Kidnap Unit. This is their case now, I'm afraid.'

'Who called them in?'

'It's protocol, Charlie.'

'But we need Bogdan to tell us where his brother is.'

'Nothing I can do. My hands are tied. SCD9 will take over from here. They say this is a huge bust we've stumbled on. Each of the phones we recovered had the details of the victim's working name and brothel location taped to them. They're organising more raids in Barnet, Camden, Haringey, Tower Hamlets and Islington on the strength of this.'

'Doesn't help us though, does it?'

'One of them must know where Nicolai is.'

'Perhaps he really is back in Bucharest, sir. We have no proof he's in London.'

'No, has to be him. Don't worry, Bogdan will deal eventually. Once he realises how much time he has coming, and the CPS offer him a way out, he'll take it.'

'I hope so, sir.'

Charlie watched the ghostly images on the screen. Bogdan yawned and put his hands behind his head. Not a care in the world.

'What about Mrs Popescu?' Charlie said.

'Wes and Rupinder are bringing her in now.'

'Not much joy there, she's hard as a frozen chicken.'

The DCI shrugged. 'I still say we should have picked him up at her place when we had the chance. Oh well, never mind,' he said, but by his tone, Charlie knew he didn't mean it.

CHAPTER THIRTY-FIVE

Salvador Cruz opened a bottle of 2012 Côte Rôtie and poured two fingers into a yellow-tinted Versace Arabesque wine glass. He took a moment to savour the aroma; spice and blackberries. He paused in front of *God the Father*, a reproduction of the oil by Cima da Conegliano he had seen once in the Courtauld Institute Gallery. He smiled.

A beautiful space. The moon was framed by the window high in the converted chancel and a single spotlight illuminated the shining black surface of a polished ebony Steinway. He remembered how she used to play.

She had loved music. She was the one who had introduced him to the piece playing now, on the wireless Bose speakers hidden in the barrel ceiling; Tartini's *Violin Sonata in G Minor*, the 'Devil's Trill'. He rocked his head gently to the opening movement, a languid lullaby, gentle violin lines over a harpsichord accompaniment, hinting at while disguising the darker passages to come. She had explained to him how challenging the piece was, the frequent double-stops requiring the violinist to play simultaneously on two adjacent strings.

Such art, such finesse, such cleverness, she had said. Such beautiful and skilled hands. Like yours, my darling.

He turned away, walked along the converted nave, admired the family portrait that hung on the wall above the white leather sofa, facing the door. It had been positioned that way so it would be the first thing someone saw when they walked in.

How perfectly the photographer had captured the moment; Magdalena, with her perfect smile, had she ever looked more beautiful? That little mischief, Mateus, and Arcanjo, so tiny and so precious he could just pick her out of the photograph and eat her. He smiled when he thought about the smell of her, the way her hair tickled his nose when he hugged her.

They had worn traditional costume for the occasion, Magdalena in an emerald-green *nauvari*, studded with rubies; Mateus, little showman that he was, had on a white shirt with a bow tie and braces, and black western-style trousers; Arcanjo looked just adorable in her *pano bhaju* they had had made specially for the portrait.

He stepped closer, reached out a hand to touch their faces.

The violin began a crisp bravura movement, the piece charging forward with faster and more intricate variants of the earlier melodies. He closed his eyes, let his soul be caught and enraptured. His eyes blinked open again and he dashed the contents of his glass into their smiling faces.

He hurled the glass against the wall, the crystal shattered on the brick, and he howled, tore the photograph from the wall and held it high over his head before smashing it on the floor, again and again, until the wood splintered, and glass lay in beaded shards. He stamped on it in rage, then tore it from its frame and shredded it between his fingers.

He stopped to get his breath.

When he saw what he had done, he went to the laundry to fetch a dustpan and brush, and the Dyson vacuum cleaner. It took him almost half an hour to tidy away the mess. He carried the glass and the splintered frame out to the rubbish bin around the side of the house.

When that was done he went down the steps to the basement, unlocked the heavy wooden door at the bottom and went into the wine cellar. It was humid here, and cool; it had once been a crypt, the smell of the long dead still hanging in the air after all these years. But perfect conditions for the three thousand bottles of wine he owned.

There were portraits stacked against the racks, all identical to the one that he had just destroyed. He chose one. For a moment his eye went to the chains lying in the shadows at the end of the racks, ready for the next martyr. Are you watching me, God the Father? I hope you're enjoying this.

I am.

He went back upstairs, hung the portrait on the wall and stood back to admire it. Perfect.

Tartini's sonata reached its climax, all double-stops, trills and runs, the pitch alternating from high to low and back again. The story went that the composer had dreamed the piece, that the devil himself had appeared to him, playing it on an infernal violin. Cruz closed his eyes and pretended he was conducting Lucifer through the final movement. Why let God have all the great works?

He doesn't appreciate them. Not the way we do.

The SCD9 inspector put his elbows on the desk, looking faintly bored, and laid it all out for him.

'The thing is, Bogdan, we found a considerable sum of cash in the safe, along with thirteen passports, belonging to the young girls you were keeping in the house.'

The translator told Bogdan what he had said. There was a whispered conversation between them. Finally: 'He said he put them in the safe so they didn't lose them. He said girls like that can be careless.'

'One of them, we are told, has the mental age of a ten-year-old. Another actually *is* ten.'

The translator nodded and turned to Bogdan, but something had stirred him up, and he waved him aside. 'I don't know what you're talking. Look at this girls. Health good, skin good, body good, good condition, no hurting. They want a nice life here, we have to protect them.'

'Protect them.'

He spread out his hands on the table. He was the victim here, just trying to help them make an honest buck. 'Of course, protect. Is dangerous business.'

'One of the girls says that you promised to get her a job as a housekeeper. When she arrived in London you beat her, took away her passport and kept her imprisoned in the house. She said she was forced to have sex with strangers, sometimes ten men in a day, and that you starved her. She even had to beg for a glass of water.'

'Which girl says this?'

He ignored him. 'Another of the girls claimed you lured her to your apartment in Bucharest and then kidnapped her and drove her here to London against her will and forced her to work as a prostitute.'

'She is lying.'

'We found on the premises more than forty phones and half a dozen laptops that you and your associates have been using to organise bookings for the girls. Believe me, Bogdan, you are looking at serious time here.'

Bogdan had a quick, whispered conversation with the solicitor. He was finally starting to look nervous.

'You could make things a lot easier for yourself by helping us.'

'My English not good. I don't understand.'

The inspector smiled and turned to the translator and repeated what he had just said. He's just stalling for time now, Charlie thought.

'Mr Popescu asks, in what way might he assist you?'

'First, by telling us where we can find his brother, Nicolai.'

Charlie and the DCI leaned in to the screen, held their breath, willing him to say what they wanted to hear. Charlie could almost see Bogdan's thoughts written on his face. For just a moment he thought he was going to crack.

Then his eyes went flat again. He said something to the translator.

'He doesn't know where his brother is. Have you tried asking around in Bucharest?'

CHAPTER THIRTY-SIX

It was midnight at Arlington Mansions, the frost in the car park glinting in the moonlight. The whole place was in darkness, stark against cold stars. Ben called this place the Limbo Zone, the place you came when you weren't in one place or the other. Charlie's shoes crunched on the salt on the front step, broken hip weather this. He punched in the entry code on the keypad beside the front door and made his way to the reception; no one there so he pressed the buzzer. A pretty nurse came out, he didn't recognise this one, she must be new.

'Here to see my mum,' Charlie said. 'Mrs George, room 203. I got a phone call earlier.'

The girl logged in to the computer on the desk, without looking at him. 'That was at eight o'clock.'

'I was working.'

A stiff smile. 'She's all settled now. Her son came in.'

'I'm her son.'

'Benedict?'

'Has Ben been here?'

'We called him when we couldn't get hold of you and he came right over. Lovely young man.'

Charlie knew what she was thinking, and it was so bloody unfair he started to protest but thought better of it. 'Well, he has weekends off,' was all he said. 'Mind if I put my head in the door?'

She shrugged and gave him a look: too little too late. But he headed down the corridor anyway.

A while since he had been in her room, he usually met her in the lounge or in the dining room. She had been busy, or someone had, and it occurred to him that Michael might have been down from Liverpool to see her without telling them. It looked like a church museum in here; there were framed pictures of the saints all round the walls, some of them a little more gruesome than he thought was right for an old lady to be looking at first thing in the morning and last thing at night.

She looked ancient fast asleep with her teeth out. Her hair was getting very thin now, though she still insisted on having it set every week. It wasn't the way he remembered her, of course. In his mind she was still the feisty livewire with the curly red hair and stout shoes who had dragged him up, him and his brothers, with no help from her husband, or from anyone really.

Whenever anything went wrong for him, he would still hear her voice in his head: 'I didn't raise the none of you to be quitters!' There was no crying allowed when he was a kid, not for them or for Jules; even when he broke his ankle coming off his bike she'd yelled at him for making a fuss and carried him inside so he didn't embarrass her with his caterwauling, as she called it. The only time he ever saw her cry herself was at his brother's funeral.

He stroked her cheek and kissed her on the forehead. His eye caught the photograph beside her bed. Now why did she still have that bastard's photograph there? He was useless as a father and worse as a husband and still she had him in pride of place. No accounting for it, was there?

CHAPTER THIRTY-SEVEN

Winter dragged itself through January, its collar up, bent into the wind, snow leaking into Charlie's boots. He saw Geri whenever she could get away, but for some reason he didn't tell Ben about it. Arsenal lost three games and drew one, and dropped out of the top four, in keeping with club tradition.

He took down the handful of Christmas cards on the mantle under his framed and signed Arsenal shirt, commemorating the Invincibles of 2003. They didn't find Nicolai Popescu, though their latest intelligence suggested he was back in Romania. His brother and the two other men they arrested inside the pop-up brothel were remanded for trial at the Old Bailey on sex trafficking charges.

He worked another duty roster, closing out two homicides in the same week. One was a woman found stabbed in her home in Muswell Hill, it turned out to be a routine domestic and he had her husband banged up inside twenty-four hours.

A few days later a man died after receiving a gunshot wound on a street corner in Enfield on a Wednesday night. That case took them a little longer, but inside forty-eight hours he had a main suspect and, once they had the forensics results, he had enough to charge him and hand the case to the CPS. Hollywood wasn't going to make a movie out of either case, but it did his stocks inside the MIT no harm, and boosted his enthusiasm and confidence again after the debacle around the O'Meara and Morton homicides.

Those cases still remained open.

Rom had to go back into hospital for more tests. Greene came back to work, but there was something different about him. He didn't seem as full of himself. Strange, Charlie thought, what one death can do to someone, even after he had seen so many in his career. He had made jokes about the poor bastard they had found tortured to death in Barrow Fields, but seeing a teenager get hit by a bus had blown him out of the water. There had been no charges laid by Internal Affairs, and not even the DCI really blamed him for that one.

People. Go figure.

They were still looking for Nicolai Popescu. The DCI, with the approval of the chief super and the assistant commissioner, had initiated a massive manhunt, using Interpol and the Romanian police. Catlin had leaned on all of her contacts inside the media to keep the story in the spotlight and Romanian community leaders in London had helped them in the search through social media. But wherever he was, the bastard had so far managed to evade them.

Before he knew it, it was February.

'So, we've found him,' the DCI said. 'Popescu.'

They were in his corner office on the fourth floor. FONC didn't look like he thought this was good news; rather, he had the look of a bloke who had just totalled his car and then discovered his insurance had lapsed.

'Where did we find him?' Charlie said.

'Bucharest. He was arrested last night.'

'Great. Can we get him extradited?'

A shake of the head. 'Unfortunately, no. We would need a European Arrest Warrant and the CPS has advised me that to do that we would need sufficient evidence to charge him. We don't have that.'

'So, what happens now?'

'It's not all bad news, I suppose. He was arrested by the Romanian police on a separate offence.'

'For doing what?'

'He raped a fifteen-year-old girl.'

'Lovely. What's that worth over there?'

'If he's found guilty? Eight to ten years.'

'And so he's off the hook?'

'If that's the way you want to look at it. Naturally, we will liaise with the Romanians and the National Crime Agency to try and secure his return to the UK when he's released, but that is going to be difficult.'

'So that's it then, sir?'

'He remains the prime suspect in the case. We have no other leads, do we?'

'No.'

'I will be flying over there in the next couple of days to talk to my counterpart in Bucharest and interview Popescu. I'm not optimistic about the outcome.'

No, Charlie thought, but I've heard Bucharest is a nice city and I'm sure you'll have a good time.

'I appreciate eight years is a reasonable amount of stir, but he could still walk out of Bucharest Scrubs or wherever he goes and come back here and start up again.'

'We'll be out of the EU by then. It will be easier to stop criminals from outside the UK coming here.'

'Yeah that'll do it, sir. After Brexit we'll fix illegal immigration straight away. Boris and Nigel said so and they'd never lie about anything.'

'Let's not get into the politics of it. I'm just saying we have gone as far as we can with Operation Galilee. I'll not authorise any more hours spent on it unless new evidence comes to light. All right, Charlie?'

'All right,' he said. So that was that, then. After everything that had happened, it seemed like such an anti-climax.

He went back downstairs in the lift. Never mind, he had a stack of paperwork to finish for his two latest homicides before he went home.

* * *

It was after eight when he finished up. He still had to collate witness statements and forensics reports for the CPS for the second of the two homicides, but they wouldn't need those until Monday. He decided to come in early Saturday morning, finish them off then.

As he was locking up, he saw Lovejoy, still at her desk. Always the last one to leave, he'd noticed.

'Go home,' he said to her. 'You don't get any brownie points for this.'

'Still a lot to learn, guv.'

'You must have a home to go to.'

She gave him the sort of smile that could mean anything.

'Got plans for your weekend?'

'Not much. What about you, guv?'

'Not really. Taking tomorrow off instead.'

'You? I thought you were nailed to the floor.'

'Going to Brighton.'

'Literally or metaphorically?'

'Don't use long words like that in here. And yes, literally. Want to see my sister and her kid without Wayne Rooney getting in the way.'

'Bring us back a stick of rock.'

'What century are you living in, Lovejoy? Only thing people come back with after a weekend in Brighton is a packet of organic mung beans and a tattoo of George Michael.'

'I'd heard you had a girlfriend down there.'

'Only girls have girlfriends who live in Brighton. They have Doc Martens and orange hair.' He realised he probably shouldn't have said that; it sounded homophobic and the jury was still out on just how offended she was likely to be.

'Well. Have a good time.'

'Yeah, you too. Goodnight.' He thought she was looking at him funny. For a minute he swore she was thinking what he was thinking, but she couldn't be. Not with that haircut.

* * *

Charlie decided not to drive down to Brighton, there would be nowhere to park anyway. He had a leisurely breakfast at a local greasy spoon, then got the tube to Embankment and the District and Circle to Victoria. He tried not to look as he put his card in the machine for a return ticket to Brighton on Southern Rail. Christ, he could get a new pair of calf-leather Italian shoes for that.

On the way down, he thought about Father Andrew O'Meara and PC Stephen Morton. It ate at him, not getting a result on either of those. He always felt like he'd done a public service when he actually had some low-life banged up, even though some of the scrotes he caught never did enough time, his opinion. But at least there was some semblance of justice done. It could never give Morton's wife and family back their husband and their father, but they would at least feel like whoever did it had paid in some way.

He stared out of the window, over the rooftops of Croydon, the view no cure for sour thoughts. His spirits only started to lift when the train sped through the Surrey Hills and into the Green Belt.

You did your best, he told himself. You can't work miracles.

He got out at Brighton, greeted by the unique sights and sounds of the English seaside; the screech of seagulls and the sight of someone's half-digested pizza from the night before splattered all over the pavement outside the exit.

Tel and Jules lived about a ten-minute walk from the station. Someone who was just leaving held the door open for him when he arrived; Charlie thought it made the security system a bit pointless, but he nodded and smiled anyway, and went through.

Jules and Terry lived on the first floor. He could hear them screaming at each other through the front door. He gave a loud knock and waited.

Jules threw open the door and the first thing he did was

check her face for bruises. She seemed more embarrassed than beaten, which was something. 'I forgot you were coming,' she mumbled and led him through to the kitchen. Tel was leaning against one of the granite worktops, all gnarly-looking in a wife-beater and bling. He flushed when he saw Charlie.

'Hello Tel. Thought you'd be at work.'

'Got the day off.'

Code, Charlie thought, for I got sacked again for being late.

'I'll see you later,' Tel said. 'I was just on me way out.'

'I hear there's a new gay bar on the corner.'

He shoved past and left. Charlie tried to stay benevolent, kept his hands firmly in his pockets.

'Was that a Burberry baseball cap he was wearing?' Charlie said, after the door slammed shut behind him.

'He's scared of you.'

'Good. What were you fighting about?'

'The usual shit.'

'Jules, tell me honestly, why did you marry that oxygen-thieving Asbo?'

'Don't call him that. You don't know him like I do.'

'That's what they all say.'

'What who say?'

'Beaten wives. I come across quite a few in my line of work, unfortunately.'

'I'm not an abused wife.'

'That's what they all say, as well.'

'For God's sake,' she said and stormed out of the room.

Charlie winced. Well, that clearly wasn't the right thing to say. Why couldn't he keep his stupid mouth shut? It never did any good.

He followed her into the living room. There was a plasma television big enough for a Multiplex, a mirror that looked like it had been blagged from a French chateau, and a large white moulded cat. Jules fiddled with a packet of cigarettes, lit up.

'Thought you'd given up.'

250

'I had.'

'Sorry if I upset you.'

She blew out a long, blue stream of smoke, and gave him her Look.

'How is he?' Charlie said. 'Rom?'

'All right. Kept him home from school last week, all the kids have got colds, I don't want him getting sick again.'

'How many weeks of school has he missed this year?'

'Better off at home than in hospital.'

'I didn't mean that.'

She chewed on a hangnail. 'They've got these new drugs they're giving him, trying to build up his immune system.'

'More drugs.'

'They keep him alive.'

'Poor little bugger.'

'Yeah, but don't you say that around him. I don't want him growing up feeling sorry for himself. He has to get on with things.'

'Where is he?'

'In his room, like always, on the computer. Don't know what we'd do without Game Boy.'

'Read?'

'Fuck off, Charlie.'

'Must be so hard for him. When I was his age, I was never home, I was always outside getting into trouble.'

'Any age you were out getting into trouble. Why don't you go in and say hello? He loves it when you come down.'

Charlie stopped outside Rom's door. There was some yellow police tape he had given him sticky-taped to the handle. He hesitated, then went back into the living room.

'Sorry, Jules. Didn't mean to piss you off.'

'Doesn't matter, Charlie.'

'Been a bit stressed.'

'Work?'

He shrugged.

'What's been happening?'

'Closed out two cases this month.'

'That's good, then.'

'Needed a bit of a boost.'

'You ever catch the bloke who did for that copper in Hampstead?'

He shook his head. 'A one in five.'

'One in five what?'

'One in every five murders in Britain doesn't lead to a conviction. Morton will go the way of Jill Dando and all the other high-profile murders, I suppose. We think we know who did it but he's banged up overseas for something else.'

'Not like you to let the job get to you.'

Another Look. Ben's been talking to her, Charlie thought. Here I am telling Jules to pull her personal life together and I'm not so much better myself. But he didn't want to talk about that right now. 'I'll go and see Rom.'

'Are you staying for lunch?'

'Will Tel be joining us?'

'I doubt it.'

'In that case, why not?'

It took him a moment to get used to the dark. Rom had all the curtains drawn, a lumen of ghost-green flickering from the monitor on the desk in the corner. The idiot trill of the VGM repeated itself in an endless loop. Rom was sitting on a chair in the corner in a tracksuit and beanie, bent over his PlayStation.

'Don't you come out and say hello to your Uncle Charlie?'

'Hello, Uncle Charlie.'

'No good saying it now, is it? What have you got all the curtains drawn for, then?'

'I can't see the screen, can I?'

'You don't want to sit here in the dark though, do you? Not enough hours in the day as it is. Not living in the North Pole.'

He drew the curtains so there was a bit of a gap. The room was a mess, the bed unmade, a cereal bowl with Weetabix cemented hard to the rim, video game covers scattered across the floor. There was an inflatable zebra head on the wall. 'Who got you that?'

'Uncle Ben.'

'What for?'

'He said it's cool.'

'You don't want to listen to your Uncle Ben, he's mad, he is.'

Rom looked pale, thinner than he was when he'd last seen him at Christmas. Jules was right, no point letting him feel sorry for himself, but the kid had a raw deal any way you looked at it. Why was it some kids never got sick, went around stealing bikes and scrawling graffiti on trains, and good kids like Rom spent half their lives in hospitals? Life made no kind of sense.

There was a huge unfinished Lego man sitting on a chest of drawers. It was made of red, white and blue bricks. 'What's this, then?' Charlie said.

'It was going to be Darth Vader.'

'Darth Vader's black.'

'I don't have black.'

'He looks like my guv'nor, he's got Lego feet like that. So, what are you playing, then?'

'Minecraft.'

'Don't you want to play FIFA?'

'Do you want to play?'

'Course. Long as I can be the Arsenal.'

'You were them last time,' Rom said and hunted for his FIFA pack among the pile of games on the desk. 'You can be Tottenham, if you like.'

'I'd rather jump head first into a bath full of your farts,' Charlie said, and that made Rom giggle.

'You can be Real Madrid, then.'

'Arsenal don't have a chance against Real Madrid.' Charlie

found a chair under a pile of clothes and rolled it over to the desk next to Rom.

'I've got seventy-seven million to spend on transfers.'

'You'll need about a billion to make any difference at Arsenal.'

'I want to get Lewandowski but I'll have to sell first. Or I could get Dybala for fifty and then play Sánchez on the left.'

'I'd do something about the defence first.'

'I've got the big fucking German.'

'Watch your language. You can't go round using that word.'

'That's what everyone was singing the day you took me to see them play. "We got a big fucking German!"'

'Just because they sing it at the football doesn't mean you can say it at home.'

'My dad does. He says "fucking" all the time.'

'Yeah well, you don't want to do everything he does.'

'You don't like my dad, do you?'

Charlie pretended to concentrate on the screen. 'You reckon I should play Benzema up front or Morata?'

'Morata's at Chelsea now, this is the old version. You can play Benzema, you'll probably beat me anyway. I'm crap at this.'

'Don't say "crap" either. And why are you no good at this game? I thought you had plenty of time to practise.'

'I've got no one to play with.'

'You can play against the computer.'

'It's not the same, is it? You've got to play against *someone* or there isn't any game. Innit?'

Charlie thought about that on the way home on the train that night. *You've got to play against someone or there isn't any game.* He wondered if what happened to the priest and that copper was all part of a game.

If it was, and if it was that personal, what was the game, and what were the rules?

CHAPTER THIRTY-EIGHT

A rough night, a cutting wind straight from the Arctic sending crisp packets and empty plastic bags flying into the air along the High Street. 'About time you were away home,' Agatha said to Jackson.

Jackson said he'd walk her home but she said, away with you, it's just down the street there and if you don't hurry, you'll miss your bus.

'My mother, she will kill me if she finds out I left you here.'

'She may be your mother, but nuns outrank mothers, lad, so that overrides anything she says. I'm fine, it's just down there. Look, I can see your bus coming. Now run along, I'll not have you walking home on my account.'

Jackson hesitated, then ran back towards the High Street, his dreadlocks bouncing in his Rasta snood. Agatha heard the rattle of the last train on the other side of the station, looked at her watch, she had stayed out longer than she intended. No one out in this part of London so late, except those with no home to go to and mad nuns like me.

Jackson was right, it wasn't safe, not even with the Almighty looking out for her.

Still, she was only two minutes from the convent house.

She was hurrying past the Boots chemist when she heard groaning, saw a shadow in the doorway. She knew she should ignore it, but she couldn't help herself. She took out the little plastic torch she kept in her pocket and shone it on the bundle of cardboard and blankets and empty Coke bottles.

'Oh, good Lord, it's you. I thought we'd seen the last of you, you scoundrel.'

'Lord save us and if it's not the angel of mercy with a moustache.'

She bent down, winced at the metallic reek of super-strength lager. 'What have you been doing to yourself? You stink to high heaven.'

'I got into a little fight.'

'A little fight.' She shone the torch on his face. 'May the saints preserve us. Someone gave you a right hiding. Who did it?'

'Just some young lads. They were out for a bit of fun.'

She fished in her pocket for her first-aid kit, took out her saline and squirted it on to the cuts, cleaned them up best she could with a bit of gauze and antiseptic. 'Where did this happen?'

'Down outside the Job Centre.'

'Now didn't I get you a place at the hostel, Mick?'

'I didn't like it there. They yell at you if you don't do things right and some of the others that stay there, they're not right in the head.'

'You won't be right in the head if you take many more beatings like this.' He squealed and wriggled. 'Still now, it's just a bit of Betadine, you don't want to get these cuts infected. They really did a job on you.'

'I'll be all right. I'll just lie here nice and quiet and sleep it off. It doesn't hurt none.'

'It doesn't hurt because you're soused.'

She put a wound dressing over the worst of the cuts and taped it all up with Micropore and told him to come by the church in the morning and get it looked at it in the daylight. 'You're a wonder is what you are,' Mick said.

'Just stay out of trouble. I wish I had a bed for you on a night like this.'

'I've seen worse than this, sister. You don't have some small change, do you?'

'What would you be wanting with that? The off-licence is closed.'

'Is it that late?'

'Just make sure you come and see me in the morning,' she said.

She was almost home when she heard what sounded like someone crying. An inhuman sound it was, and it sent a shiver right through her. It was coming from the shadows across the street. She took a few steps closer, there was someone just down the lane at the side of the convent house.

'Are you all right there?' she said.

Yes, she could see them now, some poor soul all wrapped up in their sleeping bag, on their side, their knees drawn up to their chest, facing the wall. She went over and crouched down. God in heaven whoever it was, they smelled really bad, they were filthy and doused in drink. She took out her torch.

'My name's Sister Agatha, I'm from the convent here. Can I help you now?'

Still crying, they were. She put a hand on the poor soul's shoulder, and felt fingers grip her wrist tight and they twisted around, moved so fast she couldn't even see their face, she felt something sharp go into her leg, just above her knee. Something hit her hard in the chest, a clenched fist perhaps, it knocked her backwards, and then whoever it was ran off, down the lane.

She gave a little cry and scrambled backwards against the wall. 'Oh my Lord, oh my Lord,' she said. She was too shocked to do anything for the moment. Her heart felt like it was going to barrel out right through her ribs. She pursed her lips to try and slow her breathing, shone the torch on her leg. What was it they'd done, had they tried to stab her?

Well, there was no blood. She seemed all right. Perhaps it was a needle then, but that was hardly better.

She managed to get herself to her feet, her knees still

shaking. She would get back to the convent and see about the wound there, wash it with disinfectant, then take herself off to the hospital.

She started to walk, staggered, reached out for the wall for support. She was feeling quite light-headed now, quite strange. There was a gargoyle staring at her from the roof of a nearby building. It craned its neck at her; it had a beak like a vulture and piercing red eyes. Wait, no, what was she thinking? There were no monsters in London. It was just a satellite dish.

She shook her head, tried to clear it. Feeling very strange indeed, now. Her body felt numb, it occurred to her there might have been drugs in the needle. She tried to think how long they might have been in her system, but now she couldn't remember quite where she was or how long ago the incident with the man in the doorway had happened. It was as if she was watching herself from the roof, bouncing against one wall, then the other, before she stumbled and dropped to one knee.

She saw him then, he was coming back, he had something with him, what was it in his hand, ropes or ties of some sort. He wasn't crying now, he was calling out to her. What was it he was saying? He called her Saint Agatha.

She tried to get up, get away from him, but she couldn't move her legs, and then he was standing over her and she thought he must be Jesus and she looked up and smiled. Such a beatific smile he had, so much compassion in it. She must be dead and with the angels, she thought. The Lord has come to take me home.

Even through the haze of the half-dozen Tetley Rhinos that he'd drunk earlier that evening, Mick wasn't so out of it that he couldn't hear the noises coming from the lane beside the convent house. Now that couldn't be right. What was going on down there? He was better off staying out of it, he reckoned, one good kicking a night was enough for anyone.

But then he thought about Sister Agatha. How long ago had she been by? He reached up a hand and touched his eye, felt the dressing she'd stuck on. He hoped something wasn't happening to her. For a moment he hesitated, scared.

No, he had to go and look, make sure she hadn't got herself in a scrape.

He kicked off the sleeping bag and dragged himself upright. He groaned and held on to the glass door of the chemist's shop for a bit of support, he didn't know if it was the beer or the bashing, everything was going round in a right funny way.

He staggered across the street, made it to the wall on the other side, by the halal butcher. He staggered a few more yards, peered down the lane. There was a white van parked there. You weren't supposed to park that way, the delivery trucks came down there, he'd seen lots of cars getting towed.

A pair of headlights flicked on, blinding him for a moment, and he put up his hands to shield his eyes, and next thing he heard an engine roar to life. A squeal of tyres and it was coming straight for him. He ducked out of the way just in time.

'Fuck me,' Mick said. What was that all about? He looked back at the convent house, but the lights were all out. He wondered if he should go over and knock and see if the Sister was all right, but he didn't want to get the old girls out of bed and, besides, they wouldn't answer to the likes of him this time of night, not even Sister Agatha.

He went back to Boots' doorway and crawled into his sleeping bag and curled into a ball. He slept the sleep of the damned until seven o'clock, when the store manager got in for work, and told him to fuck off or he would call the police.

They all said that.

CHAPTER THIRTY-NINE

It had been a church as recently as the war, or that was what the estate agent said. It had been partially destroyed by a bomb during the Blitz and left as a ruin until the seventies, when a property developer had bought it for a negligible sum, and brought in an architect to remodel it.

The day he first saw it, he had especially loved the inscription on the great curved arch above the chancel: 'Blessing and honour and glory and power be unto him that sitteth upon the throne.' It was from Revelations, chapter five, verse thirteen. He had been a great advocate of the Revelation once, thinking himself immune from apocalypse. Now he felt only unbridled contempt for the man he was then.

The main living area was once the nave, the choir had been retained as a mezzanine, and extended to incorporate the bedrooms and an upstairs entertaining area. The vaulted ceilings and the Lamb of God in the stained-glass window above the tabernacle had looked down on many lamb suppers. Magdalena had been a wonderful cook. Really, there was nothing she did not excel at, yet she always retained such humility, such kindness, such devotion.

He went upstairs to his bedroom, hesitated outside his daughter's bedroom, about to go in. He tried the handle and found it locked. The key, he remembered, was at the bottom of the local reservoir, a precaution he had taken to prevent such moments of weakness.

There was yet the chance he might waver. He could not

260

afford to dilute his purpose with sentiment, not now, with so much to be done.

He went into his bedroom and stripped off his suit and shirt and tie. He was relieved to be done with Doctor Salvador Cruz for another day. He was becoming tiresome.

He slid aside a glass door and stepped into his dressing room. His suits had been hung in geometric precision along one side, shirts and ties on the other; the shirts were on ebony hangers, sorted from white through to powder blue; his ties on a rack beside them, arranged by colour.

He ignored them, chose instead a long white gown, and put it over his head. Then he reached for the long brown wig, human hair, bought online and not cheap, from Gisela Mayer. He positioned it carefully then reached for the crown of thorns he had made himself from grapevine wreath. Lastly there was the theatrical beard he had bought on Shaftesbury Avenue.

He stood back to survey the enemy in the full-length mirror. It was fit for purpose, he supposed. The look of smug self-satisfaction was difficult to master, of course. But he would do. It was just a game, after all. He wasn't fooling anyone, least of all her.

He went downstairs, paused by the entertainment centre and flicked through his iPod to choose a suitable hymn. 'For All the Saints', sung by the choir of King's College, Cambridge seemed suitable. He listened for a moment to the children's voices soar around the vault, then went down to the cellar.

Sister Agatha had been tied hand and foot with cable ties, wrists in front. She lay on her side on the uneven stone floor, not moving. Her coat and grey dress had been stripped off, leaving her in a white slip.

She made a whimpering sound with each inward breath. She had worked loose a piece of yellow brick from the wall and was crumbling it between her fingers, without really knowing that she was doing it.

261

There were smells, of dust, of ancient death. She had wet herself in her terror and the urine made the inside of her thigh sting.

Someone was coming. She could hear music coming from somewhere, beautiful voices, then footsteps coming closer. A bolt slid across the door, and someone turned on a light. She tried to shield her eyes with her hands, best she could.

A shadow fell over her face. She squinted at the figure standing in the light; it was Jesus, smiling as he did in all the paintings she had ever seen of him, but there was also a hint of sadness about him.

'Am I dead?'

'No,' he said. 'No, you're not dead, Agatha, not yet. It's all right, you will be soon.'

She remembered now, there was a needle. It was the drugs, that was what it was. None of this was happening. It was all just a dream.

'Who are you?'

'Don't you recognise me? You've seen my face enough times. I thought you'd know.'

He was holding something in his right hand, a glass. He had water, oh dear God, he had water. He knelt beside her and hauled her upright, held the glass to her lips. She gulped at it, so desperate she almost choked on it. It spilled down her front, but she drank and drank until the glass was empty.

She dared look around. There were long racks of dusty wine bottles around the bare brick walls, steep steps led up to an ancient rotted door. The light came from a single bulb on a long flex. How had she got down here, what had happened to her?

She had been doing her rounds, that was it, she remembered now saying goodbye to Jackson, watching him run for his bus. What had happened after that? She couldn't for the life of her remember.

Jesus sat down on the stone steps, smiling at her oh so kindly. 'Are you a good person, Agatha? I've heard that you are.'

262

'I've tried to be a good person. All my life.'

'I believe you. One of God's little angels, aren't you? A saint, or so some might say.'

'Who are you? What is happening?'

'You are suffering for your faith, I suppose you would say. Is that a bad thing, Agatha? I thought you would glory in it.'

'What are you talking about?'

'You think I look like your Saviour, don't you? I'm afraid not. Quite the opposite in fact. I cannot save you, Agatha. No one can save you now, not even God.'

'Untie me, please, you've had your fun. Enough now. Let me go.'

'Fun? You think that is what this is?'

'You put a drug in me, didn't you?'

'Ketamine, it's called. It facilitates certain anaesthetic procedures, though I believe some people use it recreationally. It will give you nasty dreams, it's true, but its effects will have worn off by now. So, I'm afraid all this is very real. It is really happening.'

'What do you want with me?'

'I want nothing from you. You are just a pawn. But then we're all pawns, aren't we, pawns in a vicious, nasty little game. Until now, God has been in charge of the game, but now, now I've decided to start playing the game right back.'

Dear God, he was mad. Words came to her, unbidden, the twenty-third psalm. She closed her eyes and started to pray. *Yea, though I walk through the valley of the shadow of death . . .*

'How touching. You think God is going to help you. In my experience, your naivety is almost . . . tragic.' He grabbed her by the hair and forced her head back, put his face close to hers. 'Where is your God, Sister Agatha? Is he going to appear with a knife and cut these ties for you? I don't see him, do you?'

'Please.'

'You think I don't believe in him like you do? Oh, but I do, every bit as devoutly as you. I believe he is indeed watching, watching every move we make, hearing every thought we think. But he won't help you. It's faith that is all a sham. He doesn't care, you see, not about you and not about me. It's a lie and I shall prove it to you.'

She could feel his hot breath on her face and she tried to pull away, but his grip was unrelenting. *Surely goodness and mercy shall follow me all the days of my life.*

'Yea, though I walk through the valley of death, is that the prayer you're clinging to? The twenty-third psalm. You are so predictable, you people. Fear no evil, is that what you think? Yet there is so much evil that you have to fear, Sister, and there is no rod, and no staff, to comfort you. There never was.'

'Who are you?'

'You know who I am. I am Lucifer. Do you know about Lucifer?'

'The devil.'

'No, not the devil. I was an angel, God's angel, once. Just not any more.'

'Please, please, let me go. You don't have to do this, we can pray together, we will find an answer to your pain.'

'Pain? What do you know of pain?' He stood up. She clutched at the hem of his robe and he had to tear it away from her. 'Oh, but you will know pain, very soon you will have your fill of it, I promise you.'

'God can help you!'

'Help me? If God had wanted to help me, he would have done. He chose to turn his back on me and I will never give him another chance to betray me.' He started back up the stairs. 'You are so stupid. God is not your friend, he is the enemy.'

He turned off the light, leaving her in darkness again.

'I'm afraid I have been called in to work this morning. This will have to wait until later. You should pray until I return.'

The door slammed shut and the bolt drew back across the rusted latch.

Cruz went back upstairs. He could still hear her wailing down there, even after he had locked the cellar door. It was only when he closed the door that led from the kitchen that he finally got some peace. He listened to the final notes of the King's College choral, his eyes closed, and then remembered the frittata he had put in the oven. He hoped it had not burned, though he supposed there would be a certain irony if it had.

CHAPTER FORTY

The thing Charlie hated about murder was the paperwork. If people just knew how many forms there were to fill in afterwards, they'd be amazed. They had to chop down a Brazilian rainforest every time some gangbanger got sliced on the estates.

Put your knife away, save a tree.

He'd come in early to catch up, so he wasn't happy when the phone rang five minutes after he'd sat down. He stared at it, irritated. It was a Saturday morning, he wasn't even supposed to be here. He snatched it up. 'DI George.'

'Sergeant Dempster, sir, at reception. There's a woman down here says she needs to speak with you directly.'

'What's her name?'

'She gives her name as Sister Barbara from the convent in Holroyd Street.'

Holroyd Street. That was where Sister Agatha lived. 'I'll be down,' he said. He got his jacket from the back of the chair and headed towards the lifts, locking his office behind him.

The reception area was quiet for a Saturday morning; a woman with blue hair was leaning on the front desk, while a sergeant wrote out a report; someone in an anorak was pacing up and down the tiled carpet, shouting into a mobile phone.

Sister Barbara sat on one of the plastic moulded chairs under a Missing Persons poster. She wore a grey knee-length dress and a good warm coat. Unlike Sister Agatha, she had on a white coif with a grey veil at the back. A proper nun, his mother would have called her.

'Can I help you?' Charlie said.

'You're Inspector George.'

'I am. Did Sister Agatha send you?'

'Not exactly. You see, I live at the convent in Holroyd Street, there's only the two of us left these days.'

'Is there a problem?'

'Yes, there is. You see, she didn't come home last night. I'm worried to death about her.'

'I see. You'd better come through, then.'

He buzzed them through on the keypad by the security door, and led her to an interview room. He got a pad and a pen from the main desk and sat down.

'I'd better get some details.'

'I've already spoken to two policemen who came to the convent last night. But Sister Agatha told me, if anything should happen to her, I was to contact you straight away. She said you were a good man.'

'Well it's part of her job to be charitable.'

'She said you were the only one she could trust.'

'Just to be clear, you say you've reported this already?'

'Last night, when she didn't come home. I stayed up till almost one in the morning waiting for her and then I rang the volunteer who went out with her, Jackson, and he said he'd left her just before midnight. That's when I knew something was wrong and I called the local police station and told them something must have happened to her.'

'Right. What did they do?'

'They said to wait and if she wasn't back in an hour to call them again. That's what I did. They sent these two policemen in a patrol car. Terrible young they were.'

'What did they say they would do?'

'They said there was nothing much they could do until the

267

morning. I'm so worried. I couldn't just sit there. First thing, I got on the bus and came to see you, just like Agatha told me to.'

There was a telephone on the desk, Charlie picked it up and rang up to DI Cargill's office. Cargill's MIT22 was rostered on this week; if the MisPers report had been prioritised, he would know about it.

'Tony, it's Charlie. I'm downstairs. I've got someone here worried about a sister who has gone missing from the convent on Holroyd Street. Know anything about it?'

'This is not Sister Barbara, is it?'

'That's the one.'

'We've been looking everywhere for her. I got the report first thing this morning, and I went out to talk to her but she wasn't there. Bring her up, will you?'

'This way,' Charlie said to Sister Barbara and led her down the corridor to the lifts.

Cargill was waiting for them by the lifts. He introduced himself to Sister Barbara then turned to Charlie. 'Christ, you're a lifesaver, mate. When she wasn't at Holroyd Street I thought I was going bleedin' mad. Was she downstairs the whole time?'

'She thought the two uniforms last night didn't take her seriously so she came here to see me.'

'Course they took it serious, their sergeant made them do a couple of laps of the area then they rang it through to the duty inspector last night and he passed it to me first thing. I've organised some uniforms to go down there and do a door-knock and start handing out leaflets. Sister, will you come this way please?' He led her into his office, said he'd get her a cup of tea. He and Charlie walked back to the kitchen together.

'This is what happened to Father O'Meara,' Charlie said.

'Don't say that.'

'It's a fact though, innit?'

'Just one step at a time.'

'We have to let the DCI know about this.'

Cargill looked at his watch. 'He's not in yet. Let me talk to this Sister Barbara and then we'll both go and talk to him, OK?'

'What about this volunteer she said she was with. Sounds like he was the last one to see her alive.'

'I'm on it. Got two of my team out there talking to him now.'

'All right. Well, I'll leave it with you. You can find me in my office when you want to talk to FONC.'

Charlie went back to his office, turned his monitor back on and stared at the screen. It was no use. He couldn't concentrate. Every nerve in his body told him this might be the break they had been looking for.

When Cargill had finished talking to Sister Barbara, he knocked on Charlie's door and they took the lift together to the fourth floor. When they walked in, the DCI looked up from his desk and grimaced. 'When our troubles come, they come in pairs,' he said.

'When sorrows come, they come not as single spies, but in battalions,' Charlie said. '*Hamlet*, I think.'

'Thanks for correcting my education, Charlie. I always appreciate that about you. Well, sit down, you two. By the looks on your faces, this isn't good news.'

Cargill had a file with him. He took out the photograph of Sister Agatha that Sister Barbara had given the two uniforms from Malden Street the night before. 'Another religious has gone missing,' he said.

'There could be a connection,' Charlie said, 'between this disappearance and the murder of Father Andrew.'

The DCI suddenly looked like a man who had invested too heavily in Bitcoin. 'Go on.'

'She was last seen about a hundred yards from the convent,' Cargill said. 'She had been ministering to local homeless people, much as Father Andrew did. She was in the company of a lay volunteer who left her at around 23.50 yesterday evening.'

'You've spoken to him?'

'My officers rang me just before we came up, sir. His name is Jackson Stacey, IC3, he has a stall down at Covent Garden market, makes and sells his own jewellery out of old spoons.'

'Record?'

Cargill shook his head. 'Suspended sentence for drug possession. Just a bit of weed. A drunk in charge when he was nineteen. That's it.'

'He's got a better record than I have,' Charlie said.

'That wouldn't be hard,' the DCI said. 'Still, he was the last one to see her.'

'My team asked him if he would volunteer to come to the station and provide DNA and fingerprints. They said he seemed a bit affronted, but he agreed. They reckon he came across squeaky clean.'

'That wouldn't be the first time. Did they search his premises?'

'All clear.'

'All right, good. You've checked all the local hospitals?'

'Nothing.'

'She could have just been grabbed by some bootsie and dumped somewhere. It's not necessarily linked to the other homicides.'

'No sir,' Charlie said. 'But there remains that possibility.'

'I've instituted a top-level search, sir,' Cargill said. 'I have ordered extra uniforms to search the nearby marshes, and actioned a door-knock in a mile radius of the convent.'

'You have thoroughly checked the convent? You do know how many people are found hiding in the garden shed?'

'All due respect, sir, the convent doesn't have a shed. And the two uniforms from Malden Street assure me they did a thorough search.'

'Tell them to do it again.'

'I will need your authorisation to requisition extra resources, sir,' Cargill said. 'We'll need to put a POD in the High Street, tracker dogs, police divers too. There's a lake not half a mile away.'

'I'll have to let the super know about this. God's sakes. There's no chance this Sister Agatha has just got old-timer's disease or something?'

'I interviewed her a couple of times in relation to the Father O'Meara homicide,' Charlie said. 'She's sharp as a tack.'

A pinched frown. He turned and looked out of the window. 'I had hoped this was all over.'

Charlie took a breath. 'Do we reactivate Operation Galilee, sir?'

'No Charlie, we don't. DI Cargill here knows how to conduct a MisPers inquiry, don't you Tony? And for now, that's all this is. The newspapers will crucify us if they think there's any connection between this and the other two murders. Besides, we have nothing to go on. It will just create unnecessary panic.'

Charlie said nothing, even though it was killing him.

'All right, get out of here and get this thing sorted. I'll have to ring the super and let her know. This is going to be fun.'

He gave Charlie a malevolent look as he went out of the door. I shouldn't have corrected his Shakespeare, he thought. He always hates it when I do that.

Charlie volunteered to drive Sister Barbara back to the convent. Can't let her get the bus, he said to Cargill, wouldn't be right. She sat in the passenger seat, worrying the prayer beads at her neck the whole way.

'Sister Agatha said you'd help if she needed it,' she said.

'I didn't do anything, Sister. Given the nature of the disappearance, my colleagues had already prioritised the investigation.'

'She said you were humble, as well.'

271

'I think she must have got me mixed up with someone else. Believe me, everyone is doing everything they possibly can to find her.'

'I cannot help thinking about Father Andrew. Do you think the same evil that overtook him might also have befallen her?'

'There are other explanations.'

'What, in your experience, is the most common reason for someone to just disappear like this?'

'Usually, when people go missing for an extended period of time, there's a mental health issue involved.'

'You have met Sister Agatha, Inspector. Does that explanation seem likely to you?'

'No, it doesn't.'

'I pray and pray to the good Lord that she is found alive. But I fear the worst. Good does not always prevail, does it?'

Charlie turned off the High Street and down Holroyd Street. There wasn't much room to manoeuvre, there were cars parked either side.

'We have to stay— Jesus fucking Christ.'

A bearded man in an anorak and beanie walked straight out into the road in front of them, waving his arms. Charlie braked hard, didn't hit him with any force, he fell against the bonnet and slid down on it on to the road. Charlie jumped out.

The bloke had a bottle in a brown paper bag, he grinned at Charlie and took a swig. 'I am about to make a comeback,' he said.

'Are you all right, mate, you hurt?'

He started to sing the first verse of 'Sweet Caroline'.

'Goodness, it's Mick,' Sister Barbara said.

'You know him?'

'He's one of Sister Agatha's lost lambs. I haven't seen him around for a while.'

Mick didn't seem to be too badly hurt. Charlie heard someone pounding their horn. He looked around; there was a builder's van in the street behind him, getting impatient. The driver leaned out and swore at him. Charlie took out his badge and told him to pull his head in and that seemed to do the trick. Still, he couldn't block the Queen's thoroughfare all day.

'Are you hurt?' Charlie asked Mick a second time.

'Only because my public has forgotten me.'

Charlie pulled him to his feet and helped him back on to the footpath. He sat him against the wall and then jumped back in his car and pulled into a driveway. When he got back Sister Barbara was kneeling down next to Mick, patting him on the shoulder.

What an old soak, Charlie thought. Red wine had stained his grey beard, and he had the alcoholic's telltale spider-web of veins on his nose. His breath stank like a vat.

'There was a white van,' he said.

'You saw a white van?' Charlie said, his nerves suddenly taut.

Charlie leaned over him, and the old boy grabbed him by the collar. 'You've got to find the white van.'

'What white van?'

For a moment, he thought he was about to say something else, something important. 'Did you ever hear the story about the frog who dreamed of being a prince and then became one?'

'Tell me about the white van.'

'I'm writing a new album. I'm going to sing it with Barbra Streisand.'

'It's no good,' Sister Barbara said. 'He has the schizophrenia. He thinks he's Neil Diamond.'

There was a fresh dressing over his eye, scabs on his lip and his nose from a recent fight. 'Who did this?' he said to him. When he didn't answer, he turned to Sister Barbara. 'He's been in a fight and someone's tried to fix him up.'

'Agatha kept a first-aid kit with her. She was trying to help out these old fellows when they hurt themselves.'

'Can you remember who patched you up, Mick?'

'The angel of mercy has a moustache.'

'The drink doesn't help him,' Sister Barbara said. 'She's tried to get him somewhere they can help him but it's near impossible.'

'It could be concussion. Did he hit his head when he went down, do you think?'

Charlie reached into his pocket and pulled out his phone. He'd get the old boy an ambulance, have him admitted somewhere they could keep an eye on him. Just my luck, he thought, I finally get an eyewitness and it turns out to be an old soak who thinks he's a seventies rock star with bad hair.

When Charlie got back to Essex Road he was struck by the buzz about the place. Cargill had drafted extra civilians and uniforms in to take calls on the police hotline. The HOLMES inputters and analysts were already at their terminals in IR1 – they had to upload the latest intel so it could be actioned.

Cargill was talking with his intel team. Charlie waited, staring at the picture of Sister Agatha on the whiteboard. After Cargill had finished the briefing, Charlie took him aside, asked him how things were going.

'By the end of the day her photograph will be in all the papers along with a description of what she was wearing and where she was last seen. The DCI has agreed to do a piece on camera at six o'clock to appeal for witnesses.'

'No one saw anything?'

'We must have taken a hundred statements from homeless in the area already. We're still doing house-to-house in a mile radius, and we've had search dogs out there as well. I'm getting some flyers printed with her photo on. We'll start handing them out in the High Street.'

'No luck on telephony?'

'The signal on her phone vanished at 23.56.'

274

'He switched it off or dumped it. Look Tony, I have something that might be of interest.' He told him about the vagrant called Mick, and how he had run in front of his car. 'He kept muttering about a white van. You know the white van was prominent in our investigations on Operation Galilee.'

'Where is this bloke now?'

'They've taken him to Homerton. I told the ambulance crew he suffered an LOC so with any luck they'll keep him in for observation. But I don't know how long he'll be in there. You might want to send a uniform over there in case he happens to get lucid when he sobers up. Not my case, I don't have the authority.'

'You think he really saw something?'

Charlie shrugged. 'How did you go with CCTV?'

'We haven't been looking for a white van.'

'Just a thought, mate.'

As he walked away, Cargill called to him: 'Have you noticed what O'Meara and Morton and this nun have in common?'

'They all have a social conscience?'

'They've all been in the news recently. O'Meara had that documentary aired about him a few months ago, Morton had that bit in the paper, so did Sister Agatha.'

'Yeah, I know. What do you think it means?'

'I don't know. I hope it doesn't mean anything. I hope we're going to find this nun walking around the local shopping centre with a dazed look on her face.'

'So do I. Better let you get on with your job, mate. Let me know if you find a body.'

'Don't worry, if that happens, it will be all over London in five minutes.'

Charlie didn't drive straight home that night. Instead he found himself cruising the streets around the Holroyd Street convent. It was winter and already dark by four o'clock, just another dreary inner London borough with cracked pavements and run-down terraced houses and tired-looking shops. Cars glittered with frost under the tungsten glow of street lamps.

Already there were homeless bedding down for the night in dark shop doorways with their bits of cardboard and dirty sleeping bags. What a night to be sleeping rough. He remembered one of Jay's suspect jokes. Q: What is the definition of homeless? A: Something a Tory steps over on the way to the opera.

It wasn't ever meant to be that funny really, it was social commentary. Innit? For all the outrage the homeless epidemic had created, he supposed London had always been like that, a place for the very rich and the destitute to stare at each other in incomprehension in the street.

He remembered what Sister Agatha had told him about the Good Samaritan. She was right, what they all needed wasn't more religion, it wasn't Brexits or Bitcoins or another Tony Blair or Margaret sodding Thatcher; what the world needed was just more people like her, good Samaritans, and not just in London but everywhere.

He saw a parking space and pulled in, and it was a couple of minutes before he realised what he'd done. This was his street, of course, the street where he grew up, and that down there used to be his house. It was a bit more upmarket than when he'd lived there; the owners had bricked over their front gardens so they could park their Ford Mondeos.

That was where he was born, up there, top right window. It was his mother that had insisted she have him at home; she didn't hold with hospitals, she said. It was frightening the risks she took, but then marrying the old man was the biggest risk of the lot. He wondered if the neighbours had ever heard them going at it when they had one of their famous rows. You would have thought so, the racket they made.

He still remembered that one day his old man went crazy, started shouting and breaking things, threatening to kill

276

her, he must have still been in short pants and he hid in his room and prayed and prayed, like they had taught him in Sunday school, prayed for the police to come and save them all.

But if they came at all, they always came too late, and by then the old man was over whatever it was and he always managed to sweet-talk his way out of it. Except for that one time, that time he gave his mother a black eye, that time he took off his belt and told Liam he was going to belt him with the buckle end and Charlie stood between them and shouted don't you touch him, thinking: this is it, this is it.

They got there just in time that day, the one who came to the door was a big sergeant who looked a bit like Tom Hiddleston; he got the old man in a headlock and dragged him off to the police car. Other kids had heroes like Tony Adams or David Rocastle. His hero was that sergeant and he never found out his name.

That was the day he knew what he wanted to do with his life; he wanted to be the bloke who put the bully in a headlock. Of course, it never quite worked out that way. How many times had he been called to a domestic and found some bloke battering his wife, and the minute he put the cuffs on, his wife would come at him, black eye and all, and try to brain him with a skillet for hurting her darling husband?

And then there was the murder squad; a couple of times he'd had blokes in headlocks, but it was all too late because their battered wives had already been battered just once too often and were lying in the morgue with a tag on their toe.

But one day, he promised himself, one day he would be on time.

It was getting late and he was doing no good driving around in circles. If Sister Agatha was anywhere on the street, the sniffer dogs and the uniforms would have found her by now. As he drove back down the High Street he passed the POD caravan, the lights still on, a couple of eager young constables still passing out flyers to anyone who held their hand out. A TV crew was doing a live cross outside the convent. There was a solitary light on in an upper-floor window, he imagined Sister Barbara busy at her prayers.

He supposed that if Sister Agatha was still alive, she would be busy at hers, as well.

CHAPTER FORTY-ONE

Ma was sitting in a chair in a corner of the room, staring at the television. There was just a grey screen; it wasn't turned on. The bedside lamp threw her face into shadow. He walked in and said a cheery hello, saw the look of vague concern on her face as she tried to remember who he was. Then it came to her.

'That woman stole my purse.'

'What woman, Ma?'

'That woman who keeps coming into my room.'

'You mean the nurse?'

'No, not the nurse. What do I need a nurse for, nothing wrong with me. Am I in hospital?'

'Have you told them at the front desk that you lost your purse?'

'I didn't lose it, she stole it.'

'I'm sure she didn't do that. They pay her a pittance for the job she does but she still wouldn't steal your purse. Have you looked everywhere?'

Charlie noticed that although she was in her nightdress, she had her bag on her lap as if she was ready to go shopping.

'Of course I've looked. It's not here. You should ask that woman where it is.'

There was a small refrigerator in the corner of the room. He squatted down and opened the door. Inside there was a small carton of milk, a tin of condensed milk and a purse. 'So this is where you keep your cold, hard cash.'

'What?'

'Your purse. It's in the fridge, where it always is.'

'What did she put it in there for?'

'She didn't, Ma.'

'I should report her, and serve her right.'

Charlie noticed the fresh hothouse flowers on her chest of drawers. 'Has Ben been in?'

'Yes, he is a good boy. He always comes to visit despite the hours he works.'

'The hours he works? He makes a couple of phone calls, stares at a computer for a couple of minutes and then bonks someone he just met on Tinder in his lunch hour.'

'What's Tinder?'

'Oh never mind.'

'Why haven't you got your uniform on?'

'I got out of uniform bloody years ago, Ma.'

'I liked you in your uniform. Your dad would have been so proud.'

'No, he wouldn't. He hated the Old Bill, we were the bane of his life.'

She smiled at him, like she always did when she put up the walls. Was it some misplaced sense of maternal loyalty, he wondered, or did she really believe all the rubbish she talked? He looked at the walls, she'd hung up a few more pictures since last time he was there.

'Looks like the London Dungeon in here. What are these pictures, they are new, aren't they?'

'They've always been there.'

'No they haven't. It was Michael, wasn't it? Has he been down to see you and not told the rest of us?'

'Where is Michael? Is he with you?'

'He lives in Liverpool, Ma. He's a priest, remember?'

She gave him that special smile she reserved for very small children and people she thought might be mad.

'You haven't drunk your tea,' he said, seeing the empty cup on her nightstand.

'I don't like tea,' she said, even though she had drunk tea all her life. Charlie sat down on the edge of the bed.

'How is Michael anyway?'

'Who's Michael?'

'Your son, Michael.'

A blank look. It was a terrible thing, this disease. If he asked her about someone she knew thirty years ago, she could tell him their middle name and the colour of their eyes. Something that happened yesterday had long disappeared into the fog.

'So, this picture, here. Who's this, then?' Charlie asked.

'That's Saint Lawrence. He's a holy martyr. They're all holy martyrs.'

'What's he holding, a comb? Not much use to him, he looks like he's bald.'

'It's called a gridiron. They roasted him to death on that. All the saints carry around with them things to show how they died.'

'Oh lovely.'

'When they had him over the fire he said, turn me over, I'm done on this side.' She patted her bag, a sign that she approved. 'He's the patron saint of cooks.'

It always staggered him, the Catholic sense of humour. What also surprised him was how lucid his mother could be when she talked about religion. She left her purse in the refrigerator, but ask her about one of the blessed saints and she could spout chapter and verse.

'That's Saint Hippolytus. He was torn apart by horses.'

'I suppose he's the patron saint of betting, then.'

'No,' she said, and didn't even smile. 'And that's Saint Ignatius. He was torn apart by lions.'

'Lot of tearing apart in the old days, innit? Who's this, then?'

'That's Saint Andrew. Didn't they teach you anything at Sunday school?'

'I know it's surprising, being Catholic and everything, but

Father Riley seemed strangely reticent about teaching small children how to torture blokes to death.'

'What did you do then?'

'Weird that we should be having this conversation now. Why, do you want your money back?'

'We didn't pay for Sunday school.'

'It was a joke, Ma. We studied the Bible at Sunday school, we had to practically memorise it.'

'I should think so, too.'

'This Andrew, is it true he was crucified on an X-shaped cross?'

'He told the judge he didn't feel worthy to be martyred on the same cross as Our Lord,' she said, as if she had been there and witnessed the whole thing herself. 'Your uncle Will from Aberdeen said they still have a bank holiday up there on Saint Andrew's Day.'

'When's that?'

'The thirtieth of November.'

Charlie tried to think when it was that Father O'Meara died. He took out his Nokia and went back through the log. Here it was, he got a call from the duty officer early in the morning on the thirtieth.

Odd.

'Who's this bloke here, then? The one with the aubergines on his head.'

'Don't you be blasphemous. That's Saint Stephen.'

'How did he go, then? They battered him to death with eggplants?'

'They're rocks, not aubergines. He was stoned to death.'

'When is his holy day?'

'You should know all this. It's Boxing Day.'

'December the twenty-sixth.'

'When I was a little girl, the young boys used to go round town all dressed up – wren boys we called them; they'd get a little bird and tie it to the end of a pitchfork and we'd all have to give them tuppence so they'd let it go at the end of the day.'

'Sounds like the mafia.'

'They gave all the money they collected to charity.'

But Charlie wasn't really listening. He was still staring at Saint Andrew and Saint Stephen. There was a wild thought running around his head, and he wanted to get rid of it. He thought about the two crosspieces that had been tacked to the timber piece that Father O'Meara had been crucified on; so was that meant to be a Saint Andrew's Cross?

He looked around the room until he found the picture he was looking for. 'And who's this one?'

'That's Saint Agatha. She dedicated her virginity to God. They sent her to a brothel, but she wouldn't do anything, so they martyred her.'

In other circumstances Charlie would have found a one-liner in that. Instead he said: 'And when's her feast day?'

'It's tomorrow.'

It took a moment to sink in, that. When it did, he felt a strange sort of tingling all down his back, the elation of discovery mixed with numb horror.

Tomorrow. He supposed it was what he had been hoping for, in a way; another crime scene, a new set of evidence markers, fresh leads to follow, new lines of investigation. But at what cost? He remembered Sister Agatha down by the marshes with the old Polish blokes: '. . . like I said, you're a true believer.' Was he? But true believers showed up on time, like that big sergeant that arrested his old man.

'What's this she has on the plate? Looks like two puddings.'

'They're her breasts,' his mother said, like she was proud of her, come home from school with a good report.

'Has that got to do with how she died?'

'When she wouldn't give up God and do what they wanted, they cut off her breasts and then they burned her alive. Don't you remember?'

283

Charlie stood in the car park outside the Arlington Mansions, letting the cold snow fall on his burning cheeks.

They cut off her breasts and then they burned her alive.

Charlie got out his phone, took a deep breath and dialled the DCI's number.

Finally: 'What's this, DI George?'

'Sorry to wake you.'

'Do you know what time it is?'

'This could be important.'

'It had better be.'

'It's about Operation Galilee.'

'Go on.'

'I think I've found the link between the deaths of Father O'Meara and PC Morton, and the disappearance of Sister Agatha.'

He told him about the saints' days and how they had died. When he had finished, he waited. The silence stretched.

'Sir?'

'If your lurid, messianic fantasy is right, in what way exactly does it advance our investigation?'

'We can't just ignore this possibility.'

'Again: how does it advance our inquiry?'

Fair play, Charlie thought. Even if he was right, there wasn't anything for the skipper to action out of it; if he was wrong, or if they never identified a main suspect, it would make them all look like clowns.

'Look, Charlie, you're a mad bugger, and perhaps there's something in this, I don't know. But what do you want me to do?'

Charlie stared at the night sky, couldn't think of a damned thing.

'I'm not saying you're wrong, but this isn't the sort of thing I can take to Gold group, is it? It's not exactly a lead. It's just a theory, and if the press got hold of it, they'd crucify us, no pun intended.'

'Yes, sir.'

'Run with it, if you like, but don't whisper any of this to anyone until you have something I can action.'

The line went dead.

Charlie got back in his car, sat behind the wheel for a long time, staring at the wall. *Parking for friends and relatives of clients of Arlington Mansions only. Offenders will be towed.*

Why would anyone find really good people and then murder them on saints' days? You'd have to be mad. You'd also have to be clever as fuck to get it done.

But there wasn't anything he could do with this, or at least, nothing he could think of right now. Besides, every cop in London was out looking for her already. What they needed was a tip-off from the public and later, perhaps, he would see if his theory fitted. Right now it was as useful as tits on a bull.

He heard the first few bars of 'The Ride of the Valkyries', took out his iPhone, stared at the display, thought for a moment about not answering.

'Charlie,' he said and waited for her voice.

'I've been thinking about you,' Geri said, sounding whispery and breathless.

'Have you?'

'It's been a long time since I've seen you. Have you been avoiding me?'

Sort of. 'I've been bloody busy at work, Geri.'

A beat. He could imagine her, lying in the spa, more likely sitting on the sofa with a bottle of wine, running a fingernail along a cushion.

'Simon's gone up to Scotland to see his family. He's taken the kids, I'm all on my own.' And then, kittenish: 'You know how I hate being on my own.'

Don't do it, he could hear Ben shouting at him inside his brain. Do you want to be sloppy seconds your whole life?

'Charlie?'

'I'm thinking.'

'Are you driving?'

'Just been to see my mum.'

'How is she?' Geri said, and he thought: what are you asking for, you don't even know her.

'You want to come down?'

'Come down?'

'We could meet. There's a pub called the Pig and Goose just outside Sevenoaks.'

He winced.

'Come on, Charlie. You're not working tomorrow.'

'How do you know that?'

'Because I spoke to your detective sergeant at the station this afternoon. I asked him and he told me.'

'I don't want you calling me at the nick.'

'Relax, he thought it was to do with work.'

No, he doesn't, Charlie thought. The skipper isn't that stupid. He's from up north, they're sharp that lot. 'What time?' he said.

'I've booked the restaurant for 12.30. Bring your toothbrush.'

'Why, is the food that bad?'

'They have rooms upstairs. I could do with a night in the country.'

'You live in the country.'

'My bedroom doesn't have a view of a duck pond. And my bed doesn't have you in it.'

'Well everyone needs a view of a duck pond.'

'See you tomorrow, Charlie. Don't be late.'

He hung up the phone and drove home, there was nothing else to be done. He got into bed and lay on his back, wide awake, listening to the thumping bass of a party over the road. He had the Nokia on the bedside table. He watched the rhythmic blinking of the light on the ceiling, waiting for it to trill to life; any moment he would get the call from Cargill or one of his team: we've found a body, badly burned, we're doing DNA tests, but we think it might be her.

286

It was almost five when he finally gave up trying to sleep and got up to make himself a cup of coffee. There were lights burning in the flat over the road, they were still playing music. Some people, he thought, they just don't give a fuck about anyone else.

The city was still dark, the morning star bright in the sky. Another day in the life. He supposed he should be looking forward to it.

CHAPTER FORTY-TWO

The Pig and Goose was a sprawling place just outside Sevenoaks, all crooked low beams and stone walls, next to the local church. He supposed it appealed to Geri's romantic side; the website said it used to serve pilgrims on their way to Canterbury and that Dick Turpin had hidden there once, trying to stay one step ahead of the hangman.

The pub had come a long way since those days; it even had a Michelin star, with confit duck leg and fig tagliatelle on the menu. Oh, and not one, but two ghosts. Just as well, Charlie had told her, where I grew up eating wildfowl without an earth-bound spirit was not acceptable.

She was already there, sitting at a table by the Tudor fire. She had squeezed into a simple little black number, and her eyes were shining. There was a hint of very expensive perfume as she kissed him chastely on the cheek.

'It's good to see you, Charlie. I've ordered an Aperol spritzer. Shall we order a bottle of wine with lunch?'

Charlie turned to the waitress. 'I'll have a pint of the Westerham Grasshopper.'

'That's a no, then.'

'Not in the mood for wine.'

'Hope you're not going to sulk all day. I thought you'd enjoy getting out of London. All those dead bodies and hypodermic needles.'

'Archway may not be Kent, but it's not that bad.'

'Well I wouldn't want to live there.'

'That's because you can afford not to. Have you ordered?'

'No, I was waiting for you. You're late.' She leaned forward and said in a whisper: 'This is my second of these. Don't let me drink too many, will you?'

He looked around. It was a proper pub restaurant this one, no communal knives and forks and plastic salt and pepper shakers; this had polished wine glasses, proper silver on the tables, and the regulation farm implements hanging on the brick walls had all been buffed until they shone, even the wooden bullock yoke.

He scrolled down the menu. The prices were eye-watering. 'What are you having?'

'I have my eye on the sea scallops with crisp sea purslane.'

'Purslane, also known as pigweed. Good to see it making a comeback. Persians used it a lot.'

'Charlie, you never cease to astonish. How do you know these things?'

'I'm widely read. Also very curious. Spend way too much time looking things up on Google.'

'You'd be great at a quiz night.'

'You have to be proper clever to win at quiz nights.'

'Charlie, you are such a liar. That one time I met your brother, he told me you have a degree in English Literature.'

'You don't want to listen to Ben, he opens his mouth and the wind blows his tongue about.'

There was a retriever curled up by the fire. People were stepping over it and around it, women and small children bending down to pat it, but it still hadn't moved. Every now and then it would open one eye, and then because it was just so exhausted from its hard morning by the fire, it shut it again.

'Do you reckon they hire him for the day?' Charlie said. 'Nothing like a cute dog to bring in the customers.'

'Did you ever have a dog, Charlie?'

'When I was a kid. I had a spaniel, he was called Floyd. Best dog in the world, he was, he thought he was human. I could

289

talk to him, I swear he understood every word I said, his only problem was he couldn't talk back, you could see it frustrated him sometimes. But it was probably just as well, I feel he would only have made highly critical comments about my lifestyle.'

'What happened to him?'

'He was a dog. He passed, didn't he? Dogs don't live as long as us.'

'You must have been sad.'

'I still am. That's the thing about dogs, they're too easy to love. They're uncomplicated, not like people. If they love you, they lick your face, no matter what mood you're in.'

'Would you like me to lick your face, Charlie?'

'If you love me, you can.'

She finished her Aperol, didn't say anything to that, just watched him over the rim of her glass. So much for the court-trained junior barrister, sometimes she wasn't as nimble on her feet as she thought she was.

He looked out of the window, there was a thin crust of snow on the wooden tables in the beer garden. The branches of the maple tree on the sun terrace were bare. Hard to believe they sat out there only last summer, sheltering from the sun under the broad leaves.

'What is it, Charlie?'

'Thinking about work.'

'Do you ever not think about work?'

'Not really. You know that about me.'

'When I walk out of the office, I'm done with it.'

'See, I envy that. Nothing is ever unfinished in your job. You either win or you lose, but you have a schedule every day. You don't ever think, I should be at work doing something. If something needs to be done, you do some overtime and that's it. Finished.'

'What should you be doing?'

'See, that's it, I don't know. I just have this feeling I'm missing something and if I was smarter, I'd know what it was.'

The waitress interrupted them for their order. Geri had the scallops, Charlie predictably had the pork, apple and cider sausages with mashed potato – bangers and mash in anyone's language.

'I was afraid you were going to ask for extra tomato sauce,' she said, after the waitress had left with the order.

'I knew I forgot something,' he said, and grinned, and for a moment the tension thawed. As they ate, they talked in murmurs about the people in the room, guessing who was having an affair, who was on a first date, who was gay, who was sick to death of the person they were with, what sort of jobs people had.

'What do you think people say about us?' Geri said.

Charlie shrugged. She reached across the table and their fingers touched. She gave him one of her delicious smiles; a lock of her hair had strayed from its French braid and hung across her cheek, perhaps accidentally, perhaps not. He stroked it away with his hand.

'I've booked a lovely room,' she said. 'It has a four-poster bed and a spa bath.' He took his hand away. 'What's the matter, Charlie?'

'Are the scallops all right?'

'My dish of the day is absolutely perfect.'

'See, the trouble is, you're married.'

'So are you, Charlie. To the Met. We're both spoken for.' She leaned in and he heard her barrister voice. 'You knew what this was from the very start. You knew I wasn't single.'

'I just don't think I can do this any more.' He fiddled with his napkin. 'Have you paid for the room?'

'Yes, of course.'

'Will they refund it?'

She stared at him. 'Don't you fucking dare do this to me, Charlie George.'

'Sorry.'

For a moment he thought he was going to wear the Aperol

291

spritzer, but she was too classy for that. Instead, she threw her napkin on the table and her chair scraped on the oak floor-boards as she stood up. She put her bag over her shoulder and walked out of the room. He got a few looks. Charlie stared back and the rubberneckers immediately turned away.

He waited a few moments and then he went to the reception to settle up. But Geri was still there, she must have been in the Ladies, perhaps her mascara had run. She clattered past in her heels and the door slammed behind her as she went out to the car park.

'Everything all right, sir?' the maître d' said.

'Fine. I think there was a touch too much tomato sauce with her purslane.'

He heard the tyres of her X5 spin on the gravel as she drove off. Well, there was his dirty weekend ruined. There was a part of him that was relieved, another part of him that wanted to bang his head against the wall. He thought about having another pint of Grasshopper, but instead he decided to be a good boy and get in his car and drive back to London. What would he do when he got there?

He had no idea.

CHAPTER FORTY-THREE

It was a Sunday and it was winter so he decided to chance the Blackfriars Bridge. He still hadn't made up his mind whether he should head home to Archway or go into the Essex Road nick, like a poor sad bastard, and sit around in his office doing nothing on his day off.

The bridge was where they found that Italian banker – what was his name, Calvi. God's banker. He died the year Charlie was born, he only read about it later in books. He had been shocked by what came out of it, about the Vatican, the venality of it all; when he told his ma about it she said she never believed anything she read in the newspapers.

It was the first time he realised what a lot of bollocks it all was, how much money the Church had and there was his mother putting coins in the plate every week. They should have been giving her money, his opinion. And what did they do with it? Calvi used it to buy missiles for the junta in Argentina to sink British destroyers in the Falklands, the rest was syphoned off to those fancy Mafia blokes in P2.

He supposed, looking back, that was when he lapsed.

The bridge looked upbeat in its Arsenal red and white, but down to two lanes now from three; there were new concrete barriers with black piers because some medieval nut job thought running people off bridges would get him to the front of the queue in Paradise and more lap dances with dusky-eyed virgins than Harvey Weinstein. Seemed to him the whole idea of God was more grief than it was worth.

Not many people on the bridge this time of day; a street cleaner in a dirty hi-vis jacket, a few cyclists, buses and taxis crawling towards Unilever House and Saint Paul's. The sun hung in a dirty white sky brushed with mare's tails. A crisp packet flipped end over end across the road in front of him, tumbled by the Arctic wind.

He supposed that the view of the frozen duck pond and Geri in her Victoria's Secret underwear would have left this for dead. What were you thinking, son?

'You were thinking your kid brother is right,' he heard Ben say to him, in the dark behind his eyes. 'You were thinking you can't keep doing this to yourself. It's like the fags, you can't keep saying oh I'll quit next week, the only time to stop is right now.'

'All right, all right,' Charlie said, to the Ben who wasn't there.

He saw the Oxo Tower for a moment in his rear-view mirror. That's where he'd met her, in some fancy, overpriced bar with overpriced, fancy drinks. She had been up there drinking with some CPS legal eagles, he'd been invited over with some other MIT guys from Essex Road, they'd got talking and the next thing he knew he had her number. He'd only found out about Simon later and that should have stopped him but it hadn't.

The Oxo Tower vanished and then there was just him in the mirror, with his haunted, guilty look. 'Charlie,' he said, 'you're as much use as a chocolate fireguard. Get a grip, mate.'

Salvador Cruz had been saving the 1983 Château Palmer Margaux for a special occasion. He opened it in the kitchen, sniffed the cork, and took down a wine glass. He was dressed in orange overalls and a fleece balaclava.

He unlocked the heavy wooden door to the basement and paused at the top of the steps before switching on the light. Sister Agatha lay curled in a ball on the floor. She blinked at the light and then started to moan softly through the gag he had been forced to apply. All that screaming, he had worried someone might hear her.

'I'm sorry, you're probably wondering where Jesus is. I'm afraid he cannot be with us today. I told you, he has abandoned you, Agatha. He won't be back.'

He went to a low brick shelf and laid the bottle and the glass carefully on top of it. 'Expensive,' he said. 'Do you know I paid over five hundred pounds a bottle for this? So we must do things properly. We have to let it breathe, as I am letting you breathe before you are finally consumed.'

There was a large wooden crucifix, almost the height of his waist, leaning against the wall beside the wine racks. He pointed to it. 'Do you see this Agatha? This used to hang in the hall. There is a family portrait there now. He has been super-seded.' He smiled at the thought. 'What do you people all say about this man? "He died for our sins." Well, I am sure you have appreciated his sacrifice. So, now you are going to die for his.'

He undid the buttons on his overalls and leaned back with a grimace of relief as he urinated on the crucifix, paying special attention to the figure on the cross itself. When he had rebut-toned himself, he turned around; she was staring at him, eyes wide and white.

'Sorry, did you find that disrespectful? No, wait, what is the correct word? Blasphemous. Well, that is my purpose in life now; to be profane, to be irreverent. And why is that? Because I no longer revere him, I suppose you would say. Not just that. I hold him in contempt.'

He poured some of the rich ruby-red wine into a glass. He held it up to the light. 'It is made with Cabernet Sauvignon, Merlot, and Petit Verdot grapes. It's an extraordinary wine.' He swirled it in the crystal glass and put it to his nose and inhaled. 'So delicate, these floral undertones, aromatic, elegant. Something that should be lingered over and savoured. I have so few such pleasures now. This wine is one of them. You are the other.'

He squatted down beside her, held the glass in front of her face. '"This is my blood, which will be given up for you." Poetic, isn't it? If you don't know what it really means. Still, shall we drink to that?'

He sipped the wine, closed his eyes as he held it on his tongue for a moment, then swallowed. 'You are wondering, where does all this hate come from? But hate is only pain translated into action. Oh, but I see you want so badly to say something, no doubt you want to engage me in theological debate. Such things bore me. Still, it is only fair that I let you have your say. I shouldn't hog the conversation.'

He untied the gag around her mouth.

Sister Agatha drew as deep a breath as she could, and then the words tumbled out of her. 'Don't do this, please; if you won't show some mercy to me, then do it for your own immortal soul. The Bible tells us that murder leads to the soul's damnation for all eternity.'

He frowned, as if she had presented him with a complex mathematical puzzle. 'Yes, but you see, I fear that my soul is already in eternal torment, so there seems so little to lose. The sticking point, you see, is forgiveness.'

'If you ask him, God will forgive anything.'

'Oh I don't want him to forgive me, Sister Agatha. The problem, you see, is that I am not prepared to forgive *him*.'

He stood up, there was a number of framed pictures stacked against the wall, covered with a canvas sheet. He drew back the edge of the sheet so that she could see what was underneath. Then he bent down and ran a tender finger across the faces of the people in the photograph at the very front.

'You see this woman, these two children? They are the three most beautiful people the world could ever imagine.'

'Is that your family?'

His proud smile twisted into a grimace. He quickly covered the picture up again. 'Never mind,' he said. 'Are you ready for your martyrdom?'

CHAPTER FORTY-FOUR

Charlie found himself sitting in the car park at the Essex Road nick. He hadn't planned to come here; it was as if the car drove itself. But in the end, he wasn't really surprised. 'You're tragic, Charlie,' he said to himself as he punched in the security code and buzzed himself in. He rode the lift to the third floor.

There was a real buzz about the place for a Sunday. The Incident Room was packed, Cargill's team busy manning phones, three officers in the CCTV room, staring at the screens, even the civilians the DCI had authorised were working double time as well.

He headed towards his office, saw Lovejoy sitting at her computer terminal. At least he wasn't the only sorry case.

'What are you doing here?' he said to her. 'Haven't you got a life?'

'No guv, not really. How about you?'

He made a face. 'I've got one, but I don't approve of it much. What are you doing?'

'I've been thinking about Operation Galilee.'

'Haven't we all?'

He told her what he'd told the DCI, about the holy martyrs and saints' days; that today was Agatha's day.

How he thought she was going to die.

'Then we haven't got long.'

'No, Lovejoy, not long at all. In fact, he might have already done it. But let's not be pessimistic. Any ideas?'

'Perhaps.'

'Enlighten me.'

'Well, it just seems to me that instead of reacting to him, like we've all been doing, trying to find leads after the crime, our best chance could be to try to anticipate him.'

'How do you plan to do that?'

'Well, the first murder, he chose the site very carefully, right?'

'A tableau, I think DS Greene called it.'

'The second homicide, well that was Hampstead Heath, that was random, we had no chance. But if Sister Agatha is connected, well she's another religious, so I'd expect there to be context.'

'Context? Interesting word. Go on.'

'Whoever is behind this, they want it to mean something, if not to anyone else, then it must mean something to *them*.'

'And perhaps their victim as well.'

'That's what I mean about trying to get a step ahead. What if they still have Sister Agatha and plan to kill her somewhere similar to the Barrow Fields chapel.'

'A derelict church.'

'Something like that.'

'Are there many in London?'

'Depends what you mean by many, guv. It's an imprecise term.'

'That sounds like something I would say, Lovejoy.' He pulled up a chair and sat down next to her at her desk and studied what she had on her monitor.

'I've been researching derelict church sites. I've found about two dozen. There could be more.'

'Where's this one?'

'It's in Poplar, guv. It was built in the 1870s, the Germans couldn't hit it during the Blitz, but rising damp forced it to close in 1975. Its nemesis was a portable camping stove about twenty years ago.'

'What was that doing in there?'

'It was being used as a women's refuge by some charity

group. The fire gutted it, it's just a shell now, I gather it's held up by bits of scaffolding.'

'What's around it?'

'Some football club trains there, it's got a funny name, Senrab FC.'

'A lot of big players came from Senrab. Bobby Zamora played for them.' He did his best Dean Martin: 'When you're back in row Z, and the ball hits your head, that's Zamora.'

'Is that a real song?'

'We used to sing it at Arsenal when we played Fulham. Never mind, it's a possible. We should go and have a look. Any more?'

'There's this one.'

'A scout hall in Walthamstow? Forget it. Next.'

'This one's a proper church. It was built during the Wars of the Roses, it's not been used since 1961. There's plans to develop it as a gym.'

'That is just as creepy as Barrow Hill. Where is it?'

'In Brentford.'

'That's an hour's drive. How many more have you got?'

'A few.'

'You shouldn't use imprecise terms, Lovejoy.'

She tapped the screen. 'This is a workhouse chapel, it was designed in the nineteenth century for people who couldn't find work through age or disability.'

'Like the civil service.'

'It was a hospital after, got closed down in 1997. But the chapel's still there, says here it's been vandalised over the years and was partly destroyed by fire a few years ago. It's up for demolition.'

'Put it on the list.'

'Then there's this, in Catford, it's a Dissenters' Chapel, like the one in Barrow Fields. And there's this, the ruins of a chapel in Stepney that was used by the Plymouth Brethren. It was bombed during the Blitz.'

He shook his head.

'A church hall in Dulwich?'

'I don't get the feeling that a church hall will cut the mustard with this nut job, do you?'

'There's this old church in Hampstead.'

'No, not private enough. There's a hospital right next door.'

'How do you feel about a tin tabernacle then?'

'A what?'

'It's like a sort of pop-up church, they were bought as pre-fabs in the nineteenth century. Tin tabernacles they called them, or tintabs. There's one at Ponder's End.'

'Enfield, the place that time forgot. Don't tell me there's more.'

'One in Croydon, a chapel in Hounslow that looks likely, and a paupers' cemetery with a derelict chapel not that far from White Hart Lane.'

'Don't tell me I have to go over there and rummage around in dead Spurs supporters.'

'Orpheus descending into the underworld, guv.'

'Something like that.'

'Last, there's this one, in Elmscroft Road, you've already checked it once, it was where we got the hotline report from the bloke who lived over the back of it.'

She leaned forward and touched the mouse, brought it up on the tab. He was suddenly aware how close they were to each other. She smelled very nice. He pushed the chair back on its rollers, as if he hadn't noticed.

'You've forgotten one.'

'What's that, guv?'

'Barrow Hill. No reason he can't go back there, if your theory's right. So how many is that?'

'That's ten, guv.'

'It'll be midnight before we finish driving around all of those.'

'We can do it separately: I'll put my hand up for the colonies, guv, if you do Enfield.'

'Means I have to go to Tottenham. You strike a hard bargain.' He crossed his arms over his chest and thought about it. 'One condition, Lovejoy, if you find anything, don't go playing the hero.'

'Heroine, guv. And don't worry about me trying out for the Police Medal, I won't even get spiders out of my own bathroom.'

'I never picked you for one of those.'

'One of what?' she said, and he watched her bristle.

'An arachnophobe.' There was a hint of a smile. He stood up and put his coat back on. 'All right, let's get moving.'

They went down in the lift together. He studied her out of the corner of his eye. He realised she wasn't half pretty. It was a pity she batted for the other team.

'I found out what FONC stands for,' she said.

'What?'

'Friend of no cunt.'

'Where did you get that from? That is scandalous, that is.'

'Is it true?'

'Do you think I or any of my fellow officers in the team would refer to our superior officer so disrespectfully? Nobody thinks that of DCI O'Neal-Callaghan.'

'So, I'm wrong.'

'Absolutely. Who told you that?'

She shrugged.

The elevator doors opened. They went out into the biting cold of the car park and made their way to their cars. 'Next time we get a case, you can be my deputy. It has nothing to do with anything you just told me. It is just so you can get more experience, very quickly, no other reason.'

'Yes, guv.' She climbed into her Sierra.

'Keep your phone charged and turned on. Anything you see, anything at all, ring me straight away.'

'It's a long shot, this.'

'Better than sitting around here doing nothing.'

302

He looked up at the sky. It was already getting dark. What were the chances?

Cruz bent down to replace the gag in Agatha's mouth. As he stood up and turned away she kicked him as hard as she could in the back of the knee. His right leg buckled and he gasped and dropped the wine glass, which shattered on the cellar floor.

She kicked out again, sweeping his legs out from under him and he went down hard. She wriggled across the floor on her back, kicked out with her heels into his face but couldn't quite connect. She tried to get closer, so that she could use her weight to crush him, he didn't look to her as if he was very big or very strong. Perhaps if she could get her hands on one of those shards of glass, she could cut him.

She tried to wrap her legs around his face and neck but already she had lost the advantage of surprise and now he caught her by the ankles and twisted her to the side. She was heavier and probably bigger and stronger, but her hands and feet were tied, so there was no chance she could wrestle him.

He rolled away from her and scrambled to his feet; he was breathing hard but he seemed more concerned that his hand was bleeding than that she had tried to overpower him. 'I have to operate tomorrow!' he shouted at her, almost hysterical with outrage, and kicked out with his green wellington boots. He caught her on the side of the head and for a moment she could not think or move. He did it again and she blacked out.

When she opened her eyes again he was standing right over her, shouting at her, but she couldn't make out what he was saying because of the ringing in her ears. His face swam in and out of her vision.

'That wasn't very Christian, was it?'

He wrapped a piece of rag around his hand, and it quickly stained with blood. 'I shall have to sweep up,' he said. He went upstairs and reappeared a minute later with a dustpan and brush and started to clear up the tiny shards of broken glass. 'What a waste! That was one of the finest red wines money can buy.' He finished cleaning up the glass and stood up again. 'Well it's a lesson learned. Not all saints are saintly. I shall go upstairs and get the van ready. The hardest part is not getting you in here, it's getting you out again.'

He looked up. There was a trapdoor directly above her head and she could make out a glimmer of electric light. 'I think a big woman like you will put a lot of strain on the engine and the winch.'

He reached into his pocket and took out a small vial and a hypodermic syringe. He unwrapped the needle from the packet and then plunged it through the cap of the vial. He checked there were no air bubbles.

'This is going to hurt you a lot more than it hurts me,' he said, and smiled.

Sister Agatha tried again to wriggle away but he was quick and, besides, all he needed to do was plunge the syringe into her thigh and step back. 'The effects aren't immediate, as you know. Conversely, they don't last long. I'd hate you to miss your moment of glory in the sight of God. Not long to go. Stay cheerful for me.'

He went up the stairs, ripping off his balaclava and putting it into his pocket. He unwrapped the rag and glanced at his hand. Look at what the bitch had done.

The doorbell rang. He looked up, startled. Who could this be, five o'clock on a Sunday? He had no intention of answering it until he saw some fool putting their head up to the window and peering in.

He threw open the door. There was a small Asian woman standing there, a tall fair-haired man in a cheap suit a step behind her.

'What do you want?'

'Hello, my name is Sue and this is Bryan. We are calling on you and your neighbours with an interesting article,

"Why do good people suffer?" It's in this magazine, called the *Watchtower*. Do you know it?'

He stared at them, dazzled by their effrontery and their ignorance.

'Oh, you've cut yourself,' the woman said.

He looked down. The blood had soaked into the rag and was oozing down his wrist and on to the marble tiles.

'I'm busy,' he said.

'Would you like to know the truth about the Bible?'

'The truth?' He stared at her in astonishment.

She opened her magazine and almost put it in his face. 'With all the terrible things happening today, many people wonder if God really exists or cares what happens to the human race.'

'Of course he doesn't.'

Perhaps she didn't hear him. 'But we're bringing you the good news of Jesus,' she said.

Did they know how ridiculous they sounded, how ridiculous they looked? Like little children. 'Have a nice evening,' he said and shut the door in their faces. He looked down at his hands. He was shaking.

He waited until they were off his property and then went outside to the gated courtyard at the side of the house. It was bitterly cold and frost glittered on the roof of his black Mercedes. He pointed the remote at the garage doors and they swung up. The garage had been the presbytery before the place had been restored.

The Transit was parked front end in, just in front of the timber trapdoor. He bent down and swung it open. He saw her down there, just a shapeless lump in the dark. She had started moaning again. They didn't make martyrs like they used to, he thought. She didn't look like they did in the paintings.

He pressed the release for the hook, started the engine and then lowered the cable on the winch. He waited to hear the clink as it touched the basement floor then pushed the stop button on the control. He opened the van's rear doors and took out the mover's trolley. He made sure everything was ready: the timber crosspieces, the petrol, the scalpels.

He went outside, checked the sky. A storm coming, he could see inky black clouds piling up in the north and blotting out all the stars. A beautiful night to make another martyr.

CHAPTER FORTY-FIVE

Charlie got to the end of the close, debated with himself whether he should get out and take a better look. The steeple seemed to be all that was left of the church, there were just the ribs of the roof and the two end walls. It was surrounded by flats and a rather grim-looking development in shit-coloured brick.

He could see the towers of Canary Wharf in the distance, through the dreary grey of the evening; one of those lights could be his brother's flat, sorry, apartment, all glass and metal and multiple-orgasmic girls who liked to ski.

He drove around a bit, decided this wasn't the place, it would be too difficult to get into the church, you couldn't wheel a stupefied nun tied to a mover's trolley down the street, not even in Stepney. He turned on the GPS and headed to Enfield. He could hardly find the place in the dark; when he got there it turned out to be a burned-out tin shed behind a brick wall. If their perpetrator wanted to make a statement, sorry tableau, this wasn't the place he would do it, Charlie decided.

He drove back into London. By the time he got to the Tottenham Park Cemetery it was proper teeming down, dark and freezing cold. He turned up the collar of his Stone Island jacket and got out, switched on his Maglite and checked the padlocks on the gate, only the long dead in there, and they were best left alone.

He ran back to his car. He was soaked through. He punched in Lovejoy's number on the Nokia on the cradle. A flurry of rain hit the windscreen.

'How you doing, Lovejoy?'

'Just on my way to Catford, guv.'

'No luck?'

'You know what, I really thought that place in Hounslow might be it, looked right creepy, but it was all locked up and couldn't see a soul, not there or Brentford either.'

He smiled to himself. So that was why she had volunteered for all the driving, she thought she was going to be the one to find him and she didn't want to share the glory. Fair play, he sort of liked that in her. 'Have a good time in Dartford.'

'That's a contradiction in terms, guv. Where are you headed?'

'I'm off to Elmscroft Road then Barrow Fields.'

'Then what?'

'Then I don't know. I might do another circuit. I feel like a goose, to be honest. It's my day off. All the normal people are at home eating crisps in front of the television.'

'They're bored.'

'They're dry.'

He hung up. He drove out to the church on Elmscroft, the rain eased off for a minute and he got out and checked the gate. No one had tampered with it, he eased it open as far as it would go on its chain, shone his torch through. The beam settled on what he thought was a gargoyle, it gave him a bit of a shock when it launched itself into the sky and he realised it was a bat.

He was disappointed, he'd had a feeling about this place. But detectives shouldn't work on their feelings, at least that's what his old guv'nor had taught him before he retired, they relied on forensics and facts.

He got back in his Golf, wiped away the condensation on the windscreen. He turned the de-mister on and backed out, headed back down Elmscroft towards the High Street. As he headed past the off-licence and the Indian take-away, a white Transit van waited for him to pass and then turned right, back the way he had come.

* * *

308

Charlie drove past the Salvation Army store and the Morrison's and pulled up in front of the Barrow Fields cemetery gates. No one had driven in, that was clear, the chain out the front was still intact, anyone taking to that with bolt cutters would have the High Street watching them. He tried the gates, just to be sure, but it was all locked up for the night, no one getting out and no one getting in.

He was starving. He needed a break, decided to find something to eat, it was getting well past dinner time. He went back to his car, crawled along behind a bus on the High Street, he could barely see a thing through the windscreen, it was raining so hard.

He heard the first few bars of 'The Ride of the Valkyries' from his pocket. He pulled over to the side of the road, stared at the display, debated with himself whether to answer.

He picked up.

'Charlie, are you there?'

'I'm here.'

'I can't believe you did that.'

He didn't answer.

'Where are you?'

'I'm in the car.'

'Do you want to know where I am? I'm at home, I'm here all on my own. Do you know what I'm wearing?'

'I have no idea.'

'Nothing.'

'There's lots of nights I'm in my place on my own thinking about you. I don't ring you.'

'You knew the score when we started this.'

'Not only did I not know the score, I'm not sure I even understood the rules.'

'We need to talk.'

'Do we?'

'Call me when you get home.'

He didn't answer. She hung up.

309

He stared at the phone. What is it you want, Charlie? Do you want someone at home worrying about where you are on a wet night or do you want to just be able to walk out during lunch to go cruising the East End for serial killers when the mood takes?

Can't have both.

He found the nearest Wetherspoon's on Google Maps, went in and ordered a pint of Doombar and a hamburger with chips and onion rings. He asked the bloke behind the bar if they had any purslane to go with it and got a funny look.

He sat at a table on his own and stared at Sky Sports, exhausted. The football had finished, there was a round-up, Gary Lineker and a couple of Manchester United players from the eighties and nineties he couldn't remember. Arsenal had shipped five goals against Manchester City. That made four defeats in five games, Arsenal's usual New Year collapse; it was almost comforting in a way, a tradition, like the Queen's speech and Bonfire Night.

His phone rang and he snatched it up. 'Lovejoy. Where are you?'

'Dartford.'

'No luck?'

'Nothing.'

'What are you going to do?'

'I'm thinking of going back to Brentford.'

'It's dark and it's late.'

'We can't give up on this, guv. If it is connected, the last two murders were around midnight, weren't they?'

'You want to drive around all night?'

'If it was you he grabbed, you'd want me to, wouldn't you?'

Charlie stared at the screen. The Sky Channel had segued to the news: two blokes had used their 4WD to skittle into some pedestrians in a shopping mall in Sydney; there were people covered in blood lying around the footpath, some spiteful little dick-splash lying face down in the road with his hands cuffed behind his back, a squad of armed coppers in Kevlars on top of him.

He turned away. He'd rather watch the chavs in the corner sculling their pints of Heineken than look at that.

'What if we're wrong?'

'You got anything better to do, guv?'

'Not tonight I haven't. It could be one of the places I crossed off your list.'

This Lovejoy, he thought, she was like a breath of fresh air. Like a dog with a bone, she was; once she had an idea she wouldn't let it go. She's going to be one of my good ones.

'Where are you now, guv?'

'Stopped for refreshment.'

'You're in a pub.'

It sounded accusing. 'I'm on my day off.'

'I'm in a pub, too.'

'In Dartford?'

'They do have pubs in Dartford.'

'Is there sawdust on the floor?'

'Blood, and a bit of sand, no sawdust. Once I've had my shandy, I'm back out there.'

'Yeah, me too. I'll check in with you in an hour.'

Someone had left a *Sunday Telegraph* lying in the booth. He read the headline: POLICE STILL SEARCHING FOR MISSING NUN. There was a picture of Sister Agatha, the same one they had in Cargill's Incident Room. He remembered her standing in the field in the Hackney Marshes in her stout brown shoes: 'Look what the cat dragged in.'

'I'm going to find you, I promise,' he murmured under his breath, finished his Doombar and walked out.

She woke shivering with cold, scarce able to breathe. She tried to remember where she was, what had happened to her.

'The trouble I have been to,' a voice said. She tried to focus. It was dark, there was a candle burning on the ground,

311

somewhere close by, and there was a strong smell of petrol. She couldn't move her arms, they were pinioned above her head, she tried to touch the ground with her toes, but she couldn't quite reach. She struggled, desperate to get the air out of her lungs so she could breathe. The pain of it was unimaginable.

A bearded face swam into her vision. He was wearing orange overalls.

'I could let you die like this, it wouldn't take too long.' He looked at the slim watch on his wrist, as if he were pressed for time. 'But death, that just isn't the point, is it? Suffering is what martyrdom is all about.'

She tried to answer, but the gag was still in her mouth, she kicked her legs. 'Here, does this help?' he said and removed the gag.

'Please . . .' she gasped.

'It just doesn't seem fair, does it? After all you've done, all the good you've put into the world. Doesn't it seem to you that you deserve a better fate than this?' He stood closer. 'And that is exactly how I felt. I did everything, everything he asked of me, and what was my reward?'

He looked up at the darkness in the vault.

'Can you see her, down here? You want martyrs, you can have them. I'll make them for you, as many as I can!'

He picked up the candle, held it closer to his face; it looked demonic in the glow of it. 'Look at me, do I look like a bad man to you? Some people think me a saint.'

He threw his head back and shouted towards the vaulted ceiling. 'But you! You have power over everything and you used that power to take everything from me, everything I ever loved. Was that my reward? How dare you!'

He took a few breaths to calm himself, then turned to Agatha again. 'I'd better not come too close with the flame, not with all the petrol you have on you. We don't want to jump to the final act before we have even started the play.' He placed the candle down carefully, back where it had been. He chose something from the darkness, a black briefcase, and snapped it open. There was a gleaming array of instruments, cushioned in foam. He selected one with great care and held it up so that she could see it.

'I am not a man who likes to weep and cry. It is not the way a man should do things. When someone has done you an injustice there is only one thing to do. You must take action. No matter *who* has done you wrong.'

Sister Agnes had ceased her wriggling, exhausted. There were black spots in front of her eyes. She was sure she was going to pass out and she almost welcomed it. She heard him kick something towards her, a box or a crate, and he manoeuvred it until it was under her feet, and she could rest them on it. She pulled herself up and took a single gasping breath, could not help herself.

'Let me ask you this, Sister. All your life, as part of your vocation, you have believed in a merciful almighty God. I believed in that, too, once, and I still believe he is almighty. But he is not merciful, is he? People say he is just and kind. I see no evidence for that.'

She tried to concentrate on what he was saying, perhaps there was a clue in the rambling, something that would help her, something she could use to persuade him to let her go. She took another gasping breath. She couldn't feel her hands.

He was staring up into the darkness. What was up there? Something fluttered out of the rafters, a bat, its black wings flapping.

'I can and I will destroy anyone that ever served you,' he shouted into the dark. 'I will cripple and ruin every one of your saints on earth, everyone you love, everyone. Just as you did to me! Are you watching me?'

The bat was still fluttering around them, trapped by the walls, panicked by the light. Agatha did not know if it was its wings she could hear or the sound of her own blood in her ears.

She had to stay him, stall him somehow, but she couldn't get her breath. She felt wetness run down her leg as she lost control of her bladder again. She could not imagine such agony.

He held the scalpel in front of her. 'I am considered an artist in my chosen profession. I have brought so much healing with one of these.' He turned the blade so that it caught the candlelight.

'All I asked, all, was a family of my own to love and be loved. Was this too much to ask?' He leaned in, lowered his voice to a whisper. 'God broke his contract with me so there is no further compunction on me to do good. I will harm and hinder everyone who loves him, make him cry for his, as I wept for mine.'

Despite the cold, there was a sheen of sweat on his forehead. He drew a breath, squared his shoulders. He touched the edge of the blade to her skin. A pearl of blood appeared. 'But enough. Shall we begin?'

He turned away, put on a surgical apron and goggles. He held up the scalpel in his right hand. With his left he examined her breasts. 'They are quite heavy, this will not be quick. I shall have to make my first incisions here and here. It won't kill you, by the way, the blood loss is significant, but it will not prove fatal. And afterwards you won't suffer long, not like the real Agatha. We will move quickly to incineration.'

He stepped back again; despite his protestations, he was in no hurry to begin.

'My wife, you know, would not have approved. She was such a tender spirit. Angelic is the word many people used to describe her. My son was not angelic. He was a little monster. But so full of life! And I still remember how little Arcanjo would curl up on my lap with her nose pressed into my neck. If I close my eyes I can still smell her, still feel her arms around my neck.'

He did, in fact, close his eyes for a moment.

'I love you, Daddy,' he whispered, in a baby voice.

For a moment, there was stillness, just the smells of candle grease and petrol, the fluttering of the bat, the distant murmur of thunder.

His eyes snapped open. 'But you never married, and you never had children, so you cannot understand the geography of my pain. Do you know what inconsolable means? It means there is nothing in this world or the next that can console me. Except revenge.'

CHAPTER FORTY-SIX

Charlie pulled up in the lane beside the church, waited for the rain to ease, but it was clear it wasn't going to. He took the Maglite from the glove box and went to the gates. He tried the chains again without really expecting anything to happen and then stared in surprise as they slid through the bars and on to the ground.

He eased one of the gates open and peered through; the church itself should have been in darkness but he saw a lumen of light through one of the boarded-up windows. Another inch wider and he was able to put his head around the gate and he saw a white Transit van parked in front of the vestibule.

'Fuck,' Charlie murmured.

He froze, for a moment. He had never really expected that he and Lovejoy would actually be right about this.

He went back to the car and called her.

'Hello guv. Still on my way back to Brentford.'

'Forget about that. Get me back-up.'

'You've found him?'

'The church in Elmscroft Road.'

'OK, wait, I'm pulling over. I'll call it in now. Where are you?'

'I'm outside, in the car.'

'Wait there.'

'I'm not waiting, Lovejoy. And I'm your boss, so don't give me orders. Christ knows what he's doing in there. If I was going to wait, why would I be ringing you?'

'It could be dangerous.'

'Of course it's dangerous. So you'd better tell them to send me uniforms and some armed police ASAP.'

He hung up. He searched for a weapon in the car but all he had was the Maglite. Well, that would have to do. He took a deep breath and got out. He inched open the gate, it was rusted and squeaked on its hinges.

He was soaked before he went ten yards, there was rain streaming into his eyes, it was hard to see anything. He went to the van and shone the torch over it, clocked the winch mounted over the front bumper bar. Then he checked the back and swung open the door, shone the torch around. There were two cross-beams lying on the floor of the van, like the ones he'd seen at Barrow Field. The metal ramp was out; he imagined a mover's trolley going down it with Sister Agatha strapped to it.

There was the rumble of thunder, sheet lightning over the rooftops. He hoped it would drown out the sound of his footsteps on the gravel. He stepped into the vestibule. There was an ancient wooden door, the lock had been split apart, only a crowbar could have done that.

He edged it open.

CHAPTER FORTY-SEVEN

Rainwater splashed on to the ground from the rusted guttering above the vestibule. He looked up, lightning flashed again, illuminating the belfry on the east wing of the church. He waited, listened for the sound of police sirens, but he couldn't hang around all day for uniforms, he flicked off the Maglite and pushed through the door.

The first thing that hit him was the smell of petrol. Scared him, that did, more than a bullet or a blade, he didn't want to get burned. There was no option. He squatted down, took off his shoes. Surprise was the only thing he had in place of a proper weapon.

He heard a high keening sound, terrible, and then a man's voice, murmuring really low. He took a step further, water had come through the roof and left freezing pools on the stone flags.

He could see the flicker of a candle, monstrous shadows playing along the sacristy wall, but he couldn't see who was there, his view of things was obscured by the dark and the stone pillars running down the middle of the nave.

There was another lightning flash and he saw them clearly. Thunder rumbled across the sky. 'A tableau,' he heard Greene say in his head; a half-naked woman tied to a pillar with her hands above her head, a man standing in front of her in overalls and green wellington boots, the kind surgeons wore.

He saw him only for a moment, but it was vivid, he knew he

318

had seen that face somewhere before. Was he acting alone, that was the thing. Here he was, walking right up to him, what if he had a partner somewhere?

Candlelight flashed on the blade, he knew he couldn't cover the space between them in time to save her. If there was someone else, he was toast, but he had to do something before Sister Agatha was sliced apart.

As the target stepped towards Agatha, Charlie pointed the Maglite at his face and flicked it on. 'Armed police, drop your weapon.'

It sounded stupid, shouting that out when he only had a torch in his hand, but it was the only thing he could think of that might work, in the circumstances. He got down in a firing stance, the torch held straight out in front of him as if it was one of those M5s the SFOs used.

But the target wasn't falling for it, or else he didn't give a toss either way. He turned towards the candle; Charlie knew he intended to set her alight.

He yelled and ran towards him, threw the torch as hard as he could at his head. It hit the target on the temple and Charlie heard him grunt and then he went straight down. The Maglite bounced away, the light shining towards the wall, the wrong way. Where was the blade?

Charlie threw himself at him, felt a searing flash of pain in his shoulder and he scrambled clear. He fumbled on the ground for the Maglite.

As soon as he had it in his hand he rolled over, backing away, shining it into the dark behind him, thinking he would see the mad fucker standing over him with the blade. But he was still over there, kicking his legs, trying to get up.

Charlie grabbed for the candle and killed the flame with his fingers. Then he shone the Maglite around in another arc, searching for the bloke with the blade, but he wasn't there; he wasn't anywhere.

He felt a surge of panic, he could imagine that scalpel slicing into an artery. He backed away, didn't stop until he felt the sacristy wall behind him, he sat there swinging the Maglite left to right, right to left, trying get his breath back.

There was something warm running down his arm. He looked down, the blade had slashed clean through the upper sleeve of his jacket. He shone his torch on the gash, was that bone he could see, that blade had sliced clean through the skin and muscle. He felt a bit faint, but it didn't hurt, at least not yet. Can't afford to pass out, Charlie son, not now.

He heard sobbing, twisted the torch towards the pillar, saw Sister Agatha, her eyes wide, sobbing through the gag. He got up, easy as he could, tore the gag out, he could only get it to her chin, it was tied tight at the back of her head.

'Un . . . tie,' she gasped.

'Where did he go?'

But she was sobbing so hard he couldn't understand her, her eyes were rolling about in her head, she was only half conscious.

'Sister, tell me where he went!'

For a moment it seemed like she heard him, she turned her head to the right, he shone the torch towards the archway leading off the east transept, saw some narrow stone stairs leading up to the belfry.

'Let me . . .' Another gasp. '. . . down.'

'I can't let you down, I haven't anything to cut the rope with. My back-up's going to be here any minute.'

'Don't . . .' Then the merest whisper: '. . . leave.'

Another sweep with the torch, at the bare stained walls, the stone pillars, looking for the target.

Those stairs, was that where he was?

He heard Ben, he heard Lovejoy, they were in his head, shouting at him: *leave it!* But he couldn't leave it, there wasn't a bone in his body that could just leave it.

* * *

320

He shone the torch beam up the narrow stone stairs. His left arm was throbbing now, it felt numb and heavy, hung useless at his side. He inched up the steps, leaning on the wall for balance. What if he comes at you with that fucking blade? He looked down, there were spots of blood on the stone steps. The target was bleeding, too, he must have sconed him proper with the Maglite.

There could only be one reason the target was headed up to the belfry, and that was to jump. But he didn't want him to jump, he wanted to talk to him, wanted to understand why he had done all this, wanted it all to make sense.

The storm cracked right over his head, he imagined he felt the belfry shake. There was another streak of lightning, twice, three times, and through the jagged flashes Charlie looked up and saw him up there, almost like he was waiting for him.

He was sitting on the rail, one leg over. The bell had gone, long since been sold for scrap he supposed, and the housing boarded over with planks.

The target put up a hand. 'Put the torch down or I'll jump.'

Charlie lowered the torch just a fraction, searching for the blade. He had one arm hanging over the edge of the rail, it must be in that hand.

'How did you find me?'

Charlie was surprised at how refined he sounded. It wasn't an English accent, but it was cultured all the same, certainly not from his end of town.

'Luck, mate,' Charlie said.

'Your modesty insults my intelligence.'

'One of my colleagues managed to get inside your head.'

'Did they indeed? I feel sorry for them.'

'My back-up is on the way,' Charlie said. 'Put your hands where I can see them and step away from the edge.'

'Who are you?'

'My name's Detective Inspector George. I'm with the Murder Investigation Team at Essex Road.'

'What do you mean, you got inside my head? Are you religious?'

'Come away from the edge.'

'Now come on, we both know I'm not going to do that.'

'Step away!'

'Don't come any closer, please.'

Charlie had been edging in, but he hesitated, he didn't want to panic him. He had to stall him somehow.

'You don't have to jump, mate.'

'Really? You think that my life means anything to me? God has brought me unbearable pain, and death is my only possible release from it. Believe me, I'm ready to have it out with him face to face.'

The cavalry had arrived. Charlie got a better view of the target's face in the flickering blue lights: dark, slicked-back hair, glasses, a tidy goatee beard.

Definitely familiar; where had he seen him before?

'Your colleagues are out in some force. I'm flattered. Did you call out the army as well?'

Charlie calculated the distance between them. He might be able to grab him but what if he was still holding the blade?

'There are other ways.'

'There are no other ways,' he said. 'I am the angel that fell. I have to jump.' And in one movement he swung his legs over the side and was gone.

CHAPTER FORTY-EIGHT

Charlie and the DCI stood in front of the family portrait in Doctor Salvador Cruz's home in Hampstead, in papery white hooded suits, watched Crime Unit go about their business, taking photographs, carrying out evidence bags, dusting for prints.

'Looks proper like a wine bar,' Charlie said, admiring the Carrera marble and the leadlight windows and the stainless steel. He thought the rose window at the apex of the chancel was a nice touch.

'Used to be a church once,' the DCI said.

'You can do a lot with a church if you have the money.'

'He was a cardiac surgeon, so money wasn't much of an issue. On the board of several charities and a lifelong member of the local Catholic church. No one can quite believe it.'

That photograph in the entrance, him with his family, it all looked so normal, so wholesome. Just goes to show, he thought. Doctor Cruz had been clean shaven then, so the goatee must have been an affectation, a playful attempt to make himself look more like the devil.

'What happened to his wife and kids?'

'Killed by a drunk driver on Christmas Eve three years ago.' He turned away and looked at Charlie, his arm in a neoprene arm sling. 'How are you feeling?'

'They reckon there could be nerve damage, I might need an operation.'

'Take all the time you need, Charlie.'

323

'Do we know how he got the Transit van?'

'Seems your builder friends, the Morans, they did some renovation work here. I would venture that Cruz found out that Dravid needed the money to go back to India and talked to him on the QT and made him an offer. All this took a hell of a lot of planning.'

'Well, I suppose three years is long enough to think things through.'

'Before you got here, Jack's crew found two locked doors upstairs. When they went in, they found it was his kids' bedrooms. They hadn't been touched for years, they reckon. He must have locked them up straight after they were killed.'

Charlie thought about Dr Cruz, half over the steeple rail, the look on his face: *I'm ready to have it out with him face to face.*

'Crime Unit found everything we need?'

'Pretty much. End of the day, Charlie, we'll have all this tied up with a bow, shoe prints, tyre prints, brick particles from the cellar. All that's left is the paperwork.' He leaned in, lowered his voice. 'Just a friendly word of warning, you could be getting a reprimand from upstairs.'

'For catching him?'

'For leaving the victim unprotected and soaked in flammable liquid.'

'How could I have cut her down, I didn't have anything sharp.'

'The scalpel was lying on the ground, two feet away from her.'

'It was dark, I couldn't see it. I thought the target still had it in his possession.'

'And then the perpetrator committed suicide because you cornered him. You should have waited for professionals, there might have been a happier outcome.'

'If it wasn't for me and Lovejoy, Sister Agatha would be dead. Isn't that happy enough?'

'Just a heads-up that the super's looking into it, that's all.'

'You put in a word for me, of course.'

'I'm on your side, Charlie, but it's best you know what she said. I admit it was good work tracking him down, full marks there.'

'Well, most of the credit should go to DC Lovejoy. It was her idea to do the search.'

A shrug. 'Duly noted.'

'Do we know why he did it, sir?'

'Sister Agatha may be able to help us on that score, when she's recovered. You're not the only one that would like to know what was going through the mad bastard's head.'

Jack from Crime Unit went past them on the way to his van. He held up something in a plastic bag.

'It's a Jesus suit,' he said.

The DCI raised an eyebrow. 'See what I mean?' he said.

They met on Blackfriars Bridge. She'd rung him a few times through the day, she'd heard about what had happened at Elmscroft Road, of course.

'Hello Charlie. How's the war wound?'

He wiggled his fingers. 'It's all right.'

'I heard all about your exploits. Should be worth a promotion.'

'You never know. Maybe.'

'It's been all over the newspapers. I didn't see your name. Being modest?'

'No, being shunted out of the limelight. It was the boss's operation, after all. I was merely an officer who could not be named for operational reasons.'

'It will have to stay our secret, then. In light of everything, I suppose I'd better forgive you.'

'For what?'

'For running out on me on Sunday afternoon. Another woman might never talk to you again. Want to come for a drink? There's a few of us going to the bar in the Oxo Tower. You remember, it's where we first met.'

'I don't think so.'

'You're not still sulking?'

'No, I'm letting you go.'

She sniffed and pulled her red scarf up to her chin. 'Are you serious?'

'If you ever decide to leave him, call me.'

'You're letting the job get to you, Charlie. When I met you, I thought you were quite the lad, but I suppose this is for the best. You've got a bit intense lately.'

'Well the job can be intense. People dying and such. Know what I mean?'

He turned and walked away before he did something stupid and changed his mind. He knew he would probably regret this in the morning.

But next week, maybe the week after, he would start feeling a whole lot better about it.

It started to snow, one of those featherlight falls that gave the domes and bridges and embankments a light dusting and made London look like it did in the postcards. He stopped and looked back over his shoulder; Geri had gone.

Everything changed, didn't it? In his grandfather's day, the spires and the churches still dominated the skyline; now they were dwarfed by monoliths with jokey nicknames, the Gherkin, the Shard, the Cheesegrater, monuments to the almighty Quid. Hard to know which god was better. Neither of them had ever really worked for him, and now other men's wives were off the list too. So what would make him happy?

'And so the search goes on,' he said aloud, and dropped a fiver in the Starbucks take-away cup of a homeless bloke and his dog on the other side of the bridge. A common act of charity, wasn't nearly enough of them these days.

ACKNOWLEDGEMENTS

My heartfelt thanks to my agent, Kelly Falconer, for your encouragement, and for your determination and persistence in making this book happen. To my editor, Krystyna Green: thanks for your faith in me. And thanks also to Penelope Isaac and Rebecca Sheppard at Little, Brown for dusting off all the fingerprints.